# Soldier of the Mist

# Gene Wolfe

# Soldier of the Mist

**TOR**

A TOM DOHERTY ASSOCIATES BOOK

SOLDIER OF THE MIST

Copyright © 1986 by Gene Wolfe

A TOR Book

Published by Tom Doherty Associates, Inc.
49 West 24 Street
New York, N.Y. 10010

Cover design by Carol Russo

ISBN: 0-312-93734-2

Library of Congress Catalog Card Number: 86-50324

Printed in the United States

0  9  8  7  6  5  4  3  2

This book is
dedicated
with the greatest respect and affection
to
Herodotos of Halicarnassos

First there was a struggle at the barricade of shields; then, the barricade down, a bitter and protracted fight, hand to hand, at the temple of Demeter. . . .

—Herodotos


Although this book is fiction,
it is based on actual events of 479 B.C.

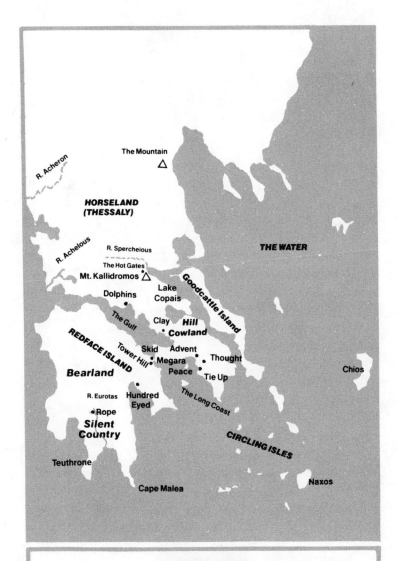

The Mountain

HORSELAND
(THESSALY)

R. Acheron

R. Achelous

R. Spercheious

The Hot Gates
Mt. Kallidromos

THE WATER

Dolphins

Lake
Copais

Goodcattle Island

The Gulf

Clay    Hill
        Cowland

REDFACE ISLAND

Tower Hill

Skid   Advent
Megara        Thought
    Peace
        Tie Up

Chios

Bearland

R. Eurotas   Hundred
              Eyed

The Long Coast

Rope

Silent
Country

CIRCLING ISLES

Teuthrone

Cape Malea

Naxos

# HELLAS
## Showing the Principal Places
## Mentioned in the First Scroll
┝━┿━┿━┿━┿━┥
### 500 STADES

# FOREWORD

About two years ago, an urn containing scrolls of papyrus, all apparently unused, was found behind a collection of Roman lyres in the basement of the British Museum. The museum retained the urn and disposed of the scrolls, which were listed in Sotheby's catalogue as *Lot 183. Various blank papyrus rolls, possibly the stock of an Egyptian stationer.*

After passing through several hands, they became the property of Mr. D_____ A_____, a dealer and collector in Detroit. He got the notion that something might be concealed in the sticks on which the papyrus was wound and had them X-rayed. The X-rays showed them to be solid; but they also showed line after line of minute characters on the sheet (technically the *protokollon*) gummed to each stick. Sensing himself on the verge of a discovery of real bibliotic importance, he examined a scroll under a powerful lens and found that all its sheets were covered on both sides with minute gray writing, which the personnel of the museum, and of Sotheby's, had apparently taken for dust smears. Spectrographic analysis has established that the writing instrument was a sharp "pencil" of metallic lead. Knowing my interest in dead languages, the owner has asked me to provide this translation.

With the exception of a short section in passable Greek, this first scroll is written in archaic Latin, without punctuation. The author, who called himself "Latro" (a word that may mean brigand, guerrilla, hired man, bodyguard, or pawn), had a disastrous penchant for abbreviation—indeed, it is rare to find him giving any but the shortest words in full; there is a distinct possibility that some abbreviations have been misread. The reader should keep in mind that all punctuation is mine; I have added details merely implied in the text in some instances and have given in full some conversations given in summary.

For convenience in reading, I have divided the work into chapters, breaking the text (insofar as possible) at the points at which "Latro" ceased to write. I have employed the first few words of each chapter as its title.

In dealing with place names, I have followed the original writer, who sometimes wrote them as he heard them but more often translated them when he understood (or believed he understood) their meanings. "Tower Hill" is probably Corinth; "the Long Coast" is surely Attica. In some cases, Latro was certainly mistaken. He seems to have heard some taciturn person referred to as having Laconic manners (Greek Λακωνιεμός) and to have concluded that *Laconia* meant "the Silent Country." His error in deriving the name of the principal city of that region from a word for rope or cord (Greek σπάρτον) was one made by many uneducated speakers of his time. He appears to have had some knowledge of Semitic languages and to have spoken Greek fairly fluently, but to have read it poorly or not at all.

A few words about the culture in which Latro found himself soon after he began to write may be in order. The people no more called themselves Greeks than do the people of the nation we call Greece today. By our standards they were casual about clothes, though in most cities it was considered improper for a woman to appear in public completely naked, as men often did. Breakfast was not eaten; unless he had been drinking the night before, the average Greek rose at dawn and ate his first meal at noon; a second meal was eaten in the evening. In peacetime even children drank diluted wine; in wartime soldiers complained bitterly because they had only water, and often fell ill.

Athens ("Thought") was more crime-ridden than New York. Its law against women's leaving their homes alone was meant to prevent attacks on them. (Another woman or even a child was a satisfactory escort.) First-floor rooms were windowless, and burglars were called "wallbreakers." Despite the modern myth, exclusive homosexuality was rare and generally condemned, although bisexuality was common and accepted. The Athenian police were barbarian mercenaries, employed because they were more difficult to corrupt than Greeks. Their skill with the bow was often valuable in apprehending suspects.

Although the Greek city-states were more diverse in law and custom than most scholars are willing to admit, a brisk trade in goods had effected some standardization in money and units of measure. An obol, vulgarly called a spit, bought a light meal. The oarsmen on warships were paid two or three obols a day, but of course they were fed from their ship's stores. Six obols made a drachma (a handful), and a drachma bought a day's service from a skilled mercenary (who supplied his own equipment) or a night's service from one of Kalleos's women. A gold stator was worth two silver drachmas. The most widely circulated ten-drachma coin was called an owl, from the image on its reverse. A hundred drachmas made a mina; sixty minas a talent—about fifty-seven pounds of gold or eight hundred pounds of silver.

The talent was also a unit of weight: about fifty-seven pounds. The most commonly used measure of distance was the stade, from which comes our *stadium*. A stade was about two hundred yards, or a little over one-tenth of a mile.

Humanitarians accepted the institution of slavery, realizing that the alternative was massacre; we who have seen the holocaust of the European Jews should be sparing in our reproaches. Prisoners of war were a principal source of supply. A really first-class slave might cost as much as ten minas, the equivalent of thirty-six thousand dollars. Most were much more reasonable.

If the average well-read American were asked to name five famous Greeks, he would probably answer, "Homer, Socrates, Plato, Aristotle, and Pericles.'' Critics of Latro's account would do well to recall that Homer had been dead for four hundred years at the time Latro wrote, and that no one had heard of Socrates, Plato, Aristotle, or Pericles. The word *philosopher* was not yet in use.

In ancient Greece, skeptics were those who thought, not those who scoffed. Modern skeptics should note that Latro reports Greece as it was reported by the Greeks themselves. The runner sent from Athens to ask Spartan help before the battle of Marathon met the god Pan on the road and conscientiously recounted their conversation to the Athenian Assembly when he returned. (The Spartans, who well knew who ruled their land, refused to march before the full of the moon.)

—G. W.

# PART I

# CHAPTER I

## Read This Each Day

I write of what has just occurred. The healer came into this tent at dawn and asked whether I recalled him. When I said I did not, he explained. He gave me this scroll, with this stylus of the slingstone metal, which marks it as though it were wax.

My name is *Latro*. I must not forget. The healer said I forget very quickly, and that is because of a wound I suffered in a battle. He named it as though it were a man, but I do not remember the name. He said I must learn to write down as much as I can, so I can read it when I have forgotten. Thus he has given me this scroll and this stylus of heavy slingstone metal.

I wrote something for him in the dust first. He seemed pleased I could write, saying most soldiers cannot. He said also that my letters are well formed, though some are of shapes he does not know. I held the lamp, and he showed me his writing. It seemed very strange to me. He is of Riverland.

He asked me my name, but I could not bring it to my lips. He asked if I remembered speaking to him yesterday, and I did not. He has spoken to me several times, he says, but I have always forgotten when he comes again. He said some other soldiers told him my name, "Latro," and he asked if I could remember my home. I could. I told him of our house and the brook that laughs over colored stones. I described Mother and Father to him, just as I see them in my mind, but when he asked their names, I could tell him only "Mother"

3

and "Father." He said he thought these memories very old, perhaps from twenty years past or more. He asked who taught me to write, but I could not tell him. Then he gave me these things.

I am sitting by the flap, and because I have written all I remember of what he said, I will write what I see, so that perhaps in time to come I can sift my writing for what may be of value to me.

The sky is wide and blue, though the sun is not yet higher than the tents. There are many, many tents. Some are of hides, some of cloth. Most are plain, but I see one hung with tassels of bright wool. Soon after the healer left, four stiff-legged, unwilling camels were driven past by shouting men. Just now they returned, laden and hung with red and blue tassels of the same kind and raising a great dust because their drivers beat them to make them run.

Soldiers hurry by me, sometimes running, never smiling. Most are short, strong men with black beards. They wear trousers, and embroidered tunics of turquoise and gold over corselets of scales. One came carrying a spear with an apple of gold. He was the first to meet my eyes, and so I stopped him and asked whose army this is. He said, "The Great King's," then made me sit once more and hurried off.

My head still gives me pain. Often my fingers stray toward the bandages there, though the healer said not to touch them. I keep this stylus in my hand, and I will not. Sometimes it seems to me that there is a mist before my eyes that the sun cannot drive away.

Now I write again. I have been examining the sword and armor piled beside my couch. There is a helmet, holed where I received my wound. There is Falcata too, and there are plates for the breast and back. I took up Falcata, and though I did not know her, she knew my hand. Some of the other wounded looked afraid, so I sheathed her again. They do not understand my speech, nor I theirs.

The healer came after I wrote last, and I asked him where I had been hurt. He said it was near the shrine of the Earth

Mother, where the Great King's army fought the army of Thought and the Rope Makers.

I helped take down our tent. There are mules for the litters of those who cannot walk. He said I must keep with the rest; if I become separated, I must look for his own mule, who is piebald, or for his servant, who has but one eye. That is the man who carries out the dead, I think. I told him I would carry this scroll and wear the round plates and my sword on my belt of manhood. My helmet might be sold for its bronze, but I do not want to carry it. They have loaded it with the bedding.

We rest beside a river, and I write with my feet cooling in its stream. I do not know the name of this river. The army of the Great King blackens the road for many miles, and I, having seen it, do not understand how it could have been vanquished—or why I joined it, since where there are so many men no one could count them, one more or less is nothing. It is said our enemies pursue us, and our cavalry keeps them at bay. This I overheard when I saw a party of horsemen hurrying to the rear. The men who said it speak as I to the healer, and not in these words I write.

A black man is with me. He wears the skin of a spotted beast, and his spear is tipped with twisted horn. Sometimes he speaks, but if ever I knew his words, I have forgotten them all. When we met, he asked by signs if I had seen such men as he. I shook my head, and he seemed to understand. He peers at these letters I make with great interest.

The river was muddy for a time after so many had drunk. Now it runs clear again, and I see myself and the black man reflected. I am not as he, nor as the Great King's other soldiers. I pointed to my arm and my hair and asked the black man if he had seen another such as I. He nodded and opened two little bags he carries; there is white paste in one and vermilion in the other. He showed me by signs that we should go with the others; as he did, I saw beyond his shoulder another man, whiter than I, in the river. At first I thought him drowned, for his face was beneath the water; but he smiled and waved to me, pointing up the river, where the Great King's army marches, before he vanished swiftly downstream. I have told the black man I will not go, because I wish to write of this river-man while I can.

His skin was white as foam, his beard black and curling, so that for a moment I thought it spun of the silt. He was thick at the waist, like a rich man among the veterans, but thick of muscle, too, and horned like a bull. His eyes were merry and brave, the eyes that say, "I will knock down the tower." When he gestured, it seemed to me he meant we would meet again, and I do not want to forget him. His river is cold and smooth, racing from the hills to water this land. I will drink again, and the black man and I will go.

Evening. The healer would feed me if I could find him, I know; but I am too tired to walk far. As the day passed, I grew weaker and could walk only slowly. When the black man tried to hurry me, I signed that he should go forward alone. He shook his head and I think called me many vile names; and at last flourished his spear as if to strike me with the shaft. I drew Falcata. He dropped his spear and with his chin (so he points) told me to look behind us. There under the staring sun a thousand horsemen scoured the plain, their shadows and the clouds of dust more visible than the riders. A soldier with a wounded leg, who could walk even less than I, said the slingers and archers with whom they warred were the slaves of the Rope Makers, and if someone he named were still in the country of the sun, we would turn and rend them. Yet he seemed to fear the Rope Makers.

Now the black man has built a fire and gone among the tents to look for food. I feel it can bring me no strength and I shall die tomorrow, not at the hands of those slaves but falling suddenly and embracing the earth, drawing it over me like a cloak. The soldiers I can understand talk much of gods, cursing them and cursing others—ourselves more than once—in their names. It seems to me I once knew gods, worshiping beside Mother where the vines twined about the house of some small god. Now his name is lost. Even if I could call on him, I do not think he could come at my bidding. This land is surely far, very far from his little house.

I have gathered wood and heaped it on our fire to make light so I can write. For I must never forget what happened, *never*. Yet the mist will come, and it will be lost until I read what I now write.

I went to the river and said, "I know no god but you. I die tomorrow, and I will sink into the earth with the other dead. But I pray you will give good fortune always to the black man, who has been more than a brother to me. Here is my sword, with her I would have slain him. Accept the sacrifice!" Then I cast Falcata into the water.

At once the river-man appeared, rising from the dark stream and toying with my sword, tossing her in his hands and catching her again, sometimes by the hilt, sometimes by the blade. With him were two girls who might have been his daughters, and while he teased them with her, they sought to snatch her from him. All three shone like pearls in the moonlight.

Soon he cast Falcata at my feet. "I would mend you if I could," he said to me. "That lies beyond me, though steel and wood, fish, wheat, and barley all obey me." His voice was like the rushing of great waters. "My power is but this: that what is given to me I return manyfold. Thus I cast your sickle on my shore again, new-tempered in my flood. Not wood, nor bronze, nor iron shall stand against her, and she will not fail you until you fail her."

So saying, he and his daughters, if such they were, sank into the water again. I took up Falcata, thinking to dry her blade; but she was hot and dry. Then the black man returned with bread and meat, and many tales told with his fingers of how he had stolen them. We ate, and now he sleeps.

# —— CHAPTER II ——
## At Hill

WE have camped, and I have forgotten much of what happened since I saw the Swift God. Indeed, I have forgotten the seeing and know of it only because I have read it in this scroll in which I write.

Hill is very beautiful. There are buildings of marble, and a wonderful market. The people are frightened, however, and angry with the Great King because he is not here with more of his soldiers. They fought for him, thinking he would surely best the armies of Thought and Rope—this though the people of those cities are sons of Hellen just as they themselves are. They say the people of Thought hate their very name and will sweep their streets with fire, even as the Great King swept the streets of Thought. They say (for I listened to them in the market) that they will throw themselves upon the mercy of the Rope Makers, but that the Rope Makers have no mercy. They wish us to remain, but they say we will soon go, leaving them no protection but their walls and their own men, of whom the best, their Sacred Band, are all dead. And I think they speak the truth, for already I have heard some say we will break our camp tomorrow.

There are many inns here, but the black man and I have no money, so we sleep outside the walls with the other soldiers of the Great King. I wish I had described the healer when I first wrote, for I cannot find him among so many. There are many piebald mules and not a few one-eyed men, but none of the one-eyed men will say he is the servant of the healer.

Most will not speak with me; seeing my bandages, they think I have come to beg. I will not beg, yet it seems to me less honorable to eat what the black man takes, as I just did. This morning I tried to take food in the market as he does, but he is more skilled than I. Soon we will go to another market, where I will stand between him and the owners of the stalls as I did this morning. It is hard for him, because the people stare; yet he is very clever and often succeeds even when they watch him. I do not know how, because he has shown me many times that I am never to watch.

While the black man speaks with his hands and the rest argue, I write these words in the temple of the Shining God, which stands in the agora, the great market of Hill. So much has happened since I last wrote—and I have so little notion of what it may mean—that I do not know how I should begin.

The black man and I went to a different market after we had eaten the first meal and rested, to the agora, in the center of the city. Here jewelry and gold and silver cups are sold, and not just bread and wine, fish and figs. There are many fine buildings with pillars of marble; and there is a floor of stone over the earth, as though one stood in such a building already.

In the midst of all this and the thronging buyers and sellers, there is a fountain, and in the midst of the fountain, pouring forth its waters, an image of the Swift God worked in marble.

Having read of him in this scroll, I rushed to it, thinking the image to be the Swift God himself and calling out to him. A hundred people at least crowded around us then, some soldiers of the Great King like ourselves, but most citizens of Hill. They shouted many questions, and I answered as well as I could. The black man came too, asking by signs for money. Copper, bronze, and silver rained into his hands, so many coins that he had to stop at last and put them into the bag in which he carries his possessions.

That had a bad effect, and little more was given; but men with many rings came and said I must go to the House of the

Sun, and when the black man said we would not, said the Sun is the healer and called upon some soldiers of Hill to help them.

Thus we were taken into one of the finest buildings, with columns and many wide steps, where I was made to kneel before the prophetess, who sat upon a bronze tripod. There was much talk between the men with rings and a lean priest, who said many times and in many different ways that the prophetess would not speak for their god until an offering was made.

At last one of the men with many rings sent his slave away, and when we had waited longer still, and all the men with many rings had spoken of the gods and what they knew of them, and what their fathers and grandfathers and uncles had told them of them, this slave returned, bringing with him a little slave girl no taller than my waist.

Then her owner spoke of her most highly, pointing to her comely face and swearing she could read and that she had never known a man. I wondered to hear it, for from the looks she gave the slave who had brought her she knew him and did not like him; but I soon saw the lean priest believed the man with many rings hardly more than I, and perhaps less.

When he had heard him out, he drew the slave girl to one side and showed her letters cut in the walls. These were not all such letters as I make now, and yet I saw they were writing indeed. "Read me the words of the god who makes the future plain, child," the lean priest commanded her. "Read aloud of the god who heals and lets fly the swift arrows of death."

Smoothly and skillfully the slave girl read:

> "Here Leto's son, who strikes the lyre
>     Makes clear our days with golden fire,
>   Heals all wounds, gives hope divine,
>     To those who kneel at his shrine."

Her voice was clear and sweet, and though it was not like the shouting on the drill field, it seemed to rise above the clamor of the marketplace outside.

The priest nodded with satisfaction, motioned the little slave girl to silence, and nodded to the prophetess, who was at once seized by the god they served, so that she writhed and shrieked upon her tripod.

Soon her screams stopped, and she began to speak as quickly as the rattling of pebbles in a jar, in a voice like no woman's; but I paid little heed to her because my eyes were on a golden man, larger than any man should be, who had stepped silently from an alcove.

He motioned to me, and I came.

He was young and formed like a soldier, but he bore no scars. A bow and a shepherd's staff, both of gold, were clasped in his left hand, and a quiver of golden arrows was slung upon his back. He crouched before me as I might have crouched to speak with a child.

I bowed, and as I did I looked around at the others; they heard the prophetess in attitudes of reverence and did not see the golden giant.

"For them I am not here," he said, answering a question I had not asked. His words were fair and smooth, like those of a seller who tells his customer that his goods have been reserved for him alone.

"How can that be?" Even as he spoke, the others murmured and nodded, their eyes still on the prophetess.

"Only the solitary may see the gods," the giant told me. "For the rest, every god is the Unknown God."

"Am I alone then?" I asked him.

"Do you behold me?"

I nodded.

"Prayers to me are sometimes granted," he said. "You have come with no petition. Have you one to make now?"

Unable to speak or think, I shook my head.

"Then you shall have such gifts as are mine to give. Hear my attributes: I am a god of divination, of music, of death, and of healing; I am the slayer of wolves and the master of the sun. I prophesy that though you will wander far in search of your home, you will not find it until you are farthest from it. Once only, you will sing as men sang in the Age of Gold to the playing of the gods. Long after, you will find what you seek in the dead city.

"Though healing is mine, I cannot heal you, nor would I if I could; by the shrine of the Great Mother you fell, to a shrine of hers you must return. Then she will point the way, and in the end the wolf's tooth will return to her who sent it."

Even as this golden man spoke he grew dim in my sight, as though all his substance were being drawn again into the alcove from which he had stepped only a moment before.

"Look beneath the sun. . . ."

When he was gone I rose, dusting my chiton with my hands. The black man, the lean priest, the men with many rings, and even the child still stood before the prophetess; but now the men with many rings argued among themselves, some pointing to the youngest of their number, who spoke at length with outspread hands.

When he had finished, the others spoke all together, many telling him how fortunate he was, because he would leave the city; whereupon he began once more. I soon grew tired of hearing him and read what is written here instead, then wrote as I write now—while still they argue, the black man talks of money with his hands, and the youngest of the men with many rings (who is not truly young, for the hair is leaving his head on both sides) backs away as if to fly.

The child looks at me, at him, at the black man, and then at me once more, with wondering eyes.

# CHAPTER III

## *Io*

THE slave girl woke me before the first light. Our fire was nearly out, and she was breaking sticks across her knee to add to it. "I'm sorry, master," she said. "I tried to do it as quietly as I could."

I felt I knew her, but I could not recall the time or place where we had met. I asked who she was.

"Io. It means *io*—'happiness'—master."

"And who am I?"

"You're Latro the soldier, master."

She had thrice called me "master." I asked, "Are you a slave, then, Io?" The truth was that I had assumed it already from her tattered peplos.

"I'm your slave, master. The god gave me to you yesterday. Don't you remember?"

I told her I did not.

"They took me to the god's house because he wouldn't tell them anything till somebody brought a present. I was the present, and for me he seized the priestess so she just about went crazy. She said I belonged to you, and I should go with you wherever you went."

A man who had rolled himself in a fine blue cloak threw it off and sat up at that. "Not that I recall," he said. "And I was there."

"This was afterward," Io declared. "After you and the others had left."

He glanced at her skeptically, then said, "I hope you

13

haven't forgotten me as well, Latro." When he saw I had, he continued, "My name is Pindaros, sir, son of Pagondas; and I am a poet. I was one of those who carried you to the temple of our patron."

I said, "I feel I've been dreaming and have just awakened; but I can't tell you what my dream was, or what preceded it."

"Ah!" Reaching in his traveling bag, Pindaros produced a waxed tablet and stylus. "That's really rather good. I hope you won't mind if I write it down? I might be able to make use of it somewhere."

"Write it down?" Something stirred in me, though I could not see it clearly.

"Yes, so I won't forget. You do the same thing, Latro. Yesterday you showed me your book. Do you still have it?"

I looked about and saw this scroll lying where I had slept, with the stylus thrust through the cords.

"It's a good thing you didn't knock it into the fire," Pindaros remarked.

"I wish I had a cloak like yours."

"Why, then, I'll buy you one. I've a little money, having had the good fortune to inherit a bit of land two years ago. Or your friend there can. He collected quite a tidy sum before we took you to the House of the God."

I looked at the black man to whom Pindaros pointed. He was still asleep, or feigning to be; but he would not sleep much longer: even as I looked, horns brayed far off. All around us men were stirring into wakefulness.

"Whose army is this?" I asked.

"What? You a soldier in it, and you don't know your strategist?"

I shook my head. "Perhaps I did, once. I no longer remember."

Io said, "He forgets because of what they did to him in that battle south of the city."

"Well, it used to be Mardonius's, but he's dead; I'm not sure who commands now. Artabazus, I think. At least, he seems to be in charge."

I had picked up my scroll. "Perhaps if I read this, I'd remember."

"Perhaps you would," Pindaros agreed. "But wait a moment, and you'll have more light. The sun will be up, and we'll have a grand view across Lake Copais there."

I was thirsty, so I asked if that was where we were going.

"To the morning sun? I suppose that's where this army's going, if Pausanius and his Rope Makers have anything to say about it. Farther, perhaps. But you and I are going to the cave of the Earth Goddess. You don't remember what the sibyl said?"

"I do," Io announced.

"You recite it for him, then." Pindaros sighed. "I have a temperamental aversion to bad verse."

The slave girl drew herself up to her full height, which was small enough, and chanted:

> "Look under the sun, if you would see!
> Sing! Make sacrifice to me!
> But you must cross the narrow sea.
> The wolf that howls has wrought you woe!
> To that dog's mistress you must go!
> Her hearth burns in the room below.
> I send you to the God Unseen!
> Whose temple lies in Death's terrene!
> There you shall learn why He's not seen.
> Sing then, and make the hills resound!
> King, nymph, and priest shall gather round!
> Wolf, faun, and nymph, spellbound."

Pindar shook his head in dismay. "Isn't that the most awful doggerel you ever heard? They do it much better at the Navel of the World, believe me. This may sound like vanity, but I've often thought the sheer badness of the oracle in our shining city was meant as an admonition to me. 'See, Pindaros,' the god is saying, 'what happens when divine poetry is passed through a heart of clay.' Still, it's certainly clear enough, and you can't always say that when the god speaks at the Navel of the World. Half the time he could mean anything.''

"Do you understand it?" I asked in wonder.

"Of course. Most of it, at least. Very likely even this child does.''

Io shook her head. "I wasn't listening when the priest explained.''

"Actually," Pindaros told her, "I provided more of the explanation than he did, thus drawing this trip upon myself; people suppose that poets have all of time at their disposal, a sort of endless summer.''

I said, "I feel I have none, or only today. Then it will be gone.''

"Yes, I suppose you do. And I'll have to interpret the god again for you tomorrow.''

I shook my head. "I'll write it down.''

"Of course. I'd forgotten about your book. Very well then. The first phrase is 'Look under the sun, if you would see.' Do you understand that?''

"I suppose it means I should read my scroll. That's best done by daylight, as you pointed out to me a moment ago.''

"No, no! When *sun* appears in the utterances of the sibyl, it always refers to the god. So that phrase means that the light of understanding comes from him; it's one of his best-known faculties. The next, 'Sing! Make sacrifice to me!' means that you are to please him if you wish for understanding. He's the god of music and poetry, so everyone who writes or recites poetry, for example, thereby sacrifices to him; he only accepts rams and rubbish of that sort from boors and the bourgeois, who have nothing better to offer him. Your sacrifice is to be song, and it would be well for you to keep that in mind.''

I told him I would try.

"Then there's 'But you must cross the narrow sea.' He's an eastern god, having come to us from the Tall Cap Country, and he's symbolized by the rising sun. Thus that's where you're to make your sacrifice.''

I nodded, feeling relieved that I would not have to sing at once.

"On to the next stanza. 'The wolf that howls has wrought you woe!' The god informs us that you've been injured by one whose symbol is the wolf, and points out that the wolf is one of nature's singers—thus the form of your sacrifice, if you are to be healed. 'To that dog's mistress you must go!' Aha!"

Pindaros pointed a finger dramatically at the sky. "Here, in my humble opinion, is the single most significant line in the whole business. It is a goddess who has injured you—a goddess whose symbol is the wolf. That can only be the Great Mother, whom we worship under so many names, most of which mean mother, or earth, or grain-giver, or something of that sort. Furthermore, you are to visit a temple or shrine of hers. But there are many such shrines—which is it? Very conveniently the god tells us: 'Her hearth burns in the room below.' That can only be the famous oracle at Lebadeia, not far from here, which is in a cavern. Furthermore, since we wouldn't want to use the coast road with the ships of Thought prowling the Gulf, it lies on the safest road to the Empire and the Tall Cap Country, which clinches it. You must go there and beg her forgiveness for the injury you did her that caused her to injure you. Only when you've done that will the god be able to cure you—otherwise he would make an enemy of her by doing so, which he understandably doesn't want."

"What about the next line?" I asked. "Who is the God Unseen?"

Pindaros shook his head. "That I can't tell you. There was a shrine to the Unknown God in Thought, and that's surely Death's Country now that the army's destroyed everything again. But let's wait and see. Very often in these affairs, you have to complete the first step before you really understand the next. My guess is that when you've visited the Great Mother in Trophonius's Cave, everything will be clear. Not that it's possible for a mortal—"

Io shouted, "Look down there!" her child's voice so shrill

that the black man sat bolt upright. She was shielding her eyes against the sun, which was now rising above the lake. I rose to look, and many of the other soldiers stopped what they were doing to follow the direction of her eyes, so that our part at least of the whole great encampment fell silent.

Music came, very faintly, from the shores of the lake, and a hundred people or more capered there in a wild dance. Goats were scattered among them, and these skipped like the dancers, made nervous, perhaps, by two tame panthers.

"It's the Kid," Pindaros whispered, and he motioned for me to come with him.

Io caught my hand as we joined the stream of soldiers going to the lake for water. "Are we invited to their party?"

I told her I did not know.

Over his shoulder Pindaros said, "You're on a pilgrimage. It wouldn't do to offend him."

And so we trooped down the gentle hillside to the lake shore through sweet spring grass and blooming flowers, Pindaros leading, Io clasping my hand, and the black man scowling as he followed some distance behind us. The rising sun had turned the lake to a sheet of gold, and the dawn wind cast aside her dark garments and decked herself in a hundred perfumes. Behind us, the trumpets of the Great King's army sounded again, but though many of the soldiers hurried back to follow them, we did not.

"You look happy, master," Io said, turning her little face up to mine.

"I am," I told her. "Aren't you?"

"If you are. Oh, yes!"

"You said you were brought to the god's house as an offering. Weren't you happy there?"

"I was afraid," she admitted. "Afraid they'd cut my neck like they do the poor animals, and today I've been afraid the god sent me to you to be a sacrifice someplace else. Do they kill little children for this Great Mother the poet is taking us to see?"

"I've no idea, Io; but if they do, I won't let them kill you.

No matter how I may have injured her, nothing could justify such a sacrifice.''

"But suppose you have to do it to find your home and your friends?''

"Was it because I wanted to find those things so much that I came to the god's house?''

"I don't know,'' Io said pensively. "My old master and some other men made you come, I think. Anyway, you were there when the steward brought me. But we sat together for a little while, and you talked to me about them.''

Her eyes left mine for the line of celebrants that traced the shore. "Latro, look at them dance!''

I did. They leap and whirl, splashing in the shallows, watering the grass with their flying feet and with the wine they drink and pour out even as they dance. The shrilling of the syrinx and the insistent thudding of the tympanon seem louder now. Though masked men leap among them, the dancers are mostly young women, naked or nearly so save for their wild, disordered hair.

Io has joined them, and with her the black man and Pindaros, but I watch only little Io. How gay she is with the vine crown twined round her head, and yet how intent on imitating the frenzy of the hebetic girls, the nation of children left far behind her for so long as the dance lasts.

Pindaros and the black man and I have left it forever, though once long ago it must have been friends and home to them. As for me—though I have left it too, it seems near; and it holds the only home and the only friends I can remember.

# ── CHAPTER IV ──
## Awakened by Moonlight

I tried to read this scroll; but though the moon shone so brightly that my hand cast a sharp shadow on the pale papyrus, I could not make out the shadowy letters. A woman slept beside me, naked as I, and like me wet with dew. I saw her shiver, the swelling of her thigh and the curve of her hip more lovely than I would have thought anything could be; and yet she did not wake.

I looked about for something with which to cover her, for it seemed to me that we two would surely not have thrown ourselves upon the grass, thus to sleep with no covering where so many others slept too. My manhood had risen at the sight of—oh!—her. I was ashamed by it, so that I wished a covering for myself, also, but there was nothing.

Water glimmered not far off. I went to wash myself, feeling that I had just started from a dream, and that if only I could cool my face I would recall who the woman was and how I came to lie upon the grassy bank with her.

I waded out until the water was higher than my waist; it was warmer than the dew and made me feel I was drawing a blanket about me. Splashing my face, I discovered that my head was swathed in cloth. I tried to pull these wrappings away, but the effort seared like a brand, so that I desisted at once.

Whether it was the water or the pain that awakened me a second time I cannot say, but I found that though the dreams I had half recalled were gone, nothing replaced them. The murmuring water lapped my chest. Above, the moon shone like a white lamp hung to guide some virgin home, and when I looked toward the bank again I saw her, as pure as the moonlight, a bow bent like the increscent moon in her hand and arrows thrust through the cestus at her waist. For a long while, she picked her way among the sleepers on the bank. At last she mounted the hill beyond, and at its very summit vanished.

Now came the sun, striking diamonds from the opalescent crest of each little wave. It seemed to me I saw it as I had seen it rise across the lake before (for I could see by daylight that the water was indeed a lake), though I could not say when. Since then I have read parts of this scroll, and I understand that better.

Even as the moon had awakened me, the sunlight seemed to rouse the rest, who stood and yawned and looked about. I waded back to the bank then, sorry I had stayed to watch the virgin with the bow and not sought farther for some covering for the woman who had slept with me. She slept still, and I cast the shards of the broken wine jar that lay beside her into the lake. Beside this scroll, I discovered a chiton among weapons and armor I felt were mine, and I covered the woman with it.

A grave man of forty years or so asked me if I was of his nation, and when I denied it, said, "But you are no barbarian— you speak our tongue." He was as naked as I, but he had a crown of ivy in place of my own head wrappings; he held a slender staff of pine, tipped with a pinecone.

"Your speech is clear to me," I said. "But I cannot tell you how it came to be so. I . . . am here. That is all I know."

A child who had been listening said, "He does not remember. He is my master, priest."

"Ah!" The priest nodded to himself. "So it is with many. The God in the Tree wipes clean their minds. There is no guilt."

"I don't think it was your god," the child told him sol-

emnly. "I think it was the Great Mother, or maybe the Earth
Mother or the Pig Lady."

"They are the same, my dear," the priest told her kindly.
"Come and sit down. You are not too young to understand."
He seated himself on the grass. At his gesture, the child sat
before him, and I beside her.

"By your accent, you are from our seven-gated city of
Hill, are you not?"

She nodded.

"Think then of such a man as you must often have seen in
the city. He is a potter, we will say. He is also the father of a
daughter much like yourself, the husband of such a woman as
you shall be, and the son of another. When our men march to
war, he takes up his helmet, his hoplon, and his spear; he is a
shieldman. Now answer this riddle for me. Which is he?
Shieldman, son, husband, father, or potter?"

"He's all of them," the child said.

"Then how will you address him when you speak to him?
Assuming you do not know his name?"

The child was silent.

"You will address him according to the place in which you
and he find yourselves and the need you have for him, will
you not? If you meet him on the drill field, you will say,
'Shieldman.' In his shop, you will say, 'Potter, how much for
this dish?'

"You see, my dear, there are many gods, but not so many
as ignorant people suppose. So with your goddess, whom
you call the Lady of the Swine. When we wish her to bless
our fields, we call her the Grain Goddess. But when we think
of her as the mother of all the things that spring from the soil,
trees as well as barley, wild beasts as well as tame, Great
Mother."

The child said, "I think they ought to tell us their names."

"They have many. That is one of the things I would like to
teach you, if I can. Were you to go to Riverland, as I went
once, you would find the Great Mother there, though the
People of the River do not speak of her as we do. A god—or

a goddess—must have a name suitable for the tongue of each nation."

"The poet said your god was the Kid," the child told him.

"There you have a perfect example." The priest smiled. "This poet of whom you speak called him the Kid when he spoke to you, and was quite correct to do so. A moment ago, I myself called him the God in the Tree, which is also correct— Why this is extraordinary! Most extraordinary!"

Turning to look where he did, I saw a man as black as the night coming toward us. He was as naked as we, but he carried a spear tipped with twisted horn.

"As I have often told the maenads and satyrs of his train, such rites as we performed yesterday bring the god nearer. Now here is such proof as to be almost miraculous. Come and sit with us, my friend."

The black man squatted and feigned to drink.

"He wants more wine," the child said.

"He does not speak our tongue?"

"I think he understands a little, but he never says anything. Probably somebody laughed once when he tried."

The priest smiled again. "You are wise beyond your years, my dear. My friend, we have no more wine. What we had was drunk last night to the honor of the god, or poured out in libations. If you wish to drink this morning, your drink must be of water." He cupped his hand and turned it over as if pouring wine onto the ground, then pointed to the lake.

The black man nodded to show he understood but remained where he was.

"I was about to say," the priest continued, "when the unfathomable powers of the god produced our friend as an illustration, that our god is commonly called the King from Nysa. Do you, either of you, know where Nysa lies?"

The child and I admitted we did not.

"It is in the country of the black men, up the river of Riverland. Our god was conceived when the Descender noticed in his travels a certain Semele, a princess, daughter of the king of our own seven-gated city. We were a monarchy in those days, you see." He cleared his throat. "The Descender disguised himself as a king merely earthly, and visiting her father's palace as a royal guest won her, though they did not wed.''

The child shook her head sadly.

"Alas, his wife Teleia learned of it. Some say, by the by, that Teleia is also the Earth Mother and the Great Mother; though I believe that to be an error. Whether I am correct or not, Teleia disguised herself also, putting on the form of a certain old woman who had been the princess's nurse. 'Your lover is of a state more than earthly,' she told Princess Semele. 'Make him promise to reveal—' ''

A handsome man somewhat younger than the priest had joined us, bringing with him a woman whose hair was dark like other women's, but whose eyes were like two violets. The man said, "I don't suppose you remember me, do you, Latro?"

"No," I said.

"I was afraid you wouldn't. I'm Pindaros, and your friend. This girl"—he nodded to the child—"is your slave, Io. And this is . . . ah . . . ?"

"Hilaeira," she said. By then my eyes had left her own, and I saw that she sought to conceal her breasts without appearing to do so. "It's not customary to exchange names during the bacchanalia. Now it's all right. You remember me, don't you?"

I said, "I know I slept beside you and covered you when I woke."

Pindaros explained, "He was struck down by the Great Mother. He forgets everything very quickly."

"How terrible for you!" Hilaeira said, and yet I could see she was glad to learn I had forgotten what we must have done the night before.

The priest had continued to instruct Io while we three spoke among ourselves. Now he said, "—gave to the child god the form of a kid."

Io must have been listening to us; she turned aside to whisper, "He writes things down to remember. Master, yesterday you sat by yourself and wrote for a long time. Then this woman came to you, and you rolled up your book again."

"Teleia, Queen of the Gods, was not deceived. With sweet herbs and clotted honey, she lured the kid away, coming at last to the isle of Naxos, where her bodyguard waited under the command of her daughter, the Lady of Thought."

The last of the worshipers were rising now, many appearing so exhausted and ill that I wondered whether a beaten army could have looked worse. I felt I had seen such an army once; but when I tried to recall it, there was only a dead man lying beside the road and another man, with a curling beard, putting the horse-cloth on his mount.

The black man, who must soon have grown bored with what he could understand of the priest's story, had gone to the lake to drink. Now he returned and gestured for me to rise.

Indicating Pindaros, Hilaeira whispered, "He said the child was your slave. Are you this man's?" When I did not answer she added, "A slave can't own a slave; any slave he buys belongs to his master."

"I don't know," I told her. "But I feel he's my friend."

Pindaros said, "It would be discourteous for us to leave while your young slave is being taught. Afterward we can go looking for the first meal."

I motioned for the black man to sit with me, and he did.

Hilaeira asked, "You really don't remember anything, or know whether you're slave or free? How is that possible?"

I tried to tell her. "There is a mist behind me. Here, at the back of my head. I stepped from it when I woke beside you and went to the lake to drink and wash. Still, I think I'm a free man."

"But the Lady of Thought," continued the priest, "is not called so for nothing. She's a true sophist, and like her city follows her own interests alone, counting promises and honor as nothing. Though she had helped her mother, she saved the heart of the kid from the pot and carried it to the Descender."

He continued so for some time, his voice (like the wind)

toying with the fresh grass, while his followers gathered about us; but I will not give the whole of his story. We must go soon, and I do not think it important.

At last he said, "So you see, we have a particular claim upon the Kid. His mother was a princess of our seven-gated city, and it was through the blue waters of our lake—right over there—that he entered the underworld to rescue her. Yesterday you helped celebrate that rescue." Then silence fell.

Pindaros asked, "Are you finished?"

The priest nodded, smiling. "There is a great deal more I could say. But little heads are like little cups, soon so full they can hold no more."

"Then let's go." Pindaros stood up. "There should be some peasants around here who'll be happy enough to sell us a bite."

"I will lead the worshipers back to the city," the priest told him. "If you wish to wait for us, I'll point out the farmhouses that feed us each year."

Pindaros shook his head. "We're on our way to Lebadeia, and we must put a good many stades behind us today if we're to reach the sacred cavern tomorrow."

Hilaeira's violet eyes flashed. "You're on a pilgrimage?"

"Yes, we've been ordered to go by the oracle of the Poet God. Or rather," Pindaros added, "Latro has, and a committee of our citizens has chosen me to guide him."

"May I go with you? I don't know what's happened—you certainly don't want to hear about my personal life—but I've been feeling very religious lately, much closer to the gods and everything than I ever did before. That's why I attended the bacchanal."

"Certainly," Pindaros told her. "Why, it would be the worst sort of beginning if we were to deny a devotee our protection on the road."

"Wonderful!" She sprang erect and brushed his lips with hers. "I'll get my things."

I put on this chiton and these back and breast plates, and took up the crooked sword and the bronze belt I found with them. Io says the sword is Falcata, and that name is indeed written on the blade. There is a painted mask too; Io says the priest gave it to me yesterday, when I was a satyr. I have hung it about my neck by the cord.

We have stopped at this house to eat cakes, salt olives, and cheese, and to drink wine. There is a seat here where I can spread this scroll across my knee in the proper way, and I am making use of it to write all these things down. But Pindaros said a moment ago that we must soon go.

Now there are swarthy men with javelins and long knives coming over the hill.

# CHAPTER V

## Among the Slaves of the Rope Makers

IT is the custom to beat and abuse captives. Pindaros says this is because the Rope Makers despise their slaves but count us as equals, or at least as near to equals as anyone who is not a Rope Maker can be.

Me they beat more than Pindaros or the black man until we found the old man sleeping. Now they do not beat me. They do not beat Hilaeira or her child much, either; but both weep, and they have done something to the child's legs so that she can scarcely walk. When my hands were freed, I carried her until we halted here.

A moment ago a sentry took this scroll from me. I watched him, and when he left the camp to relieve himself I spoke to the serpent woman. She followed him and soon returned with my scroll in her mouth. Her teeth are long and hollow. She says she draws life through them, and she has drunk her fill.

Now I must write of the earliest things I remember from this day, before they too are lost in the mist: the brightness of the sun and the billows of soft dust that lifted with each step to gray my feet and my legs too, as far as my knees. The black man walked before me. Once I turned to look back and saw Pindaros behind me, and my shadow, black as the black man's, stretched upon the road. I was beaten with a javelin shaft for that. The black man called out, I think telling them not to strike me, and they beat him also. Our hands were

28

bound behind us. I feared they would strike my head because I could not protect it, but they did not.

When the beating was over and we had walked a few steps more, I saw an old black man asleep near the road, and I asked Pindaros (for I knew his name) if they would bind him like the black man with us. Pindaros asked what man I meant. I pointed with my chin as the black man does, but Pindaros could not see him, because he lay half-concealed in the purple shade of a vineyard.

One of the slaves of the Rope Makers asked me what man it was I spoke of. I told him, but he said, "No, that is only the shadow of the vines." I said I would show him the sleeping man if he would allow me to leave the road. I spoke as I did because I thought that if the old black man awakened he would wish to aid the black man with us and might tell someone of our capture.

"Go ahead," the slave who had spoken to me said. "You show me, but if you run, you'll join our friends. And if there's nobody there, you'll pay for them again."

I left the road and knelt beside the sleeping man. "Father," I whispered. "Father, wake up and help us." Because my hands were tied, I could not shake him, but I dropped to one knee and nudged him with the other as I spoke.

He opened his eyes and sat up. He was bald, and the curling beard that hung to his belly was as white as frost.

"By all the twelve, he's right!" the slave who had come with me called to the rest.

"What is it, my boy?" the old man asked thickly. "What's the trouble here?"

"I don't know," I told him. "I'm afraid they're going to kill us."

"Oh, no." He was looking at the mask that hung about my neck. "Why, you're a friend of my pupil's. They can't do that." He rose, swaying, and I could see that he had fallen asleep beside the vineyard because he had drunk as much as he could hold. The black man gleams with sweat, but this fat old man shone more, so that it seemed there was a light behind him.

To the slave who had come with me, he said, "I lost a
flute and my cup. Find them for me, will you, my son? I've
no desire to bend down at the moment."

The flute was a plain one of polished wood, the cup of
wood also; it lay upon its side in the grass not far from the
flute.

Several of the slaves of the Rope Makers crowded around
staring. I believe the black man was the first such they had
ever seen, and now they had seen two. One said, "If you want
to keep your flute and cup, old man, you'd better tell us who
you are."

"Why, I do." The old man belched softly. "I do very
much indeed. I am the King of Nysa."

At that the little girl piped, "Are you the Kid? This
morning a priest said the Kid was the King of Nysa."

"No, no, no!" The old man shook his head and sipped
twilight-hued wine from his cup. "I'm sure he did not, child.
You must learn"—he belched again—"to listen more carefully. Otherwise you will never acquire wisdom. I'm sure he
said my pupil was the King *from* Nysa. King *of* Nysa, King
*from* Nysa. You see, he was put into my hands when he was
yet very young. I tutored him myself, and he has rewarded
me"—he belched a third time—"as you behold."

One of the slaves laughed. "By giving you all the wine
you wanted. Good enough! I wish my own master would
reward me like that."

"Exactly!" the old man exclaimed. "Precisely so! You're
a most penetrating young fellow, I must say."

It was then I noticed that Pindaros stood with head bowed.

The oldest slave said, "That's a nice flute you have, old
man. Now hear my judgment, for I command here. You must
play for us. If you do it well, you can keep it, for it offends
the gods to take a good musician's instrument. If you don't
play well, you'll lose it, and get a drubbing besides. And if
you won't play at all, you've had your last carouse." Several
of the others shouted their agreement.

"Gladly, my son. Most gladly. But I won't flute without
someone to sing to my music. What about this poor boy with

the broken head? Since he found me, may he sing to my fluting?''

The leader of the slaves nodded. "With the same laws. He'd better sing well, or he'll screech a lively tune when we thwack him.''

The old man smiled at me, his teeth whiter even than his beard. "Your throat will be clogged with the dust of the road, my boy. You'll need a swallow of this to clear it.'' He held his cup to my lips, and I filled my mouth with the wine. There is no describing how it tasted—as earth, rain, and sun must taste to the vine, I think. Or perhaps as the vine to them.

Then the old man began to flute.

And I to sing. I cannot write the words here, because they were in no tongue I know. Yet I understood as I sang them, and they told of the morning of the world, when the slaves of the Rope Makers had been free men serving their own king and the Earth Mother.

They told too of the King from Nysa and his majesty, and how he had given the King of Nysa to the Earth Mother to be her foster son, and to the Boundary Stone.

The slaves of the Rope Makers danced as I sang, waving their weapons and skipping and hopping like lambs in the field, and the black man and Pindaros, and the woman and the child danced with them, because the knots that had bound them had been only such as little children tie, knots that loosen at a shaking.

At last the song died at my lips. There was no more music.

Pindaros sat with me for a time beside this fire, while the rest slept. He said, "Two of the lines of the prophecy were fulfilled today. Did you remember?''

I could only shake my head.

" 'Sing then! And make the hills resound! King, nymph, and priest shall gather round!' The god—he was a god, you realize that, don't you, Latro? The god was a king, the King of Nysa. Hilaeira was a nymph last night when we danced to the honor of the Twice-Born God. I'm a priest of the Shining God, because I'm a poet. The Shining God was telling you

that you should sing when the King of Nysa called upon you.
You did, and he took away the cords that bound us. So that
part's all right.''

I asked him what part was not all right.

"I don't know," he admitted. "Perhaps everything's all
right. But—" He stirred the coals, I suppose to give himself
time to think, and I saw his hand shake. "It's just that I've
never actually seen an immortal before. You have, I know.
You were talking of seeing the River God, back in our
shining city.''

I said, "I don't remember."

"No, you wouldn't, I suppose. But you may have written
about it in that book. You ought to read it.''

"I will, when I've written everything I still remember
from today.''

He sighed. "You're right, that's much more important.''

"I'm writing about the King of Nysa, saying he was a
black man like the black man with us.''

Pindaros nodded. "That was why he came, of course. As
King of Nysa, he's that man's king, and no doubt that man's
his faithful worshiper. The Great King's army, that's retreating toward the north, levied troops from many strange nations.''

Pindaros paused, staring at the flaming coals. "Or it may
be that he was following the Kid. He's rumored to do it, and
the mysteries we performed yesterday may have called the
Kid to us. They're intended to, after all. They say that where
the Kid has been, one finds his old tutor asleep; and if one
can bind him before he wakes, he can be forced to reveal
one's destiny.'' He shivered. "I'm glad we didn't do that. I
don't think I want to know mine, though I once visited the
oracle of Iamus to ask about it. I wouldn't want to hear it
from the mouth of a god, someone with whom I couldn't
argue.''

I was still considering what he had said first. "I thought I
knew what that word *king* meant. Now I'm not sure. When
you say 'the King of Nysa,' is it the same as when you say
the army of the Great King is retreating?''

"Poor Latro." Pindaros patted my shoulder as a man

might quiet a horse, but there was so much kindness in it I did not mind. "What a pity it would be if you, who can learn nothing new, were to lose the little you know. I can explain, but you'll soon forget."

"I'll write it out," I told him. "Just as I'm writing now about the King of Nysa. Tomorrow I'll read it and understand."

"Very well, then." Pindaros cleared his throat. "In the first days, the nations of men were ruled by their gods. Here the Thunderer was our king in the same way the Great King rules his empire. Men and women saw him every day, and those who did could speak to him if they dared. In just the same way, no doubt, the King of Nysa ruled that nation, which lies to the south of Riverland. If Odysseus had traveled so far, he might still have found him there, sitting his throne among the black men.

"Often the gods took the goddesses in their arms, and thus they fathered new gods. So Homer and Hesiod teach us, and they were skilled poets, the true enlightened singing-birds of the Shining God. Often too the gods deigned to couple with our race; then their offspring were heroes greater than men— but not wholly gods. In this fashion Heracles was born of Alcmene, for example."

I nodded to show I understood.

"In time, the gods saw that there were no thrones for their children, or for their children's children." Pindaros paused to look at the starry sky that mocked our little fire. "Do you remember the farmhouse where we ate, Latro?"

I shook my head.

"There was a chair at the table where the farmer sat to eat. His daughter, that curly-headed imp who dashed about the house shouting, crawled into it while I watched. Her father didn't punish her for it, or even make her climb down; he mussed her hair instead and kissed her. So it was between the gods and their children, who became the kings of men. The kings of the Silent Country, to which we're being taken, still trace their proud lines from Alcmene's son. And if you were to travel east to the Empire instead, you'd find many a place where the Heraclids, the sons and daughters of Heracles, ruled not long ago; and a few where they rule yet, vassals of the Great King.''

I asked whether the farmer would not someday wish to sit in his chair again.

"Who can say?" Pindaros whispered. "The ages to come are wisest." After that he remained silent, stroking his chin and staring into the flames.

# ──── CHAPTER VI ────
## Eos

THE lady of the dawn is in the sky. I know her name because a moment ago as I unrolled this scroll she touched it with her shell-pink finger and traced the letters for me there. I have copied them just where she drew them—look and see.

I remember writing last night, and what I wrote; but the things themselves have vanished. I hope I wrote the truth. It is important to know the truth, because so soon what I write will be all I know.

Last night I slept only a little, though I rolled up this beautiful papyrus and tied it with its cords so I might sleep. One of the slaves of the Rope Makers woke me, sitting cross-legged beside me and shaking me by the shoulder.

"Do you know who I am?" he asked.

I told him I did not.

"I am Cerdon. I let you leave the road when you saw . . ." He waited expectantly.

"I'm tired," I told him. "I want to sleep."

"I could beat you—you know that? You've probably never had a real beating in your life."

"I don't know."

The anger drained from his face, though it still looked dark in the firelight. "That's right, you don't, do you? The poet told me about you. Do you remember what you saw under the vines?"

It was lost, but I recalled what I had written. "A black man, an old man and fat."

35

"A god," Cerdon whispered. His eyes sought the heavens, and in the clear night found innumerable stars. "I'd never seen one before. I never even knew anybody who had. Ghosts, yes, many; but not a god."

I asked, "Then how can you be sure?"

"We danced. I too—I couldn't stand still. It was a god, and you saw him when none of the rest of us could. Then when you touched him, all of us could see him. Everyone knows what happened."

Very softly the serpent woman hissed. She was beyond the firelight, but it gleamed in her eyes as in beads of jet. They said, "Give him to me!" and I heard the scales of her belly like daggers drawn from their sheaths as she moved impatiently over the spring grass. "No," I said.

"Yes, we do," Cerdon insisted. "Then I saw him as I see you now. Except that he didn't look like you. He didn't look like any ordinary man."

"No," I said again, and let my eyes close.

"Do you know of the Great Mother?"

I opened them again, and because I lay face down with my head pillowed on my arms, I saw Cerdon's feet and the crushed grass on which he sat. The grass looked black in the firelight. "No," I said a third time. And then, "Perhaps somewhere I have heard of her."

"The Rope Makers call us slaves, but there was a time when we were free. We pulled the oars in the galleys of Minos, but we did it for silver and because we shared in his glory."

Cerdon's voice, which had been only a whisper before, fell lower, so low I could scarcely hear him, though my ears were so near his lips. "The Great Mother was our goddess then, as she is our goddess still. The Descender overcame her. That's what they say. He took her against her will, and such was his might that she bore him the Fingers, five boys and five girls. Yet she hates him, though he woos her with rain and rends her oaks to show his strength. The Rope Makers say the oaks are his, but that can't be. If they were his, would he destroy them?"

"I don't know," I said. "Perhaps."

"The trees are hers," Cerdon whispered. "Only hers. That's why the Rope Makers make us cut them down, make us dig out their stumps and plow the fields. The whole Silent Country was covered with oak and pine, when we were free. Now the Rope Makers say the Huntress rules Redface Island— because she's the Descender's daughter, and they want us to forget our Great Mother. We haven't forgotten. We'll never forget."

I tried to nod, but my head was too heavy to move.

"We've been slaves, but we're warriors now. You saw my javelins and my sling."

I could not remember, but I said I had.

"A year ago, they would have killed me if I touched them. Only they had arms, and the arms were guarded by armed Rope Makers, always. Then the Great King came. They needed us, and now we're warriors. Who can keep warriors slaves? They will strike him down!"

I said, "And you wish me to strike with you," because it was plain that it was what he had come for.

"Yes!" His spittle flew in my face.

"There's no Rope Maker with you now." I sat up, rubbing my eyes. "Is there? Is this the country of the Rope Makers?"

"They have no country, they have only their city. The Silent Country is ours. But no, we're not there. It's far to the south, on Redface Island."

"Then why go back? You have friends and weapons."

"Our wives are there, and our children. No, you must come with us. You must find the Great Mother and touch her. We will kiss the ground at her feet then, because to kiss the ground is to kiss her lips. We will drive the Rope Makers back into the sea, and she will be our queen. I have your sword, and I'll give it to you again if you'll lead us. You will be her chief priest."

"Then I'll lead you," I said. "In the morning, when we're rested and ready to march."

"Good! Good!" Cerdon smiled broadly, and I saw that

some blow had deprived him of three teeth. "You won't forget?"

"I'll write it in this scroll."

"No," he said. "Don't write it, someone may see it."

But I have written anyway, so I will not forget. This is everything Cerdon said and all I said.

When he had gone to another place and stretched himself to sleep, the serpent woman came, saying, "Won't you give him to me?"

"Who am I," I asked, "that I should say yes to you, or no?"

"Give him something of yours," the serpent woman instructed me. "Bathe him or touch him. If you only touch him, it may be enough to make him real."

"He's real now," I said. "A man of blood and bone, just as I am. You aren't real." What she had said had made me think about those things.

"Less than his dreams," the serpent woman hissed. A tongue of blue fire with two points emerged from her mouth when she spoke. "What is it you wish? Perhaps I can bring it to you."

"Only to sleep," I said. "To sleep and to dream of home."

"Touch him for me then, and I will go away. The fauns bring dreams, and should I meet one, I will order him to bring you the dream you wish."

"Who are you?" I asked her, for I was still thinking of such matters.

"A daughter of Enodia." Her eyes sought out the refulgent moon, riding just above the horizon cradled in a woman's slender arms.

"Is that who holds the moon?" I asked. "I see her, and I would not call her dark."

"Now she is the Huntress," the serpent woman hissed, "and Selene. You may see more of both than you like before you're done."

Then she was gone.

I tried to sleep again, but Sleep would not come, though I

saw him standing with closed eyes at the edge of the fire-light. In a moment, he turned away to walk among the shadows. I thought then of writing in this scroll but felt too tired. Holding it as near the flames as I dared, I read it for a time.

Pindaros came. "I see you can sleep no more than I," he said. "That's an evil thing, for slaves. A slave must learn to sleep whenever he can."

"Are we slaves?" I asked.

"We are now. No, worse, for we are the slaves of the slaves of the Rope Makers. Soon they will take us to their masters, and then perhaps we'll only be slaves of the Rope Makers. That will be better, if you like, but I won't celebrate it."

"Will we have to twist their ropes for them?"

Pindaros chuckled. "They don't really make rope," he said. "Or anyway, no more than anyone else does. If we're very unlucky, we'll be driven into the mines. That's the worst thing that can befall a slave."

I nodded to show I understood.

"I don't think that will happen to me. The People of Thought may destroy our shining city and take my property—they hate us—but I have friends even in Thought, and certain talents."

"You're worried about the little girl and me." I looked across the fire at the sleeping child.

"And Hilaeira, and the black man too. If I'm freed, I'll buy freedom for all of you if I can. But it might help if you could sing for the Rope Makers as you sang today to the playing of the god. They love choral music, and they don't much value soloists; still no one could resist that, and no one would keep such a singer a slave. Can you do it?"

Hoping to please him, I tried; but I could not recall the words I had sung, nor any tune.

"It will be all right," Pindaros said. "I'll get us all freed some way. You don't remember, I know; I could see it in your eyes. It was a miracle, and you've forgotten it."

"I'm sorry," I told him, and I was.

"You haven't offended me." He sighed. "And I'm sorrier for you, Latro, than for any other man I know."

I asked whether he recalled the words.

"No," he said. "Not really. But I remember how they sounded, that great rushing swing like waves beating upon a cliff that ended in larks and thunder. That's the way poetry ought to sound."

I nodded because he seemed to expect it.

"As my own never has. But after hearing your song, I think I may be getting a bit closer. Listen to this:

"Arrows have I for the hearts of the wise,
    Straight-drawn by Nature to bear off the prize,
    But lift I my bow to the crowd on the plain,
    The fools hear but wind, and some fool must explain.

"Do you like it?"

"Very much," I said.

"Well, I don't. But I like it better than anything I've done before tonight. In our shining city, there are—there were, I ought to say—half a dozen of us who tried our hands at verse now and then. That was the way we put it, 'tried our hands,' as though there were no difference between composing poetry and weaving mats beside the fire. We met monthly to sing our latest lines to one another, and pretended not to notice that none of them was ever heard again. If mine had seemed the best to me when our dinner was over, why, I was the cock of the walk—in my own eyes—for the month that followed. How proud I was of my little ode for the Pythia's games!"

I said, "I suppose everyone's vain in one way or another. I know I am."

Pindaros shrugged. "Your good looks are real, and so is your strength, as you proved just today. But as for us—now I see that we were only noisy boys, when we should have been men or been silent. After hearing the god this afternoon, it may be that I will be a man someday. I hope so. Latro, I wouldn't boast to you like this—and that's what it is, boasting—if I didn't know you'll forget everything I've said."

"I'll write it down," I told him.

"To be sure!" Pindaros laughed softly. "The gods have their revenge, as always.

"We call for night to hide our acts,
But Night, a god, gives God the facts."

"I like that, too," I said.

"Composed for you this moment and thrown hot from the forge. Still, there may be something in it. 'We've need of night . . .' "

"Pindaros, is there really a god of night?"

"There are at least a dozen."

"With a body like a snake's and a head like a woman's, a woman with black hair that has never seen a comb?"

He stared at me for a moment in silence, and at last stirred the fire as he had before. "You've seen that, haven't you? No, that's no goddess—it's a monster of some kind. Heracles was supposed to have rid this part of the world of them; but Heracles has been on the Mountain for four hundred years, and I suppose they're creeping back. Do you see it now?"

I shook my head.

"Good. I was hoping to get some sleep before these slaves stirred their lazy legs. If you see your monster again, don't touch it. Promise?"

"I promise." I almost said that if I were to touch him, that might be enough; but I did not.

He rose and stretched. "Then I'll try to sleep. A sleep without dreams, I hope. Empty of horrors. I ought to copy you and write myself a note forbidding me to talk to you in the dark. Alas, I lack your diligence. Good night again, Latro."

"Good night, Pindaros."

When he was gone, a small arm circled my waist. "I know you," I told its owner. "You're Io. I've been reading about you in this scroll."

"You're my master," the child said. "They had no right to do what they did to me. Only you."

"What did they do?" I asked, but she did not answer. Putting my arm about her shoulders, I looked at her face in the firelight and saw how many tears had furrowed those dusty cheeks. "If the serpent woman comes again, I'll tell her she can't have you."

She shook her head. "It's not that. I ran away, and now I've been punished for it."

"Did you run away from me, little Io? I wouldn't punish you if you did."

She shook her head. "From the Bright God. And I lied when I said he'd given me to you."

"Perhaps he did," I told her. Holding her close, I watched the silent figures in the shadows for some sign, but there was none. "The gods are not at all like us, little Io."

# PART II

# CHAPTER VII

## Beside the Beached Ships

THIS little tent seems small indeed. When I woke a short time ago, I discovered this scroll. Being barred from leaving by the sentry at the door and not wishing to disturb the black man who shares this tent with me (he was busily carving a doll), I resolved to read it from the beginning.

I had hardly started when a man in a fine corselet of bronze came in, and I supposed him to be the healer of whom I had just read. He disabused me of that notion at once, saying, "My name's Hypereides, fellow. Hypereides the Trierarch, and I'm your master now. How can you pretend not to know me?"

I said, "I'm afraid I forget very quickly."

He scowled ferociously and pointed a finger at me. "Now I've got you! If you forget, how can you remember that?"

I explained that I had just read it and pointed to the place where it says, "The Healer says I forget very quickly, and that it is because of a wound I suffered in a battle."

"Wonderful," Hypereides said. "Wonderful! You've an answer for everything."

"No," I said. "I only wish I did. If you're not the healer, can you tell me where I am now?"

There was a stool in one corner of the tent. (I am using it now to write this.) He pulled it over and sat down, motioning for me to sit on the ground before him. "Armor's heavy stuff," he said, "something I never considered as a youngster, when I used to watch the soldiers ride past in the

45

Panathenaea. You learn soon enough to sit when you can and as high as you can, so it's not too hard to stand up." He took off his helmet with its gorgeous crest of blue horsehair and scratched his bald head. "I'm too old for this sort of thing, let me tell you. I fought at Fennel Field, my boy, ten years ago. There was a battle! Would you like to hear the story?"

"Yes," I said. "Very much."

"You really would? You're not just saying that to please a man older than yourself?"

"No, I'd like it. Perhaps it would recall to me the battle in which I was wounded."

"You don't remember my telling you yesterday? No, I see you don't. I didn't mean to cause you such pain." He cleared his throat. "I'll make it up to you, my boy. I'm a wealthy man back home, though you mightn't think it to see me parading about in this stuff. I'm in leather, you see. Everybody in leather knows Hypereides." He paused and his smile faded. "Three ships the Assembly laid on me."

"Three ships?"

"Build them, outfit them, pay the rowers. It cost . . . well, you wouldn't believe what it cost. Want to take a look at them, my boy?"

"Yes. I'm sure I've seen ships before, somewhere, and they were very interesting."

"Certainly," Hypereides said. "You too."

Looking around, I saw that the black man had laid down the doll and his little knife and was asking by signs whether he might go with us.

"It's all right," Hypereides told the guard at the door. "In fact, I don't think we'll need you here any more. Go find Acetes and ask him what he wants you to do."

Three ships had been drawn up on the beach, and their red-painted sides were covered with men hammering hair and pine tar into their seams.

"We were hit by a blow rounding Cape Malea," Hypereides explained. "It loosened them up, and by the time we got to Tower Hill we were taking on more water than I liked. A man *does* learn a bit about ships in the leather trade, I'll admit; and I thought it better to caulk them now than to try to take them back home as they were, and for all I know be handed some urgent message and told to put to sea again at once. Certainly it wouldn't do to run into a few stray barbarians and find them in better shape than we are."

"Who are these barbarians?" I asked.

"Why, the Great King's navy, of course. With the help of Boreas, we beat them in the Strait of Peace, let me tell you. There was a battle! I wish you could see our rams, my boy; the bronze itself is scarred. There was a time—I don't expect you to believe this, yet it's the plain fact—when there was so much blood in the sea we floated a span deeper than usual, just as if we were running up an estuary. I'm telling you, every man you see here fought like a hero and every oar rose like a slaughtering spear."

He pointed. "That's my personal command in the middle there, *Europa*. A hundred and ninety-five men to pull her oars. A dozen soldiers besides myself, and four Sons of Scoloti to draw the bow. The soldiers don't have to be paid, being citizens like me or foreigners who live with us. But the rowers, my boy! Great gods, the rowers! Three obols a day for every stick, and their food. And wine for their water! A drachma every day for each Son of Scoloti. *Two* for the kybernetes. That's almost a dozen owls a day, just for *Europa*. With the other ships, it comes to twenty."

He paused, frowning down at the sandy ground, then looked up and smiled. "Did you catch the signification of her name, my boy? Europa was carried off by the Thunderer in the shape of a bull. So when people see *Europa,* they think of a bull—wait till you see her mainsail! And what does a bull make them think of? Why, leather, of course. Because the best and strongest leather is bull's hide. And let me tell you, my boy, there'll be a lot of shields to be refitted when this war's over. Leather—bull, bull—Europa, *Europa*— Hypereides. Besides, Europa gave her name to the whole continent, bigger than her brother's place and Libya's combined, and the barbarians come from the other side. Europe—

Europa. *Europa*—Hypereides. So who're you going to buy
your leather from when the war's over?''

"You, sir, I promise." But I was looking at the ships and
thinking I could never have seen anything made by men half
so lovely, though they smelled of tar and lay on their sides
like three beached logs. I said, "If Europa the woman was
as slender and graceful as your ships, it's no wonder the
Thunderer ran away with her. Any man would want to." I
did not want him to guess I could not remember who the
Thunderer might be.

Hypereides had put his helmet on, pushed back so the
visor seemed the bill of a cap. Now he took it off again to
rub his head. "I've always thought she must have been on
the weighty side, myself," he said. "I mean, what sort of
woman would a god want to turn himself into a bull for?
Besides, he carried her on his back, and his choosing a bull's
shape for that makes it appear cargo was a consideration."

He laid his arm across my shoulders. "It's quite wrong,
my boy, to think that for a woman to give you pleasure she
has to be as lissome as a lad from the palaestra. When we get
back home, I'll introduce you to a hetaera called Kalleos.
Then you'll see. Besides, a girl with some flesh on her is
easier to catch; when you get to be my age you'll appreciate
the importance of that."

While we stood looking at the ships from a distance, the
black man had run down to them and poked about. As
Hypereides spoke of the hetaera, he came leaping back to
squat before us, pointing with his chin to the ships and the
sparkling sea and making many little marks in the sand with
his fingers.

"Look there," Hypereides said. "This fellow's seen the
barbarian navy. Both of you must have, because you were
with their army, and their ships followed it clear around the
Water."

"Were there really so many?" I asked him.

"More than a thousand, and that's not counting the traders
that carried food for the troops, or the special ships the
Great King had built for his cavalry horses. Why, in the

Strait of Peace you couldn't see the water for blood and wreckage."

He squatted beside the black man. "Here's the Long Coast. Right here's Tieup, where my old warehouse stood before they burned it; Megareos, my manager, is captain of *Eidyia* now. The man I had on Ceos has *Clytia.*

"Tieup's where our navy was before it went up to Artemisium. Here's the island of Peace over here, and here's Peace. We only had about three hundred ships, and we beached 'em in these three bays on the island the night before. Mine were in this bay here—all our city's were. You can keep a trader at sea half a month, my boy, but a warship has to touch land nearly every night, because there's so many aboard you can't carry enough water for 'em."

I said, "I see."

"Themistocles was with the navy, and he had a slave of his swim the channel and demand an audience with the Great King. This slave said Themistocles had sent him, which was true enough, and Themistocles wanted to be satrap of the Long Coast. Then he warned the Great King that our navy was going to slip off the next day to reinforce Tower Hill." Hypereides chuckled. "And the Great King believed it, too. He sent all the ships from Riverland around to the other end of the bay to cut us off.

"Then the strategists—mostly Themistocles and Eurybiades the Rope Maker, from what I've heard—sent the ships from Tower Hill to make sure the Riverlanders, over there, didn't come up behind us. A lot of people in the city still think the ships from Tower Hill deserted, and you can see why: the rumor the slave started, and then their leaving the rest of the fleet."

The black man pointed with his chin, and I saw a sailor striding up the beach toward us. Hypereides conferred with him for a moment, then told us to return to this tent. "I'm putting you on your honor," he said. "I don't want to have to keep you two chained like the others, but if you try to leave, I'll have to do it. Understand?"

I told him I did.

"But you'll forget—I forgot that." He turned to the sailor and said, "Stay with them until I send somebody to relieve you. I don't think you'll have any trouble; just don't let them wander away."

He is with us now; his name is Lyson. He asked whether Hypereides had told me about the Battle of Peace. I said he had begun but had been called away, and I was eager to hear the rest.

Lyson grinned at that and said Hypereides had taken us to see his ships the day before as well and had recounted the events of the battle while we looked at them. Lyson had been whittling pegs then and had heard most of it. "He took you to see the other prisoners too, because he wanted to ask them questions about you. The little girl gave you that book, and Hypereides let you keep it; and he let that fellow have a knife like mine because he showed he wanted to whittle."

I asked why these other prisoners were kept chained when we were not.

"Because they're from Cowland, of course. But you, you're Hypereides's ideal audience, one he can tell his stories to over and over." Lyson laughed.

I said, "I suppose the crews of all three ships are making fun of me."

"Oh, no. We've got too much to do for that. Anyway, we're mostly laughing at Hypereides, not at you. And we wouldn't laugh at him if we didn't like him."

"Is he a good commander?"

"He worries too much," Lyson said. "But yes, he is. He knows a lot about winds and currents, and it's good to have somebody on a ship who worries too much. He's an able merchant too—that's why we were sent here—and so he gets good food for us cheap and doesn't stint as much as most of them."

"It seems strange to have a merchant commanding warships," I said. "I'd think a horseman would do it."

"Is that how it would be in your own country?"

"I don't know. Perhaps."

"In Thought we keep the horsemen on their horses where

they belong. But listen here, if you weren't lying to Hypereides and you really don't know where you're from, you've only to look for a city where a horseman would be put in charge of warships. It's someplace in the Empire, I suppose."

I asked where that lay.

"To the east. Who'd you think we were fighting in the Strait of Peace, anyway?"

"The Great King, so Hypereides said."

"And the Great King rules the Empire. You were in his army. We've got your sword and pot-lids now. How'd you think you got that wound?"

I shook my head and somewhere found the memory that had once been painful to do so, though it was no longer. "In a battle. Other than that, I don't know."

"Of course not, poor stick. Somebody ought to look at it for you, though. Those bandages are dirty enough to beach on."

The black man had been listening to us, and though he did not speak, he seemed to understand what he heard. Now he said by signs that if he were allowed to, he would take off my bandages, wash them (vividly pantomiming how he would scrub them on a stone and beat them with another), dry them in the sun, and replace them.

"Ah," Lyson said, "but if I go with you, this one'll wander off."

The black man denied it, clasping my hand and saying by signs that he would not leave me, nor I him.

"He'll forget."

The black man cocked his head to show he did not understand the word.

Lyson pointed to his own head and traced the ground with his finger as though writing or drawing, then smoothed the imaginary scratches away.

The black man nodded and pretended to draw too, then with his finger indicated the course of the sun across the vault of heaven, and when it had set rubbed the drawing out.

"Ah, it takes all day."

The black man nodded again and unwound my bandages, and the two of them went off together, fast becoming friends.

As for me, I finished the reading of this scroll I had earlier begun. Now they have returned, and I write but feel I know less than ever. So many strange things—events I cannot credit—are described here. So many people are mentioned whom I have forgotten. Surely Io was the little girl who gave me this yesterday; but where are Pindaros, Hilaeira, and Cerdon? Where is the serpent woman, and how did the black man and I come to be where we are?

# ——— CHAPTER VIII ———

## At Sea

OUR ship rolls in a way that makes it hard to write, but I am learning to allow for it. The sailors say it is often much worse and I must walk and write and drink on board, and do everything else, before the sea grows rougher. "When we round Cape Malea, forget your home," they say; but I remember it, though I have forgotten every other place.

Our ship is the *Europa*, the largest of the three, with triple-banked oars. The men who sit highest have the longest oars, and they think themselves the best because they can spit on the rest; but all get the same pay. Now we are under sail, and they have no work, save for one or two who are bailing and the like. Soon there will be work enough, they say. Some are sleeping on the rowing benches, though all slept, I think, last night.

I am writing in the bow, leaning comfortably back against the high, straight post that marks the front of our ship. Below it (I remember, though I cannot see it from where I sit) is our ram. It does not look like a real ram at all—the dark eyes painted on the bow make the green metal look like the bill of an angry bird, at least to me. I can see the ram through the water when I stand and look over the bow. The water is sky-colored and very clear; but there is a second sky below, and I cannot see to the bottom.

A big rope runs from my bow post to the very top of the mast, and there are more such ropes there, going to both sides of the ship and to the stern, all to brace the mast against the pull of the sail. The one above my head bends a trifle, but the rest are stretched as straight as spears; the wind is behind us now, and our rowers are idling on their benches while the wide sail labors for them.

This sail hangs from a long, tapered yard raised almost to the top of the mast. There is a bull painted on it, not just a head like the carved bull's head on the sternpost, but every part; and I think I like him best of all our decorations. He is black, his nose is gold, and his blue eye rolls to see the woman sitting on his back. He has a brave tail, and it seems to me that if I were on one of the other ships it would appear that his golden hoofs ran upon the sea.

The woman who rides him has red hair and blue eyes, and two chins. She smiles as she rides; her hands stroke the bull's horns.

The long, narrow deck runs from the place where I sit to the stern, where two sailors hold the steering oars and the kybernetes watches them and the sail. The prisoners are chained to the mast where it goes through the deck.

Our captain's name is Hypereides. He is a man of middle years, bald and thick at the waist but erect and energetic. Not as tall as I. He came to talk with me, and I asked him the name of the country to our left. He said, "That's Redface Island, my boy."

It surprised me and I laughed.

"Not much of a name, is it? But that's all the name it has. Named for old Pelops, who was king there hundreds and hundreds of years ago."

"Did he have a red face?"

"That's what they say. The satirists make jokes about him, saying it was red from drinking, or that he was always angry, stamping up and down and sneezing. If you ask me, neither can be right. How could his mother know he was going to drink too much? Maybe he was angry all the time as a baby—the gods know a lot of them are—but who ever heard of one's being named for it? If you ask me, my boy, he was born with one of those red patches on his face that some children have. Anyway, that's where Tower Hill is, and the Rope Makers' city."

Then he told me about the Battle of Peace and how his ships had been hidden in a bay on the isle of Peace. Very early in the morning, when there was still fog on the water, the barbarians' ships had come into the strait. A lookout had seen them through the fog and heard the chants of their rowers, and he sent a signal. Hypereides and his ships, and all the other ships of the city came out then, and the Rope Makers' ships too. "You should have seen us, my boy— every man shouting out the Victory Hymn, and every oar bent like a bow!"

They met the barbarians ram to ram, and the ships from Peace came out of the bay behind the Dog's Tail and caught the barbarians in the flank; but there were so many barbarian ships that even when they fled they were a great fleet. No one knows where they are now, and most of the ships from Thought and Rope, and all the ships from Tower Hill, are hunting them among the islands.

Hypereides said that I must have fought for the Great King, and I asked him if I were a barbarian. "Not a real barbarian," he said. "Because you talk like a civilized man. Besides, there were a lot of us fighting for the Great King— almost as many as were on our side. See those people I've got chained up? They're from Hill—you can tell by the way they talk. Their city fought for him, and we mean to burn it around their ears, just as he burned ours."

The sun was high and hot, but the base of the mast was in the shadow of the sail; so when Hypereides went to talk to the kybernetes, I went to talk to the prisoners. One of the bowmen was watching them, and he looked to Hypereides to see whether he minded. Hypereides had his back to us, and the bowman said nothing.

I want to write about the bowmen before I forget that I intended to. They wear leggings and tall fox-fur caps. Their clothes look very uncomfortable, and while I was talking to the prisoners the bowman watching them took off his cap to fan himself.

Their curved bows are of wood and horn, and they bend backward now because they are not strung. It seems to me the right way to carry arrows is over the back, but the bowmen have their quivers at their waists. The quivers have a beard at the top that folds over the opening to keep out the spray.

The bowmen have cheeks that come straight up to their fierce eyes, like the cheek-pieces of a helmet. Their eyes and hair are lighter than ours, and their beards are longer. They cut the hair from their enemy's dead and wear it on their belts and wipe their hands on it. They cannot speak the tongue I speak to Hypereides and the rest as well as I can, and they cannot speak the tongue in which I am writing this at all. They smell of sweat. That is all I know of them.

No, there is one thing more, which is why I wrote all I just did. It is that the bowman who watches the prisoners watches me as no one else does. Sometimes I think he is afraid, sometimes that he wants some favor. I do not know what his look may mean; but I thought I should write of it here, to read when I have forgotten.

The prisoners from Hill are a man, his wife, and their daughter. When I came to them, they called me Latro. At first I thought they believed me such a one—a hired soldier or a bandit. But they have nothing to steal, and who has hired me? Then I understood that *Latro* is my name and they knew me. I sat on the deck beside them and said that it was cooler there and if they wished I would bring them water.

The man said, "Latro, have you read your book?"

I glanced about and saw it in the beakhead where I had left it. I told the man I had been examining the ship and had not.

The woman saw it too, and looked frightened. "Latro, it will blow away!"

"No, it won't," I told her. "The stylus is heavy, and I've put it through the cords."

"It's very important that you read it," the man said. "You offered to bring us water. I don't want water—they gave us enough earlier. I want you to bring me your book instead. I swear by the Shining God not to harm it."

I hesitated, but the child said, "Please, master!" and there was something in her voice I could not resist. I got it and brought it back, and the man took it and wrote a few words on the outside.

I told him, "That's not the best way. Unroll it like this, and you can write on the inner surface. Then when the book's closed, the writing's protected."

"But sometimes the scribe writes where I have written too, when he wishes to leave some message for a person who otherwise would not open the book. He might write, 'Here are the laws of the city,' for example."

"That's so," I admitted. "I'd forgotten."

"You speak our language well," he said. "Can you read what I've written?"

I shook my head. "I think I've seen letters like those before, but I can't read them."

"Then you must write it yourself. Write, 'Read me every day,' in your own language."

I took the stylus and wrote what he had told me, just above his own writing.

The child said, "Now if you'll read it, you'll know who you are and who we are."

Her voice pleased me, and I patted her head. "But there is so much to read here, little one. I've unrolled it enough to see that it's a long, long scroll, and the writing is very small. Besides, it was written with this and not with ink, and so the writing is gray, not black, which makes it hard to read. You can tell me these things, if you know them, much faster than I could read about them."

"You have to go to the house of the Great Mother," the child announced solemnly. Then she recited a poem. When it was over she said, "Pindaros was taking you there."

"I'm Pindaros," the man told me. "The citizens of our shining city designated me as your guide. I know you don't remember, but I swear it's the truth."

A black man who had been sleeping with the sailors rose and climbed from his bench to the deck where we sat. It seemed to me that we had met before, and he looked so friendly and cheerful that I smiled to see him now.

He exclaimed, *"Hah!"* when he saw me smile. Some of the sleeping men stirred at the sound, and those who were not asleep stared at us. The bowman, who had been watching and listening, put his hand to the knife in his belt.

"You must be less noisy, my friend," Pindaros said.

The black man grinned in reply and pointed from his heart to mine, and then, triumphantly, from mine to his.

"You mean he knows you," Pindaros said. "Yes, perhaps he does, a bit."

I said, "Is he a sailor? He doesn't look like the others."

"He's your comrade. He was taking care of you before Hilaeira and Io and I met you. Perhaps you saved his life in the battle, but he was using you to beg when I first saw you." To the black man he said, "You got a great deal by your begging, too. I don't suppose you still have it?"

The black man shook his head and pretended to gash his arm with his knife. Filling his hand with the unseen blood, he counted it out as money, making a little click with his tongue for the sound made by each imaginary coin as he put it on the deck. When he was finished he indicated me.

The child said, "He gave it to the slaves that night when we camped, while you were writing poetry and talking to Latro. It was for the slaves Latro killed, because the slaves were going to kill him when we got to the Silent Country."

"I doubt if the Rope Makers would have let them. Not that it matters; I had ten owls, but they got them in Tower Hill. I'd rather we were prisoners in Rope than in Tower Hill, but even Tower Hill would be preferable to Thought." Pindaros sighed. "We're their ancient enemies, and they are ours."

Hypereides had been telling me how the ships of Thought had fought the barbarians, implying that I was a barbarian myself; now I asked Pindaros if his city and Thought were worse enemies.

His laugh was bitter. "Worse by far. You forget, Latro, and so perhaps you've forgotten that brothers can be enemies more terrible than strangers. Our fields are rich, and theirs are poor; thus they envied us long ago and tried to take what was ours by force. Then they turned to trading, growing the olive and the vine, and exchanging oil, fruit, and wine for bread. They became great makers of jars too and sold them everywhere. Then the Lady of Thought, who loves sharp dealing, showed them a vein of silver."

The black man's eyes opened wide, and he leaned forward to catch every word, though I do not think he understood them all.

"They had been rich. Now they grew richer, and we proved no wiser than they and tried to take what was theirs. There is hardly a family in our shining city that is not related to them in some way, and hardly a man in theirs—except the foreigners—who's not a cousin of ours. And so we hate one another, and cease to hate every four years when our champions give their strength to the Descender; then we hate again, worse than ever, when the games are done." He pursed his mouth to spit but thought better of it.

I looked at the woman. She had eyes like thunderheads and seemed far more lovely to me than the woman painted on our sail. I did not wish to think this, but I thought that if Pindaros was a slave, I might somehow buy her and her child. "And are we friends," I asked her, "since we've traveled together?"

"We met at the rites of the God of Two Doors," the woman said. She smiled then, remembering something I could not recall; and I felt she would not object, that she would be content to live with me and leave her husband wherever his fate might take him. "Then the slaves of the Rope Makers came," she said, "and while Pindaros and the black man faced their first antagonists, you killed three. But the others were going to kill Io and me, and Pindaros stepped in front of you and made you stop. For a moment I thought you were going to cut him down, and so did he, I think. Instead you dropped your sword, and they bound your hands and beat you, and made you kiss the dust before their feet. Yes, we're friends."

I said, "I'm glad I've forgotten that surrender."

Pindaros nodded. "I wish I could forget it too; in many

ways, your state is a most enviable one. Nevertheless, now that the Shining God has directed you to the Great Mother, you'd better go to her and be cured if you can.''

"Who is this Great Mother?'' I asked him. ''And what does the child's poem mean?''

Then he told me of the gods and their ways. I listened intently as he spoke, just as I had to Hypereides's account of the Battle of Peace; but though I do not know what it was I hoped to hear from each, I knew when each was finished that I had not heard it.

Now the sun is hidden behind our sail, though I sit in the bow again; the ship rocks me as a mother rocks her child. There are voices in the waves, voices that laugh and sing and call out one to another.

I listen to them too, hoping to hear some mention of my home and the family and friends I must surely have there.

# CHAPTER IX

## *Night Comes*

A CROSS the sea, black shadows race like chariots. Though it will soon be too dark for me to write here, I will write as much as I can, and if I cannot write everything where I am, I will go to one of the fires and write there, then sleep.

I had hardly put away this stylus when the kybernetes spoke to the sailors, who stopped gambling and talking to furl the sail, strike the mast, and run out their oars.

It is wonderful to travel in such a slim, swift ship under sail; but it is far more so when the rowers strain at the oars and the ship leaps from the water at every stroke and falls back shouting. Then the wind is not behind the ship, but the ship makes her own, which you feel full in your face though silver spray blows across the bow.

Then too the flute boy plays, and the sailors all sing to his piping to keep the stroke; their song calls up the sea gods, who come to the surface to hear it, their ears like shells, their hair like sea wrack. For a long time I stood in the bow watching them and seeing the land brought ever nearer, and I felt that I myself was a god of the waters.

At last, when the land was so close I could see the leaves on the trees and the stones on the beach, the kybernetes came and stood beside me; and seeing that he meant to give no order for a few moments more, I ventured to tell him how beautiful I thought his ship and the others, which we had outdistanced and now saw behind us.

"There's none better," he said. "Hardly one as good. Say

what you please about Hypereides, but he spared no expense on *Europa*. You may say it was to be expected, because he meant to take the command himself; but there's many another who did the same and got his timber cheap anyhow. Not Hypereides. He's got the wit to see that his honor's gone aboard her as well as his life.''

"He must be brave too," I said, "to take charge of this ship himself when he could have stayed safely at home."

"Oh, he couldn't have done that," the kybernetes told me, glancing at the beach. "They're foolish enough in the Assembly at times, but never such fools as to let the men who supply the army and navy stay clear of the fighting. Not that Hypereides would have been safe in the city anyway; the barbarians burned it. Still, he could have served on land if he wanted. A good many did. But look at *Clytia* there. She's a fine ship too. My brother's kybernetes on her. Do you know what that poet said to me?"

Not knowing who the poet might be, I shook my head.

"He said her oars, with the foam on them, made her look like a bird with four white wings. And it's true—just look. He may be a pig from Cowland, but he's a fine poet all the same. Were you there when he sang for us last night?"

I said, "I'm afraid I don't remember."

"Ha, ha! You drank too much and fell asleep!" He slapped my back. "You've the soul of a sailor. We'll train you to the oar when that head wound heals."

"Were they good poems?"

The kybernetes nodded. "The men couldn't get enough of him. I'm going to ask Hypereides to make him perform for us again tonight. Not that I'll have to ask, I expect." He raised his voice. *"Easy now! Easy!"*

"Are you going to beach the ships here?"

"Bet on it, stick. The wind's favoring, so we *might* round the cape before sundown; and if we hadn't a day to spare, I'd try it. But if there was trouble, we'd have to spend the night at sea, and that's no joke. I told Hypereides we ought to put in, and he agreed. There's a little place called Teuthrone

not far from here, and we may be able to buy some fresh
food—what we got from Tower Hill's about gone.''

He shouted another order, and all the oars on one side
remained raised when they left the sea. The ship spun about
like a twig in an eddy. In a moment more, the oars were
backing water, rowing us backward to the shore. Half a
dozen sailors dove from the stern and swam to the beach like
seals. Two more threw them coils of rope.

"*Ship oars!*" the kybernetes shouted. Then: "*Over the
side!*"

I must have shown how astonished I was, because he
rubbed his hands and said, "Yes, it's a good crew. I chose
most of them myself, and the rest are men who worked for
Hypereides before the war."

By that time there was hardly a score of people left aboard—
the kybernetes and I, the soldiers (whose breastplates and
greaves would have sunk them like stones had they dived into
the sea), the bowmen, the black man, the three prisoners, and
Hypereides. Without her crew, the ship seemed so light I was
afraid she might turn over.

"Come here!" the kybernetes called. He waved, and the
soldiers and prisoners joined us in the bow, making the stern
rise a bit more.

Ashore the sailors were heaving at their ropes. I felt the
keel scrape, come free, then scrape again. The deck began to
tilt and we grabbed the railing.

"Don't jump now," the kybernetes said, seeing that I was
considering it. "That's a rock bottom."

The deck was almost too steep for us to keep our footing
when we made our way aft, but from there it was easy to climb
over the taffrail and onto the beach without so much as
getting our feet wet.

By the time I stood on land, the sailors were already
gathering driftwood for a fire and the other ships were backing water a stade or so from the beach. The black man and I
helped collect wood, having seen that it was a point of honor
with the sailors to get the best before the crews of the other
ships reached shore.

This coast is low and rocky, with a few scrubby trees; and yet it cannot really be said that beauty ends where the clear seawater comes to shore. While I watched, a hawk came racing down the ridge, caught the updraft from the sea, and soared on it like a gull, never moving a wing; when I saw it, I saw this rocky land too for what it is, a finger of the forest on a hand held out to the sea.

Hypereides took three soldiers and a score of sailors and went into the village to buy supplies. Acetes posted two more soldiers on the ridge as sentries. The rest of us threw off our clothes and plunged into the water to swim and wash. Even the prisoners, I noticed, were allowed to wash, though because of their chains they could not swim. I myself swam only a little, careful to keep the bandages on my head out of the water. I noticed that the bowmen went some distance away so they might wash out of sight of the rest of us.

When I returned to the beach, the child was sitting on a stone beside my possessions. I thanked her for watching them, and she said, "I didn't want anyone to take your book, master. Then you wouldn't know who you are, or who I am."

"Who are you?" I asked her. "And why do you call me master?"

"I'm your slave Io."

I explained that I had thought her the daughter of the couple with whom she had been chained.

"I knew you did," she said. "But we only met them a little while ago. I'm your slave, given you as your personal property by the Shining God when you were in Hill."

I shook my head.

"That's the truth, master, I swear by the club of Heracles. And if you'll just read your book you'll find out all about it, and about the curse the Great Mother laid on you. Then you'll see it isn't right for me to be like this"—she held up her chain to show me—"when you're free. I should be free too, to serve you."

I tried to recall what the woman had told me this

morning. "The soldiers captured us when we were going somewhere."

"Not these soldiers, master. Those were the slaves of the Rope Makers. They beat you, and they treated me like a woman and made me bleed there, though I'm not a woman yet. Hilaeira says I won't have a baby, but she might." Io sighed, recalling much pain and weariness, I think, that I have forgotten.

"Then we met some real soldiers, shieldmen with helmets and big spears. They made the slaves of the Rope Makers give us up. I hid your book because I was afraid they'd take it from you, and they made us go to Tower Hill, but I don't think the people in Tower Hill wanted to keep us—they're afraid of the Rope Makers like everybody else, and they didn't want to have prisoners that were taken from them. But they're afraid of the People of Thought too, and the soldiers from my city helped burn theirs. So after a while they gave us to Hypereides. He separated us, but I could see he liked you, so when you came to talk to me I gave your book back. I had it under my peplos, with the cords around my waist. Did you read it? I told you to."

"I don't know," I said.

"Maybe you did. But if you didn't write anything afterward, it doesn't matter now."

"You're a very knowing little girl," I told her, pulling on my chiton.

"It hasn't helped me much. I was owned by a pretty nice family back in Hill. Now I'm here, and all I've got out of the trip is a bath. Will you talk to Hypereides and ask him to let me take off my chain?"

While I tied my sandals, I said, "You can't take off a chain as though it were one of these."

"Yes, I can. They have them to chain up bad sailors and barbarian prisoners, so they aren't made to fit somebody as little as me. It's tight, but I can get my foot out. I did it last night."

"Show me."

She crossed her chained foot over her knee, stuck out her

tongue, and tugged at the shackle, which was indeed too large. "I was sweating a little then," she said. "I guess that made it easier. Now it's got sand under it."

"You'll take the skin off."

"No, I won't. Master, put your hand right here, and your thumb against my heel. Then pull with your fingers and tell me what you think."

I did so, and the shackle slipped from her foot as easily as an anklet. "You were joking," I said. "Why, you might almost have stepped out of it."

"Maybe I was, a little bit. You're not angry at me, are you, master?"

"No. But you'd better put it back on before someone sees you."

"I don't think I can," she told me. "I'll say it fell off in the water, and I couldn't find it."

"Then you'd better hide it under one of those stones."

"I know a better place. I found it while you were swimming around. Look at the edge of this big rock."

It was a hole the size of a man's head. When I thrust my arm into it, I discovered that it went almost straight down.

"I wouldn't do that," Io said. "Something smells bad down there." She dropped the chain and shackle into it. "I don't think they'll put another one on me. They'll be afraid that will get lost too."

One of the sailors who had reboarded the ship had returned now with a bronze fire-box. I was surprised to see how bright its vents seemed. The sun was setting behind the finger of land, plunging the beach into shadow.

"I'll go and get our food, master," Io said happily. "That's one of the things I ought to do for you."

"It won't be ready yet!" I called after her, but she paid no attention. I had picked up this scroll and started to follow her when someone tapped my shoulder.

It was one of the bowmen. I said, "She'll do no harm; she's only a child."

He shrugged to show he was not concerned about Io. "My

name is Oior," he said. "I am of the People of Scoloti. You are Latro. I heard the man and woman speak of you."

I nodded.

"I do not know this land."

"Nor I, either."

He looked surprised at that but went on resolutely. "It has many gods. In my land we sacrifice to red fire and air the unseen, to black earth, pale water, sun and moon, and to the sword of iron. That is all. I do not know these gods. Now I am troubled, and my trouble will be the trouble of all who are here." He looked around to see whether anyone was watching us. "I do not have much money, but you will have all I have." He held out his hand, filled with bronze coins.

"I don't want your money," I told him.

"Take. That is how friends are made in this land."

To please him, I took a single coin.

"Good," he said. "But this is no good place to talk, and soon there will be food. When we have eaten and drunk, go high up." He pointed to the ridge, between the sentries who stood black against the sky to the north and south. "Wait for Oior there."

Now I am waiting, and I have written this as I wait. The sun has set, and the last light will soon leave the western sky. The moon is rising, and if the bowman does not come before I grow sleepy, I will go to a fire to sleep.

# ─── CHAPTER X ───
## Under a Waning Moon

I write beside the fire. When I look about, it seems that no one is awake but the black man and me. He walks up and down the beach, his face turned to the sea as if waiting for some sail.

Yet I know many are awake. Now and then one sits up, sees the rest, and lies down again. The wind sighs in the trees and among the rocks; but there are other sighs, not born of the wind.

I asked Hypereides whether we would bury the dead man in the morning. He said we would not, that there is hope we will reach the city soon. If we do, the dead man can lie with his family, if he has one.

But I should return to the place where I stopped writing only a short time ago. Io carried food and wine to me, though I had eaten already, and we shared it with our backs against one of the highest rocks of the ridge, watching the moon rise over the sea and enjoying the spectacle provided by the fires of driftwood and the ships drawn up on the beach.

Hypereides was generous with food, and because no one had remembered I had eaten already, Io had received full portions for both of us. While I pretended to dine a second time, she piled what she did not want of her own meal onto my trencher, so there was a great deal there still when I drained the cup, wiped my fingers with bread, and laid it at my feet.

68

"I would like something of that."

I looked around to see who spoke. What I had thought only a stone resting by chance upon a larger stone was in fact the head of a woman. As soon as she saw I had seen her, she rose and came toward us. She was naked and graceful, beyond her first youth (as well as I could judge in the moonlight), though not her beauty. The black hair that fell to her waist seemed longer, thicker, and more tangled than any woman's hair should be.

As she came nearer to us, I decided she was a celebrant of some cult; for though she wore no gown, she had tied the shed skin of a snake above her hips like a cincture, with the head and tail hanging down.

"Here," I said. I picked up my trencher again and held it out to her. "You may have it all."

She smiled and shook her head.

"Master!" Io gasped.

She was staring at me, and I asked her what was wrong.

"There's nobody there!"

The woman whispered, "She's your slave. Won't you give her to me? Touch her and she's mine. Touch me, and I am hers." She scarcely moved her lips when she spoke; and she looked away, toward the moon, when she said, "I am hers."

"Master, is there somebody here? Somebody I can't see?"

I told Io, "A woman with dark hair, belted with a snake skin."

"Like the flute-playing man?"

I did not remember such a man and could only shake my head.

"Come to the fire," she pleaded. She tried to pull me away.

The woman whispered, "I won't hurt you. I've come to teach you, and to give you a warning."

"And the child?"

"The child is yours. She could be mine. What harm in that?"

I told Io, "Go away. Run to the fire. Stay there till I come."

She flew as a rabbit flies the hooves of warhorses, leaping and skipping among the rocks.

"You are selfish," the woman said. "You eat, while I go hungry."

"You may eat as I did."

"But quick of wit, an excellent thing. Alas, that I cannot chew such food." She smiled, and I saw that her teeth were small and pointed, shining in the moonlight.

"I didn't know there were such women as you. Are all the people of this coast like you?"

"We have spoken before," she said.

"Then I've forgotten it."

She studied my eyes and sank fluidly to the ground to sit beside me. "If you have forgotten me, you must have seen many things."

"Is that what you came to teach me?"

"Ah," she said. "It is my face you do not remember."

I nodded.

"And the rest is somewhat differently arranged. Yes, you are right. That is one of the things I have come to teach you."

I looked at her, seeing how fair her body was and how white. "I'd gladly learn."

Her hand caressed my thigh, but though her fingers moved with life, they felt as cold as stones. "Someday, perhaps. Do you desire me?"

"Very much."

"Later, then, as I told you. When you have recovered from that wound. But now I much teach you, as I said I would." She pointed to the moon. "Do you see the goddess?"

"Yes," I said. "But what a fool I am. A moment ago, I thought her only a crescent lamp in the sky."

"There is a shadow across her face now," the woman told me. "In seven days, the shadow will cover it wholly. Then she will become our dark goddess, and if she comes to you, you will see her so."

"I don't understand."

"I tell you these things because I know she once showed

herself to you as a bright goddess when the moon was nearly
full. What she has once done, she will do again, so these
things are good for you to know. For a very small price, I
will tell you more—things that will be of the greatest value
to you.''

I did not ask what the price was, because I knew; and I
saw that she knew I knew. I said, ''Could you take her? Even
when she's sitting around the fire with the rest?''

''I could take her though she sat in the fire.''

''I won't pay that price.''

''Learn wisdom,'' she said. ''Knowledge is more than
gold.''

I shook my head. ''Knowledge is soon changed, then lost
in the mist, an echo half-heard.''

She rose at that, brushing the dust from her hips and thighs
like any other woman. ''And I sought to teach you wisdom.
You mocked me when you said you were a fool.''

''If I mocked you, I've forgotten it.''

''Yes, that is best. To forget. But remember me when you
meet my mistress in any guise. Remember that I helped you
and would have helped you more, if you had been as generous to me as I to you.''

''I'll try,'' I said.

''And I will warn you, as I promised. The child fled down
this hill, and fled safely; but soon one who walks this hill
will die. Listen well!''

''I am,'' I said.

''Then wait for the death. Afterward you may go in safety.''
She paused, licking her lips as she cocked her head to listen.

I listened too, and heard far off the noise a stone made falling
upon a stone.

''Someone comes,'' she said. ''I would ask you for him,
but that would be your death. Notice that I am your friend,
merciful and just, more than fair in every dealing.''

''As you say.''

''Do not forget my warning and my teaching. There is one
thing more.'' Swiftly she went to the boulder behind which

she had been waiting when I first saw her. For an instant she disappeared as she crouched to take something from the ground. Then she stood beside me again and dropped it at my feet. It clinked as coins do, tossed in the hand.

"The women here put knives beneath their children's cradles," she told me. "They tell one another they will keep us away; and though they do not—not always—it is true we do not like iron." She crouched again, this time to wipe her hands on the ground. "The reason we do not is to come."

I picked up what she had dropped. It was a chain, with a shackle at one end.

"Don't let your brat dump her rubbish into my house again," the woman said.

A man's voice, rough and deep, called, *"Latro!"* I glanced in the direction of his call, and when I looked again the woman was gone. The stone rested on the boulder as before. I went to it and picked it up. It was a common stone, not otherwise than any other; I tossed it away.

*"Latro!"* The man's voice sounded a second time.

"Over here," I called.

A tall foxskin cap came into view. "I am glad you waited," the bowman told me. "You are indeed my friend."

I said, "Yes. Soon we will walk back to the fire together, Oior." For I trusted neither the woman nor her warning, and I feared for the child.

"But not before we have spoken." The bowman paused, rubbing his chin. "A friend believes his friend."

"That's true."

"I told you I do not know the gods of this land."

I nodded; we could see each other almost as well in the bright moonlight as we might by day.

"And you do not know mine. You must believe what I say of them. A friend speaks only the truth to his friend."

I said, "I'll believe whatever you tell me, Oior. I've already seen something tonight stranger than anything you're liable to say."

He sat on the ground almost where the woman had. "Eat your food, Latro."

I sat too, on the other side of the trencher. "I've had all I want."

"As have I, Latro; but friends share food in my land." He broke a piece of bread and gave half to me.

"Here also." I ate my bread as he ate his.

"Once our land was ruled by the Sons of Cimmer," Oior began. "They were a mighty people. Their right ran from the Ister to the Island Sea. Most of all were they men mighty in magic, sacrificing the sons of the Sons of Cimmer to the threefold Artimpasa. At last their sorcerers slew even their king's son, the acolyte of Apia. She is Mother of Men and Monsters, but the boy's blood burned on Artimpasa's altar.

"But the king came to know of the sacrifice of his son, and with hands held to heaven he declared death, that no sorcerer should sacrifice again among the Sons of Cimmer. He sent forth his soldiers, saying, 'Slay every sorcerer! Leave none alive!'

"Seven sorcerers sped to the sunrise beyond the Island Sea. Death-daunted they dwelt in the desert, cutting its cliffs for their cottages and at last counting a numerous nation, the Neuri."

To show I was listening, I nodded again.

"Sorcery they sent against the Sons of Cimmer, stealing the strength from their swords. Silver they sold to the Sons of Scoloti, paid in moon-pale ponies and brides bought for their proud priests. So they learned from our lips, copied our clothes and our customs.

"Soon they said, 'Strong are the Sons of Scoloti! Why do they dwell in the desert? Strike the Sons of Cimmer, a puling people languishing in a lordly land.' Then bent we our bows and waged war.

"Scattered were the Sons of Cimmer, wider with each wind. We pastured our ponies in their palaces and tented in their temples, princes of their plains.

"Long ago, low we laid them. Careful chroniclers count the kings since we came to the country of the Sons of

Cimmer, but count them I cannot." He sighed, his recitation ended.

I felt I knew why he had given it, and I asked, "But what of the Neuri, Oior?"

"How can a simple bowman speak of the sorcerers? They live in their ancient land, east of the Island Sea. But they live among us too, and no one can say who they are. They have our speech and our clothing. As well as we they draw the bow, and with a touch, tame horses. No one knows them, unless he sees the sign."

"And you have seen it," I prompted him.

He bowed his head in acknowledgment. "Apia burned her brand on the Neuri, price of the boy's blood. Once in each year, and sometimes more than once, each changes. 'Sorcerer' is your word, Latro. *Neurian,* say the Sons of Scoloti. Apia is earth, Artimpasa the moon."

"I understand," I said. "How does a Neurian change?"

"His eyes dim. His ears sharpen. Swift then are his feet across the plain—"

A dog howled in the distance. Oior gripped me by the arm. "Listen!"

"It's a dog," I said, "singing to the moon. Nothing more. There's a town—Teuthrone, the kybernetes called it—not far from here. Where there's a town, there are always dogs."

"When the Neuri change, they drink the blood of men and eat their flesh, pawing the dead to wake them."

"And you believe there is one here?"

Oior nodded. "On our ship. You have seen our ship. Have you stood in the lowest place, where the water laps the wooden walls?"

I shook my head.

"There is sand there, and water and wine, bread, dried meat, and other good things. Often I watch the man, the woman, and the child. You understand?"

I nodded again.

"Once they thirsted, and when the rest had eaten, no one had fed them. The man spoke to Hypereides. Hypereides is a

kindly man, for he has not even put out their eyes. He told
me to go to the lowest place and bring water, wine, bread,
olives, and cheese. I got them, and I thought it might be I
would never go there again, and it might be good to see all
that was there. I was where the oarmen stand, and do not
sit."

"In the stern?" I asked. "Where the steersmen are?"

"Beneath them. A step I took with back bent. Then two,
then three. It was very dark. The food is where the oarmen
stand because the evil water runs away when the ship is
pulled onto the shore. If I had turned and gone back then, I
would not have known. I took one step more, and eyes
opened, far before mine. Not a man's eyes."

"So you believe one of the other bowmen is a Neurian?"

"I have seen such eyes before," Oior said, "when my
sister died. Eyes that were like two white stones, cold and
bright. But now when I look into the eyes of the others, I
cannot see the stones. I heard the man and the woman, and
even the child, when they talked. You are blessed by your
gods and see unseen things. You must look into the eyes of
all three."

"I am cursed by our gods," I told him, "like your Neuri.
And Hypereides will not believe us."

"Behold," Oior said, and drew the dagger from his belt.
"Apia's prayer is scribed along the blade. It will send him to
his grave, and I will heap stones upon it. Then he cannot
return unless the stones are taken away. Will you look?"

I said, "Suppose I look and see nothing? Will you believe
me?"

"You will not see nothing." Oior pointed to the crescent
moon. "There is Artimpasa. You will see her in his eyes, or
Apia's black wolf. Then you will know."

"But if I do *not* see," I insisted, "will you believe me?"

Oior nodded. "You are my friend. I will believe."

"Then I will look."

"Good!" He rose smiling. "Come with me. I will take
you to the other bowmen. I will say, 'Here is Latro, friend to

the Sons of Scoloti, friend to Oior, enemy to all that is evil.'
I will speak the names, and you will take each by the hand
and look into his eyes.''

"I understand.''

"The rest will be listening to the man in chains, but the
bowmen do not listen, because this talk is like the cackling of
geese to us. Come, it is not far, and I know the path.''

It was not easy to see the way in the moonlight, for there
was in fact no path, though Oior moved as readily as if there
were. He was five strides or more ahead of me when an arm
circled my throat.

# —— CHAPTER XI ——

## In the Grip of the Neurian

I fell backward, half-strangled. For an instant there was a long knife, its point at my chest; perhaps its owner hesitated for fear his blade would pierce his own heart.

Steel flashed and he cried out, his lips near my ear. Oior was rushing back toward us. I was flung to one side. As I drew breath, I heard bone snap—a horrible sound, but a joyful one because the bone was not mine.

When I got to my feet, Oior was wiping his dagger on the hair at his belt, and the bowman who had watched the prisoners lay dead, his head twisted to one side.

"Thank you," I gasped. "Thank you, Oior."

If he heard me, he gave no sign; his dagger cleaned to his satisfaction, he plunged it back into its sheath.

Louder I said, "Thank you, Oior. We were friends already; now we are friends forever."

He shrugged. "A lucky throw. If not . . . Indeed, the goddess was in it."

"I have no money, except for what you gave me. But I will tell Hypereides. He will reward you, I'm sure."

Oior shook his head. "As you are my friend, Latro, do not tell. To the men of this land, the Sons of Scoloti and the Neuri are one. This would bring dishonor upon all. Go to the fire. Hear the man in chains. I will dig a place here for this Neurian with his own knife and pile it with stones so he cannot rise. Tomorrow he will be here, and we will not."

77

"I understand," I said. "Oior, even what you did—
I'm afraid I may forget. But we are friends forever.
Tell me."

He held his dagger out to me and with his free hand drew
the bow from his bowcase. "Put your hand on my bow," he
said. "Put your hand on my dagger. So we swear."

I did as he asked, and he pointed dagger and bow toward
the moon. *"More than brothers,"* he pronounced. *"Though
I die."*

"More than brothers," I replied, "though I die."

"When you forget, I will tell you, Latro," he said, "and
then you will remember. Go now."

I gathered up the trenchers and cups, and turned to say
good-bye to him. I wish I had not, and perhaps I will write of
that later, when I find words to tell of what was, perhaps,
only a trick of the moonlight.

Afterward I ran, and I had nearly reached the fire when I
heard shouts and groans. A party of sailors was carrying
something along the beach. Those who had been sitting about
the fire rose and went to them, and I went too.

Blood still seeped from the dead man's ragged wounds. I
turned aside from the sight, and the sailors from the fire
crowded around him. In truth, I was thankful I could see him
no longer.

Hypereides and the kybernetes pushed through to look at
him. I heard the kybernetes ask where he had been found,
and someone said, "At the edge of the water, sir."

The kybernetes must have felt the dead man's hair, though
I did not see him do it. "And dripping wet. Washed up. He
went for a swim at an unlucky time, I'm afraid. I've seen
things pulled from the sea—" If he finished the thought, I
did not hear him.

Hypereides said, "You, there. Go to the ship. There's a
roll of sailcloth in the supplies. Cut off a piece big enough to
wrap him in."

A sailor darted away.

The black man appeared beside me, asking by signs
whether I had seen the dead man, or whether I knew what

had befallen him; I could not be sure which. I shook my head.

Hypereides shouted, "We need an altar, and fast! Get to it, the rest of you. Pile up these rocks. Right here's as good a place as any."

I think the sailors were happy to have work to do. The altar semed almost to lift itself from the ground, a heap of stones as high as my waist, as long as my outstretched arms and nearly as wide.

Pindaros joined us, bringing the woman and Io. "Where have you been?" he asked me. "Io said you were up on the ridge, and she seemed worried about you. I tried to go, but Hypereides wouldn't let me, or our friend here either; afraid we'd run off, I suppose." He lowered his voice. "He was right, too, at least so far as I was concerned."

I explained lamely, "There was someone Io couldn't see. And other things."

The woman said, "You and she had better stay with us in the future."

Hypereides came to speak to Pindaros. "I know some prayers, but if you could compose something special . . . ?"

"I'll try," Pindaros said.

"You won't have long to work on it, I'm afraid."

"I'll do the best I can. What was his name?"

"Kekrops. He was an upper-bank man, if that helps." Hypereides hesitated. "Something short enough for me to remember after hearing it once or twice."

"I'll try," Pindaros said again. He turned away, lost in thought.

The dead man was laid before the altar and a fire of driftwood kindled upon it. Ten sailors who had sworn they had good voices and no blood guilt sang a litany to the sea god: *"Horse-Breaker, Earth-Shaker, Wave-Maker, spare us! Ship-Taker, Spring-Maker, Anchor-Staker, care for us!"* And so on.

When they were finished, Hypereides, in full armor with his blue crest upon his helmet, cast bread into the fire and poured wine from a golden cup.

> "Third brother of the greater gods,
>   By destiny, Death's king,
>   Accept for suffering Kekrops's sake,
>   The food, the wine we bring.
>   He labored for thy brother,
>   Thy brother used him sore.
>   Accept a sailor cast adrift,
>   Beached on thy river's shore."

Some beast howled nearby, and little Io, sitting on my right, pressed herself against me. "It's only a dog," I whispered. "Don't be frightened."

The black man reached across her to touch my shoulder. When I looked at him, he shook his head and bared his teeth.

Hypereides finished the poem in a thundering voice I would not have believed he commanded.

> "Yet should the old man slacken,
>   You'll find no better oar,
>   To row such souls as Ocean rolls
>   Unto Death's bitter shore."

"By all the Twelve," whispered Pindaros. "He remembered the whole of it. I wouldn't have bet a spit on him."

Hypereides then cast beans, mussels, and meat into the fire, with other things. Two sailors rushed forward with leather buckets of seawater to quench it. Two more quickly wrapped the dead man and carried him away.

"It was a wonderful poem," I told Pindaros.

He shook his head. The men around us were rising and drifting back to the big fires nearer the ships.

"Surely it was. See how many of them are crying."

"They were his friends," Pindaros said. "Why shouldn't they weep? May the Gentle Ones snatch you! Poetry must shake the heart." There were tears in his own eyes; and so that I would not see them he strode away, his chain dragging after him in the sand.

My thoughts were still upon the fight on the ridge, and I

glanced at the ragged skyline it showed against the stars. A tall figure with a staff stood there with a shorter figure, like a boy, beside him.

The woman who had sat beside Pindaros took my arm. "Come, Latro, it's time to go."

"No," I told her. "You take Io. I'll come soon. I think this is someone I should speak with."

She and the black man followed the direction of my gaze, but it was clear they saw nothing. Holding the chain that bound her leg in one hand, the woman took Io's hand in the other. They and the black man hurried off, followed by a bowman who was not Oior.

Alone, I watched the tall figure come down from the ridge. After him trailed the smaller one, who seemed often to stumble. A light surrounded the tall figure; the lesser one had no such luminosity but seemed translucent, so that I sometimes dimly glimpsed the rocks and trees behind him. Neither cast a shadow in the moonlight.

When the tall figure had come near, I saluted him, calling, "Hail!" By then I could see that his hair and beard were gray, his face stern and dark.

"Hail," he answered, and lifted his staff. His voice was deep and hollow.

I asked him, as politely as I could, whether he had come for Kekrops, and offered to lead him to the body.

"There is no need," he told me, and he pointed with his staff to the foot of the altar, where Kekrops had been laid out. I was startled to see that the body was still there; it rose despite its wounds and stumbled across the sand to him.

"You fear the dead," the tall figure told me, seeing my look. "You need not; no one will do you less harm."

The smaller figure had left the slope of the ridge; while we spoke, it crossed the beach toward us. It was a bowman dressed like those on our ship, and I asked the tall one if he was the man who had tried to kill me.

"Yes," he said. "But he will not do so now. Until he is freed, he is my slave."

"He is a murderer," I said. "I hope you will punish him for what he did."

The bowman shook his head. It swung loosely, like a blossom on a broken stalk.

"He cannot speak," the tall figure told me, "unless you first speak to him. That is my law, which I lay upon all my slaves."

I asked the dead bowman, "Didn't you kill Kekrops? Can you deny his murder when he stands beside you?" Now that I must write that, it seems strange. I can only say it did not seem so then.

"Spu killed only in war," the dead bowman murmured. He held a finger to his eye. "Spu would kill you, Neurian, in justice for him."

"We must go," the tall figure told me. "It is not right that they should remain on earth, and I have much to do. I have lingered only to tell you that my wife's mother sends her to speak with you. Do not forget."

"I'll do my best not to," I promised.

He nodded. "And I will remind you of it when I can. I do not understand mercy, and thus I am as I am; but perhaps she will be merciful to you, and I can learn from her. I hope she is at least just." He took a step forward, and it seemed to me that he stood upon a stair I could not see. With each step, he sank more deeply into the ground; the sailor and the bowman followed him.

"Good-bye," I called. And then to the bowman, I cannot say why, "I forgive you!" He smiled at that—it was strange to see the dead mouth smile—and touched his forehead.

Then all three were gone.

"There you are!" It was the kybernetes, with a sailor carrying a javelin in tow. "You shouldn't go off by yourself, Latro. It's dangerous for you." He lowered his voice. "I've just learned that one of the bowmen plans to kill you. A man of mine who knows a bit of their gabble overheard them talking. Do you remember this stick?"

He pointed to the sailor, and I shook my head.

"I chose him because he's a stout fellow and he watched

you before. His name's Lyson. He's not to leave you . . . and you're not to leave him, understand? Those are my orders.''

"Was the bowman who wants to kill me named Spu?" I asked.

"Why, yes," the kybernetes said. "How did you know?"

"I was talking to him as you came up. He was a simple, decent man, I think.''

The kybernetes looked at Lyson, and Lyson looked at the ground, shaking his head.

The kybernetes cleared his throat. "Well, if you meet Spu again before we find him, try to remember that he may not be so friendly the next time. I just hope Lyson's with you—and he'd better be.''

Now Lyson is indeed with me, though he sleeps. Only I am left awake, and the black man, and the sentries Hypereides has set around us and the ships. A moment ago, a lovely young woman left the largest ship, and seeing that I saw her, halted to speak with me. I asked who she was.

She smiled at that. "Why, Latro, my name's been on your lips half the day. Would you like to see me fatter, with red hair? I can do that, if you wish.''

"No," I told her. "You are so much more lovely than your picture on the sail.''

Her smile faded. "Yet plain girls are luckier. Ask your little Io.''

I did not understand her, and I believe she knew it; yet she did not explain. "I only stopped to tell you I am going to the Great Mother," she said. "I was her priestess once; and though I was taken from her long ago, it may still mean something to her, if only a little. Because you've loved my beauty today, I'll ask her to be kind to you.''

"Is she merciful?" I asked, remembering what the tall lord of death had said.

Europa shook her head. "Sometimes she is kind," she told me. "But we are none of us merciful.''

She has walked into the ridge, which opened a door for her. There is another woman on the ship now. I see her pace

the deck in the moonlight, as if deep in thought. She wears a
helmet with a high crest, like Hypereides's, and her shield
writhes with serpents.

Her face recalls to me the face of Oior, Oior's face not as I
saw it at any other time, but as I saw it when I looked back
upon leaving him and saw him bent over the dead bowman.
When I had met him on the beach and when we had talked at
the top of this narrow ridge of land, his sun-browned face
had been as open as the faces of the sailors, though without
their vivacity and native cunning, a face as strong and as
simple as the face of a charger or a bullock. It was a face
much like my own, I think, and I liked him better for it.

And yet when I turned back to look at him as I descended
the slope, it had changed utterly, though all its features were
the same. It had become the face of a scholar of the worst
kind, of the sort of man who has studied many things
hidden from common men and grown wise and corrupt. He
smiled to see the dead bowman, and he stroked the livid
cheek as a mother strokes her child.

I must remember that.

# ─── CHAPTER XII ───

## The Goddess of Love

THE Lady of the Doves once blessed this place. Her statue was thrown down by the barbarians and both its hands broken off. When we came, the black man and I set it upon its base again—an act of piety, so says Pindaros, that must surely win us her favor. Though her hands lie at her feet with her doves still perched on their fingers, she is a most lovely goddess.

But there are a great many earlier things I wish to record here while I still remember them.

We came into the Bay of Peace about midmorning, I believe, though that is lost in the mist. The first thing I can recall clearly from this day is seeing the huts stretching far up the hillsides of Peace, many unroofed.

It was on that island, so Hypereides told me, that the poor of his city found refuge when the Great King's army came, and where they remained for the most part even after the Battle of Peace, for fear it might come again. Now that a decisive victory has been won on land, they are abandoning their huts and returning to the city.

There are three bays on the east coast of the island, and the city of Peace is on the southernmost. The richest families that came to Peace are there, having paid heavily for their lodgings. We put in at the middle bay, Hypereides hoping, as he said, to ferry some poorer folk back.

"Besides," he told me, "this is where we were before the battle. The families of a lot of my men are here, and other people who helped us out in various ways."

Pindaros, who was listening to Hypereides with me, put in, "You were wounded in the battle that freed them to go home, Latro. But since you were on the wrong side, you'd better not tell anybody that."

"And you'd better not go ashore at all," Hypereides told him. "Once they hear that Cowland tongue of yours, they're apt to stone you. Didn't you fight, too? You can't be much more than forty, and you look able enough."

Pindaros grinned at him. "I'm thirty-nine, Hypereides— the best time of a man's life, as I'm sure you remember. But as for fighting, you know what Archilichos wrote:

"Some lucky lout has got my noble shield.
I had to run, and dropped it on the way;
So 'tis with us who fly the reeking field.
Who cares? Tomorrow's loot is what I lost today."

Hypereides shook his finger at him. "You're going to get yourself in trouble, poet. There are many in the city who won't honor your supple mouth. Or tolerate it, either."

"But if I should get into trouble, good master, why, you're in trouble too. So why don't you free me? Then in the next war you may be my prisoner instead of I yours. I'll treat you royally, I swear."

We were under oar already, for the wind was in the southwest and the strait runs due south; thus it was easy to bring all three ships into the wind to enter the bay. By that time I could see the crowd on shore, and the kybernetes came forward to suggest we stow our mast and sail.

Hypereides wet a finger and held it up. "There's not much of a blow. Don't you think it might swing north later?"

The kybernetes shrugged. "I've seen it happen, sir. I wouldn't count on it."

"Neither would I, but let's not count it out, either. Besides, these fellows should welcome the chance to sweat a bit and show their wives how hard they're working."

"There's something in that. But if I were you, Hypereides,

I'd put a couple of soldiers at the gangplank. Otherwise you'll get enough women on board to capsize her."

"I've already ordered it," Hypereides told him. "Still I'm glad you mentioned it. It won't hurt to lie to for a bit here, will it? I've got a speech to make to the crew."

"We'd have to, to unship the mast."

"Good." Going aft to face the crew, he waved for their attention and bellowed, *"Up oars! In oars!* Waterman, you can pass the dipper while I'm talking. Men, how many of you have families still on the island? As far as you know?"

About half the hands went up, including Lyson's.

"All right. We don't want to lose a lot of time here, so those who don't, stay on your benches. The kybernetes will call the ones who do to the gangplank by oar groups, one from port, one from starboard. That's no more than six at a time, ever. If you see 'em—that's wives, children, parents, or your wife's parents, and nobody else—tell 'em to come to the gangplank and the soldiers will let 'em board. If you don't see 'em, they're probably back home already, so go back to your bench so the next oar group can come up. I have to go ashore—"

There were a few muttered groans.

"—to consult with the authorities. Acetes and his men will keep order; if you know what's good for you, you'll do as they say. While they're on this ship, your wives and families are your responsibility. Keep 'em in hand or they'll be put ashore, and not on the mainland, either. Otherwise nobody's to leave the ship till we get to Tieup. I should be back by the time your families are on board and the kybernetes has found places for 'em and got 'em settled down, and as soon as I'm back, off we go. I want to make Tieup before nightfall, *you hear me?"*

That brought a rousing cheer.

*"And I won't be denied!* So get some rest, because you may have to break your backs before we do. Now— *Out oars! Mind the count!"* He beat the rowing rhythm with one hand on the other as the flute boy readied his instrument. *"I*

*love my wife, and she loves me! But all I do is stir this sea! I
love my girl, and she loves me! But all I do is stir this sea!"*

The rowers took up the chant, and soon men with mooring
lines were leaping to the quay, where a thousand slatternly
women greeted our ships by calling out names that might
have been anybody's, holding up their babies, and waving
rags of every color, and many that were of no color at all.
Hypereides, whose armor I had polished with similar rags,
could hardly get a foot on the gangplank for the press of
them, and at length the soldiers had to drive them back with
the butts of their spears to permit him to leave.

Astonishingly (or so I thought) a few of these women were
actually the wives of various rowers. When the first hugs and
kisses were done with, the kybernetes made them sit on the
thalamite benches (which run completely across the ship
under the storming deck) and threatened to put them on the
ballast if the ship became unstable, as he assured them it
would if they let their children run loose.

A bowman came aft to join us as we watched. "I am
Oior," he said. "You do not remember?"

When I shook my head, Io pulled at my chiton, whispering, "Watch out, Latro. You know what Lyson said."

"Oior does Latro no harm. Spu was the Son of Scoloti
who wished harm to Latro, and Spu is gone."

Pindaros drawled, "I heard about that. Hypereides thinks
he jumped ship at Teuthrone. What do you think, Oior?"

The bowman laughed. "Oior is a Son of Scoloti. Oior
does not think. Ask any man of your people. But tell me, does
it not make you sad to see so many men who now greet their
families again, when you do not?"

"I don't have much of one, for which I thank the gods,"
Pindaros told him. "If I did, somebody else would have
claimed my estate. Let's just hope that our noble enemies
here leave me in possession—otherwise, I'll need a few rich
relations to take care of me, and I haven't got them."

"Sad for you. Oior has wife." He held out his hand at
waist level with the thumb folded and all four fingers extended. "So many sons. Many, many daughters, too many

for any man. You want girl? Play with this one, take care of
her when older. You choose. Oior sell very cheap."

Hilaeira gasped, "Would he? Really do that? Sell his own
children?"

"Of course," Pindaros said. "All barbarians will, except
for the kings. And very wise of them too, I'd say. Children
are easily got and lots of trouble afterward. I'm with you,
Oior."

"Easily got by men," Hilaeira snapped. "Not by us. Not
that I know for myself, but I've helped others. Why, my
aunt—"

"Is somebody we don't want to hear about now," Pindaros
told her.

"You talk to captain very much. Oior wants to know what
you think this ship will do."

"Go to Tieup and get refitted. She's in pretty good shape
now, so that shouldn't take more than a couple days. After
that, perhaps join the fleet, which I should imagine is hanging about the Circling Isles hoping for a chance at the Great
King's navy. Or the strategists may cook up another special
task for Hypereides. One never knows."

"And you? Not just you only, this girl, this woman, this
man, black man."

"We'll be left in the city, all of us. Those of us from the
shining city will be sold as slaves, I think we can depend on
that. If they've left me my estate, I'll buy our way out, and
if they haven't, they haven't. Latro and the black man may
be sold too—if they are, I'll buy them and free them, so that
Latro can obey the oracle of the Shining God. If they're held
as prisoners of war, well, I'll see what I can do."

Hilaeira said, "I don't want to be a freed slave. I'm a
freeborn citizen."

"Of a conquered city," Pindaros reminded her dryly.

"Bowmen go ashore in Tieup?"

"Certainly. I imagine you'll be paid there, at least if you
ask for it. Then you can go home, if you like."

"Oior will maybe leave this ship, go on some other."

I asked him whether fighting for anyone who would hire him were the only way he had to earn his living.

"You also," he said. "So this man speaks."

"I know," I said. "I wanted to learn about you because I thought it might tell me something of myself. You have a wife and children; do you have a house too, and a farm?"

He shook his head. "The Sons of Scoloti do not have those things. We live in wagons, follow grass. Oior has many, many horses, many cattle also. Here in south you have pigs and sheep. We never see them if not we come. They are slow to walk. They could not live in my land."

Pindaros asked, "Is the sun in your eyes, Oior?"

"Yes, yes. Light from the water." He seemed to stare at the deck. "Eyes are the bowman. I go now."

When he had left, Pindaros remarked, "That was rather strange, don't you think?"

I said, "For a bowman to have weak eyes? I suppose so."

Io murmured, "They were only weak when they looked at you, master."

Hypereides returned as the last of the sailors' families were being settled, just as he had promised. With him were a dozen attractive women, finely dressed in gowns of yellow, pink, and scarlet, with much silver jewelry and some gold. Several held flutes or little drums, but their many bags and boxes were carried for them by porters whom their leader paid.

This was a plump woman somewhat younger than Hypereides, with red hair and cold blue eyes. She came aft with him as we pushed off from the quay, now riding so deep that the greased boots of the thalamites' oars were almost in the water. "Well, well," she said, looking at me. "Here's a likely boy! Where'd you get this one?"

"Picked them all up at Tower Hill after we left Dolphins, as I told you. He's the perfect confidant—forgets everything overnight."

"Really?" I would not have believed those hard eyes could be sad, but for a moment they were.

"I swear it. I'll introduce you to him, but tomorrow he

won't know your name unless he notes it down. Will you, Latro?''

Wishing to please her and discountenance him, I said, "How could I forget it? No one could forget such a woman, whom once seen must remain in the eye of the mind forever.''

She dimpled and took my right hand between hers, which were small and moist. "I'm Kalleos, Latro. Do you know you're quite the figure of a man?''

"No," I said. "But thank you.''

"You are. You might pose for one of the sculptors, and perhaps you will. In fact, you'd be just about perfect, if only you had money. You don't, do you?''

"I have this." I showed her my coin.

She laughed. "One spit! Where'd you get it?''

"I don't know.''

"Is this a joke, Hypereides? Will he actually forget who I am?''

"Unless he writes it in that book he carries, and remembers to read what he's written.''

"Wonderful!" Smiling at me still, she said, "What you have there isn't really money, Latro, only change. A daric or a mina, that's money. Hypereides, will you let me have him?''

He shook his head as though in despair. "This war's ruined the leather trade. In the old days, certainly. But now . . .'' He shrugged.

"What do you think it's done for us, cooped up on Peace with a bunch of refugees? Latro, you look strong enough. Can you box or wrestle?''

"I don't know.''

Pindaros said, "I've seen him with a sword—no spear and no hoplon. If I were a strategist, I'd trade ten shieldmen for him.''

Kalleos looked at him. "Don't I know you, pig?''

He nodded. "Some friends treated me to a dinner at your house just before the barbarians came.''

"That's right!" Kalleos snapped her fingers. "You're the

poet. You got Rhoda to help you with a love lyric. It ended up being a little, uh—''

"Paphian," Pindaros supplied.

"Exactly! Pinfeather . . . What's your name?''

"Pindaros, madame.''

"Pindaros, I'm sorry I called you a pig. It's the war, you know—everybody does it. Hypereides will let you come with him tonight, if he knows what's good for him. I don't know if my house's still standing, but we'll make it up to you whether it is or not. No charge. If you need money, I could even lend you a few drachmas till you get home again.''

I do not think Pindaros is often without words, but he had none then. At last Hilaeira said, "Thank you. That's very, very kind of you, madame.''

"Wait!'' Pindaros leaped into the air, waving his hands. "I've got it—the city's saved!'' He whirled about, arms wide, to address Hilaeira and Io. "Our freedom! My estate! We get to keep them!''

"It's true, Hypereides,'' Kalleos told him. "It's the Rope Makers. Our people wanted to burn Hill and take Cowland, but the Rope Makers wouldn't stand for it. They want to make sure we'll always have an enemy in the north.''

# ── CHAPTER XIII ──

## Oh, Violet Crowned City!

Pindaros exclaimed, "Oh, bright bulwark of our nation, ruined!" A thin blue smoke overhung what had been the city of Deathless Thought; and though it was set well back from the sea (Tieup, at the edge of the water, had fared much better) the clear air and bright summer sunshine mercilessly revealed how little remained.

"Oh, violet crowned!" Pindaros turned away.

Hilaeira asked, "How can you sing its praises? This is what these people would have done to us."

"Because we chose to surrender," Pindaros told her. "And lost even when we fought for the Great King. They chose to resist, and won even with us against them. We were wrong, and they were right. Their city was destroyed; ours deserved it."

"You can't mean that."

"I do. I love our shining city as much as any man can love his home, and I'm delighted it's endured. But I studied here with Agathocles and Apollodoros, and I won't pretend this was the justice of the gods."

The black man pointed to himself and me to indicate we had assisted in the destruction. I nodded to show I understood, hoping no one else had seen him.

Hypereides came aft rubbing his hands. The wind had veered north as soon as we left the bay, so he felt certain he enjoyed divine favor. "What a ship! Loaded to the gunnels and still outreaching the others. That's the Long Coast whiz-

zing past, my boy, the land that bore her and us. If I'd
known she'd be this good, I'd have had three triremes instead
of one and the triacontors. Well, too bad for their skippers, I
say. This'll teach 'em their old boss's still the boss.''

Io piped, "*Clytia* has her oars out, sir. Now *Eidyia*'s
putting hers out too.''

"They think they can beat us like that, little sweetheart,
but don't you bet on it. We can match 'em trick for trick.''

In a few moments more, our own crew was hard at work.
*"I love my boy, and so does he! But all I do is stir this sea!"*
They stirred it well enough; we reached the boathouses a
ship's length ahead of *Eidyia* and three before *Clytia*.

I went forward to join Kalleos while the sailors were
unshipping the masts. She was keeping watch over her women,
who were alternately snubbing Acetes's soldiers and joking
with them. "Wasn't that a lovely sail?" she asked. "I'll tell
you, I hate to see it put away.''

"Not half so beautiful as the original, madame.''

Her blue eyes shone. "Latro, you and me are going to get
along.''

"Am I to go with you, then, madame?''

"That's right. Hypereides hasn't signed a bill of sale yet,
but we've hooked fingers on the deal, and he'll draw one up
tonight. You see, Latro, in my business I need a man who
can keep order. It's better if he doesn't have to fight, but he
has to be able to. I used to have a freedman. Gello, his name
was. But he had to go in the army, and I hear they got him in
the winter skirmishing. Be polite, do your work, don't bother
my girls unless they want to be bothered, and you'll never
feel the whip. Get me mad, and . . . well, they always need
a few good men in the silver mines.''

"I'll write what you say here," I told her. "Then I won't
forget." Yet even as I spoke, I was thinking that I am no
one's slave, no matter how these people talk.

As soon as the masts were down, we had glided into the
boathouse. Now sailors and sailors' families were crowding
ashore. I started to go with them, but Kalleos stopped me.
"Wait till they're gone. If you think I'm going to walk to the

city with them, you don't know me as well as you're going to. I'll hire a sedan chair if I can. Otherwise I plan to take my time, and I don't want their brats climbing all over me."

I said, "If you'll tell me how much you want to promise the bearers, I'll hire a chair for you now and have them bring it to the ship."

She cocked her head at me. "You know, you may turn out to be a nicer buy than I thought. But I've a better idea yet. Turn left out of the boathouse and go down the narrowest street you see. Three doors on the left, and there's a man who used to rent them. He may still have his chairs, even if most of his bearers are in the navy. Tell him Kalleos sent you, and you'll pay a spit for a chair without bearers, to be returned by you in the morning. If he won't agree, throw down the spit and take a chair. Here's a spit, and a drachma too, in case he wants a deposit. Bring the chair here, and we'll hire one of these sailors to carry the other end."

"I think I can get someone who won't have to be paid, madame, if you'll feed him."

"Better and better! Go to it."

I waved to the black man, and together we had no difficulty in persuading the chair owner to let us have a light one with long poles and a painted canopy.

"I lost a little flesh on the island," Kalleos told us as she took her seat. "I can tell by the way my gowns fit. Lucky for you I did."

While I had been gone, she had hired a dozen sailors to carry the bags and clothes boxes; so there was quite a procession, the gaudily gowned women following us, and the sailors following them with the baggage. The women were in a cheerful mood, happy to return to the city even if the city was destroyed. When we reached the stones that marked its borders, Kalleos had them strike up a tune on their drums and flutes while a tall, handsome woman called Phye strummed a lyre and sang.

"She has a lovely voice, hasn't she?" Kalleos said.

She had, and I agreed. The black man was carrying the front of the chair, and I the back.

"Two drachmas a night I could get for her, if only she'd learn philosophy," Kalleos grumbled. "But she won't. You can't get it through that thick skull of hers. Last year I got one of the finest sophists in the city to lecture her. After three days, I asked her to tell me what she knew, and all she'd say was, 'But what's the *use* of it?' " Kalleos shook her head.

"What is the use, madame?"

"Why, to get two drachmas a night, you big ninny! A man won't pay that kind of money unless he thinks he's sleeping above himself, no matter how good-looking the girl is, or how accommodating, either. He doesn't want her to talk about Solon or whether the world's all fire or all water; but he wants to think she could if he felt like it.

"Solon!" Kalleos chuckled. "When I was younger, I used to know an old woman who'd known him. You know what he wanted? A girl who could drink with him cup for cup. That's what she said. They finally found one, a big blond Geta who cost them a fortune. She drank with him all night, slept with him, and thanked him—still in the bed—by signs when he paid her and tipped her and went home. Then the owner and the fancy man—that's you, Latro—told her to get out of bed, and she fell on her face and broke her nose."

I had been looking at the smoke over the city. I asked how it could still be burning, when it had been destroyed, as I understood it, last autumn.

"Oh, those aren't the fires the barbarians lit," Kalleos told me. "That's just dust raised by the builders, and people burning wreckage to be rid of it. A few went over as soon as the Great King's army left, then more when the weather turned good this year; and now all the rest after the victory at Clay. The best people are coming home from Argolis too, and all that means that the customers will be here, not on the island. So here we are, and the playing and singing is to let them know we're back."

She pointed. "They'll be building a new temple for the goddess up there on the sacred rock—that's what I hear—when the war's over and they can raise the money."

"It will be a beautiful site," I said.

"Always has been. There's a spring of salt water up there that was put there by the Earth Shaker himself in the Golden Age, when he tried to claim the city. And up till last year, the oldest olive tree in the whole world, the first olive tree, planted by the goddess in person. The barbarians cut it down and burned it; but the roots have put up a new shoot, that's what I hear."

I told her I would like to see it, and that I was surprised the citizens had not fought to the death to defend such things.

"A lot did. The temple treasurers, because there was so much they couldn't get it all away, and a lot of poor people who were left behind by the last ships. Before the Great King's army got here, the Assembly sent to the Navel to ask what to do. The god always gives good answers, but he usually puts them so you wish he hadn't. This time he said we'd be safe behind walls of wood. I guess you understand that."

She looked back to see whether I did, and I shook my head.

"Well, neither did we. Most people thought it meant the ships, but there was an old palisade around the hilltop, and some people thought it meant that. They strengthened it quite a bit, but the barbarians burned it with fire arrows and killed them all."

After that she did not seem to wish to talk, and I contented myself with listening to the women's music and looking about at the destruction of Thought, which had not—or so it seemed to me—been very large to begin with.

Soon Kalleos directed the black man to turn down a side street. There we halted at a house with two walls still standing, and she stepped out. Her head was proud as she walked through the broken doorway, and she turned it neither to the right nor the left; but I saw a tear roll down her cheek.

The women stopped their playing and singing, and scattered to search for possessions they had left behind, though I think none of them has yet found much. The sailors laid down their burdens and demanded their pay, an obol apiece. The black man and I explained (he by signs and I with words) that we had nothing and went inside too, to look for Kalleos.

We found her in the courtyard kicking at rubbish. "Here you are at last," she said. "Get busy! We'll have guests tonight, and I want all this cleared out, every stick of it."

I said, "You haven't paid the sailors, madame."

"Because I've got more work for them, you ninny. Tell them to come in here. No, get to work, and I'll talk to them myself."

We did what we could, saving those things that appeared repairable or still usable and burning the rest, as a thousand others were doing all over the city. Soon the sailors were at work too, patching the door and setting brick upon brick to rebuild the walls. Kalleos asked how many urns had been left whole. There were only three, and I told her.

"Not nearly enough. Latro, you can remember for a day or so—isn't that what Hypereides said?"

I did not know, but the black man nodded in agreement.

"Fine. I want you to go to the market. Most of the people selling there will have stalls or a cloth on the ground. Pay no attention to those. Find a potter who's selling out of a cart. You understand?"

"Yes, madame."

"And find a flower-seller with a cart too. Tell them to follow you. Bring them and their carts back here, and I'll buy everything they have. There's nothing like flowers when you don't have furniture. Your friend's to stay here and work, understand? And you're not to loiter, either. We've a lot to do before tonight."

I did as Kalleos had told me, but on the way back I was stopped by a man of unusual and rather less than prepossessing appearance. The chlamys that draped his narrow shoulders was of a pale hyacinth; he carried a tall, crooked staff topped with the figure of a woman, and his dark eyes were so prominent they seemed about to leap from his head.

With his staff held to one side, he bowed very low in the Oriental way. It seemed to me there was something of mockery in it; but then there seemed something of mockery—lent by his eyes, his tall, lean frame, and his disordered hair—in all he said and did.

"I should be most grateful for a trifle of information, good sir. May I inquire whom it is who has need of so many urns and blossoms? That it's none of my affair, I well understand; but surely it will do no harm to tell me. And who knows? Soon I may be in a position to do you, sir, some little favor in return. It is the mouse, after all, that gnaws the net that binds the lion, as a certain wise slave from the east taught us long ago."

"They're for Kalleos, my mistress," I told him.

His mouth opened so widely when he grinned that it seemed he showed a hundred teeth. "Kalleos, dear old Kalleos! I know her very well. We're good friends, Kalleos and I. I wasn't aware she had returned to this glorious city."

"She came back only today," I said.

"Wonderful! May I accompany you?" He looked around as though reconciling the destruction with the city as he had known it. "Why, her house is only a few doors away, I believe? Tell her, fellow, that an old admirer who would pay his respects awaits her leisure. I am Eurykles the Necromancer."

# ── CHAPTER XIV ──

## How Strange a Celebration

PINDAROS said, "Was there ever anything like it?" He waved at the banks of flowers, with the broken walls beyond them only half restored. "Now it's the city of the Lady of Thought indeed, Latro. The people are here again, yet her owls roost in the ruins. What a poem I shall make of all this!"

Behind him, Hypereides said, "When you write it, don't forget to say I was here, and that I drank my wine and cuddled my wench as of old."

"You're no fit subject for great poetry," Pindaros told him. "No, stop, I'll make you so. For a thousand years, your name will be linked with Achilles's."

I had tallied them in my mind as they trooped in, six in all: Pindaros, Hypereides, the kybernetes, Acetes, and two others I did not recognize, the captains of *Eidyia* and *Clytia*. Now Acetes was holding out the bundle he had carried into the house. "Here, Latro, Hypereides said you should have these."

I unwound the sailcloth and found bronze disks for the breast and back, and with them a hooked sword and a bronze belt. It was strange to touch the cool metal of the sword and belt, because I, who remembered nothing else, felt I remembered them, though I could not have told where I had worn them or even when I had lost them. I buckled them on, knowing they had been mine before, but no more than that.

When I had put the disks in the room Kalleos had given me, I returned to the courtyard, where she had greeted her

100

guests and was making them comfortable on the couches she bought this afternoon. "Hypereides," she said, pouring his wine herself, "I've a proposal to make to you."

He smiled. "No one can say he found Hypereides unready for business."

"I told you there'd be nobody here tonight but you and your guests. If you'll look around, you'll see I've kept my word."

"You've cheated me already," Hypereides told her. "The stars are coming. But never mind, I won't ask for my slave back. Only for the black one, whom you took without a by-your-leave."

"Certainly," Kalleos said. "I thought he was a free sailor when I borrowed him. He can return with you in the morning. But Hypereides, a friend of mine dropped in today when he heard I was back in the city. He's as merry a fellow as you'll ever meet, full of jokes and stories, I promise you. If you don't want him to join your party, just say so and I swear you'll never see him. But if you've no objection, I'll be forever grateful. And of course there'll be no charge to him or you. His name's Eurykles of Miletos."

At that moment, one of the women came to tell me the food had arrived, and I went to the rear entrance to help the cookshop owner and the black man unload.

Kalleos came just as we were finishing. "Good, good! They're all hungry. Do you know anything about food, Latro?"

"I don't remember," I told her.

"I suppose not." She looked at the trays I was making up. "At least you're doing well enough so far. The girls will carry them in, understand? You don't go in again unless there's trouble. I don't expect any tonight, but you never can tell. Try to stay awake and don't drink, and everything will be fine. Sometimes a girl screams and sometimes she *screams*. You know what I mean?"

"I think so."

"Well, don't go in unless one *screams*. Got it? If all of them start screaming, come fast. Don't draw that sword unless you have to, and don't use it no matter what. Where'd you get it, anyway?''

"From the Swift God," I said, and only when I had spoken realized I did not know what I meant by what I had said.

"You poor boy." Kalleos kissed me lightly on the cheek. "Phye, dear, get some of those lazy sluts in here to take these trays so the man has room to work. Tune your lyre if you haven't already, and tell the flute girls to fetch their whistles. But wait till the trays have been brought in before you start."

"I know," Phye said. "I know."

Turning back to me, Kalleos shook her head. " 'Wine, music, and women—what else does a man need?' That's what your friend the poet asked me. And do you know, I nearly told him. Meat, for one thing; veal and lamb, and they cost me— I won't say, it isn't polite, but a lot. Not to mention some nice fish, three kinds of cheese, bread, figs, grapes, and honey. And tomorrow you'll sweep half of it off the floor. You didn't come free, Latro, let me tell you." She paused, studying me. "You know, I used to be a slave myself. From up north."

I said, "I wondered, because of your coloring. Very few people here have red hair or blue eyes."

"I'm a Budini, or I was. I don't even remember their words any more. Somebody stole me, I think, when I was just a little girl." She paused again. "Do you want to be free, Latro?"

"I am free," I told her. "It's only that I don't remember."

She sighed. "Well, as long as you don't, you're going to have to have somebody around who does and will tell you what to do. I suppose it might as well be me."

When all the food was ready, I went to the courtyard arch to listen to the flutes; but in a few moments Pindaros came out and drew me back into the kitchen. "Hypereides has sold you to Kalleos," he said.

"Yes, I've been working for her."

"That puts me in serious difficulties, as I hope you understand."

I told him that until I found my home and friends I would be as happy in this place as in any.

"Your happiness—permit me to speak frankly—doesn't much concern me now. The pledge I made in the temple of the Shining God does. I promised to take you to the shrine of the Great Mother. I've done my best so far, and I must say the Shining God's rewarded me handsomely: I've heard the playing of a god and your singing. That's a privilege given few, and it's improved my own poetry almost beyond belief. But if I return to my city without fulfilling my vow . . ."

"Yes?" I asked.

"He may take it away—that's what I'm afraid of. And even if he doesn't, someone's bound to ask about our visit to the shrine. What am I to say? That I've left you here a slave while I raise the money to buy your freedom? What will they think of me? We've got to work out something."

"I'll try," I told him.

He patted my back. "I know you will, and so will I. And if I can get you to the shrine, perhaps you'll be cured. Then we'll worry about your happiness, both of us. Probably you'll want to return to your homeland, as you say, and I'll arrange passage for you on some trading ship. The war's nearly over now, and the merchants will be sailing again."

"I'd like that," I said. "To return home and find people I won't forget."

Over Pindaros's shoulder, I saw the rear door swing back very quietly. For an instant, the black man looked in. When he saw us, he held a finger to his lips, then gestured for me to join him and shut the door again.

"You'd better go back in there," I told Pindaros. "Before you're missed. I'll remember."

"It doesn't matter," he said. "They think I'm relieving myself."

"Pindaros, is your Shining God a very great god?"

"One of the greatest. He's the god of music and poetry, of

light, sudden death, herds and flocks, healing, and much
more.''

"Then if he wishes me to visit this shrine, I will do so. He
trusted you to guide me; I think you should trust him to guide
us.''

Pindaros shook his head as if in wonder. "Is it because
you can't remember the past that you're so wise, Latro?''

We chatted for a few moments more, he telling me about
the refitting of Hypereides's ships and I telling him of the
work the black man and I had done for Kalleos.

"You've accomplished wonders,'' Pindaros told me. "It's
almost as though I were at some dinner in our own city. Do
you think they'll ask me to recite?''

"I imagine so,'' I said.

He shook his head again. "That's the trouble with being a
poet: your friends all think you're a public entertainer. Worse
luck, I don't have anything suitable. I'll dodge it if I can—
propose singing or games.''

"I'm sure you'll think of something.''

Turning away, he muttered, "I'd a hundred times sooner
think of a way to get you to the shrine.''

As soon as he had left, I hurried to the rear door. The
black man grinned at me from the darkness outside and held
up a sleeping child. "Io.''

I nodded, for I recalled her from this morning when we were
still on Hypereides's ship.

He stepped into the kitchen, where there was more light,
and walked his fingers through the air, holding her cradled in
one arm.

I said, "All that way? No wonder she's tired. I suppose
she followed Pindaros and the rest, staying far enough behind
to keep out of sight.''

The black man motioned for me to come, and carried her
to one of the roofless sleeping rooms. There he laid her on
some discarded gowns and put his finger to his lips.

"No,'' I told him. "If she wakes without knowing how
she got here, she'll be frightened.'' I do not know how I

knew that. I knew it as I know many other things. I shook her gently, saying, "Io, why did you come so far?"

She opened her eyes. "Oh, master!"

"You should have stayed with the woman," I told her.

She whispered, "I don't belong to her. I belong to you."

"Something bad might have happened to you on the road, and in the morning we'll have to send you back to the ships."

"I belong to you. The Shining God sent me to take care of you."

"The Shining God sent Pindaros," I told her, "or so he says."

Sleepily, she rolled her head from side to side. "The oracle sent Pindaros. The god sent me."

It seemed futile to argue. I said, "Io, you must be quiet and stay in this room. See, I'm covering you with some of these so you won't get cold. If Kalleos or her women see you, they may make you leave. If they do, go to the back of the house and wait for me."

She was sleeping again before I finished. The black man laid a wooden doll beside her and stretched himself beside the doll.

"Yes," I said. "It's better that she have a protector."

He nodded—and fell asleep himself, I think, before I had left the room.

Now I sit on a broken chair near the courtyard door, where I can hear Phye's songs. There is a lamp here with a good wick and a fine, bright flame, so here I watch the stars and the waning moon; and write everything that has happened today, so I will not sleep. If Kalleos were to beat me, I might kill her; I do not wish that, and I too might die. It is better to write, though my eyes water and burn.

It is later, and Phye no longer sings. Pindaros suggested they play kottabos, and I, not knowing how it was played, stood under the lintel for a time to watch. Pindaros drew a circle on the floor and a line at some distance from it.

Everyone stood behind this line; and as each drained his cup, he threw the lees at the circle.

When several rounds had been played, Eurykles proposed that the loser of the next tell a tale, and Pindaros seconded him. Hypereides lost, and I sit listening to him (though I do not think I shall trouble to record his tale here) while I write.

# —— CHAPTER XV ——

## The Woman Who Went Out

PHYE'S tale had not yet begun when a shout of laughter woke me. No doubt she had missed the circle purposely, or perhaps one of the men had pinched her as she threw, or jostled her arm. I give here as much of it as I recall:

Once there was a woman whose husband was very rich but would never give her any money. They had an estate outside the city and a fine house in it, with many slaves and so on, but her gowns were still the gowns she had brought from her father's house, and her husband would not buy her so much as a comb.

One day when she lay weeping on her bed, her maid discovered her there. Now her maid was a Babylonian and as clever as all the people of that city are, and so she said, "My lady, I can guess easily enough why you weep. It's because all the other ladies hereabout have lovers to entertain them, and buy them silver bracelets and curios from Riverland, and talking birds that tell them how beautiful they are even when their lovers aren't around to do it. While you, poor thing, have only that ugly old fool your husband, a skinflint who never gives you so much as a sparrow."

"No," said her mistress, "it's because he never gives me any money."

"That's what I said," said her maid. "For we women, men and money are the same thing, after all. Have I ever told you how we girls get our dowries in Babylon?"

"No," said the mistress again. "But please do, even if it isn't a very good story. Because hearing even a poor story would be better than lying on this barren bed crying away my life."

"Why, it's no story at all," said her maid, "but the plain truth. When a girl in my city approaches the age of marriage, she sells herself to whatever men she likes for as much as they'll pay. In that way the best looking soon accumulate a great deal of money and so get a handsome husband, and soon after, many comely children. By the same token, homely girls get none, and thus it is that we Babylonians are the best-looking people in the whole world." (Here Phye, whom I was watching by this time through the doorway, patted her hair to considerable laughter and applause.) "Though you, my lady, would be thought lovely anywhere, I must say."

"That's extremely interesting," said her mistress, "and I certainly never knew it. But it doesn't do me the least good; I'm married already, so I don't need another dowry."

"True," said her maid. "But suppose you were to go out at night and make whatever handsome men you meet the same sort of offer our Babylonian girls do? You'd have a handsome lover for the night, and very quickly a great deal of money."

"It's certainly a most attractive idea," her mistress admitted, "but it seems to me that it's out of the question. My husband sleeps with me every night. If he were to wake and find me gone . . . Now that you mention it, I suppose it *might* be possible to administer some sort of mild and harmless medication that would assure him of a good night's sleep. Do you happen to know of a dealer in such preparations?"

Her maid shook her head sadly. "Most of them are ineffective, my lady, and even the worst cost a great deal. But I know a trick worth a dozen of them, if you can tell me where to find the last resting place of an amorous woman."

"Really?" said her mistress. "Magic? How fascinating!

You know, my cousin Phyllis's grave is only a short walk from here. Would that do, do you think?''

"I don't know," said the maid. "Was she fond of men?''

"Extremely," said her mistress. "And when she died, one of my uncle's he-goats wouldn't eat for a month.''

"Then she'd be perfect," said the maid. "Here's all we have to do. At dinner tonight, you must slip something into your husband's food that will make him ill—''

"Night soil, you mean?'' her mistress suggested.

The maid shook her head. "Too obvious. . . . I have it! He's accustomed to rancid oil—it's the only sort he'll let us buy for the kitchen. Give me that old pin to take to the market, and I'll trade it for the freshest, purest oil I can find. That should make him sick, and he'll sleep overnight in the temple of the Healing God in the hope of a cure. When he's gone, you and I will dig some earth from the garden and take it to your cousin's grave. There you'll moisten it with a certain fluid I'll indicate to you—you have a plentiful supply— and we'll make a doll of clay, kneading a lock of your hair into it.''

Her mistress clapped her hands with delight. "Why, this is *much* better than crying!''

"Then," her maid continued, "we'll lay the doll on her grave and engage in a recitation in which I shall prompt you. After that, whenever you want to leave at night, all you'll have to do is put the clay doll in your bed in your place. If your husband wakes, he'll see you beside him. And if he embraces the doll, he'll meet with such a reception as will endear you to him forever.''

"Wonderful!'' exclaimed her mistress, and that very night they carried out their plan with complete success.

The next night the lady waited until her husband was asleep, put the doll in their bed beside him, and enjoyed a succession of fascinating adventures in the city that left her a great deal wealthier than she had been before.

All went well for some time, she adventuring almost every night and her husband never complaining, though she noticed the clay doll was losing its proper shape. Early each morning when she returned, she would pat it until it looked as it had when she and the maid had formed it. But every night when she took it out again, she found that the clay had shifted downward in a most alarming fashion; and at last she told her maid the problem.

"Alas, my lady," said the maid. "I feared this might occur. In Babylon, we fire these figures in a potter's furnace—then there's no further trouble. But since you had no money and I didn't know of a potter here who'd be likely to cooperate without it, I neglected that step."

"What are you talking about?" said her mistress. "What's the matter with the doll?"

Her maid sighed. "It's a condition in which you would not, I think, wish to find yourself, my lady. If nature is allowed to take its course, there will soon be *two* clay dolls instead of one."

"How horrible!" said her mistress. "What can we do? Can't we bribe a potter to fire it now?"

"My lady," said her maid, "it would only crack later. I believe the best thing would be for us to bury the doll again in the place where we dug it up. You'll have to sleep with your husband—at least for a time—but that can't be helped. Do you by any chance remember the spot?"

"Why, yes," said her mistress. "It was under the apple tree."

"Then that would be the best place to put it," said the maid.

And so they did, and the woman began sleeping with her husband once more.

One day one of his rivals in business, a man as penurious as himself, found him moping about the market. "What's the matter?" he said. "Has someone cheated you?" For he would have been sorry indeed to hear that the husband had been cheated by anyone other than himself.

"No," said the husband. "It's my wife."

"Ah," said his rival. "There's a great deal of that going around these days, you know."

"Not long ago," said the husband, "she was as passionate as any man could wish. But now . . ."

"I can well imagine," said his rival. "Not that I've ever experienced the same thing myself."

"It's like embracing a woman of clay," said the poor husband. "And all I can think of is how I used to go to dinner parties and have a fine woman every night. I thought that when I married it would be better—because I used to have to give a party myself now and then, and it was so costly—but honestly I think the old days were better, and in fact I know it."

"Then all you have to do is return to them," said his rival. "Send her back to her father."

"And refund her dowry?" asked the husband. "You must be mad!"

"Then I can teach you a spell that will serve your turn," said his rival, who had no faith in such spells himself. "At least, my grandfather swore by it. You must find a blossoming tree in green and ardent health."

"Why, the apple tree in our garden has been blooming for days," said the husband. "I declare, you've never seen a tree doing better."

"Exactly the thing, then," said his rival. "You must lop off a limb and hide it under your bed. Whenever you want to go out and amuse yourself, take out the limb and put it in the bed in your place, saying,

> "Stick I cut, so brave and bright,
> Stick be straight and strong tonight!

"Believe me, as long as your wife doesn't light the lamp, she'll never know the difference." Then the rival went away, chuckling as he wondered whether his grandfather's spell would work.

But the husband ran home, and noting that the apple tree in his garden was still in flower, he immediately ordered his gardener to saw off its largest limb.

"It'll be the death of it," said the gardener, shaking his head.

"I don't care," said the husband. "It quite spoils the symmetry all natural objects should possess; so cut it off."

And thus it was done, and the husband carried the limb to the bedroom he shared with his wife and put it beneath the bed.

That night, the woman noticed that her husband's hair smelled of apple blossoms, which it certainly never had before. "Why, he's trying to make himself attractive for me," she said to herself. "And who knows what may come of that. . . . I should encourage him."

She gave him a kiss on the cheek, one thing led to another, and she was embraced ardently all night, until at last she fell into an exhausted sleep.

At dawn her husband returned, put the limb under the bed once more, and lay down congratulating himself.

This went on for several nights, until at last, in the very heat of love, the woman said, "Although you're stout and strong all night, dear, I notice you're always exhausted in the morning. You'd better get some rest when we're finished."

To this, the limb replied, "I wilt not, stepmother." Which so surprised the woman that she lit the lamp.

You may imagine her delight then, for she saw in her bed not the withered old husband she had expected, but a blooming youth with fair red cheeks. She blew out the lamp at once, and for some time they came together each night as happily as any pair could.

It was not to continue. One night she rolled over meaning to embrace her lover and found, to her great disgust, that she was caressing her husband instead. Thereafter the same thing occurred more and more frequently, for her husband had discovered that he was no longer so young as once he had been, and he was sorely pained by the inroads his nighttime adventures were making in his fortune.

But when her husband had occupied the bed every night for nearly a month, the woman smelled apple blossoms again.

Then, kissing her lover, she exclaimed, "If only he were dead! I'd have his money, and we could live together for the rest of our lives. You wouldn't be niggardly to me, would you, darling?"

"Never, stepmother," said her lover. "Every spring I would furnish our house new, and each fall I would shower upon you the fruits of the earth."

That sounded promising, and by this time the woman had convinced herself that "stepmother" was only her lover's pet name for her, he being at least in appearance somewhat the younger. Thus she said, "Do it, then! Do it tonight!"

"I will, stepmother."

And the next morning the man and his wife were found dead by the gardener, hung with the same rope. A noose had been tied in each end and the rope thrown over the largest limb of the apple tree in the garden.

The gardener and the lady's maid were accused of murdering them and tried on the Areopagus; but their deaths were ruled a double suicide, and husband and wife were buried beneath the apple tree.

There was laughter and applause when Phye's tale was told, and Hypereides said, "I'll have to be careful not to tell that one to my crew around the fire some evening. Do you know, I think half of 'em would swallow the whole rigmarole as solid fact. Why, on this past voyage, there was talk of a werewolf aboard."

The kybernetes shook his head ruefully. "It's our mixing with the Orientals that's done it, Captain. We used to be a reasonable people, believing in the Gods of the Mountain and nothing else. Now there's more gods up and down the Long Coast than along the River in Riverland. A god for wine, and all sorts of nonsense."

"Are you saying," Pindaros snapped, "that you don't credit the God in the Tree? I can tell you, sir, you're badly mistaken."

Kalleos intervened. "Gentlemen! Aristocrats! It's a rule of

this house that there are to be no religious arguments. Tolerant discussion, if you like. But no fighting."

"I assure you," Pindaros said stiffly, "that I speak from personal experience."

"So do I," Kalleos told him. "I've seen men who've been the best of friends for years at each other's throats. The gods are stronger than we are, so let them do their own fighting."

"Words of wisdom," said Eurykles. "Now if I may shift the conversation to what I hope will be a somewhat less touchy topic, it's my opinion that such tales of magic as Phye has just amused us with should not be discounted wholly, Hypereides. It's quite possible for we poor mortals to peep a bit into the future, for example—and I do not refer exclusively to quizzing some god or other at an oracle."

"Perhaps," Hypereides admitted. "I've heard some things along that line that make a man think."

"Lo!" exclaimed Eurykles, regarding Hypereides with admiration. "There's the mark of an open mind for you, friends. Your true man of reason never accepts or rejects without evidence, unless the thing is foolish on the face of it, like that business with the apple branch."

The kybernetes chuckled. "And the clay doll."

"No, no!" Eurykles raised a hand. "I won't say it can be done. But there's certainly something real behind it. Spirits *can* be summoned from a grave, and I urge you as reasonable men not to mock what you don't understand." He drained his cup. "My dear, I'd like quite a bit more of that."

"Trinkets!" said the kybernetes.

"What, sir?" asked Eurykles thickly. "Do you deny that such things can be? Why, I myself, in the practice of my profession—" He belched. "Excuse it. I have often called the dead to stand before me while I questioned them."

The kybernetes laughed. "Since I've no wish to be asked to leave by the lady of this house, I offer no comment."

"You don't believe me, but your captain here is a wiser man than you. Aren't you, sir?"

"Perhaps not wholly," Hypereides said.

"What?" Eurykles reached into the neck of his chiton and produced a leather purse. "Here I have ten birds. Yes, ten little owls nesting together. They're here to testify that I can do what I say."

"And it's easily said," said the kybernetes, "where we are now. But it can't be proved."

"There's a burial ground not far from here," Eurykles told him. "Surely this good wine—and I wouldn't in the least object to another drop, my dear—has given you the courage to come along with me."

"If you're proposing a bet," said the kybernetes, "I'd like to see what's in there."

Eurykles loosed the strings and shook out the jingling coins, arranging them in a row with one uncertain finger.

The kybernetes examined them and said, "I'm not a wealthy man, but I'll cover three, with the provision that I'm to judge whether a ghost has been produced."

Eurykles shook his head, nearly falling from his couch in the process. "Why, what protection would I have then? You might faint or run, but declare afterward . . ." He seemed to lose his thoughts, as drunken men often do. "Anything," he finished weakly.

Kalleos said, "I'll hold the money and judge. If you admit there was a ghost, you lose. Or if you run or faint, as Eurykles says. Otherwise, you win. Fair enough?"

"Absolutely," the kybernetes told her.

Eurykles mumbled, "That's only three. What of the other seven? Hardly worth my while."

The captain of *Eidyia* announced, "I'll cover one."

"And one for me," said the captain of *Clytia*.

"And the rest?" Eurykles looked at Pindaros. "You, sir? I'll make my fortune tonight, if I can."

"I haven't a copper," the poet told him. "As Kalleos will testify. Even if I did, I'd be betting with you rather than against you."

Hypereides said, "In that case, I'll cover the remaining five. Furthermore, I'll bet two with you, Pindaros—on trust.

I go to Hill now and then, and the first time I do, I'll come by to collect.''

"If you win," Pindaros told him. "Kalleos, if we're going to the burial ground, may I ask that we have Latro for a guard? The streets are dangerous by night, and we've all had a bit to drink.''

# —— CHAPTER XVI ——

## In the City

ONLY soldiers are supposed to carry arms, so Kalleos told me. She gave me Gello's old gray cloak to cover my sword.

Eurykles had said the burial ground was not far from Kalleos's house, but it seemed far to me. I wondered whether I would be able to find the house again, or if the others could find it, for they were all somewhat drunk, and some were very drunk. Of the women, only Phye had come with us, Kalleos saying she would not walk so far to see a god, far less a ghost, and the rest admitting frankly that they would be frightened out of their wits if Eurykles won his bet.

Kalleos had provided two torches. I carried one and Phye the other. It was good she had it, for there were stones and fallen bricks everywhere, and yet the remaining walls (and many still stand) cast shadows that seemed blacker for the faint moonlight around them. I walked at the front of our procession. After me came Eurykles to direct me; Kalleos had given him a fowl for a sacrifice, and he carried it under his cloak, from which it voiced faint protests. In what order the rest walked, if there was any, I do not know, except that Phye brought up the rear.

When we reached the burial ground, Eurykles asked Hypereides whether there was any person there with whom he wished to speak. "If so," he said, "I'll attempt that first, as a courtesy to you. I reserve the right to raise another to settle our bet if I'm unsuccessful with the first. Have you a

117

parent buried here, for example? Or anyone else whom you wish called home from the realm of shadow?"

Hypereides shook his head, and I thought he looked frightened.

I whispered to Pindaros, "Isn't it strange to see so many people in this place?"

"All of us, you mean," he said.

"And the rest." With my free hand I indicated the others who stood about us.

"Latro," Pindaros whispered, "when your mistress's friend Eurykles performs his ceremony, you must help him."

I nodded.

"If there's someone standing close by who seems attentive to the ceremony, but who did not come with us from Kalleos's house, you must touch him. Just reach out and touch him. Will you do that?"

Eurykles continued, "None of you, then, have any particular person in mind?"

All three captains shook their heads; so did the kybernetes.

"Then I'll search for a grave that appears to offer a good subject. I shall attempt that subject, and upon the result the whole of our bet depends. Is that understood?"

They murmured their agreement.

"Good. Phye, come with me. I must look at the graves and read the stones. You, boy, whatever your name is. You come too."

For some while we moved from grave to grave, our feet rustling the dry stalks of the grain that had been planted there, Eurykles hesitating a long time over many of the graves, sometimes tracing the letters in the stones with his fingers, sometimes scraping soil from the grave to sniff or taste. A wandering wind brought the odors of cooking and ordure from the city, and the smell too of freshly dug earth.

Phye screamed and dropped her torch, clutching Eurykles for protection. The fowl flew squawking from his cloak, and he slapped Phye, demanding to know what the matter was.

"There!" she said, and pointed with a trembling arm.

Lifting my torch higher, I saw what she had seen and went over to look at it.

A grave had been opened. The grave soil was thrown back in a heap, the withered remains of the funerary wreaths lay upon it, and the coffin had been pulled half out of its place and smashed. The body of a young woman, thus exposed, lay with feet and legs still within what remained of the coffin. The shroud had been torn away, leaving her naked except for her long dark hair. The smell of death was on her; I stepped away from it, feeling I had known it before, though I could not have said where or when.

"Take the reins!" Eurykles ordered Phye. "This is no time for your womb to dance." She only sobbed and buried her face in his cloak.

Acetes said, "Something terrible has happened here. What we see is desecration." His hand was on his sword.

"I quite agree," Eurykles told him. "*Something* has happened, but what is it? Who did it?"

Acetes could only shake his head.

I stroked Phye's hand and asked whether she was feeling better. When she nodded, I got her torch and relit it for her from my own.

Eurykles told the others, "I'm only a foreigner in your city, but I'm grateful to my hosts, and I see my duty plainly here. We must discover what has occurred and inform the archons. My own talents and training—most of all the favor with which I am regarded by the chthonic gods—lay an obligation upon me. I will raise the spirit of this poor girl, and from it we will learn who has done this, and why it has been done."

"I can't," Phye whispered.

Faintly though she spoke, Eurykles heard her and turned. "What do you mean?"

"I can't watch. I can't stay here while you do—whatever you're going to do. I'm going back." She drew away from him. "Don't try to stop me!"

"I won't," Eurykles told her. "Believe me I quite understand, and if I could be spared I'd take you back to Kalleos's house myself. Unfortunately these other gentlemen—''

"Have entered into a wager they regret," one of the captains said. "I'll go back with you if you want, Phye. As for the bet, I stand with my old master, Hypereides. If he wins, so do I. I lose if he loses."

"No!" Phye glared at him with so much hatred in her eyes that I thought she might fly at his face. "Do you think I want your filthy hands under my gown all the way back to Kalleos's?" She spun on her heel and strode off, her torch zigzagging as she threaded her way among the silent people.

Eurykles shrugged. "I was wrong to allow a woman to come with us," he said. "I can only apologize to the rest of you."

"That's all right," Hypereides told him. "If you're going to do something, let's get on with it." He drew his cloak more tightly about him.

Eurykles nodded and said to me, "See if you can find that bird, will you? It won't have flown far in the dark."

A small cypress grew a few steps away. The fowl was roosting in its branches, where I caught it easily enough.

When I returned to the men waiting beside the opened grave, Eurykles had a knife. As soon as I gave him the fowl, he cut its throat with a quick slash, pronouncing words in a language I did not understand. Three times he walked around the grave with slow, bobbing strides, scattering the fowl's blood; as he completed each circuit he called softly *Thygater*, which I suppose must have been the woman's name. As he made the third circuit, I saw her eyes open to watch him; and remembering what Pindaros had told me to do, I crouched and reached into the grave to touch her.

At once she sat up, pulling her feet from the broken coffin.

I heard the indrawn breath of Hypereides and all the rest, and I confess I was startled too, so that I jerked back my hand. Eurykles himself was staring at her slack-jawed.

Once standing, Thygater remained where she was, looking not at Eurykles or Pindaros or any other.

"You've won," Hypereides whispered, his voice shaking. "Let's go."

Eurykles threw back his head and extended his thin arms to the moon. *"I triumph!"* he shouted.

"Be still," the kybernetes hissed. "Do you—"

*"I triumph!"* Eurykles pointed to the ground at his feet. "Here! Stand *here,* Thygater! Present yourself to your master!"

Obediently, the dead woman climbed from her grave and stood where Eurykles had pointed. Though she walked, there was nothing of life in her; a doll with jointed limbs, moved by a child, might have walked so.

"Answer!" Eurykles ordered her. "Who disturbed your sleep?"

"You," the dead woman said. A coin fell from her mouth as she spoke, and her breath reeked of death. "And this man"—without turning her head to look at me, she pointed—"whom my king says must go as he was sent."

"Yes, I woke you, and this man with his torch. But who dug here and broke the coffin in which you lay?"

"I did not lie there," the dead woman said. "I was very far away."

"But who dug here?" Eurykles insisted.

"A wolf."

"But a man must have broken your coffin."

"A wolf."

Pindaros said softly, "She speaks as an oracle, I think."

Eurykles nodded, the inclination of his head so slight that I was not certain I had seen it. "What was the wolf's name? Speak!"

"His name was Man."

"How did he break your coffin?"

"With a stone."

"Held in his hands?" Eurykles demanded.

"Yes."

The captain who had offered to escort Phye said, "That girl was right. I'm going back." Everyone except Eurykles and me stepped away from the opened grave.

Eurykles said, "Don't you know she can prophesy for us,

you fools? Listen, and you'll hear the veil of the future torn
to shreds. *Thygater!* Who will win the war?''

"Wolves and ravens win all wars.''

"Will Khshayarsha, whom your people call the Great
King, ever rule this country?''

"The Great King has ruled our country.''

"That's what the oracle of Dolphins said,'' Pindaros told
Eurykles.

> "Wait not for horse and war,
>     But quit the land that bore you.
>     The eastern king shall rule your shore,
>     And yet give way before you.''

I do not think Eurykles heard him. "Thygater! How may I
become rich?''

"By becoming poor.''

Hypereides announced, "I've seen a wonder tonight, but it
was something I'd sooner not have seen, and I can't believe
the gods smile on such things. I'm going back to Tieup.
Anybody who wants to hear more can do it and take the
consequences for all I care. Eurykles, tell Kalleos I lost and
went back to my ships; I'll tell her myself the next time I see
her.''

"I'm coming with you,'' the kybernetes said, and Acetes
and both captains nodded.

"Not so fast,'' Pindaros put in. "Hypereides, you bet me
two owls, and Kalleos isn't holding those stakes.''

Hypereides dropped them into Pindaros's outstretched palm.
"If you want to come with us, you can share my room in
Tieup.''

Pindaros shook his head. "Latro and I are going back to
Kalleos's. Tomorrow I'll come for Hilaeira and Io.''

It was on my tongue to tell him Io was already there, but I
bit it back.

Eurykles spat on his hands and rubbed them together. "As
you desert us, Thygater and I are going into the city. I've

certain patrons there who'll be most gratified to behold my victory. Come, Thygater!''

"Wait," Pindaros told me. "Our way lies with theirs, but we need not walk with the dead woman."

I watched them go, and Hypereides and the other to the west. "Pindaros," I asked, "why am I so afraid?"

"Who wouldn't be? I was terrified myself. So is Eurykles, I think, but ambition overrules it." He laughed nervously. "You saw through his little trick, I hope? I meant you to give Eurykles more than he bargained for, but you came over us both and gave me more than I'd bargained for as well."

"I'm not afraid of the dead woman," I said. "But I'm afraid of something. Pindaros, look at the moon. What do you see?"

"It's very thin," he said. "And it's setting behind the sacred hill. What about it?"

"Do you see where some columns are still standing? The moon is tangled in them—some are before her, but others are behind her."

"No," Pindaros said. "No, Latro, I *don't* see that. Shall we go now?"

I agreed. When we had left the burial ground and were about halfway to Kalleos's, Pindaros said, "No wonder you weren't frightened by the dead girl, Latro. You're more frightening than she. The wonder is that she didn't seem afraid of you. But perhaps she was."

The door was barred, and our knocking brought no one to open it; but it was not difficult to find a place where the wall had been thrown down and not yet rebuilt. "My room has half a roof," Pindaros told me. "Kalleos showed it to me earlier. The best in the house, she said; and except for her own it probably is. You're welcome to share it if you like."

"No," I told him. "I have a place."

"As you wish." He sighed and smiled. "You got a cloak out of our adventures tonight, at least. I got two owls, and I had a woman; I've gone farther and come away with less. Good night, Latro."

I went to this room where the black man and Io are

sleeping. Io woke and asked if I was all right. When I said I was, she told me Phye had come back sometime earlier, and Kalleos had beaten her terribly.

I assured her that no one had beaten me, and we lay down side by side. She was soon asleep, but I was still frightened and could not sleep. Against all reason, the moon that had been setting when Pindaros and I were walking had climbed high in the heavens again, looking like the dead woman's eye when it opened a slit to see Eurykles.

Dawn came through the broken roof, and I sat up and wrote all that has happened since I wrote before. This is the last, and I see that upon the outside of my scroll it is written that I am to read it each day, and so I begin. Perhaps then I will understand what the dead woman meant, and where I am to go.

# —— CHAPTER XVII ——
## On the Way to Advent

THERE are many inns. Though we arrived by daylight, it was too late to go to the house of the god; Pindaros has taken a room for us in this one only a few stades away. The inn is a hollow square with two stories all the way around. We have a double room—like a man's bent arm, but wider.

The first thing I can remember from this day is eating the first meal with Kalleos and the other women. I knew her name then from some earlier time, for I called her by it when I brought out the boiled barley meal and fruit, and the wine and water, asking Kalleos whether I could carry food to Io and the black man. Kalleos said to bring them to the courtyard, where the long table stood. (I think the black man and I must have put it there, because when the time came to take it down we knew how to do it.)

The women were talking about how happy they were to be in the city again, and of going to the market to buy jewelry and new clothes. Though the sun was at its zenith, I think most had just risen. Another man came, still yawning and rubbing his teeth with a cloth. I made room for him, and he said, "I'm Pindaros. Do you remember me, Latro?"

I answered, "Yes. I remember our parting last night, and this morning I read my scroll. Your name is written there often. Pindaros, I must find the healer from Riverland."

When I mentioned Riverland, the women fell quiet to listen. Pindaros said, "Who is that?"

"The man who treated me just after the battle. He told me

my name; he'd learned it from the men of my maniple. Do you see how important that is? Those men knew who I was, so they must know where I came from."

"And you want to find out?" Pindaros asked. "You haven't talked about it much before."

"Yes!"

He said to Kalleos, "He's been getting better all the time. This is the best yet. Latro, you must go to the Great Mother. Did you read that in your book too?"

I told him I had read the words of the Shining God: "By the shrine of the Great Mother you fell, to a shrine of hers you must return."

"There you are, then."

One of the women asked, "Who's the Great Mother?" But Pindaros waved her to silence.

"I don't trust the gods of this land," I said.

Pindaros shrugged. "A man must trust the gods. There's nobody else."

"If the scroll is true, I've seen many more than you," I told him. "You've only seen the Black God—"

The black man nudged me and opened and closed his hands to show that there were twenty black gods at least.

"I believe you," I said. "But the scroll tells only of your seeing one, and the same for Pindaros. Have you seen more?"

He shook his head.

Kalleos asked, "Are you saying you've actually seen a god, Latro? Like they used to appear to people in the old days?"

"I don't know," I told her. "I've forgotten, but I wrote of many in my scroll."

"He has," Pindaros told her. "He's seen one at least, because I was there and saw him too. So did little Io— remind me to ask how you got here, Io—and our comrade there. I think he's seen many more. He's told me about them at various times, and after seeing the King of Nysa, whom he just called the Black God, I believe him."

"Then believe me also when I say no one should trust

them. Some are better than others, no doubt: the Swift God, the Shining God, and the King of Nysa. But I think . . ."

"Yes?" Pindaros bent toward me, listening.

"I think that even the best act in some twisted way, perhaps. There's malice even in those who would be kind, I think even in Europa. In the serpent woman it burned so hot that I felt it still when I read what I had written of her."

I do not think Kalleos had been listening to me. She said, "But you remember, Pinfeather. And you, honey. You've got to tell us about it."

Then Pindaros and Io told of meeting the Black God. I remember thinking that it was much as it was written in this scroll, so I will not give their words here. I remember too that I was glad it was they who spoke and not I, because I was hungry and it gave me time to eat.

They were still talking when I finished my barley porridge and bit into an apple. When there was a knock at the door, I went.

A pretty woman with blue eyes darker than Kalleos's waited there. "Hello, Latro," she said. "Do you remember me?"

I shook my head.

"I'm Hilaeira, and we're old friends. May I come in?"

I stood aside and told her I had read of her in my scroll that morning.

She smiled and said, "I'll bet you didn't read that you're handsomer than ever, but you are. Hypereides says this house is full of women. I don't see how they can keep their hands off you. Do you remember Pindaros?"

"Yes," I said. "He's eating the first meal. I think perhaps Kalleos will invite you to join us if you like."

"I'd love to. I just came from Tieup, and that's no stroll."

We went into the courtyard, where I told Kalleos, "This is Hilaeira. May she join us?"

"Of course, of course!" Kalleos said. "Hilaeira, dear, I ought to have introduced myself on *Europa,* and I'm sorry I didn't. You can sit beside me—move over, Eleonore—and help yourself. Like I said, I would have offered to help you yesterday, but I thought you were Pinfeather's wife. How'd you get to the city?''

"I walked," Hilaeira told her. "Hypereides says it's against the law here for a woman to go out alone, but Io was gone—"

Io called, "Here I am!"

"Why, so you are! Anyway, Hypereides wouldn't send anybody. He didn't want to spare them, and he thought Pindaros would come. Pindaros didn't, so I decided to risk it. I thought I'd probably meet him on the road, but of course I didn't. Hypereides gave me a letter for you." Hilaeira reached into the neck of her gown and drew it out. "It's a little damp, I'm afraid."

"No matter. Read it to me, will you, dear? This sunlight would have my poor eyes weeping like Niobe."

Hilaeira broke the seal and glanced at the writing. "Are you sure you want me to? It looks rather personal. I—"

The women all laughed.

"Go ahead, dear. We've no secrets in this house."

"All right. 'My darling sweet: May I say once more how fine it was for this weary old sailor to rest his salt-rimed head upon that divine white bosom of yours—' "

At this point Hilaeira was interrupted again by the women's laughter, and some of them beat the table with their spoons. There were more such interruptions subsequently, but I shall take no more notice of them.

" 'When I began my voyage to the Navel and Tower Hill, I quite agreed with the Assembly's decision to send ships instead of going overland, but what a weary steed a ship is!

" 'And yet the return paid for all. Thank you, dearest Kalleos. The second part of your payment must await my return, alas, for we are being dispatched to join the fleet. Send my slave back with the chair *today*.' That's underlined," Hilaeira added.

Kalleos looked at the black man. "You have to take the chair back, understand? Then go to the sheds and find Hypereides. If you don't, he'll have the archers after you."

The black man nodded, his face expressionless, then turned

to me, pretending to write upon the palm of his hand and cocking an eyebrow as he does when he wants to ask a question. I said, "You want to know whether I read of you in my scroll. Yes, I did. You were my first friend; I know that."

He left the table, and I have not seen him since.

" 'Be kind to poor Latro,' " Hilaeira continued, " 'and you will find him anxious to do whatever lies in his power to help you. At least, I have always found him so.

" 'Pindaros Pagondas of Cowland will already have told you what happened last night. I think it was the worst adventure of my life. May all the Twelve preserve me from such another! I lost, and you may pay the money I and the others left with you to Eurykles. When you have done so, I urge you never to see him again. Believe me, O sweetest Kalleos, if you had been one of us last night, you would not.

" 'And now farewell—' "

"Wait up!" Kalleos exclaimed. "Pinfeather hasn't told me anything. What happened, poet?"

"In a moment," Pindaros said. "Let her finish."

" 'And now farewell from your grateful lover Hypereides, darling Kalleos. The Rope Makers say a man who goes to war must return with his hoplon or upon it. I've tested mine and it won't float, so I mean to carry it back. Till then I remain your loving Hypereides.' "

When the women had subsided somewhat, Pindaros asked, "Do you really want me to tell you what happened last night? In front of everyone here? I warn you, if I do I'll tell the truth. You've been a generous hostess, Kalleos, so if you'd prefer to hear it in private . . ."

"Go ahead," Kalleos told him.

"From the beginning?"

She nodded.

"All right, then I'll start by saying that when Eurykles made his bet it struck me that Phye's tale had been very convenient for him. When she said she'd come with us— alone out of all these women—I felt sure something was in the wind. Maybe I hadn't drunk quite as much as the others, or maybe I've got a stronger head. I don't know. How much were you supposed to get, Phye?''

Kalleos said, "Never mind that," and Phye, through bruised lips, "An owl.''

"We found an opened grave," Pindaros continued, "and at first I thought Eurykles had done it himself; later I realized it would have been too great a risk. Phye was frightened, and she went to him for protection. That told me she knew Eurykles better than any of the rest of us, and that she was really afraid. If she'd been faking it, she would almost certainly have grabbed Hypereides, since he'd bet the most money.''

"Go on," Kalleos said grimly.

"When we were here, Eurykles had seemed very drunk. I suppose you have to seem drunk to bet that you can raise the dead. But at the burial ground, he was the soberest of all, except for Latro, who hadn't been drinking. Phye said she was leaving, and it seemed to me she meant it; but it also seemed that Eurykles either thought it was part of some plan or wanted her to believe he thought that, so that she'd go ahead with it when she got her nerve back.''

"She didn't," Kalleos told him grimly. "She came here.''

"I can see that. Phye, I'd put a slice of cucumber on that eye, if I were you.''

"Nothing you've talked about would have horrified Hypereides," Kalleos said. "Get on with it.''

"All right, I will. Eurykles raised the woman from the grave. She stood up and talked to us, but she was quite clearly dead. Her face was livid, and her cheeks beginning to fall in.''

Kalleos leaned toward him, her eyes narrowed to slits. "He *did* it?''

Pindaros shrugged. "He sacrificed a cock, and she stood up and spoke. When the rest of us left, she followed him into the city.'' He turned to Phye. "What were you supposed to do? Supply the voice, or actually appear as the ghost?''

She said, "You knew. Even when we were back here, you knew.''

"Because I bet with Hypereides? I knew enough to know who was going to win a strange bet proposed by a stranger. So does Hypereides, I imagine, when he's sober."

By then the women were all talking at once. Hilaeira whispered across the table, "Latro, did you touch her? Do you remember?"

I nodded.

"Which brings us to Latro," Pindaros said to her. "I can't go back to our shining city until I've taken him to the shrine of the Great Mother. I won't blame you if you don't want to come, though you're welcome to if you wish."

Hilaeira said, "My father—he's dead—had a business connection here. I thought perhaps he'd let me stay with him a while."

"Certainly," Pindaros said.

"This is so near Advent, where they have the mysteries of the Grain Goddess, and I'd love to be an initiate. They'll take me, won't they? Despite the war?"

"They'll accept anyone who hasn't committed murder, I believe," Pindaros told her. "But there's quite a period of study involved—half a year or so. Kalleos, what do you know of the mysteries? Is there any reason Hilaeira couldn't be initiated?"

Kalleos shook her head, smiling again. "Not a reason in the world. And Hilaeira, dear, I heard what you said about your poor uncle, or whoever it was. Believe me, dear, you don't need him. You're welcome to stay right here with me for as long as you like."

"Why, that's very kind of you," Hilaeira said.

"It does take a while, you understand. But you're lucky, because it's right about now that they start. You'll have to go down to Advent every so often all summer, and there are fasts and ceremonies and whatnot. I've never gone through it, but I know people who have."

"Did it change their lives?" Hilaeira asked.

"Hm? Oh, yes, absolutely. Gave them a whole new outlook, and a better one too, I'd say. And it's ever so useful socially. Where was I? Washings—there's a lot of them, mostly in the Ilissus. In the fall they admit you to the lesser mysteries. After that would be the time for you to go home, if you want to. Then a year later you come back, go through the lesser mysteries again, and then the greater mysteries. Then you're an initiate and a friend of the goddess's forever, and every year you can come back for the greater mysteries, though you don't have to. Those last four days. The lesser mysteries are two, I think. But you really ought to go down to Advent and talk to the priests."

"Is it far?"

"No. If you start when we're through eating, you . . . Pinfeather, what's the matter with you?"

"It's just that— Last night, Latro said— By all the gods!"

Hilaeira was looking at him too. "For a man who takes talking corpses in his stride, you seem a bit distraught."

"I should be. I am! I've been an idiot. Io, do you remember what the prophetess said? I want to be sure my memory's not playing me false."

"I think so," Io told him. "Let me see. 'Look under the sun . . .' "

"Further along," Pindaros told her. "About the wolf."

" 'The wolf that howls has wrought you woe!' " Io chanted. " 'To that dog's mistress you must go! Her hearth burns in the room below. I send you to the God Unseen!' "

"That's enough. 'The wolf that howls has wrought you woe, to that dog's mistress you must go, her hearth burns in the room below.' Kalleos, is there a cave at Advent?"

Kalleos shook her head. "I haven't the least idea."

"There must be. I need to borrow Latro for today and tomorrow. May I have him? I'll bring him back to you, I swear."

"I suppose so. Would you mind telling me what's going on?"

Pindaros had bitten into his apple. He chewed and swallowed before answering. "Back in our city, I took an oath to guide Latro to the place mentioned by the prophetess. I thought it meant the oracle at Lebadeia, which is only about two days' journey."

"You consulted the god at the Navel?" Kalleos asked.

Pindaros shook his head. "There's a temple of the Shining God and a prophetess in our city. We never got to Lebadeia, as you can see from our ending up here. But last night Latro said—"

I interrupted. "That we should trust the Shining God if we trusted his oracle."

"Right. Latro, I know you don't remember, but go get your book. Look at the very beginning and tell me where you were wounded. We know about the battle—where on the battlefield."

"I don't have to get it," I told him. "I read it this morning. At the temple of the Earth Mother."

Pindaros heaved a great sigh. "I thought I recalled someone's saying something about that. That clinches it."

"Clinches what?" Hilaeira asked.

"The wolf is one of the badges of the Great Mother," Pindaros told her. "That's why I thought it was the shrine of the Great Mother that was meant—it is in a cave, by the way. But don't you remember what the priest said to us beside the lake? The morning after you and I first met?"

"He explained that the gods have different names to indicate different attributes, and different names in different places, too. Of course, I knew that before."

Pindaros nodded. "And do you know how Advent got its name? Or why the mysteries are performed there?"

"I thought it had always been there."

"No, in ancient times Advent—which wasn't called Advent then—had a king named Celeos. His people lived by hunting and fishing, and gathering wild fruits. The Great Mother was looking for her daughter, who'd been carried away by the Receiver of Many. To shorten a long story, in her wanderings she came to Advent and taught Celeos to grow grain."

Hilaeira exclaimed, "I see!"

"Certainly, and I should have seen too, much sooner. The Grain Goddess *is* the Great Mother, and the Great Mother is the Earth Mother, who sends up our wheat and barley. Her greatest temple's at Advent, and it was near a temple of hers that Latro was wounded. The Shining God was telling Latro to go to Advent, and when I started to lead him in the wrong direction, he made sure we'd get to the right place after all. All I have to do now is take him there, which I can do this afternoon. Then I'll be free to return home.''

"And will I find my friends?" I asked him. "Will I be cured then?"

"I don't know," Pindaros answered solemnly. "Certainly you will have taken the first step."

# —— CHAPTER XVIII ——

## Here in the Hall of the Great Mother

I sacrificed today. About midmorning, Pindaros, Hilaeira, Io, and I went to talk to a priest. He told us that his name was Polyhommes and that he was of the family of the Eumolpides. "The high priest is always chosen from our family," he said. "Thus many of us serve our turn, hoping for a smile from the goddess." He smiled himself, and broadly, for he was one of those happy and helpful fat men one sometimes meets in the service of gods and kings, though he smelled of blood, as I suppose all priests must.

"We are the children of Demophon, whom the goddess would have made immortal if she could. I grant it's not as good as being of the line of Heracles, who actually *was* made immortal, but it's the best we can manage. Now what can I do to help you, sir? This is your wife, I take it, and your little daughter. And your son, who's been injured. A striking young man—what a pity someone struck him!" He chuckled. "This is not a shrine of healing, however, save for the spirit. I will be happy to direct you to one."

I said, "I hope it will be a shrine of healing for me," and Pindaros explained our actual relationships.

"Ah! Then we have here, in fact, two parties, though you have traveled together. Let's take the young woman first, for her case will be somewhat easier, I believe.

"You must understand, my daughter, that there are three

135

classes of persons who cannot be admitted to the mysteries.
These are murderers, magicians, and soothsayers. If you are
admitted to the mysteries—or if you so much as begin the
ceremonies for admission—and it is discovered that you belong to any of those three classes, the penalty is death. But at
this moment there is no penalty; you need not even tell me, 'I
have killed,' or, 'I am a magician.' All you have to do is
leave this room and return to the city. Nothing will be said or
done.''

"I . . ."

"Yes, my daughter?"

"Do you know how girls sometimes dip a mirror into a
spring when the moon is full? When you look into it, in the
moonlight . . ."

"What do you see?"

"Your husband's face. The man who's going to be your
husband. The Moon Virgin shows you, if you're a virgin
yourself.''

Polyhommes laughed. "Hopeless for me, I'm afraid. I've
four children.''

"I used to be good at it, or I thought I was, and I,
uh, showed some other girls how. I don't do it any more."

"I see. Did you look into the mirror *for* them, or did you
simply show them how to do it for themselves?"

"I showed them how," Hilacira said. "You can't do it for
somebody else. Each one has to do it for herself.''

"And did they pay you for your help?"

Hilaeira shook her head.

"Then you're surely not a magician or a soothsayer, my
daughter. May I take it you're not a murderess? In that case,
you may attend the initial ceremony. That will be . . ." He
paused, counting on his fingers. "Just five days from now, in
the evening. You're living in the city?"

"I'm staying with a friend."

"Then it would probably be best for you to return there.
There are good inns here, but they're frightfully expensive,
I'm told. On the fifth day you may come here just as you did
today. We'll assemble at the stele at sunset.''

Hilaeira cleared her throat, a sound like the peep of a little frog. "I said I was staying in Thought, Holiness. I'm not *from* Thought."

Polyhommes laughed again. "You're from Cowland, my daughter. You're all from Cowland, except for your young friend here, and I can't imagine where he's from. Can't you tell we speak differently here on the Long Coast? We don't double the 'fish' and the 'camel' the way you do, for one thing."

"That doesn't matter?"

Polyhommes shook his head. "I said there were three classes who were not admitted. Actually, there is a fourth— those who cannot understand our language well enough to comprehend the ceremonies. But even they are excluded only on practical grounds. If a barbarian learns our speech, he is welcomed."

"And will I have to make an offering when I come again in five days?"

He shook his head again. "Most do, but it isn't required. I take it you're not wealthy?"

"No."

"Then my advice is to make an offering, but a small one. Perhaps one drachma—or an obol, if that's all you can afford. That way you'll have something to put in the krater and need feel no embarrassment."

"May I ask one more question?"

"A hundred, my daughter, if they're all as sensible as those you've asked thus far."

"It isn't this way in our city, but here people tell me a woman isn't supposed to go out alone. Will anyone bother me when I try to come back? I don't think Pindaros will be here then, and Kalleos probably won't want Latro to come."

Polyhommes smiled. "You won't be alone, my child. Far from it. Recollect that every candidate for initiation this year will be on the Sacred Way with you. No one will molest you, I promise. Nor will the archers stop you and inquire why you've no escort. If you're nervous, you need only find some decent man and put yourself under his protection.''

"Thank you," Hilaeira said. "Thank you very much, Holiness."

"And now, young man, to you. You're not a candidate?"

Pindaros said, "He merely wishes to present himself to the goddess."

"Purity is best, just the same. I take it he's no magician or soothsayer. Has he blood guilt?"

"He doesn't remember, as I told you."

I said, "I killed three slaves once, I think, though I didn't write it down. You said so later, Pindaros, and I read about it this morning while you and Hilaeira were still asleep."

"They were slaves of the Rope Makers," Pindaros explained, "serving as auxiliaries in their army. Blood spilled in battle doesn't count, does it?"

Polyhommes shook his head. "There's no guilt. Have you an offering?"

Io whispered, "The Shining God gave me to him. He can't give me to the goddess, can he?"

"He may if he wishes," Polyhommes told her. "Do you, young man? This slave girl would make a fine offering."

"No. But I've nothing else."

"I can give him a little money," Pindaros put in.

"Good. Young man, I'd suggest you use what your friend gives you to purchase an animal for sacrifice. The town is full of people who sell them—you'll have no difficulty. If you're short of funds, a hen is acceptable."

Pindaros shuddered. "No. Not a hen."

"Fine. A more, ah, significant beast is, of course, a better sacrifice. Normally those who sacrifice here desire to improve the fertility of their fields, and a hen is often sufficient. A young pig is the most common gift."

Pindaros said, "Like Hilaeira, I have a final question. Are there caves here? I realize you can't reveal the mysteries, but caves connected with the worship of the goddess?"

Polyhommes nodded without speaking.

"Wonderful! Sir, Holiness, you've been very, very kind. We'll go and get the sacrificial animal now. Meanwhile, perhaps a small gift for yourself . . . ?"

"Would be most gratefully accepted." Polyhommes glanced at his palm and smiled. "Return at noon with your sacrifice, my son. I will be present to assist you with the liturgy."

When we were outside, Pindaros said, "I'm going to follow a hunch. Have you heard of the Lady of Cymbals?"

I shook my head; so did Hilaeira.

"That's the name under which the Great Mother's worshiped in the Tall Cap Country. Not by the sons of Perseus or Medea, but by their slaves—Lydia's people, and so on. They use the lion and the wolf as the Great Mother's badges more than we do. I know you don't remember that the oracle mentioned a wolf, Latro, unless you read that this morning too. But it did, and it said you had to cross the sea, which probably meant to the Tall Cap Country. After one's manhood, the sacrifice most acceptable to the Lady of Cymbals is a bullock."

Hilaeira asked, "Do you have enough money?"

"If we can find a cheap one. Kalleos advanced me a bit, and I won a bit more betting with Hypereides."

Most of the animal sellers had only the smaller ones. Shoats were the creatures most often sacrificed, as Polyhommes had told us, and fowls the cheapest; but there were sheep too, and eventually we came upon a yearling bull for sale.

Io said, "His horns have only just sprouted," and patted his muzzle.

"Very tender indeed, young lady," the farmer promised her. "You won't find better meat anyplace."

"That's right," Io said to Hilaeira. "We get to keep the meat, don't we? Will they cook it for us at the inn?"

Hilaeira nodded. "For a share of it. And they'll keep everything and give us something worse unless somebody watches them."

"I think he'd let me ride on his back, like Kalleos on the sail."

Pindaros bargained with the farmer and, after starting to walk away twice, bought the bullock for what he said was far too much money. "The people here laugh at us because we named our country after our cattle," he told me. "But we have some good stock, and I wouldn't trade them for all the ships on the Long Coast. You can't eat a ship, or plow anything but the sea."

There was a cord through the bullock's nose, and it followed us docilely enough while we bought a garland for its neck and chaplets of flowers for ourselves, though Pindaros refused to let Io mount.

Perhaps I should write here that the temple of the Grain Goddess is called the Royal House and that Pindaros said it was different from any other he had seen. Certainly it seems strange enough to me. It is large and square, and its interior is filled with pillars, so that one walks in it as in a forest of stone. They say the fire before the statue has been kept burning since the goddess wished to bathe the infant Demophon in its flames.

I will not give the words we spoke to the goddess before we sacrificed; I do not think it lawful. When all had been said, I put my hand on the bullock's head and begged the goddess to join my friends and me in our meal. Polyhommes poured milk in the bullock's ear, asking whether it wished to go to the goddess. It nodded, and Polyhommes cut its throat with the holy knife, which is of bronze, not iron. We cast certain parts of the carcass into the flames, and everyone relaxed.

"A good sacrifice, wouldn't you say, Holiness?" Pindaros smiled and straightened his chaplet of blossoms.

"A most excellent sacrifice," Polyhommes assured him.

Hilaeira's eyes were bright with tears. "I feel I'm a friend of the goddess's already," she said. "Once I thought she smiled at me. I really did."

"She does have a kind face," Polyhommes said, smiling up at his goddess. "Severe, but—"

Io asked, "What's the matter?"

He did not answer. He had been ruddy, but his cheeks were as white as tallow now, and the hand that held the sacred blade shook so that I feared he would drop it.

Pindaros took his arm. "Are you ill?"

"Let me sit," Polyhommes gasped, and Pindaros and I led him to the nearest bench. His forehead was beaded with sweat; when he was seated, he wiped it with a corner of his robe. "You wouldn't know," he said. "You're not familiar with her, as I am."

"What is it?" Pindaros asked.

"My family always supplies the priests . . ."

"You told us that."

"So we're always in and out of the Royal House, even when we're just children. I've seen the goddess . . . I've seen her statue I suppose ten thousand times."

We nodded.

"Now I want one of you—you, little girl—to describe it to me. I must know whether you see what I do."

Io asked, "Just talk about her? She's real big, bigger than any real woman. She wears her hair off her shoulders, I think probably in a knot at the back of her head. Should I go around and see?"

"No. Go on."

"And she's got a crown of poppies, and wheat—a sheaf of wheat, is that what they call it?—in her hand. Her other hand is pointing at the floor."

The fat priest let out his breath in a great *whoosh*. "I must see my uncle—get him to rule on this. All four of you remain here. Right here. It might be better if you didn't speak."

He hurried off, and we sat in silence. It seemed to me there should have been a feeling of peace then in the quiet temple, peace engendered by its sullen fire, its bars of sunshine and deep shadows; but there was none. Rather it seemed filled with soft yet heavy noises, as if some massive beast stirred and stamped where it could not be seen.

Polyhommes soon returned. "Our high priest has gone to the city; I'll have to decide this myself." He seemed calmer, and the heavy odor of wine was on his breath. "Very well. You must accept my statement that I have observed this statue many times, and that until today its left hand has always rested upon the head of the stone boar standing beside it."

Hilaeira's mouth opened, and even Pindaros gave a low whistle.

"A miracle—a major miracle—has taken place here today. A great sign. Did any of you see it? See the hand actually move?"

Pindaros, Hilaeira, and I all shook our heads. Io had trotted around the sacred hearth to look more closely at the statue.

"A pity, and yet move it surely did, doubtless at the very moment of sacrifice, when our eyes were on the victim." Polyhommes paused, drew a deep breath, and let it out again. "I suppose you've heard about the dead woman in the city? She's said to have walked until cockcrow and spoken to many persons, and the whole town's abuzz over it. No one knows what it may mean, and now this! Wait until word of this gets out! Can you imagine it?"

"I can," Pindaros said. "I hope I'm far away by then."

Polyhommes continued as though he had not heard him. "This is something you can see for yourself and go home and tell your children about. This is—"

Io called. "There's a clean place on the pig's head where the hand used to be. Come look!"

No doubt it was a measure of our amazement that all of us did, obedient as children to a child's command. She was right. Smoke from the sacred fire had grimed the boar's head, but the broken marble where the goddess's hand had left it was white and new.

"Think what this will mean for our Royal House." Polyhommes rubbed his hands. "For the mysteries!"

"And I was here," Hilaeira whispered.

"Indeed you were, my daughter. Indeed you were! And when you've fathomed the mysteries—well, priests are always chosen from the men of our family, as I've said. But there is a place—the highest of all—for a woman in the ceremonies.''

Hilaeira stared at him, a dawning wonder in her eyes.

"She too is customarily of the Eumolpides, but that is no insupportable obstacle. There is adoption, after all. There is even marriage. Such arrangements might be made by the high priest, and there can surely be no question now about who the next high priest will be." Polyhommes threw out his chest. "My uncle is an elderly man, and it would seem that the goddess has made her wishes regarding his successor quite clear. There was, after all, only one priest present at the time of the miracle."

Io asked, "But what does she want?"

"Eh?" He turned to look at her.

"The goddess. Why's she pointing at the floor?"

"I'm not sure." The fat priest hesitated. "When such a gesture is used by one in authority, it generally means that something or someone is to be brought to him."

Pindaros cleared his throat. "An oracle in our shining city directed that Latro be brought to the goddess."

"Ah. And he was the giver of the sacrifice—officially, at least." Polyhommes turned to me. "Young man, you must remain in this Royal House overnight, sleeping on the floor or upon one of these benches. Perhaps the goddess herself will appear in your dreams. If not, I think it likely she'll favor you with some message."

Thus I am here, sitting with my back against a column and writing these words by the light of the declining sun. I have had a good deal of time to think this afternoon; and it seems to me that more than once I have felt the spirit of a house when I, a stranger, went into that house—though I cannot retrieve from the mist those times or those houses. A temple is the house of the god who dwells there, and so I open myself to this house of the Grain Goddess, hoping to know whether it is friendly to me.

*     *     *

There is nothing—or rather, there is only the sense of age. It is as if I sit with a woman so old she neither knows nor cares whether I am real or only some figment of her disordered mind, a shadow or a ghost. A fly may light upon a rock; but what does the rock, which has seen whole ages since the morning when gods strode from hill to hill, care for a fly, the creature of a summer?

# —— CHAPTER XIX ——

## In the Presence of the Goddess

I ate the beef, bread, and fruit Io had brought me from the inn, and drank the wine. When I was finished, I spread the pallet Hilaeira had carried and lay down; but I was not in the least ready for sleep, and when the town grew quiet, I sat up again.

For a time I read this scroll (which I must try always to keep with me) by the light of the sacred fire, learning of the many gods and goddesses who have shown themselves to me; and once or twice I took up the stylus to add some conclusion to the account of today's events I had written earlier. But how can a man draw conclusions from what he does not comprehend? I knew I did not understand what occurred, and it seemed to me that it would be better to wait until the goddess had spoken. Now I sit in the same place to write this record.

An acolyte entered without taking the least notice of me and, mumbling a prayer, cast an armload of cedar into the fire. It fell with a deep booming, as though the sacred hearth were a drum and not a stone. When I dozed, that booming echoed through my dreams and woke me.

I could see the statue plainly in the firelight. The hand pointing to the floor was nearest the flames and flushed with their light, so that it seemed to glow like iron in a forge. I felt it demanded something of me, and I threw off my cloak, hoping that when I was nearer I would understand. The goddess's hand was hot to my touch, but it was only after I had drawn my own away that I looked at last and saw the thing to which she pointed.

There was a small section of floor between the coping around the sacred fire and the pedestal upon which the goddess stood. It was dirtier than the floor in other places, I think because those who cleaned it were fearful to approach her too closely, or were not permitted to do so. I knelt and brushed its surface with the tips of my fingers. Just at the place she indicated, there was a ring of bronze set in the stone, though the depression that held it was so packed with dirt I could scarcely see it.

I wished then for Falcata, but I could not have worn her in the temple, and I had left her at our inn. There had been ribs among the meat, however, and when I had worked the point of the sharpest under the ring, it came up easily enough. I cast the rib into the fire as an additional offering and pulled at the ring with both hands.

The slab rose more readily than I had expected. Beneath it was a narrow stair and close beside it a pillar of flame; for the sacred hearth was not, as I had assumed, at the level of the temple floor, but here below it. I descended the stair, keeping away from the flames as well as I could.

"Your hair is singed." The voice was that of a woman. "I smell it, Latro."

I looked through the fire and saw her seated upon a dais at the end of the low room. Young she was, and lovely, wreathed in leaves and flowers; and flowers and leaves had been woven to make a chiton and a himation for her. And yet for all her youth and beauty, and the colors and perfumes of so many blossoms, there was something terrifying about her. When I reached the floor, I circled the sacred hearth, bowed low to her, and asked whether she was the Great Mother.

"No," she said. "I am her daughter. Because you are no friend of my mother's it would be best for you to call me the Maiden."

She rose from her seat as she spoke and came to stand

before me. Slender and fragile though she looked, her eyes were higher than mine. "My mother cannot be everywhere, though she is in many places together. And so, because you have meddled in my realm, I offered to speak with you for her." She touched my hair, brushing away the scorched ends. "My mother does not wish to meet you again in any case. Would you not rather treat with me instead?"

"But I must meet with her," I said. I had read in this scroll what the Shining God had said and what the prophetess had chanted, and I told the Maiden of them.

"You are mistaken," the Maiden told me. "The Wolf-Killer said only that you must go to a shrine of my mother's, not that you need speak with her. As for the sibyl, her words were but a muddle of the Wolf-Killer's, cast in bad verse. Here is the hearth. You stand in the room below, though it was not always thus. You wished to speak with my mother, but I am before you in her place, more beautiful than she and a greater goddess."

"In that case, goddess, may I beg you to heal me and return me to my friends and my own city?"

She smiled. "You wish to remember, as the others do? If you remember, you will never forget me."

"I don't want to," I told her, but I knew even as I spoke that I lied.

"Many do," she said. "Or at least many believe they do. Do you know who I am?"

I shook my head.

"You have met my husband, but even he is lost now among the vapors that cloud your mind. I am the Queen of the Dead."

"Then surely I must not forget you. If men and women only knew how lovely you are, they wouldn't dread you as they do."

"They know," the Maiden told me, and plucked a lupine from her chiton. "Here is the wolf-flower for you, who bear the wolf's tooth. Do you know where it was born?"

I understood and said, "Beneath the soil."

The Maiden nodded. "If ten thousand others had not

perished, this flower could never have been. It is the dead—trees and grasses, animals and men—who send you all you have of men, animals, trees, and grasses.''

"Goddess, you say I've meddled in your realm. I don't remember; but restore my memory, and I'll do whatever you want of me to make amends.''

"And what of the injury you did my mother?''

"I don't recall that, either,'' I told her. "But I am sorry from the bottom of my heart.''

"Ah, you are no longer so stiff-necked as once you were. If this were my affair and not hers, I would do something for you now, perhaps. But it is hers, not mine.'' She smiled the infinitely kind smile of a woman who will not do what you ask. "I will convey your apology to her and plead your case most eloquently.''

I think she saw the fury in my eyes before I knew of it myself, for she took a step backward without turning away from me.

"No!'' My hand reached for Falcata, and I learned why the gods forbid our weapons in their temples.

"You threaten me. Do you not know that I cannot be harmed by a common mortal?''

"No,'' I said again. "No, I don't know that. Nor that I'm a common mortal. Perhaps I am. Perhaps not.''

"You and your sword have been blessed by Asopus; but I am far greater than he, and your sword is elsewhere.''

"You're right,'' I said. "My hands are all I have. I'll do the best I can with them.''

"Against one entitled to your reverence as a goddess and your respect as a woman.''

"If there's no need of them, I won't use them. Goddess, Maiden, I don't want to harm you or your mother. Yet I came hoping . . .'' It seemed a bite of dry bread were caught in my throat; I could not speak.

"To be as other men. To know your home and friends.''

"Yes.''

"But by threatening me, you will only come to Death.

Then you will be mine as so many others are, your home my kingdom, your friends my slaves."

"Better that than to live like this."

The stench of the grave filled the room, so strong that it masked the smoke from the cedar fire. Death rose through the floor and stood beside her, his skeleton hand clutching his black cloak.

"I need only say, 'He is yours,' and your life is past."

"I'll face him if I must."

Her smile grew warmer. "When you die at last, some monument will read, *Here rests one who dared the gods.* I will see to it. Yet I would rather not take such a hero in his youth."

Death sank from sight as quietly as he had come.

"You asked three favors of me; I will grant one, and you may choose the one. Will you be healed? Or returned to your friends? Or would you prefer to see your home again, though you will not recall it? I warn you, my mother will have a finger in it, whichever you choose; and I will make no further concessions. If you threaten me again, you will walk in the Lands of the Living no more."

I looked into her lovely, inhuman eyes; and I could not think which to choose.

"May I offer you refreshment?" she asked. "You may sample my wine while you decide, though if you drink deep of it, you must remain with me."

Glad of any argument that might postpone the choice, I protested, "But then, Maiden, I could see neither my friends nor my city."

"Both will be mine soon enough. Meanwhile you are young and very brave; come and share my couch, that a greater hero may be born. Our wine is in the columbarium there."

She pointed, and I saw a niche in the wall. In it stood a dusty jar and a cup, once the castle of some spider queen. Fear woke my hair. "What is this place?" I asked.

"You do not know? How quickly they forget, above! Your race might beg for memory better than yourself. You stand in the megaron of King Celeos. Behold his walls, where sits Minos his overlord, painted from life when he visited Celeos here. Celeos is my subject now and my husband's, and Minos one of our chief justices; no judge could better find the guilt attached to every party in a dispute than Minos. Behind you burns the fire in which my mother would have purified Celeos's son. When at last it dies, all this land will come to us."

I could only stare about me.

"This room has waited you a whole age of the world, but I will not. Have you chosen? Or will you die?"

"I'll choose," I told her. "If I ask for memory, I will indeed know who I am. But I may find myself very far from my city and my friends, and I've noticed that those who remember are generally less happy than I. If I choose my city, without friends or memories it will be as strange a place to me as this town of Advent. So I'm going to choose to rejoin my friends, who, if they are truly my friends, will tell me about my past, and where my city lies. Have I chosen wisely?"

"I had rather you had chosen me. Still, you have chosen, and one additional drop joins the flood that whirls us to destruction. Your wish shall be granted, as soon as it can be arranged. Do not cry out to me for succor when you are caught by the current."

She turned as if to go, and I saw that her back was a mass of putrefaction where worms and maggots writhed. I caught my breath but managed to say, "Do you hope to horrify me, Maiden? Every man who has followed a plow knows what you've shown me, yet we bless you all the same."

Again, she revealed her smiling face. "Beware my half sister Auge, who has stolen the south from my mother. And keep my flower—you shall have need of it." As she spoke, she sank slowly from sight.

At once the room grew darker despite the fire. I felt that a hundred ghosts, banished from it by her presence, were returning. Beside Minos stood a naked man with the head of a bull, his hand upon Minos's shoulder. The play of the firelight upon his muscled chest and arms made it seem they moved. A moment more, and he stamped as an ox does in the stall.

I snatched up the lupine, fled up the steps, and slammed down the slab. Almost, I threw the lupine into the flames; but its blue petals shone in the firelight, and I saw that it was but a wildflower, newly blown and brave with dew. I took off my chaplet, which had held many such blossoms, and found it sadly wilted. It I put into the flames instead, and I have rolled the lupine into the last turning of this scroll.

For it seems to me that we who bless her should not wantonly destroy what she has given.

Now I have written all I recall of this day. Already the morning, when we came to this place and met with Polyhommes, is as faded as the chaplet. I have looked back to see whether I spoke with Pindaros, Hilaeira, or Io at our inn, but there is nothing. Nor do I remember the name of the inn, nor where it stands. I would go there now and tell Pindaros of the Maiden, but no doubt the doors would be bolted, even if I should find it. I have written very small, always, not to waste this scroll. Now my eyes sting and burn when I seek to read it in the firelight, and yet nearly half the sheets are gray with my writing. I will write no more tonight.

# PART III

# —— CHAPTER XX ——

## In My Room

HERE in Kalleos's house, I have decided to write again. I have just read the last of what is written on this scroll, but I do not know whether it is true or even how long it has been since I wrote it. I read because I noticed the scroll in this chest today when I got out a clean chiton, and I thought if ever I needed to write something I would use it. I will write first who I am. I think this tells only who I was.

I am *Latro,* whom Kalleos calls her man slave. There is a girl slave too, Io, but she is too small to do heavy work. There are also Lalos the cook and another cook whose name I have forgotten, but they are not slaves; tonight Kalleos paid them, and they went home. Many women live here, but they are not slaves either, I think, and they do no work—only welcome the men when they come to their couches, and eat and drink with them. Before the men came, some of them teased me, but I could see they liked me and meant no harm. Kalleos paid them this morning after the first meal.

One of them spoke to me afterward, when the rest had gone to the market. She said, "I'm going to Advent tonight, Latro. Isn't it wonderful? If you want to come, I'll ask Kalleos."

I knew Latro was my name, because that and other things are written on the door of this room. I asked her why I should want to go to Advent.

"You don't remember, do you? You really don't."

I shook my head.

"I wish Pindaros hadn't gone home and left you here," she said sadly. "Kalleos wouldn't sell you for what he had, but I think he should have stayed and sent for more money, instead of going to get it."

I could see she was concerned for me; I told her I was happy enough, and that I had eaten all I wanted when I finished bringing the food from the kitchen.

"You said the Maiden promised you'd see your friends again. I wish she were quicker."

That was when I knew I had not always been in this place, and that I must have a family and a city of my own. Once there was a very large man and a very large woman who took care of me. I remember helping the woman carry cuttings away when the man pruned our vines. They had spoken to me too; and though I could understand everything Kalleos and the rest said, and speak to them as well as they to me, I knew their words were not mine, and I could speak mine to myself. So do I write, now. I did not know then who the Maiden was, because I had not read this scroll; by the time I wanted to ask about her, the woman had gone.

I stacked the dishes from the first meal and carried a stack into the kitchen. Lalos had told me his name when I had come to get the food. Now he said, "Have you heard about the Rope Makers, Latro?"

"No. Who are the Rope Makers?"

"The best soldiers in the world. People say they can't be beaten."

The other cook farted with his mouth.

"That's what people say—I didn't say it was true. Anyway, there's a lochos of Rope Makers going from house to house asking questions. The magistrates shouldn't have let them in—that's what I think. Of course they're our allies, and I suppose the magistrates didn't want trouble. Suppose they'd said no, and the Rope Makers had fought their way in. With so many away with the army and navy, who knows what would have happened?"

The other cook said, "You do. And everything else."

I asked, "Will they come here?"

"I suppose, some of them. They're going everywhere, asking crazy questions like what did you eat at the first meal yesterday."

The other cook said, "Then we'll tell them. What's the harm in telling a Rope Maker what you had at the first meal?"

"Yes, we'll tell them," Lalos agreed. "We'd better."

I carried in the rest of the dishes, and the cooks put little Io to washing them. There was food waste, mostly seeds and apple cores, scattered around the courtyard. Kalleos told me, "I'm your mistress, Kalleos, Latro. I want you to sweep all this up. You know about answering the front door?"

I nodded and told her I had read it on my own door.

"Good. And *don't* forget to sweep again tonight when everyone's left. You can remember that, and I like it clean in the morning. And Latro, no matter what they tell you, the girls have to look after their own rooms—they'll get you to do it if they can, the lazy sluts. And their rooms have to be clean by tonight. If you see one who doesn't clean her room, you tell me."

I said, "I will, madame."

"And when you go to the door tonight, don't let in anyone who's drunk until he shows you his money—silver, not bronze or copper. Or gold. Let in anybody who has gold. But don't let in anyone who looks poor, drunk or sober. And don't draw that crooked sword of yours unless you have to. You shouldn't have to."

"No, madame."

"Use your fists, like you did on what's-his-name the other night. And when Io's finished washing up, send her to me. Don't let those two idlers in the kitchen make her do all their work—I want her to go to the market with me. I'll have most of the stuff for tonight delivered, and she can carry the odds and ends. Make the deliverymen go to the back, and don't talk to them. And make them leave—*after* you have all the goods—if they try to snoop. I'm counting on you, Latro."

Men came as soon as it grew dark, mostly bald or graying men, too old to fight. I admitted them; when they were busy with the women, I slept a bit in my chair by the door, only waking when the first left. Some stayed, sleeping with the women in their rooms. When the courtyard was empty, I carried the cups and bowls back to the kitchen for Io to wash tomorrow and got out my broom.

Many of the lamps were dark, and a man slept in one corner. I could see it would be impossible to clean the place well, but I decided to clean it as well as I could. It was very pleasant in the courtyard anyway. The thinnest-possible sliver of moon peeped between the clouds and left shadows beneath the walls, and the heat had passed. The air was soft, perfumed by the flowers Kalleos had bought that afternoon.

I was sweeping near a corner where there were many urns holding many flowers, when a woman's hand stroked my shoulder. I turned to see who she was, but her face was lost in the shadows. She said, "Come, child of war. Do that later, or never."

Knowing what she wanted, I laid my broom on the flagstones and sought her among the blossoms, not finding her until she showed herself to me by kindling a silver lamp shaped like a dove, which hung over the couch in her chamber.

I cannot remember what women I have possessed. Perhaps there have been none. I know that for me tonight she was the first—that no other would have been real beside her, that our joy endured while cities rose and fell, and that while I clasped her the breezes of spring blew perpetually.

My lover was half woman and half child, her cheeks and all her flesh rose-tinted in the roseate light from the dove, slender yet round of limb, her breasts small but perfect, her eyes like the skies of summer, her hair like fire, like butter, like night, ripe with myriad perfumes. "You forget," she said. "But you will remember me."

I nodded because I could not speak. I do not think I could have lifted my hand.

"I am more lovely than my rival. Three faces she has, but none like mine. You have forgotten her; you will never forget me."

"Never." Her chamber was hung with crimson velvet; it seemed to glow in the dim light.

"And I am lovelier far than Kore, the Maiden." Her voice grew bitter. "Not long ago, I gave my favor to a poor creature called Myrrha. Better I had withheld it. Her own father bore her down, and she became a tree, a speechless thing with wooden limbs." A horned doorman fluttered wide, white sleeves to ensure our privacy. "Yet she bore him a child, the fairest ever seen. I locked it in a chest—so you would call it—to keep it safe, for I had lovers who would have used it like a woman."

I nodded, though I would rather she had talked of love.

"I trusted her—that vile girl who calls herself the Maiden, though her legs clasp Hades. She opened the chest and stole the child. I begged for justice, but she kept it four moons each year. At last it died, and from its blood sprang this blood-red blossom where we lie."

I said, "I would lie here forever, for every kiss of yours is new to me."

"Yet you will not, O my lover. Soon, how soon you must go! But you will not forget me, nor what I say."

Then she whispered in my ear, repeating the same thing again and again in many ways. I cannot write it here, because I do not remember what it was—and it seems to me that even as I heard her words they were lost; but perhaps they only sank into some part of me where memory does not go. She showed me an apple of gold and spun the dove to make its light play upon that apple.

Then she was gone, and her chamber too, and I was left leaning on my broom in the cold court. The moon glowed high overhead, a crescent glyph cupping some meaning I did not comprehend.

I got one of the lamps and searched among the flowers for the door to her room; when I found it, it was only a crimson anemone, half-open, before which fluttered a tiny white moth.

With my hand I brushed him away and held it up, and it seemed to me the heart of the blossoms held a spark of laughter, but perhaps it was only a tear of dew.

A woman touched my shoulder. It was Kalleos, her breath heavy with wine because she had been drinking with the men.

"You don't have to worry about that, Latro," she said. "Poking among the flowers with a light. Get it tomorrow, when you can see what you're doing. Put away that broom and come with me. You're a fine figure of a man, know that?"

"Thank you," I said. "What is it you want, madame?"

"Only your arm to get me to my door. I'm ready for my bed tonight, by every god, and I'll sleep like a chalcis. I've a skin in there, Latro, and I'll give you a drink before you go. It isn't right that you should work all the time and never get to party."

I took her to her room, where she sat on her bed, her weight making the straps creak under the mattress until I thought they must break. She told me where the wineskin was and had me pour cups for us both; and while I was drinking mine, she blew out the lamp.

"I'm at that age when a woman looks best in the dark," she said. "Come and sit with me."

My hand brushed her naked breast.

"Surely you know how to put your arm around a woman?"

It was not completely dark. I had left the door open a crack, and a thread of light from the silver dove stole in, whispering something too faint for me to hear. Kalleos had let her robe fall to her hips, and I could see her white breasts and the rounded bulge that ended in the dark cloth of her robe. I felt they should disgust me now, but they did not. Rather it seemed that in some way Kalleos was the woman in the anemone, as a word written is the spoken word, and not just a dirty smudge upon the papyrus.

"Kiss me," she said. "And let me lay down."

I did as she told me, then took off her sandals and pulled her gown away from her legs.

By that time she was snoring. I went out, shutting the door behind me, and came here to my own place, where I write these words.

# CHAPTER XXI

## Eutaktos

THE lochagos knocked as I was serving the first meal today. Kalleos moaned. "That's trouble, I'm sure of it."

Zoe, who had been boasting about the big tip she had been given the night before, said, "It might be good news. You never know."

"Anything that happens before dark is bad news when you've got a headache. When you're my age, you'll understand."

The knocking grew louder. Phye said, "That's not knuckles. He's pounding with something."

It had been the grounding iron of a spear, as I learned when I opened the door. Eutaktos and half a dozen shieldmen shouldered their way in. Their hoplons and cuirasses protected their bellies, but their helmets were pushed back, and I was able to hit one in the neck and throw Eutaktos over my hip before the rest got their spears leveled. I threw my chair and drew my sword, and the women began to scream. Eutaktos was up again and had his own sword out, with Io hanging from his sword arm and crying, "Don't kill him!"

He shook her off. "We won't, unless he runs on the spears. Who's master here?"

Kalleos came forward, wearing the expression she used when the women threw food. "I am, and that's my slave you're talking about killing. If you kill him, you'll pay for him. Nine minas he cost me not a month ago, and I have a receipt signed by a leading citizen."

"You're no daughter of Hellen's."

"I didn't say I was a citizen," Kalleos answered with dignity. "I said the man I spoke of is. He's at sea in command of a squadron of our warships at this very moment. As for me, as a freedwoman and a resident foreigner I am protected by our laws."

Eutaktos looked sourly from her to me. "How many men here?"

"Right now? Three. Why do you want to know?"

"Get the rest."

Kalleos shrugged and told Phye, "Bring in Lalos and Leon."

"You there." Eutaktos pointed to me with his sword. "Quick! Name the man who sold you."

I shook my head.

Io said, "Hypereides, sir. Please don't hurt Latro—he can't remember."

The shieldmen, who had been nudging one another and winking while they stared at the women, fell silent as though someone had given a command. Eutaktos lowered his sword and sent it rasping back into the scabbard. "You say he doesn't remember, little girl?"

Suddenly abashed, Io nodded.

"We can settle this quickly," Eutaktos told Kalleos. "Do you have any books?"

Kalleos shook her head. "None. I keep all my records on wax tablets."

"None at all? Want us to search? You won't like it."

"There's a book Latro has to write in. He does forget, as Io says."

"Ah." Eutaktos glanced at one of the other Rope Makers, and both smiled. "Fetch it, woman."

"I don't know where he keeps it."

Phye said, "You won't be able to read it, Lochagos. I've tried, but he writes in some barbaric tongue." Our two cooks, who had banged the pans that morning and talked loudly, looked very small beside her. The man I had hit got to his feet rubbing his neck.

"But he can read it to me," Eutaktos said. "Latro, bring me your book."

Io said, "He's afraid you'll take it, sir. You won't, will you?"

Eutaktos shook his head. "Do you know where it is?"

Io nodded. "I know more about Latro than anybody."

"Then get it. We won't hurt him or you."

Io ran to my room and was soon back carrying this scroll.

"Good!" Eutaktos said. "And now—"

There was a tap at the door. Eutaktos told one of the shieldmen to see who it was and send him away. To me he said, "A fine book, must have cost a couple of owls. Too long for you to unroll it all between your hands?"

I nodded.

"Then do it on the floor, so I can see it. Little girl, hold down the end."

The shieldman who had been sent to the door announced, "Urgent message, Lochagos. A Milesian."

Eutaktos nodded, and the soldier ushered in a tall and very lean man with hair like a black haystack; he wore a purple cloak and many rings. This man darted a glance at me, another at Kalleos, and said to Eutaktos, "Many blessings upon you, noble warrior! I have words that are for your heroic ears alone."

Kalleos came forward smiling. "I can show you to a comfortable room, Lochagos, where you two can talk in private. We haven't tidied up yet from last night, but—"

"No matter," Eutaktos snapped. "Take us there—we won't be long. You, Latro, close your book again and keep it so. Basias, see that he does."

They were back almost at once, the Rope Maker looking pleased and the Milesian chagrined. To his shieldmen, Eutaktos said, "This fellow's come to tell us what we were about to see for ourselves." He turned to me. "Unroll your book."

I did as he had ordered, and when I reached the final sheet found a dried flower there.

Eutaktos crouched beside me. "You men, look here! Did everyone see this?"

The shieldmen nodded, and several said, "Yes, sir."

"Remember it. You may have to tell Pausanias. You heard me ask the question. You heard he couldn't answer. You saw him unroll this book, you saw the flower. Don't forget those things." He stood up. "These are high matters. It won't go well with anyone who makes a mistake."

The Milesian began, "Noble Rope Maker, if you would care—"

"I wouldn't. You Ionians are mad for gold. We win your battles for you, so you think we've got it. There isn't a man here who's any richer than the poorest slave in this house, myself included."

"In that case . . ." The Milesian shrugged and turned to go.

"Not so fast!"

Two shieldmen blocked the door.

"You'll leave when I say, not before. Obey orders or suffer for it. Latro, you're coming with us; so's the child. What's her name?"

"Io!" Io piped.

"Woman." Eutaktos turned to Kalleos. "Apply to Pausanias or either of our kings and you'll be compensated. Shut up! You talk too much—all of you do up here."

"Sir," I said, "I've got a cloak and some clean chitons. May I get them?"

He nodded. "Whatever you want, as long as that book's part of it. Basias, go with him."

Kalleos said, "Eurykles, you're not going with them too, are you?"

"Of course not," the Milesian told her.

Eutaktos turned on him. "Of course, you mean. You're from Miletos, Miletos is in the Empire, the Empire's our enemy, you're our prisoner. Curses and witchery will get your throat cut before you finish them."

I left with Basias then, and so I did not hear what else was said. When we returned, Io had a little bundle at her feet and a wooden doll under her arm. Basias looked inquiringly at Eutaktos and pointed to my sword.

Kalleos explained, "He was my watchman, Lochagos. Latro, I'll keep that for you, if you like."

"No," Eutaktos told her, "Basias will keep it. Pausanias may return it to him."

The street was hot after the shade of Kalleos's courtyard. I held my belongings at my shoulder with one hand and held Io's hand with the other; she held mine and did the same. Eutaktos marched in front of us, staring every man he saw out of countenance and spitting every time some new city stink offended his nostrils. The Milesian stumped sour-faced after us, muttering to himself.

Basias was on my right, and on my left and behind us tramped the rest of the shieldmen, all with long spears, red cloaks, and big hoplons painted with the wedge-shaped letter that the Crimson Men call the Stylus, which seems to me a most fit insignia for their Silent Country. They might have been the vanguard of an army of occupation, and the archers posted where the road left the city looked relieved when we marched past.

Among the Rope Makers each shieldman has several slaves to carry his belongings, pitch his tent, and prepare his food. These slaves had bought wine in the city, so we had a little to stir into our water (for the shieldmen had not yet eaten the first meal), as well as raw onions, boiled barley, salt olives, and cheese. Io says I forget, and I know I do; but I remembered then how much wine there had been on Kalleos's table when we left, and her melons and figs.

Before we ate, Eutaktos sent slaves into Thought to recall the other enomotia of his lochos. When the meal was over (which it soon was) he ordered the rest to break camp. I asked Basias where we were going.

"Back to Redface Island," he told me, "if that's where the prince is. He wants to see you."

I asked why, but he only shook his head.

Io said, "You don't remember, but we sailed around Redface Island with Hypereides. It looked wild—just a few little villages along the shore."

Basias nodded. "Too many pirates. Tower Hill trades for us."

The Milesian had come over to listen. He remarked, "And gets rich from it."

"That's their problem." Basias turned and stalked away.

"Odd people, aren't they?" the Milesian said. "I know you don't recognize me, Latro, but I'm Eurykles the Necromancer. You held a light for me not long ago, when I performed one of my greatest wonders."

Io said, "You came to Kalleos's and joined Hypereides's party. Rhoda told me."

Eurykles nodded. "That's right, and from it you must know I'm a good friend of Kalleos's; and Kalleos is Latro's rightful owner."

"She is not!"

He looked at her askance. He is one of those people who can raise one eyebrow a great deal higher than the other.

"Latro's a free man, and I'm *his* slave. Kalleos said I was hers, but she didn't even have a bill for me."

"Nor does Latro, I imagine. Not that it matters now. Don't talk of buying and selling to these Rope Makers, by the way. Among every other people in the world, trading's honorable and stealing dishonorable; but among the Rope Makers it's just the reverse. Stealing's glorious if you don't get caught, but trading blackens a man's name as much as keeping a stall in the market."

I said, "You don't like them."

"Nobody does. Some people admire them, and some people nearly worship them; but nobody likes them, and from what I've seen of them today, they don't even like each other."

Io asked whether he had been to Redface Island.

He shook his head. "There's no money past Tower Hill on the isthmus, not a scrap. Nothing but barley, blood, and beans. You saw how Eutaktos treated me when I came to him with valuable information, didn't you? Made me a prisoner! An officer from any decent city would have filled my mouth with silver."

I said, "You came to tell the Rope Makers about me."

"Yes, I did. It was quite clever of me, I think. You see, I had heard the Rope Makers were going through the city asking all sorts of foolish questions and paying no attention to the answers. They'd ask someone where he'd eaten dinner, and most would say in their own houses, and a few at some friend's house, and one or two at an inn or a cookshop; but it didn't seem to matter, no matter what they said. And after I'd listened to half a dozen stories like that, it dawned on me that they were looking for a man who didn't know. That had to be you."

Io asked, "What's my master ever done to you, fellow?"

Eurykles grinned. "Why, nothing. But I didn't think they were going to harm him, and I still don't. Judging from what Eutaktos says, Pausanias is just as apt to honor him. Besides, they would have found him sooner or later anyway—I was too late, actually—and I may still get something out of it."

"I thought you didn't want to be their prisoner."

"Yes, but it's their ingratitude that rankles. Anytime I really want to leave, I'll just render my person invisible and stroll away."

Then the last of the Rope Makers came out of the city and we left, each shieldman with his slaves marching behind him and carrying his hoplon, helmet, and spear, as well as the other things, and Io, Eurykles, and I behind Eutaktos as before. Now we are camped by a spring, and Io has reminded me that before I sleep I should write down what happened today. A woman with two torches and two hounds is beckoning from the crossroads, and when I have finished writing this I will go to see what it is she wants.

# CHAPTER XXII

## The Woman at the Crossroads

THE Dark Mother frightened me. She is gone, but I am still afraid. I would not have thought I could be frightened by a woman even if she held a knife to my throat; but the Dark Mother is no common woman.

When I left the fire and went to speak to her, she seemed nothing more, a woman such as anyone might see in any village. Her eyes were dark, her hair black and bound with a fillet. The top of her head came only to my shoulder. She held a torch in each hand, torches that smoked, sending up black columns to the night sky.

Her dogs were black too, and very large—I think of the kind kings use to hunt lions, though I cannot remember ever having seen such a hunt. Their muzzles came to her elbows, and sometimes their ears stood erect like the ears of wolves. Their spittle was white and shone, even when it had dropped from their flews to the ground.

"You do not know me," the Dark Mother said, "though you have seen me each night."

When I heard her voice I knew she was a queen, and I bowed.

"These dogs of mine could tear you to bits, do you know that? Do you think you could resist them?"

"No, great mistress," I said. "Because they are yours."

She laughed, and at the sound of her laughter, things

168

stirred among the trees. "That is a good answer. But do not call me *mistress**; that word means an owner of the earth, and she is my enemy. I am Enodia, the Dark Mother."

"Yes, Dark Mother."

"Will you forget me, when you see me no longer?"

"I will strive not to forget, Dark Mother."

She laughed again, and the stirring told me the things waiting among the trees were so near they could almost be seen.

"I am the woman of poisons, Latro. Of murder, ghosts, and the spells that bring death. I am the Queen of the Neurians; and I am three. Do you understand?"

"Yes, Dark Mother," I said. "No, Dark Mother."

"Today you passed many farms. There you must have seen my image, cut in wood or stone—three women, standing back to back."

"Yes, Dark Mother, I saw the image. I did not know what it meant." My teeth warred in my mouth, the teeth above against the teeth below.

"You do not remember, yet you have looked often at the moon and seen me, as I have seen you. Once when I heard a certain one called the God in the Tree, I came while you stood in water. I sought him but found he was not He whom I sought. Do you recall me as I was then?"

I could not speak; I shook my head.

As the darkness vanishes when the moon steps from behind a cloud, so she vanished. In her place stood the lovely virgin I had seen beside the lake after I had slept with Hilaeira.

"You remember now," the virgin said, and smiled. "Earth's power is great, but I am here and she is not." She held a bow, just as I remembered, and there were seven arrows in the cestus at her waist. The Dark Mother's hounds fawned on her.

"Yes," I said. "I remember. Oh, thank you!" and I knelt and would have kissed her feet but that the hounds bared their teeth at me.

---

*The word Latro used was probably *despoina* (Gk. δέσποινα). —G. W.

"I am no friend of yours, save as you are the enemy of my enemy; and when I am gone, you will forget me once more."

"Then never go!" I begged her. "Or take me with you."

"I cannot stay, and you cannot go where I go. But I have come to tell you of the place to which you will go soon. It is my country—do you understand? Call me Huntress now, for that is what they call me there, and Auge."

"Yes, Huntress."

"Once it was Gaea's. I sent my people, and they took it for me, breaking her altars."

"Yes, Huntress."

"You must not seek to loose their grasp, and because you will forget, I desire to send a slave with you who will remind you. Happily, there is someone with you who has sworn to serve me without reservation, and thus is mine wholly to do with as I choose."

"And I, Huntress."

"Hardly, though I know you mean well. Look at this." She held out her hand; in it writhed a little snake no longer than my finger. "Take her, and keep her safe."

I took it, but I had nowhere to put it. I held it in my hand, and in a moment it seemed to vanish; I held nothing.

"Good. Down that road is a farmhouse." The Huntress pointed with her bow. "It is not far, and you need not fear that the shieldman set to watch you will wake. You must go to that farm and make its people give you a wineskin and a cup. When you meet the one who has dedicated himself to me, you must make him drink, and you must put my serpent into the cup. Do you understand?"

"Huntress," I said, "I have lost your serpent."

"You will find her again when the time comes. Now go. I send my dogs before you to rouse the house."

As she spoke, they flashed from her side. For an instant I saw them streaking down the road she had indicated; then they were gone.

I turned and followed them, knowing that was what the virgin wished me to do. When I had taken fifty steps or so, the urge to see her once more overwhelmed me, and I looked over my shoulder.

I wish I had not, because she was gone. The Dark Mother stood where she had stood, holding her torches; wisps of fog and dark, shapeless things had left the trees to be with her. Someone screamed and I began to run, though I could not have said whether I ran to give aid or to fly the Dark Mother.

The farmhouse was like a hundred others, of rough brick with a thatched roof, its farmyard surrounded by a low wall of mud and sticks. The gate had been broken; I entered easily. Inside, the wooden figure of the three women had been thrown down, though the altars to either side of the door had not been touched. The door was whole, but as I approached it a man with staring eyes flung it open and ran out. He would have collided with me as one horseman rides down another, had I not caught him as he came.

I asked, "Are you the father of this hearth?"

"Yes," he said.

"Then I can take away the curse, I think; but you must give me freely a skin of wine and a cup."

His mouth worked. I think it would have foamed had there been any moisture there. The screaming inside had stopped, though a child wept.

"Give me the wine," I told him.

Without another word he turned and went in again, and I followed him.

His wife came to him, naked and weeping, her face twisted with fear and grief. She tried to speak, but only the noises of grief and fear could pass her lips. He pushed her to one side; when she saw me she clasped me for protection, and I put my arm about her.

The man returned with a wineskin and a cup of unglazed clay. "This has waited two seasons," he said. I saw that he himself was no older than I, and perhaps younger.

Telling him to comfort his wife, I went back outside. There I set up the image in its place again, poured a little wine into the cup, and sprinkled a few drops before each of the three figures, calling them Dark Mother, Huntress, and

Moon. Before I had finished, silence settled on the house, and an owl hooted from the wood.

The farmer and his wife came out to me, she now wearing a gown and leading a girl younger than Io by the hand. I told them I did not think they would be troubled again. They thanked me many times; and he brought a lamp, another skin of wine, and cups like the one he had given me. We all drank the unmixed wine, the child sipping from her mother's cup that she might sleep soundly, as her mother said. I asked them what they had seen.

The child would say only that it had been a bad thing; I did not question her further, seeing that it made her afraid. The woman said that a hag with staring eyes had sat upon her and held her motionless by a spell; she had been unable to breathe. The man spoke of a winged creature, not a bird nor a bat, that had flapped after him from room to room.

I asked whether any of them had seen a dog. They told me they owned a dog and had heard him bark. We went to look for him in his kennel behind the house and found him dead, though there was no mark upon him. He was old and white at the muzzle. The man asked whether I was an archimage; I told him only for this night.

When I left the farmhouse, a figure moved at the cross-road, and I saw many tiny lights, though the Dark Mother and her torches were gone. It was the Milesian; he started up as though frightened when I approached him, though he relaxed when he saw my face. "Latro!" he exclaimed. "There's someone else awake, at least. Do you know the Rope Makers didn't even post a guard? There's confidence for you."

I asked what he was doing.

"Just a little sacrifice to the Triple Goddess. Road crossings like this are sacred to her, provided there's no house in sight, and the dark of the moon is the best time. I hadn't thanked her properly yet for the great boon she gave me in the city—you were there and saw it, what a pity you don't remember! Anyway, this seemed a good chance to do it.

Then this fellow''—he pointed to the sacrifice, a black puppy—
"wandered up to me, and I knew it had to be propitious."

I said, "If you haven't finished . . ."

"Oh, no. I completed the last invocation just as I heard
your step." He bent and picked up the glowing things that
formed a circle around the puppy, then looked significantly at
the wineskin. "You've been buying from the peasants, I
see."

I nodded and asked whether he was dedicated to the Triple
Goddess.

"Yes indeed. Ever since I was a lad. She gives her worshipers all they ask—even old Hesiod says so in his verses,
though none of his countrymen seemed to heed him. I admit
she has some strange ways of doing it."

I knew then that he was the one of whom the Huntress had
spoken, and I loosened the thongs of the wineskin and poured
wine into the cup. "What is it you have asked of her?"

"Power, of course. Gold is only a kind of power, and not
the best kind. As for women, I've had a good many, and I
find I prefer boys."

To fill the time, I said, "Power will get you all you wish
of those. Kings have no difficulty."

"Of course not. But real power is not of this world, but of
the higher one—the ability to call back the dead and summon
spirits; the knowledge of unseen things."

I sipped from the cup, and as I lowered it, felt the little
snake stir in the hand that held the skin. When I poured more
wine into the cup, I dropped the snake in with it.

The Milesian drained it at a gulp. "Thanks. I owe you
something for that, Latro." He wiped his mouth on the back
of his hand. "I'd initiate you into the mystery of the goddess,
but you'd forget, and it can't be written down."

Side by side we walked back to the tents of the Rope
Makers. My bed was in Basias's tent; I do not know with
whom the Milesian's was. He asked if we might share another cup before we slept. I told him I had drunk all the wine
I wanted, but I would gladly give him another. He drank it
and wished me a good night.

I tried to wish him the same, but the words stayed in my throat.

"Eurykles," he told me, thinking that I had forgotten his name.

"Yes, Eurykles," I said. "Good luck, Eurykles. I know your goddess is pleased with you."

He smiled and waved before he went into one of the tents.

I lay down, and after a long time I slept. Now the sky grows light, and though I would sooner forget what happened last night, I think it best to write it here.

# ── CHAPTER XXIII ──

## In the Village

I am writing this in the courtyard of the inn. Eutaktos had been so eager to leave Thought that he did not buy provisions for the return to Redface Island. I think perhaps he believed also that he could get them more cheaply away from the city, and in that I suppose he was right. Anyway, we have halted here, and Eutaktos and some others are bargaining for food in the market. I am writing because I have not yet forgotten what took place last night, though I do not remember how I came to be among these Rope Makers.

The Milesian came to me when we halted here and said, "Let's find a wineshop. I'll repay you for what you gave me last night." I pretended to have forgotten, but he pressed me to go anyway, saying, "Basias can come with us. Then they can't say we were trying to get away."

Soon the Milesian, Basias, Io, and I were sitting very comfortably at a table in the shade; there was a jar of old wine and one of cold well water in the center of the table, and each of us had a cup before him. "You will recall that we were discussing the Triple Goddess last evening," the Milesian said to me. "At least, I hope you will. That hasn't gone yet, has it?"

I shook my head. "I can remember our camping outside this village late last night, and everything that came after that."

Io asked, "Where are we, anyway? Is this far from Advent?"

"This is Acharnae," the Milesian told her. "We're about

fifty stades from Advent, which will be our next stop. It would have been a little shorter along the Sacred Way, but I suppose Eutaktos felt there was too much danger of incurring a charge of impiety.'' He looked at Basias for confirmation, but the Rope Maker only shrugged and put his cup to his lips.

"I've been to Advent before," Io told the Milesian. "With Latro and Pindaros and Hilaeira. Latro slept in the temple."

"Really? And did he learn anything?"

"That the goddess would soon restore him to his friends."

I asked Io to tell me about that.

"I don't know much, because you didn't tell me much. I think you told Pindaros more than me, and you probably wrote more than you told Pindaros. All you said to me was that you saw the goddess, and she gave you a flower and promised you'd see your friends soon. We were your friends, Hilaeira and Pindaros and me, but I don't think she meant us. I think she meant the friends you lost when you were hurt."

Basias was looking at me narrowly. "She gave you a flower in a dream?"

I said, "I don't know."

Io told him. "He just said she gave him one."

The Milesian spun an owl on the table as if hoping for an omen. "You can never tell about goddesses. Or gods either. Possibly a dream with a goddess in it is more real than a day without one. The goddess makes it so. That's what I'd like to be."

I was surprised. "A goddess?"

"Or a god. Whatever. Find some little place, impress the people with my powers, and make them build me a temple."

Basias told him, "You'd better put more water in that."

The Milesian smiled. "Perhaps you're right."

"Drinking unmixed wine will drive a man mad—everybody knows that. The Sons of Scoloti do it, and they're all as mad as crabs."

"Yet I've heard there are little villages along your coast where the people worship sea gods who've been forgotten everywhere else in the world."

Basias drank again. "Who cares what slaves do? Or who their slave gods are?"

Io said, "We had four Sons of Scoloti on Hypereides's ship with us, Latro. But then one left the night the sailor died and never came back."

Basias nodded. "What did I tell you?"

The Milesian spun his coin again. "Not all of them are Sons of Scoloti. Some are Neurians; there was a Neurian in the city."

"Who are they? I never heard of them."

"They live east of the Sons of Scoloti and have much the same manners and customs. At least, when we see them."

Basias poured himself more wine. "Then who cares?"

"Except that they can change themselves into wolves. Or anyway they change into wolves. Some people say they can't control it." The Milesian lowered his voice. "Latro, you don't remember how I raised a woman in the city, but one of them had opened her grave. I had planned, you see, just to produce a ghost; but when I saw that broken coffin—well, the opportunity was too good to miss."

The innkeeper, who had been lounging against the wall not far away, sauntered over to join the conversation. "I couldn't help but hear what you said about men who change to wolves. You know, we had somethin' a bit odd happen just last night, right here in Acharnae. Family sleepin' peacefully in their beds, when just like a thunderclap the place was full of I don't know what you call 'em. People talk about Sabaktes and Mormo and all that, kind of like they was a joke. These wasn't, though they didn't write their names on the walls."

The Milesian said, "They vanished at dawn, I assume. I wish I might stay here another day, so I might exorcise them for those good people; my fame in that line outreaches the known world, though I hesitate to say it. But I fear the noble Eutaktos means for us to march again after the first meal."

"They're gone already," the innkeeper said. "I haven't talked to the family myself, but I know them that have, and they say a man come to the door just as they was runnin' out. He said to give him a skin of wine and he'd fix things. So they did, and he set up the figure of the three goddesses that had been knocked down and poured out a bit to each goddess. Soon as he did that, they was gone.'' The innkeeper paused, looking from face to face. "He was a real tall man, they said, with a scar on his head."

The Milesian yawned. "What happened to the wine? I don't suppose he poured it all out."

"Oh, he kept that. Some people are sayin' he probably whistled up those whatever-they-weres just to get it. I say that for a man who could do that, he was satisfied awful cheap."

"And so would I," the Milesian drawled when the innkeeper had left. He spun the owl on the table as before. "But then, it all depends on just whom the wonder's worked for, doesn't it? When I raised the dead woman in the city, I had sense enough to take her around to some wealthy patrons before cockcrow. Most of them weren't *my* patrons before they saw her, to be sure. But they were afterward. Some people despise wealth, however. I do myself."

"You don't talk like it," Basias told him.

"Do you have any money?"

"I thought this was your treat."

"Oh, it is. I just want to know whether you've got any."

"Couple of obols," Basias admitted.

"Then throw them away. They're no good where we're going, or so people tell me. Toss them into the dirt there. I'm sure that fellow who just left will be happy to pick them up."

Basias darted the Milesian a surly look but said nothing.

"You see, you don't despise *money*. Nor do I. Wealth is stuffy and stupid and arrogant, and the only good thing about it is that it has money. Money's lovely stuff—just look at this." He held up the owl. "See how it shines? On one side the owl: the male principle. On the other, the Lady of Thought: the female principle." He spun the coin on the table. "Money always gives you something to think about."

Basias asked, "Do you know what Pausanias did after the Battle of Clay?"

The Milesian looked bored, but Io piped, "Tell us!"

"We killed Mardonius and got his baggage. So Pausanias told his cooks to cook a meal just like they would have for him and his staff. He called in all our officers and showed it to them. I wasn't there, but Eutaktos was, and he told me. Pausanias said, 'See the wealth of these people who have come to share our poverty.' "

"It's perfectly true." The Milesian nodded, still spinning his coin. "By our standards, the wealth of the Empire is incalculable. His name wasn't really Mardonius, by the way. It was Marduniya. It means 'the warrior.' "

Basias said, "I couldn't say that without wrenching my mouth."

"You'll have to learn to wrench your mouth, if you hope to get rich while you're liberating the Asian cities with Pausanias."

"Who said I did?"

"Why, no one. I said 'if.' "

"You say too much, Eurykles."

"I know. I know." The Milesian rose. "But now, if you'll excuse me, kind friends, I have to—where does one do it here, anyway? In back, I suppose."

No one spoke for a moment, then Basias said, "I'd like to go with him."

I asked why he did not.

"Because I'm supposed to stay with you. But I'd like to see what he has under all those clothes. Did you ever?"

"See him naked?" I asked. "Not that I remember."

Io said, "Neither have I, and I don't want to. I'm too little for that."

Basias grinned at her. "Anyway, you know it. Half don't. But if you change your mind, I'll show you a way."

I said, "And I will kill you for it."

"You mean you'll try, barbarian."

Io said, "Latro isn't a barbarian. He talks just as good as you do. Better."

"Talk, yes, but can he wrestle?"

"You saw him throw your lochagos."

Basias was grinning again now. "I did, and it set me wondering. Want a bout, barbarian?" He drained his wine.

"Same rules they use in Olympia—no hitting, no kicking, no holds below the waist."

I stood and took off my chiton. Basias laid his sword belt on the table and took off his cuirass, then pulled his own chiton over his head. The innkeeper appeared from nowhere with half a dozen loungers in his train. "Just a friendly bout," Basias told him.

He was shorter than I by a hand, but a trifle heavier. When he extended his arm for me, it was like gripping the limb of an oak. In a moment he had me by the waist; and in a moment more, I was flat on my back in the dirt.

"Easy meat," Basias said. "Didn't anybody ever teach you?"

I said, "I don't know."

"Well, that's one fall. Three and you lose. Want to try again?"

I bathed my hands in dust to dry the sweat. This time he lifted me over his head. "Now if I wanted to hurt you, barbarian, I'd throw you into the table. But that would spill the wine."

The inn yard swung dizzily until it was where the sky should be, then slapped me as a man swats a fly.

"Two falls for me. Got anything left?"

My eyes were wet with the tears of shame, and I wiped them on the back of my arm. One of the loungers told the innkeeper, "I'll take my obol now. Why not save the time and trouble?"

Io was saying, "I'll bet you another obol," to the lounger by the time I had my knees under me.

"Bet with a child? Let me see your money. All right, but you'd be a fool if he were Heracles."

The oak limb I had imagined a moment earlier appeared before my eyes. "I can't help you up," the big man who held it rumbled. "It's against the rules. But it's not against them to take your time getting up, and you'd better do it."

I got a foot beneath me but kept one knee on the ground as I wiped my forehead.

"He's beating you by lifting you, like I beat Antaeus. You have to keep hold of him all the time. He can't lift himself."

When Basias offered me his arm again, I closed with him, gripping him under the arms as he gripped me by the waist.

"He'll try to bend you back," the man with the club said. "Twist and squeeze. Every muscle in your arm's a piece of raw hide. They're drying in the sun, pulling up. Hear his ribs creak? Dig into his neck with that sharp chin of yours."

We fell together. When I had climbed off him, Basias said, "You're learning. That's one for you. You've got to give me your arm this time."

I turned him upside down and found that his lower ribs were softer than the upper ones. His arms were no longer as hard as they had been. With one hand on his waist and one at his shoulder, I was able to get him above my head. "You didn't throw me at the table," I told him. "So I won't do it to you either."

The big man with the club pointed to the lounger who had bet with Io.

I said, "All right," and knocked the lounger off his feet with Basias.

The Milesian applauded, rapping the tabletop with his cup.

"Good!" the big man whispered. "Now let him win."

# ── CHAPTER XXIV ──
## Why Did You Lose?

Io asked her question with her eyes as I sat writing. I said, "I don't know." And then, thinking of the man with the club and why he might have spoken as he had, "Do you think we'd be better off if I'd won? Besides, it wouldn't have been fair. Suppose Basias had thrown me into the table. That would have ended the match."

He came out of the inn with grease on the place where he had hurt his arm. "Any wine left?"

Io tilted the jar and peered inside. "Almost half-full."

"I can use it. Your master's a man of his hands, girl. With some training he might do for the Games."

"You'd better water that," she told him. "It drives you mad."

"I'll spit in it. Same thing." He looked at me. "You really don't know who you are?"

I shook my head. The Milesian stirred in his sleep, groaning like a woman in love.

"You're a barbarian by the look of you. No Hellene ever had a beak like that. No helot either. That sword of yours looks foreign too. You have any armor?"

Io said, "He used to have front and back plates, round things that hung over his shoulders and tied at the waist. I think Kalleos has them now."

Basias drained his cup and filled it again. "I saw a lot of those on dead men at Clay, but they don't help me much."

I said, "Tell us about the battle. You were there, and I'd like to know."

"What happened to you? I can't tell you that without knowing where you were." He dipped a finger in his wine. "Here's our army. That's a ridgeline, see? Over here's the enemy." He poured a puddle on the table. "The plain was black with them. One of our officers—Amompharetos is his name—had been giving Pausanias trouble. He should have been asked to the council, see? Only he wasn't. Either the message never got to him, which is what Pausanias says, or Pausanias never sent it. That's what Amompharetos said. They finally got it patched up, so Pausanias put Amompharetos and his taksis back here in reserve to show he trusted him."

Io said, "It looks to me like he didn't."

"You're no man; you'll never understand war. But the reserve's the most important part of the army. It's got to go to the hottest place when the army's losing. There were more hills here on the right, with all the men from that dirty place we just left hiding behind them. We're out where the enemy can see us; then Pausanias gives the order to pull back."

Io interrupted. "Is Pausanias one of your kings? And do you really have two?"

"Sure we've got two," Basias told her. "It's the only system that works."

"I'd think they'd fight."

"That's it. Suppose there was just one. A lot of people have tried that. If he's strong, he takes every man's wife, and the sons too. He does whatever he likes. But look at us. If one of ours tried that, we'd side with the other. So they don't. But Pausanias isn't a king, he's regent for Pleistarchos."

Basias held up his cup to me. I poured a little wine from mine into his and let him do the same. "Over here's the Molois," he continued, "almost dry. Here's Hysiae and here's Argiopium, just a village around the temple of the Grain Goddess."

The grass underfoot is yellowing, the sky so light a blue it hurts the eyes. Brown hills rise at the end of the yellow plain. Dark horsemen cross and recross; beyond them the red cloaks of the enemy seep away like blood from a corpse. Mardonius is on his white stallion in the midst of the Immortals. The trumpets are blowing, and the heralds shout to advance. I try to keep our hundred together, but Medes with bows and big wicker shields press through our formation, then spearmen and bowmen with bodies painted white and red. We run across the plain, the swifter outpacing the slower, the lightly armed always farther ahead of the heavily armed, until I can see no one I know, only dust and running strangers, and ahead the shining bronze wall of the hoplons, the bristling hedge of the spears.

Little Io was pressing my forehead with a wet cloth. An enemy bent over me, his horsehair crest nodding, his red cloak falling beside his shoulders. I reached for Falcata, but Falcata was gone.

"It's all right," Io said. "All right, master."

The enemy straightened up. "How long's he been like this?" It was Eutaktos, and I knew him.

"Not long," Io said. "Basias sent one of the inn servants for you."

I tried to say I was well, but it came from my lips in this tongue, not in theirs.

"He talks a lot," Io told Eutaktos, "only you can't understand it. Most of the time he doesn't seem to see me."

I said, "I'm better now," speaking as they.

Eutaktos said, "Good, good," and knelt beside me. "What happened? Basias hit you?"

I did not understand what he meant. "We broke," I told him. "Even when they made a new shieldwall we were only a mob behind it. The Medes took the spears in their hands and broke them, died. The arrows were no good, and I can't find Falcata."

Io said, "That's his sword."

I told them Marcus was dead, and I could not find Umeri, that we should not have gone to Riverland.

Eutaktos said, "There's magic in this. Where's that magician?"

Io gestured. "Asleep outside."

"He was, maybe. Not now. I would have seen him."
Eutaktos stamped away and I sat up.

"Are you better, master?"

Io's little face looked so concerned I had to laugh. "Yes,"
I said. "And I know you. But I can't think who you are."

"I'm Io, your slave girl. The Shining God gave me to
you."

We were in a cramped, dark room that smelled of smoke. I
said, "I don't remember. What is this place?"

"Just an inn."

A tall, ugly woman with short black hair came in, saying,
"Hello, Latro. Do you remember me?"

I said, "Latro?"

"Yes, you're Latro, and I'm your friend Eurykles. Kalleos's
friend too. Do you recall Kalleos?"

I shook my head.

"I'm supposed to heal you," the woman said, "and I want
to. But I don't know what happened—I was taking a nap. It
might help if I did."

Io said, "Do you remember how he wrestled with Basias?"

"Yes. Basias threw him twice, then he threw Basias twice,
then Basias threw Latro again to end the bout. We all had a
drink on it, and Basias went in here to try to find something
to put on that bad place on his arm. Latro wanted to write in
his book—"

I looked at Io and tried to stand. She said hastily, "I have
it right here, master. Your stylus too."

"—and I got sleepy and lay down. What happened after
that?"

"Basias came back and they drank some more, and Basias
asked Latro if he had any armor." Io looked at me. "Basias
has your sword, master. He's keeping it for you."

The ugly woman said, "Go on."

"And I said he didn't. Then Latro said to tell him about
the battle. I guess he meant the one where everybody in our
Sacred Band got killed. Anyway Basias knew, and he told us
about their kings and where the armies were." Io paused for
breath.

"Then Latro shouted. He kept on shouting and knocked over the wine, and Basias got hold of him from in back and tried to throw him down, but Latro got loose. Then Basias and a lot of men from the inn caught him and threw him down and he stopped shouting. He talked a lot, but you couldn't understand him, and they carried him in here. Basias said it was because he didn't put enough water in his wine, but he did. He put a lot more in than Basias did."

The ugly woman nodded and sat beside me on the low bed. "What was the matter, Latro? Why were you shouting?"

"We all were," I told her. "Running toward the enemy and shouting. They were retreating—we had so many more than they—and it seemed as though a good push would end the war. Then they turned like an elk with a thousand points."

"I see." A few hairs sprouted from the woman's chin; she pulled at them with her fingers. "Eutaktos thinks it's witchery, but I'm beginning to doubt it; the malice of someone on the Mountain seems more likely. We might try a sacrifice to the War God. Or . . . Latro, these Rope Makers have a healer called Aesculapius. Do you know of him?"

I shook my head.

"He might be best, since you're under their protection, or ought to be. I'll talk to Eutaktos about it. I'll also compound a charm for you, calling upon certain powers with whom I have influence. Health isn't one of their concerns, usually—still, they may be able to do something."

When the ugly woman left, Io wanted to stay with me; but I would rather have her where she can discover what's taking place and return to tell me. Before she left I had her bring me a stool, so I might write this in comfort. Eutaktos has put two shieldmen at the door, but they permit it to stand open, and I am sitting so the light falls upon the papyrus.

Io has returned to say that the slaves of the Rope Makers are building an altar to the Healing God the ugly woman spoke of. She says Basias has been to this god's great temple on Redface Island, and that when Eutaktos has sacrificed for me I will have to sleep beside the altar. In her absence, I had been reading this scroll, and thus I know I slept in the temple of the Grain Goddess once in much the same way.

Io says Eutaktos intends to leave this place and go to Advent tomorrow, whether the god appears or not. From Advent there is a good road to Redface Island.

I asked her about the ugly woman who promised to make me a charm; she says there is no such woman, that it was Eurykles of Miletos, who wears a purple cloak but is a man. That seems stranger to me than any of the strange things I have read in this scroll.

The innkeeper brought my supper, and I asked for a lamp. He said he had lost a bet on me, but it was worth it to see the man he bet with knocked down. He asked a great many questions about who I was and where I came from, none of which I could answer. He says he sees many foreigners in his trade, but he could not tell me where my country lies.

I asked him to tell me the nations I was *not* from. Here is what he said: Not a Hellene. (Which I knew already, of course.) Not of Persepolis. (I asked him about this place; it is the Great King's city.) Not of Riverland. (This I knew, because I recalled thinking we should not have gone there. Plainly I have been there, and though it is not my home, it may be that someone there knows me.) Not of Horseland, the Tall Cap Country, or the Archers' Country. Not a Carian.

I am more determined to find my friends and my home than ever now, because of the things I have read here. I feel that though I may forget everything else, I will not forget that. The Queen of the Dead promised I will soon see my friends again, and I wonder if they too are not prisoners of the Rope Makers. I would try to sleep, but when I shut my eyes I see the wall of spears, the wicker shields trampled down, the bodies of the dead, and the white walls of the temple.

# —— CHAPTER XXV ——
## I, Eurykles, Write

As requested by your slave, Io, I shall describe the events of the past night and day, turning her words into such as may properly be set down. She asks this because Eutaktos the Spartiate has forbidden you should have this book, thinking that writing in it as you do has disordered your mind. She wishes a record to be kept that she may read it to you when this book is restored to you, and I form the letters better than she, and smaller.

But before I write as she has directed me, permit me to say somewhat of myself. For though it may be, Latro, that the august regent wishes you ill, it may also be that he wishes you well—as, indeed, it is my fond hope he does. How then will you recollect your friend and companion on this journey to the dour isle of Pelops, if I do not here record some outline of my person as a corrective to your errant memory? So shall I now do, after placating little Io (fiery as the gadfly), who nibbles her lips with impatience.

Very well then, and briefly: I was born in Miletos, in the lesser Asia, my father having been, as Mother always assured me, a distinguished citizen of that, my native city. When I was but eleven years of age, the Triple Goddess appeared to me in a dream, pointing out the leaves of a certain plant and urging me by their aid to escape another boy, at whose hands I had suffered many injustices. After several errors, I discovered the correct plant in the waking world and contrived to slip a young and tender leaf into a confection I feigned to eat until he took it from me. He was ill for several days preceding his death, which a wise priest summoned by his parents ascribed quite correctly to the darts of the Far-Shooting Delian.

Following this boy's demise, I made—as you, my dear friend, may imagine—many, many sacrifices; and though they were but sparrows, frogs, and suchlike boyish things, I am bold (or rather say, I have such impudence) enough to suppose that they were accepted in the spirit in which a willing heart offered them, however young. In a year or less, I heard of the great Carian temple to her, at no great distance inland from my city. Thither I journeyed, walking most of the way. There I made a prayer to that sly messenger who lends to thieves his winged heels and managed to procure a most suitable sacrifice in the form of a large black rabbit with a crescent moon of white upon its forehead. (For this animal I was complimented by a priest, a kindness I have not—O subtle reeds, bear witness—forgotten to this day.)

Upon returning to Miletos, I discovered that Mother had seized the occasion of my absence to remove herself from the city; some said to Samos, others to Chios. Here was the hand of the goddess clearly, and I resolved that she alone would be my mother henceforth. I attached myself as firmly as I could to all who were in her good graces, and offered my services to those who, like prudent Agamemnon, called King of Men, sought her favor.

To me, at least, it has been granted in full. I do not scruple to say in any company that there is neither man nor woman more skilled in her mysteries than I, or more adept at the weaving of curses, the compounding of poisons, or the raising of ghosts. You yourself were present at my greatest triumph, Latro, and I pray that divine Trioditis, who sees the past as well as the present and the future, may someday restore what you have lost, that you may give witness to it.

In my person I am a true son of Ion, far taller than the ruck of men and blessed with a dancer's frame, hardy and graceful rather than muscular. My eyes are prominent, as are the bones of my cheeks. My nose and mouth are delicate, my lofty forehead half-concealed by abundant hair. If the stamp-

ing Io soon reads you this, you may know me by my chlamys, which has been dyed a pleasing color with the juice of
mulberries.

As a frequent visitor to her city, I gained the friendship of
your mistress, Kalleos, a happy event made twice happy for
me by the triumph I have already mentioned. Suffice it to say
that you and I, in company with certain others, among whom
Io of the burning eye was not included, made our way from
your mistress's house to a certain place of burial, and there
discovered One whom I restored—for a brief time at least—to
the Lands of the Living. It was the wonder of all beholders,
and should you find it difficult to credit what I say, I urge
you to return to the city we have left, where you will find the
matter talked of by all.

For your sake, then, I have compounded a charm calcu-
lated to calm and restore your mind—this at your own request and Eutaktos's as well. And indeed I would have acted
had either of you asked alone.

For the Moon, a single white stone. For the Huntress, one
of the minute arrowheads made before the time of the gods,
which the initiate may sometimes discover. For the Dark, a
single black hair plucked from the head of one who has
dedicated himself wholly—that is to say, from my own head.
With a thorn of the white-flowered briar dipped in my own
blood, I wrote upon a scrap of cypress bark my plea for you
to the goddess. All these I bound in a circle of deerskin and
with mighty invocations hung about your neck on a thong.

The sophists would say that all these things—stone, dart,
hair, prayer, and hide—count for nothing; or at most that
they serve only to turn the minds of priest and supplicant to
the gods. Yet I have observed that those who believe so win
no favor, and thus I myself believe that they are something
more. With the charm in place (as Io urgently bids me write),
Eutaktos and I, with Io and some others, escorted you to the
altar I had ordered the slaves to build. There the holy fire was
kindled, there Eutaktos himself offered a sacrifice for you, and
there you remained, circled at some distance by sentries.

I regret I was not present when you reported to Eutaktos in

the morning; but Io was, having secreted herself nearby with that stealth and cunning so well suited to the cattle-raising half barbarians from whom she proceeds. Her description of the conversation is prolix indeed, but I shall abstract from it.

In your dream, you seemed to wake at the cracking of a stick (or so Io says you told Eutaktos) to see an elderly man, bent and swan-white of beard, approaching from the wood. You rose and asked if he was the god Aesculapius. He denied it. When you pressed him, he maintained that he was indeed Aesculapius, but no god—merely a poor mortal forced to serve them. You asked then if he would not heal you. Again he shook his head, saying that he had been sent by the murderess of his mother, whose slave he is from her temple on Euboea to the island temple of Anadyomene, but that he could do nothing; at which point he vanished.

Io says that at this Eutaktos grew angry, shouting that Aesculapius would not have employed such words to describe the goddess. This moment you chose (surely, friend Latro, you might have chosen more wisely) to ask that Eutaktos return you to your comrades, saying that you had read in this book of your visit to the Queen Below, and that Eutaktos should not take it upon himself to thwart the will of one to whom all must come at last.

At that Eutaktos grew more wrathful still. He ordered that this book be taken from you (as it was, by Basias), and we broke camp. These events you have already forgotten, or so Io and I fear. We now proceed to more recent things, which you at present know as well as we—or so we hope—but which will perhaps have escaped you when Io reads my words to you.

First as to the goddess. Aesculapius, as I have explained to you, was the son of her brother and twin, borne by a mortal woman named Coronis. While she carried his child, Coronis proved unfaithful to him; and upon learning of the disgrace, the goddess slew her. The god, however, recalling that the child she carried was his own as well as hers, saved him from her funeral pyre, snatching him both from his mother's womb and from the flames, and giving him over to the tutelage of one from whom he learned so much of the healing art as to exceed his teacher and every other mortal.

I cannot believe that he would call his rescuer's (and his father's) twin a murderess, since the right of the gods to slay mortals even as we slay beasts is everywhere unquestioned, and the woman was far from blameless. I am happy to learn, however, that Aesculapius is subject to the goddess in this part of the world. So high is she already in the eyes of her devoted Eurykles that nothing could raise her higher; and yet it may be useful to me.

Now as to recent events. You will wish to know how it is that Io and I have your book, though you do not. The answer is that Basias the Spartiate has permitted it from the good feeling he has for Io and yourself, saying that so long as you are granted no sight of it, Eutaktos will not object. Thus we now keep it from you, but write as we do.

We are halted this night upon the road to Megara, having passed through Eleusis without a halt. About Megara (or so the gossip of the soldiers has it) the regent is camped with his army. Megara is not ruled by his city in name, but it is a member of its league, and no doubt at least some of his troops are Megarians. When we reach Megara tomorrow, we may thus expect to be delivered to the regent. I have exerted myself to discover all I can concerning him, and Io agrees that I should pass my knowledge to you by this means.

He is said to be a man in his twenties, somewhat over the average height, handsome but scarred, and muscular as all these strange islanders are. He is said also to be more persuasive than most in speech, but as short and sharp of tongue as any. He is a scion of the elder of his nation's royal houses, an Agid, and thus only remotely related to that great Lycurgus, whose code of laws has set his nation apart from all others. Specifically, he is the son of Cleombrotos, who was himself the younger son of King Anaxandridas. By this connection is he the uncle of King Pleistarchos, who ascended to his father's throne only last year, and he stands regent for him. He has a wife awaiting his return to his city, and a young son, Pleistoanax.

As to his skill in battle—the thing these people value so far above all else that all else is naught to them—his victory over the Sons of Perseus, whose army was so much greater than his own, stands witness to it; it needs no other. As to the favor of the gods, what soldier can gain the victory without it?

I speak of him now with more than ordinary interest, for a runner with a message all say was his arrived not long ago and hastened to Eutaktos's tent. Soon leaving it in search of refreshment, he encountered Io and asked of you. She brought him to you, and together you three talked at some length. Then he, having satisfied himself (so Io says) that you indeed recalled nothing, wished to examine this book, and she brought him to me.

His name is Pasicrates, and he is a most comely youth, tall and well-featured as all these people are, but as stiff and sullen as the rest. At his request, I showed him your book, and I watched him discover (as others have) that he could not read it. He opened it to the end, however, and examined the flower, then replaced it carefully and rolled the book up again. He asked whether I had been present when Eutaktos found it, and I confirmed that I had and described the scene to him. He asked why Eutaktos has seen fit to bring me with you, to which I replied that he must ask Eutaktos. He wished to know what my city was, and then why I had deserted fair Ionia's shore to come across the Water. At his urging, I described my life to the best of my ability, and somewhat more fully than I have written of it here. He is himself a servant of the Triple Goddess—as he proved, turning his back to show me the scars he received when he was beaten before her altar at Orthia.

Perhaps I should explain here a custom of these people of which you are very likely unaware. Each year, when the boys of that year are about to pass from the care of their teachers into that of their officers, the best and strongest are chosen to run a gauntlet to the honor of the goddess. Much blood is spilled, and I have heard that they generally continue until one or two of the boys are dead.

It is a point of honor, I should add, among the boys not to cry out, though I cannot say what would befall a boy who did. It has been many years, I think, since such a thing occurred, and perhaps it never has. The boys who die in silence are received as sacrifices to the goddess. (How sad it is to count the places at which such sacrifices, the most pleasing of all, are still made and to find the fingers of one's hands more than sufficient!) Those who live are honored above all the rest and carry her favor for the remainder of their days.

I spoke to this Pasicrates as eloquently as I could and with all the charm I command, which some have not hesitated to call great. And I will not deny that it would please me very well to have the love of so handsome a youth, and one who is sworn to the goddess, as I am myself—though whether such a thing would please her as well, I cannot say.

But I can say, and I will, that it appeared to me that Pasicrates was not wholly insensible to the attractions of my person. (Unlike yourself, dear Latro, though I hesitate to write it.) We look upon these people, who live only for war and are forever training for battle, and think how comely they are. But what must they think, who hear for the first time, from our lips, the trumpets of eloquence and the deep-mouthed tocsins of philosophy? Must not they think us as far above common men as we think them? So (as I dare to hope) does the messenger of the great regent think your poor friend—

Eurykles of Miletos

# —— CHAPTER XXVI ——

## Pasicrates

THE regent's messenger has restored my scroll to me. He sought me out this morning and asked whether I recalled meeting with him the night before. I do not remember that now; but I must have when we spoke, since I told him I did.

He said, "Then you know I'm Pausanias's runner."

I nodded and said I was surprised he did not leave our plodding march to return with word from Eutaktos.

"The only order I brought was that he should continue the search if he has not found you, and return with all speed if he had. It's you Pausanias wants to see, not me. If I were to run back, could you keep pace with me?"

I confessed I did not know but said I would try.

"Then we'll race to the tree on that hill and see who shows the best heels."

He no sooner spoke than he was off like an arrow. I followed as fast as I could, and my legs are longer than his; but I never overtook him, and he had time to halt at the tree and turn to study me before I came pounding up.

"You might run to Megara at that," he said. "But look at this poor tortoise." It was Basias, the man whose tent I share, doing his best in his cuirass and greaves and waving his sword.

Pasicrates called, "You can't touch us with that! Get a longer blade!" Seeing that we were not deserting the column, Basias slowed to a walk.

"Want to sit here?" Pasicrates asked. "They have to

tramp up this hill anyway.'' His face had that relentless regularity we find so attractive in a statue's, but his eyes seemed as cruel as a stoat's. As though I had not seen their look, I threw myself down in the shade.

"How did you lose your memory? Do you know?''

I shook my head.

"Perhaps the child does, or that Eurykles.''

"Who are they?''

"Friends of yours that Eutaktos brought along. I talked to them yesterday. Come to think of it, Io was there when I talked with you—the little slave. She's yours, she says.''

I said, "I remember the child, but not her name.''

"What about Eurykles?''

I shook my head again.

"When I got here, I wondered why Eutaktos had bothered with them. I understand now.''

We spoke no more after that until Basias reached us.

"Just a foot race,'' Pasicrates told him. "I don't think my job's in danger, but Latro can replace me if I'm wounded.''

Basias nodded, wiping the sweat from his forehead with his finger and flinging it away. "Wrestler, too.''

"You've tried him?''

Red-faced and panting, Basias dropped beside us. "Beat him. Five falls, though. He's strong.''

"He looks it. How much do you know about him?''

"Forgets. Got a slave girl. I've got his sword. That's all.''

"I see. Latro, what's my name?''

"Pasicrates.''

"Right. How'd you know?''

"You told me,'' I said.

Basias explained, "In the morning he remembers everything after we camped. But it goes. By noon he won't remember anything before he woke.''

"And the child remembers for him?''

"He had a book. It says read this each morning, but we can't read the rest. Eutaktos had me take it.''

"I want you to give it back—I'll have a word with Eutaktos.

Latro, if you had your book again, would you read it for me?''

I said, "If you want to hear it."

"Or for Pausanias, the regent of Rope?"

"Of course."

"Good. I don't think I'll have you do it yet, because there might be something there he wouldn't wish me to know. We'll see tonight when we reach Megara. Basias, what about Eurykles? Does he help Latro too?"

"A bit. Not so much as the child."

"What do you think of him?"

Basias grinned. "He better stay out of sight in Rope. The women'll kill him."

"He bothers me," Pasicrates said half to himself.

"Hit him and he won't."

"Not like that. Latro, among us it's customary for each older man to have a younger friend. You understand? It's a good system. The younger man learns more. If he gets into trouble, he's got someone to speak for him. This isn't the same thing."

Absently, I asked what it was. I was watching a scarlet wildflower nod in the breeze; it seemed charged with meaning.

"Like a man with a daughter. Except that the daughter's the man himself."

Basias said, "Bet you've plenty after you."

"Certainly." Pasicrates had been lying on his back on the sparse grass. Now he sat up. "I'm Pausanias's protégé, and they like that. That's why it seems so familiar. And yet so strange. I wish he were a slave."

Basias asked why, but Pasicrates did not answer. After a moment he said, "His hands are cold. Have you noticed?"

Not long after, the marchers caught up with us and we fell in with the rest. I moved among them looking for the child Pasicrates had mentioned, and soon found her. To test my grasp of what I had heard, I said, "I have good news, Io. I'm going to get my scroll back."

"That's wonderful, and you knew my name!"

"Pasicrates told me."

"And he said Eutaktos is going to let you have it again?"

"Yes. Except that I don't think Eutaktos knows it. Pasicrates will order him to."

Io looked doubtful. "Eutaktos is a lot older."

"I know," I told her.

When we had walked a few more stades, a tall woman in a purple cloak handed me this scroll, with the stylus I am using thrust through the cords. "Here, Latro," she said. "The lochagos ordered Basias to return it. I'd been keeping it for him, and I said I'd bring it." She slipped an arm through mine.

"It was Pasicrates," Io whispered to her.

"Really? He's quite a handsome youth, but not as handsome as your master."

"What does that have to do with it?"

"Nothing. I was just thinking." She squeezed my arm. "You know, Latro, in a way you're rather fortunate. If you wished to change your name, all you'd have to do would be to tell your friends to call you by the new one next morning; then you'd never know you had once been someone else. I don't suppose you know whether you've ever done it?"

"I don't think so. Do you want to change yours?"

She nodded. "It means 'well talked of,' which is good enough, I suppose; but I'd like something better. What do you think of Drakon?"

"Shouldn't it be Drakaina?"

The woman laughed, and Io said, "That's good, master."

"Do either of you know where we are? Pasicrates said we were going to Megara."

Before they could reply, Basias dropped back to walk between Io and me. "We're turning off at this fork," he announced. "The three of you, me, Eutaktos, and Pasicrates. We're to see the regent while the rest make camp."

We hurried down a dusty road that looked no more important than the other; but when we reached the summit of the next hill, the whole scene changed as a nightscape does at the rising of the sun.

A thousand tents stood in orderly rows upon a rolling

plain. Beyond them, a city lifted white walls; beyond those spread sparkling blue water dotted with foam where the salt-sharp wind ruffled countless waves; and beyond the tumultuous sea rose the dim blue bulk of an island.

Io shouted for joy. "Look! Look! Is that Peace? We went there on Hypereides's ship, only he wouldn't let us off. Is it?"

Basias mussed her brown curls. "That's right. You've an eye for the lay of the land, little girl. If you were an Amazon, you'd make a strategist someday."

Io pulled at my chiton and pointed at the sea. "Latro, that's Peace Bay. Hypereides told us. It's where the ships from Thought beat the barbarians."

Pasicrates whirled on her like a panther. "Our ships fought there too, and our Strategist Eurybiades commanded the combined fleets!"

I said, "Don't shout at her. She didn't know, and neither did I."

"But she at least will remember," Pasicrates snapped, "because I shouted at her. Mild lessons are soon forgotten, and in the end the kind teacher is the cruel teacher—he doesn't teach. Enough! I'll tell Pausanias you're coming." He runs so well I think only the finest horse could overtake him. Before we had gone another hundred strides, he was flashing among the tents.

Io's dusty cheeks were streaked with tears. I picked her up and tried to comfort her. "I'm all right, master," she said. And then, "He was right, I won't forget. Not even his name."

"Eurybiades?"

She shook her head. "Pasicrates."

To distract her, I said, "Look how many tents there are! A whole army's camped here, with thousands of soldiers. Have you and I ever seen any army in camp before, Io?"

The woman whispered, "This is nothing. You should have seen the encampment of the Great King. It was like a city on the march—but no city on earth could have equaled it, except perhaps Babylon."

Eutaktos must have sharp ears, because he overheard her. "I saw that camp, and my slaves looted the pavilions of the satraps. If your Great King were here with us, he would not think this camp nothing."

Pausanias's tent is larger than all the rest, embroidered and hung with tassels of gold. I think it must have been part of the loot Eutaktos spoke of. When we came near, I could hear voices; one, I think, the voice of Pasicrates, the other harsh and flat, the speech of a young man accustomed to giving orders and to concealing any emotion he might feel while giving them. I heard Pasicrates say, ". . . a spy of the Great King's."

The other answered, "A spy is a stone that can be thrown back."

Eutaktos coughed, I suppose to let those within know we had arrived. After that I could distinguish no more words.

There are two sentries at the door, tall men no older than Pasicrates; they will not permit us to approach it. We stand to one side—or rather, Eutaktos and Basias stand so, their hands on their sword hilts. Io, the woman, and I are sitting on the ground, where I write these words, having seen by reading how good it is to write so that what has happened is not lost.

I have read of the Lady of the Doves; and I feel I then visited a realm at once higher and smaller than our own. What was it she wished of me? For I feel sure there was something. Did she obtain it? Even after reading what I wrote twice, I cannot say. I am sure she was a friend to the woman Kalleos; but was Kalleos a friend to me?

The Lady of the Doves said I would not forget her, though I forget everything. She was not wrong; when I read of her again, my flesh stirred at the memory. For love, she was surely the only woman, or all of them.

But I must put her memory aside and think of what I will say in the tent. Soon, I think, Pasicrates will come out and take us in to the regent.

# — CHAPTER XXVII —

## Pausanias

THE regent has furnished his tent with plunder. He sits upon scarlet cushions, and there are carpets rich with griffins, black bulls savaged by golden lions, and men strangely dressed, with black and curling beards. The air is perfumed by lamps of gold.

Pasicrates announced, "O royal Pausanias, this is the man Eutaktos the Lochagos brought. I have examined him, and I am satisfied he is indeed the one shown you in your dream, so far as I am able to judge."

The regent stared at me. His face is terrible with scars, but it seemed to me it would have been terrible without them, as hard and cruel as iron. Perhaps a smile touched his mouth; a scar drew up one cheek, so I could not be sure.

"The man I saw wore a chaplet of withered blossoms. Fellow! Were you wearing such a chaplet when my shieldmen discovered you?"

"I don't remember," I told him. "But I may have written of it. May I look?" I held up this scroll.

The regent's lips drew back from his teeth, which are large and not quite white. "Good. Very good. And the flower?"

Pasicrates said, "It was still there when I examined the book, Highness. The lochagos may have put it there, but I doubt that he did."

The regent pointed. "Open that to the stick."

I did as he ordered, holding the scroll so he could see the

writing. As I unrolled the last sheet, a dried lupine dropped into his hand.

Pasicrates cleared his throat. "Perhaps I ought to add, Highness, that the lochagos says they appeared to have had a dinner party the night before in the house where he found this man. There would have been flowers, naturally, and chaplets for the guests."

The regent waved this aside. "I'm satisfied. I wish Tisamenus were here, but this is the man, or we'll never find him. He looks like him as well. I couldn't see that scar in my dream, but no doubt the chaplet covered it."

I asked, "You dreamed of me?"

He nodded. "It was Kore herself, smiling and wreathed in blossoms. She said, 'For the many subjects you have given, I will show you a secret known but to the gods.' Then I saw you. What's your name, anyway?"

"Latro," I told him.

"I saw you sitting on a pallet. It was night, but there was a fire, and I could see the firelight flicker on your face. You were holding this, and you unrolled that book and put the flower into it and rolled it partway up, then wrote. The goddess was gone, but I heard her voice. She said, 'He will have forgotten everything, knowing nothing more of the past than of the future. See who is with him!' Nike stood behind you in the shadows."

"I am to bring you victory?"

Still smiling his snarling smile, the regent leaned back among his cushions. "Not many men are favored by the gods. A few heroes like Perseus, Theseus, my ancestor Heracles. Those destined to—destined for greatness." He turned to his messenger. "Where did he get that scar, Pasicrates?"

"I don't know, Highness. The lochagos brought two others with him, a slave child who remembers for him and the magician I told you of. They're outside with the lochagos and the ouragos who guarded him on the march."

"Get them in here. All of them."

Eutaktos entered first, Basias last. I think they were all a bit frightened.

The regent smiled again when he saw Io. "You know your master's history, little girl, or so Pasicrates tells me."

Io nodded timidly.

"How did he receive that scar?"

"I wasn't with him, sir."

"But you know. Don't mind this face. The faces of my conquests look far worse."

"There was a big battle. Our men went with the Great King's army, but they lost. My master fought in that, I think."

"And so do I. But you must tell me why you think as you do."

"Because it was when the army came back that they brought him to our temple. That was the first time I saw him."

"And did he have that scar then?"

Io shook her head. "There was a bandage with blood on it."

Pasicrates said, "But if he fought for the barbarians, Highness—"

"You're a handsome boy," the regent told him. "But if you want to stay where you are, you'd better learn to think. To whom did the Maiden appear? Who has her favor?"

"Ah, I see!"

"I hope so. Lochagos, I like a man who achieves his objective. Who makes no excuses because he needs none. I won't forget this."

Eutaktos stood very straight. "Thank you, Highness."

"This man with you has been taking care of . . ."

"Latro," I prompted.

"Of Latro, as I understand it."

"Yes, Highness."

"And has learned something of his ways in the process, no doubt. I'm going to detach him for the time being. You may return to your lochos."

"Thank you, Highness." Eutaktos left us, walking proudly. I have not seen him again.

"Child, do you know that your city and mine are no longer enemies?"

Io nodded. "Pindaros said so."

"A man of your city?"

She nodded again. "He said you saved us."

"He was right. It's true your men fought me, and fought very well for foreigners. But when a war's over, it's over. Or it should be. Thought's army wanted to burn your city; I wouldn't let them. Now your city and mine are friends."

Io said politely, "I hope it's always so, sir."

"And when I've more leisure, I want to talk with you. If you tell me the truth, I'll see things go well for you. You'll have food and new clothes, and other children to play with."

"Thank you, sir," Io said. "Only I don't belong to you. I belong to Latro."

"Well said, but I doubt if he'll object. Will you, Latro?"

I shook my head.

"And this soldier of mine will continue to look after you. After all three of you." He looked toward Basias, who stood like a statue, his hands to his sides. "An idiot, a child, and a spy won't be too much for you, will they, ouragos? What's your name?"

"Basias, Highness! No, Highness!"

"Good. I don't think the first two will give you much trouble, Basias. The spy may. If he does, kill him. If he won't follow orders, I don't want him alive."

The woman in the purple cloak exclaimed, "I'm not a spy!"

"Of course you are. If I hadn't known it before, I'd know it now because you were too slow to deny it. You're from Miletos, or so you told my messenger."

She nodded. "And I'm—"

"A Hellene. As we all are, save Latro. A good many Hellenes fought for the Great King."

"I didn't fight at all."

"Certainly not. Your king's no fool, and neither are his ministers. One look at that face would tell any sensible man you'd be more useful behind the enemy's line than before it. I know what happened to Miletos; the Great King tore down your walls and sent you to herd goats. I'd ask how you got out, but you've some story. Don't bother. Basias has his sword—not that he'd need it."

"I am protected—"

"You're under no law but ours, and ours says we can kill you where you stand. It would give Basias one fewer worry, and if you lie to me, he'll wring your neck."

Basias said, "He was in the Great King's camp, Highness. I heard him tell Latro."

Spreading his hands, the regent whispered, "Speak or die. Who got your report?"

Though the time had been so brief, the woman had recovered her composure. "Believe me, most royal—"

As quickly as he might have thrust with his spear, Basias grasped her arm. She raised a hand to claw his face, but a blow to her head sent her reeling across the tent.

Basias drew his sword.

"Wait," the regent told him. To me he said, "I saw that step. You would have protected your friend, if only Basias were here. What if he were not? If you had only Pasicrates and me to deal with?"

I said, "If it weren't for the sentries, I would have killed all of you, or tried to."

Io gasped, "Master, no!"

The regent waved her fears away. "Your master's a man of courage. He'll need to be, living among us."

Awkwardly, the woman got to her feet. There were tears in her eyes, but something else too.

"I don't have time for more of this," the regent told her. "You may speak and live or remain silent and die. Choose."

"Then I choose to speak," the woman said. "Who would not?" She smoothed her cloak as women do, as women keep their clothes in order though the cities burn.

"Good. A confessed spy may be useful. Useful, you may live and even prosper. Who got your report?"

"Artabazus."

"Better and better. And that report was . . . ?"

"That half a year and a few gifts would make any fighting unnecessary."

"He did not believe you?"

The woman shook her head. "He believed me, but he couldn't convince Mardonius."

Basias dropped his sword. It fell point down, piercing the carpet where he stood and sticking upright in the earth beneath it. He lifted his arm and looked at his hand with unbelieving eyes. The fingers were swollen, and there was a gray pallor on the skin.

"Let me see that," the regent said. And then, when Basias did not obey, "Come here!"

Like a doll moved by strings, Basias walked to where the regent sat and held out his hand.

"He had a poisoned pin in his hair." The regent looked at the woman. "Tell us the antidote."

"I have no pin, Highness," she said. "You may search my person if you wish."

"You hid it when you fell. You may be worth something at that. What's your name?"

"Eurykles, Highness. Others have thought so."

The regent nodded absently. "Basias, tell the sentries one of them is to take you to Kichesippos, my healer. The rest of you, come here and sit before me. I'm tired of breaking my neck. Take cushions if you want."

I got a cushion for the woman and a long one for Io and me. As I put them down before the regent, I could hear Basias talking to the sentries outside.

"You too, Pasicrates," the regent said, and his messenger seated himself upon a cushion at his right hand.

"Eurykles, tell me why you gave Artabazus that advice."

"Because it was the best I could give," the woman said. She paused to gather her thoughts. "War is only the last recourse of politics; it has no sure victories, or so I think. A king who fights when he might gain his ends by a cupful of wisdom and a handful of gold is a fool.''

The regent smiled. "You believe your Great King a fool?"

"The Great King was gone. Mardonius was a good soldier but a stupid man. If Artabazus had been in command . . ."

"If Artabazus had been in command, what then? What of the Hellenes? You're one, as you just reminded us.''

"You'd be ruled by men of our race, just as you are now, and as our cities in the lesser Asia are. What difference would there be? Why should ten myriads die?''

"You know of others who think as you do? In Thought?"

"I'm certain such men exist.''

"You're careful. So am I.'' The regent glanced at Io and me. "Let me suggest to all three of you something you may not have noticed. Perhaps I should say let *us* suggest it, because I've talked to Pasicrates and he feels as I do.''

The woman leaned toward him, her fingers playing upon her cheek. "Yes, Highness?"

"We are four men whose interests run so close they're indistinguishable. Let me speak of Rope and this whole country first. We Rope Makers are the finest soldiers in the world, and the Great King knows that now. But men who know war know it's no game; a wise man dodges it if he can, just as you said. As for glory, my uncle Leonidas won enough at the Gates to the Hot Springs to last our family till Tantalus drinks—I say nothing of my own battle. An honorable peace, then, is our only desire.''

The woman called Eurykles gave the slightest of nods, her eyes fixed upon the regent as a serpent transfixes a bird.

"Our country is divided into so many warring cities no one can count them all, or no one has bothered. Every clutter of huts on the mountainside makes its own laws, issues its own currency, and fields its tiny army to crush its tiny neighbor. Clearly, what we need is union under the noblest of our cities, which by a happy coincidence happens to be my own.''

"By a coincidence even happier," the woman said, "I have before me a member of the elder royal house of that city, who is in addition its most renowned living leader."

"Thank you." The regent nodded graciously. "Unfortunately, our city is not strong enough to unite all the rest. More, it is not rich enough. I have often thought that if only we had found the silver, instead of Thought, or if we had seized the treasury of Croesus . . ." He shrugged and let the words trail away. "But suppose we had the help—or at least the threat—of additional troops. Cavalry, let us say, because there's so little here. With that threat and gold enough to make gifts to farsighted men, a great deal might be done."

The woman nodded. "It might indeed."

Pasicrates murmured, "Highness, do you think you should speak in this way before the child?"

"Speak in what way? Say that I seek an honorable peace with the Great King and a position for Rope commensurate with its virtues? She may repeat that to anyone she may meet."

Io said, "I won't repeat anything. I don't do that, except for telling Latro. But you said all our interests went together."

"Your master is fortunate in his slave; I've seen that already. As for our interests, let's take Eurykles here first. We'll get to you in a moment. Eurykles serves the Great King, as he admitted a moment ago. More directly, he serves Artabazus. He wishes to be rewarded for his work, like any other man. The Great King wants to recover the prestige he lost here and to add to his glory. Peace and union under a leader grateful to him—"

The woman said, "Would be all he could desire, Highness, I'm sure. Someone who has the king's ear would have to be consulted, naturally."

"Naturally. Now as to you, child. Your city is allied with the Great King already, and as your friend Pindaros told you, it would have been destroyed but for my own city and my acts in its behalf. Isn't it clear that anything that helps your strongest friends helps you?"

Io shook her head. "To tell the truth, I don't care about my city. I care about Latro."

I said, "Who is a soldier of the Great King's. You think I'm an idiot because I forget, Prince Pausanias, and perhaps I am. But I've always known that, even when I did not know my name."

# — CHAPTER XXVIII —

## Mycale

A place of which most, I think, had never heard before is now on everyone's lips. The combined fleets of Thought and the Rope Makers have given the barbarians another terrible defeat there. Some say this was on the same day as the great battle in which I was wounded, others that it must surely have been after it, for it could not have taken so long for the news to reach us. To this the first reply that a ship may be delayed for any time one chooses by storms and contrary winds, and that the news came first to Thought, and only subsequently to us from there.

Io said, "Oh, I hope the black man's all right. I know you don't remember the black man, Latro, but he was your friend even before Pindaros and me. When they brought you to the temple, he was with you."

I asked her, "Do you think he was in that battle?"

"I hope not, but he probably was. When Hypereides sold you to Kalleos, he kept the black man. And Hypereides was going to take his ships back to the fleet."

"Then I hope the black man is safe, and Hypereides dead."

"You shouldn't be like that, master. Hypereides wasn't a bad man. He got us out of that dungeon in Tower Hill, just by talking, and he let Pindaros and Hilaeira go when the law said he should."

But before I write of these recent matters, I should write of earlier things, which may soon be lost to me in the mist I cannot drive from the back of my thoughts. The regent has put us in the care of his messenger, who sent his slaves to bring our possessions and Basias's tent. He showed us where his own stood, near the regent's, and told us to put up Basias's beside it. I did not think I recalled how a tent should be erected; but when I had spread everything upon the ground, the steps came to me each in turn. Io crawled beneath the oiled linen and held up the poles, and she enjoyed that so much I took three times longer about the whole business than I should.

A sword Io says is mine was with Basias's clothing in a scabbard hung from a belt of manhood. I put it on and felt better at once; a man without weapons is a slave. Io says Kalleos let me wear it when I was hers, and perhaps that is why I did not feel resentful toward her, as Io swears I did not.

Then Basias's slaves came, cowering because they thought themselves to be beaten. They had been gathering firewood when Pasicrates's slaves had come, and they had discovered what had befallen their master's baggage with great difficulty. I explained that their master was ill and ordered them to have such food as sick men eat ready for him.

That was wise, because slaves soon brought Basias in a litter. With them was an old man who told us he was Kichesippos the Messenian, but who speaks as the Rope Makers and their slaves do, making the ox long. Basias's arm was swollen and black, and it seemed to me that he was in a dream, sometimes hearing what we said, sometimes deaf to it, sometimes seeing what we could not see. Perhaps that is how I seem to others; I do not know.

Kichesippos told Basias's slaves, "Your master has been bitten by a viper, and from the breadth between its fangs and the severity of his reaction, by a larger one than I have ever seen. I have cut his wounds and drawn forth the poison as well as it can be done. Do not attempt to do that a second time; after the first, it is useless. Let him rest, see that he is warm, feed him if he will eat. Give him all he wants to eat and drink. By the favor of the goddess, he may recover. But he may die.''

Io asked if there was nothing more we could do.

"As I understand the matter, the viper has not been killed?''

I nodded, and Io said, "We never even saw one, sir. He hit somebody, and somebody else said there was a poisoned pin in his hair.''

Kichesippos shook his head. "A pin could not have held so much, and it would have left a single scratch. I will not remove the bandage to show you the punctures, but there are two.'' (Then I marveled at little Io's cunning; if she had told him it was his master, Pausanias, who had said it, surely Kichesippos would never have contradicted him.)

"If the viper were dead,'' he continued, "that might be of benefit to him. Still more if its raw flesh could be held to his wound—while it lives, it strengthens its poison as a city strengthens the army it sends forth. Other than that, I can suggest nothing.''

Io said, "Then you might examine my master. Perhaps the royal regent spoke of him after they conferred today? He can't remember.''

"I've noticed the scar. Come here, young man, I wish to touch it. Will you kneel? No act of submission is implied. Tell me if I hurt you.''

I knelt before him and felt his deft fingers glide along the side of my head. Io asked, "Are you a priest of Aesculapius? When Latro slept beside his altar, Aesculapius said he couldn't help him.''

"Nor can I, I'm afraid,'' Kichesippos told her, "without reopening the wound. That might easily kill him.'' His fingers withdrew. "You may stand, young man. Do you drop things? Do you fall or suffer dizziness?''

I shook my head.

"You are fortunate—all those symptoms are to be expected. Were you wearing a helmet when your injury occurred?''

I told him I did not know.

"That's right, you forget. Is that your only symptom?''

"Yes," I told him.

Io said, "Gods appear to him. Sometimes."

Kichesippos sighed. "Occasional hallucinations. Young man, I think some foreign object has been driven deeply into your brain. A splinter of bone is the most likely thing, judging from the visible wound; but I have known of a similar case in which the object was a small arrowhead. If it's of any comfort to you, it probably won't get any worse. Eventually the object may dissolve, particularly if it's a bone splinter. If that occurs, the damaged part may—I say *may*—reconstitute itself, partially at least.

"Don't get your hopes up. The process will take years if it happens at all, and it probably will not. As for treatment . . ." He shrugged. "Prayers are never wholly wasted. Even if you're not cured, you may receive some other benefit. There is Aesculapius, whom this child says you have petitioned already. In addition, there are shrines all over the country to heroes who are said to heal, though they killed, mostly, while they lived. One may help you. And there are the great gods, if you can get their attention. Meanwhile, learn to live with your disability. Do you recall my name?"

"Kichesippos."

Io said, "In the morning he remembers yesterday evening, but by noon he's forgotten it. He writes things down."

"Excellent."

I said, "Yet when I reread what I've written, I sometimes wonder whether I wrote the truth."

"I see." Kichesippos nodded to himself. "Have you written anything today?"

"Yes, while we were waiting to see the regent."

"And were you tempted to lie? I do not ask whether you lied, but only whether you were tempted to do so."

I shook my head.

"Then I very much doubt that you have lied in the past. Lying is a habit, you see, like drinking too much. You told the truth as you saw it, which is all any man can do."

I said I hoped he was correct.

"You must remember that in every life there occur events

so extraordinary that only the most talented and ingenious liar could have conceived them. Take the great battle at Mycale— have you heard about it?''

Io and I shook our heads.

"Word of it reached the regent only today, and the noble Pasicrates, who had it directly from my master, informed me as we conferred about your poor friend here.'' The old man paused to collect his thoughts.

"This Mycale is a place on the Asian coast. King Leotychides found the barbarian fleet beached there, the portents were favorable, and he ordered an immediate attack. The ships' crews had been reinforced by an army from Susa, and it seems to have been a hot fight. But in the long run the barbarians can't stand up to disciplined troops, and they broke. Naturally, our men held their formation; but a few men from other cities ran after the enemy, and by great good luck they were able to reach the stockade before the gates could be shut. That finished the barbarians, and we burned more than three hundred ships.'' He rubbed his palms together. "The men from a hundred ships burned three hundred and destroyed an army. In a century, who will believe it? The Great King will build more ships, no doubt, and raise new armies. But not this year, and not the next.''

"And meanwhile," I said, "he'll need every soldier he has."

Kichesippos nodded. "I imagine so."

By the time the old physician left, it was nearly dark. I told the slaves to prepare food for us, and the woman in the purple cloak joined us while we ate. "Would you mind if I had some? I couldn't help but smell it. I'm your neighbor now—did you know?''

"No," Io said. "We didn't know where you were staying."

"With the handsome Pasicrates. But he's off somewhere at the moment, and his slaves won't obey me.''

There was hardly enough food for Io, Basias, and me, so I went to Pasicrates's tent, where I found his slaves cooking a meal for themselves. One escaped, but when I had the other two by the throat I pounded the right head against the left and told them to bring food, and that I would push their faces into the coals the next time they disobeyed the woman.

When I returned to our own tent, she said, "What did I tell you? Barley, blood, and beans. And after sampling the barley and beans, I think I would prefer the blood. Well, beans are a proper food for the dead, anyway."

I asked her whether she planned to die.

"No, but we're going there. Hadn't you heard? To Rope, so the royal Pausanias can bed his wife, then to Acheron so he can consult the shades. It should be an interesting trip."

Io asked, "You mean we're going to visit the dead?"

The woman nodded, and though I felt vaguely that I had once considered her less than attractive, I could not help noticing that her face was lovely in the firelight. "I am, at least, and the regent is. You should have seen how delighted he was when someone told him who I was. He sent for me again at once, and I thought he was going to ask me to raise a few ghosts for him on the spot."

"Is it far?" Io inquired.

"To Acheron? Why, no, just the other side of the grave."

I told the woman not to tease her.

"Oh," she said, "you want to take the long road. No, not really, Io. Two or three days to Rope, and not much longer, I'd think, to Acheron, if we get a ship at the gulf, as I suppose we will. By the way, do you have a comb I might borrow? I seem to have lost mine."

Not with the best grace, Io produced a little bone comb. The woman ran it through her dark hair, which in truth could not have been more disordered if it had never been combed at all.

"I'm going to let it grow out," she said. "These Rope Makers all let theirs grow long, have you noticed? They comb it before a battle, or so I've heard. See? No poisoned pins."

Pasicrates's slaves brought a bowl of beans, some dried fish, a loaf of barley bread, and a wine bowl. I told Io to see whether Basias had eaten. She reported that he was thirsty, and I gave her a cup of mixed wine from the bowl, and half the loaf.

The woman said, "You'd better eat some of that yourself. You won't be getting anything better."

I said, "I intend to. But first, may I ask you a question? Your tongue isn't my own, and I sometimes feel I haven't learned as much of it as I'd like."

"Certainly."

"Then tell me why everyone calls you Eurykles, which is a man's name."

"Ah," she said. "That's a *personal* question."

"Will you answer it?"

"If I may ask you one."

"Of course."

"Because they haven't divined my true nature. They think me a man. So did you, in a time you've forgotten."

I said, "I'll try not to reveal your secret."

She smiled. "Speak out if you wish. It's all one to Hippocleides, if you know that expression."

Just then Io came out of the tent, the wine cup still more than half full. "He won't eat any bread," she said. "I talked to his slaves and gave it to them. They said he wouldn't eat for them, either, but he sipped a little broth."

The woman called Eurykles shuddered.

"Since you don't mind people knowing, what shall we call you?" I asked her.

"Why not Drakaina, as you yourself suggested? Drakaina of Miletos. By the way, have you heard about the battle and what the Milesians did afterward?"

"Not about the Milesians. Weren't they sent inland to herd goats? That's what the regent said."

"Oh, no. Just some people from the prominent families. And not to herd goats, not really; they were sent to Susa as hostages. But when the people of my fair city heard about Mycale, they rose against the barbarian garrison and killed them all."

"As a barbarian myself, I'm not sure I approve."

"Nor am I," Drakaina said. "Still, it puts me in a rather

dubious position, doesn't it? I like that.'' She rose and returned Io's comb.

"Aren't you going to ask your personal question?"

She shook her head. "I'll reserve it. Later, perhaps."

When she had gone back into Pasicrates's tent, Io looked at her little comb with dismay. "Now I'll have to wash it," she said.

# ── CHAPTER XXIX ──

## The Silent Country

THIS land the Rope Makers rule is a place of harsh mountains and wide, fertile valleys. Behind us are the rough hills of Bearland, where we camped last night and Basias woke me with his groaning. Io says we camped the night before outside Tower Hill, and she hid this scroll as she had when we were imprisoned there, for fear it would be taken from me. She says also that some of the soldiers were from that city, and that they left the army there.

This morning while we were still in Bearland, I wondered why this Silent Country should be called so. When we stopped in the village for the first meal, I went to one of the houses to ask the people.

There was no one there, they being (as I assumed) at work in their fields. Io says Basias is supposed to watch me, but he is too ill for that; and Pasicrates, who had watched me on the morning march, has run ahead.

Thus I went from house to house, stooping to enter the low doorways and coughing at the smoke from the hearths. Once I found a pot seething over the flames, and once a half-eaten barley cake; but there were no men, no women, and no children, and at last I began to think that they were somehow hidden from mortal eyes, or perhaps that they were the spirits of the dead, whom the Rope Makers had in some way forced to toil.

The fifth place to which I came was a smithy. Its forge still blazed, and tongs gripped a half-formed, glowing spit. When

I saw it I knew the smith could not be more than a step or two away; I found him crouched beneath his own work table, hiding behind his leather apron, which he had draped across it. I pulled him out and made him stand. His grizzled head came only to my shoulder, but he was as muscular as all are who are of that trade.

He begged my pardon many times, saying over and over that he had meant no disrespect and had only been frightened to see a stranger. I told him I would not hurt him, and explained that I merely wished to ask him a few questions about this land.

At that he grew more frightened than ever, his face the color of ashes. He feigned to be deaf and, when I shouted at him, to speak some gobbling dialect and to be unable to understand me. I drew Falcata and laid her edge at his throat; but he caught my wrist and wrenched it until I cried out, and with his free hand snatched up his hammer. Then I saw the face of Death himself, his naked, grinning skull.

In an instant Death was gone; there was only the smith's face again, more ashen now than ever, its mouth open and its eyes rolling backward into his head. The sound his hammer made as it fell from his hand and struck the earthen floor seemed too loud, like the noise that wakes us from sleep.

I let him go, and he leaned backward until his body was held erect for a moment by the javelin in his back. The point crept from his chest under the press of his weight, two fingers' width of hammered iron that shone in the light of the forge, before he slipped to one side and tumbled down.

One of the slaves of the Rope Makers stood in the doorway holding a second javelin. I said, "Thank you. I owe you my life."

Putting his foot on the body, he drew out his weapon and wiped its head on the smith's leather apron. "This is my village," he said. And then, "He made this."

"But he would have killed me, when I would not have harmed him."

"He thought you would, and it would have been his death

if he had been seen talking with a foreigner. As it will be mine if I'm seen with you."

"Then let us not be seen," I said, and we dragged the smith's body to a place out of sight of the street; when we had concealed it as well as we could, we kicked dust over the blood, and he led me through a rear door to a yard where the smithy and its heaps of charcoal shielded us.

"You don't remember me," he said.

I shook my head. "I forget much."

"So you told me after we had seen the black god. I'm Cerdon, Latro. Do you still have your book? Perhaps you wrote of me there, though I told you not to."

"Are we friends, then? Is that why you saved me?"

"We can be, if you'll keep your promise."

"If I've promised something to you, I'll do what I promised. If I haven't, I'll give you whatever you ask anyway. You saved my life."

"Then come with me to the shrine of the Great Mother tonight. It's not far from here."

I heard a faint sound as he spoke: the whisper of a woman's skirt, or the dry slithering of a serpent. Then it was gone, and when I looked I saw nothing. I said, "I'd do it gladly if I could; but we'll march as soon as the slaves have eaten. Tonight we'll be far away."

"But you'll come if you can, and not forget?"

"By tonight? No. Tomorrow I'll have forgotten, perhaps."

"Good. I'll get you as soon as the camp's asleep. Your slave won't inform on us, and the Rope Maker in your tent is too ill to notice anything." He started to rise.

"Wait," I told him. "How was it you were here when I needed your help?"

"I've watched you since Megara, knowing it was useless to talk until we got here. I knew we'd come, though, because our village is on the road to Rope, and it belongs to Pausanias. When I saw you go away without a guard, that was my chance. So I followed you, hoping to find you alone; and by her grace I did."

I did not understand. "This smithy belongs to the regent?"

"This village, the fields, and all of us. I helped bring the Rope Maker to your tent for Kichesippos. You didn't recognize me."

"No," I admitted.

"I knew you didn't. Now I must go, but I'll come tonight. Don't forget."

"What about . . ." I nodded to indicate the dead man in the smithy.

"I'll see to it," he said. "No one will care but us."

When I returned to the grove where the shieldmen had eaten, they were forming their column while a few tardy slaves covered fires or stowed pots. We marched bravely through the village to the music of the flutes; but when we reached this river, we found the bridge in flames. Though the slaves soon put out the fire, the roadway had been destroyed, and it was decided to camp here for the night. Everyone is weary after the march through Bearland anyway, and they say the bridge will be repaired tomorrow.

Basias's slaves had to carry him in a litter this morning, as well as carrying our tent and the other things. I asked if it was not too much for them. They said it was not—it was no more than they had borne when they left the Silent Country to fight the Great King, because they had to carry ten days' rations. I offered to take one end of the litter; I believe they would have liked to accept, but they were afraid they would be punished.

I asked whether Basias owned a village, and whether they came from there. They said he owned only a farm. All three live on it and work the land. It is south of Rope, and they believe they will be ordered to take him there until he is well. He has a house in Rope too, but they think the farm will be better. If he dies, the farm will pass to a relative.

They did not seem afraid to talk to me; so I told them I had gone into the village, and the people there would not. They said it is different and better in the army, and that no one will inform on them for speaking to a stranger when they must pitch the tent for him to sleep in and cook his meals; but that it would be well if I did not speak to the slaves of others. I think perhaps Basias is a kinder master than the regent, though perhaps it is only that he is not so rich. A man who has only a farm and three slaves cannot afford to lose even one.

I went into the tent then and talked to him, telling him about the burning of the bridge, because I was growing more and more curious about this strange land. Although I cannot say what customs of other nations are, I feel certain those I have known have not been like this; there is no sense of familiarity in anything I hear.

He was weak, but I think not in much pain. Io says he is feverish sometimes and thinks himself a boy again, talking of his old teachers; but he was not like that when I spoke to him.

I told him of the bridge, and he said the slaves across the river had done it hoping we would take some other route—that the slaves here would want us to pass through as quickly as possible. Naturally I did not tell him about Cerdon or what happened in the smithy. He asked about the fields we had passed, and whether they had been plowed for the fall sowing. I was surprised, thinking he would have seen them himself as we marched; but he said he had slept most of the morning, and he could not see much from his litter anyway, because of those who walked beside it. I told him the fields were still in stubble, perhaps because so many men were with the army.

"Time to plow," he murmured. "Before the rains."

"You won't be able to plow for a while, I'm afraid. I'm sure your slaves can manage it, with you there to direct them."

"I never plow. I'd no longer be a Rope Maker, see? But it's got to get done. On the Long Coast the shieldmen have farms and slaves, and work their farms too. I wish I could. We need another hand, but I have to drill."

"The war's nearly over," I told him. "That's the way people talk, at least."

He rolled his head from side to side. "The Great King'll

come back. If not, we'll go there, loot Susa and Persepolis. Or there'll be a different war. There's always another war.''

He wanted to drink. I brought water from the slow, green river and mixed it with wine.

When I held the cup for him, he said, "I won't wrestle you any more, Latro. You'd beat me today. But I beat you once. Remember that?''

I shook my head.

"You wrote when we were through. Read your book.''

Soon after that I left him, sitting before the tent in the sunshine to do as he had suggested. Not knowing where I might find the account of our wrestling, or even whether it was there, I opened this scroll halfway and read of how I had seen Eurykles the Necromancer raise a woman from the dead. I was glad then that it was day; and every few lines I lifted my eyes from the papyrus to watch the peaceful river slipping past and the thin black smoke from the timbers the slaves had pulled from the bridge.

After a time, Drakaina came to sit by me. She laughed when she saw my face and asked what I was thinking.

"What a terrible thing it must be to have memory—although I wish it.''

"Why, if it is so terrible?''

"Because not having memory, I lose myself; and that is worse. This day is like a stone taken from a palace and carried far away to lands where no one knows what a wall may be. And I think every other day has been so for me as well.''

She said, "Then you must enjoy each as it comes, because each day is all you have.''

I shook my head. "Consider the slaves in that village we passed. Every day for them must be much like the day before. If only I could find my own country, I could live there as they do. Then I'd know much that had happened the day before, even if I could not remember it.''

"A goddess has promised you'll soon be restored to your friends,'' she said. "Or so I've been told.''

Joy shook me. Before I knew what I did, I took her in my

arms and kissed her. Nor did she resist me, and her lips were as cool as the brook of shining stones where once I washed my face and paddled my feet.

"Come," she said. "We can go to Pasicrates's tent and tie the flap. I have wine there, and his slaves will bring us food. We need not come out until morning."

I followed her, never thinking of my promise to Cerdon. The tent was warm and dim and silent. She loosed the purple cords that held her cloak about her neck, saying, "Do you remember how a woman looks, Latro?"

"Of course," I told her. "I don't know when I've seen one, but I know."

The cloak fell at her feet. "Then see me." She drew her chiton over her head. The swelling of her hips was like the rolling of a windless sea, and her breasts stood proudly, domed temples roofed with carnelian and snow. A snakeskin was knotted about her waist.

She touched it when she saw my eyes upon it. "I cannot remove this. But there is no need."

"No," I said, and embraced her.

She laughed, tickling and kissing me. "You don't recall our sitting side by side on a hillside of this very island, Latro. How I hungered for you then! And now you are mine."

"Yes," I said. And yet I knew already that it was no, though I burned with desire. I longed for her as a dying man for water, a starving man for bread, a weak man for a crown; but I did not long for her as a man for a woman, and I could do nothing.

She mocked me and I would have strangled her, but her eyes took the strength from my hands; she tore them away. "I'll come to you when the moon is up," she said. "You will be stronger then. Wait for me."

Thus I sit before our fire and write this, hoping someday to understand all that has happened, watching the pale moth that flutters about the flames, and waiting for the moon.

# ──── CHAPTER XXX ────

## The Great Mother

THE terrible goddess of the slaves appeared last night. I touched her and everyone saw her. It was horrible. Now the camp is stirring, but there is no need to write quickly; the market will be full before the bridge is mended. I will have time to read this again and again, so that I will never forget.

Cerdon crept to the fire while I sat staring at the flames, and crouched beside me. "There are sentries tonight," he whispered. "We must be careful. But the Silent One has gone, and that's more than I let myself hope for."

I felt that Drakaina might yet come and that Cerdon would not grudge us a few moments together, so I asked who the Silent One was and added, "I think you are all silent here."

"The young one." Cerdon spat into the fire. "The Silent Ones are always young men, because young men haven't begun to doubt."

"I'm a young man," I said. "So are you."

He chuckled softly at that. "No, you're no Silent One. Nor I. Besides, they're younger than either of us. They're Rope Makers, chosen from the first families—families that own whole villages and many farms. Do you know about the judges?"

I shook my head, glad of another delay.

"The judges rule. The kings pretend to rule; and they lead the armies, fighting in the first rank and often dying. But five judges rule our land. Only the kings can make war; that's the

225

law. But each year the judges meet to make a war that's outside the law.''

I said, "If there's a new war each year, you must always be at war.''

"We are.'' Uneasily, he glanced over his shoulder. "The war's against us.''

"Against you slaves?'' I smiled. "People don't go to war against their own slaves.''

"So I heard when I was in the north with the army. Masters there would laugh at such a thing, just as you did. Here it's so. Each year the war's voted in secret, and it's a war against us. The judges speak to young men, to the men who were boys until the full moon, when they were whipped for Auge. They become Silent Ones, seeming just untried shieldmen but each having the ear of some judge. A Silent One may kill us as he likes. You know the Silent One, I think. His tent stands over there. Do you remember his name?''

It was the tent to which Drakaina had taken me, and I remembered what she had said. "Pasicrates?''

Cerdon nodded.

"If the identity of the Silent Ones is kept secret, how can you know?''

"There's a look about their eyes. An ordinary Rope Maker—an Equal, like the one in your tent—may kill only his own slaves. If he kills another man's, even a Neighbor's, he must pay. A Silent One looks at you, and his hand moves by a finger toward his dagger, maybe because the others respect you, maybe only because you've talked to a foreigner.'' Cerdon shook himself as men do when they wake from evil dreams. "Now it's time to go,'' he said. "Past time. You'll have to leave that sword behind.'' He rose, motioning for me to follow.

I unbuckled Falcata and laid her in the tent. Cerdon was about three strides ahead of me. "Hurry,'' he said. As he spoke something moved beside his leg, and he cried out. It was but a muffled cry, smothered behind the hand with which he covered his mouth, but Io must have heard it in her sleep. She came running from the tent as I knelt beside him.

"Master! What happened?"

I told her I did not know. I carried Cerdon to the fire and by its light saw two wounds in his leg. Five times I filled my mouth with his blood. Io brought wine and water when I was through; I rinsed my mouth, and we poured wine on the wounds. By then he was dripping with sweat.

I asked Io whether Basias's slaves were awake as well. She shook her head and offered to get them up.

"No," Cerdon gasped.

Io said, "When Basias was bitten, the regent's healer said to keep him warm." I nodded and told her to bring my cloak.

Cerdon whispered, "You must go without me."

"If you wish."

"You must go. I saved you at the first meal. Do you remember?"

"Yes," I told him. "I'll go alone, if that's what you want."

Io covered him with my cloak and tucked it in around him, then filled a cup and held it to his lips.

"Follow the river. You'll see a white stone, and a path. Follow the path. There's a wood we never cut—not even for building timber . . . a fire there."

"I understand," I said, and stood up.

"Wait. You must touch her. Touch her, and I'm repaid."

"I will."

Io said, "I'll look after him, master, and hide him if he can walk a little when it gets light. I don't think he wants us to call anyone."

I ran, partly because Cerdon had said to hurry, partly because I feared the snake. There were sentries as he had said, but it was easy to slip between them and scramble down the bank into its shadow. The river—it is called the Eurotas, I believe—was nearly dead of the summer heat; the soft earth at the edge of its water muted my steps. There was an odor of decay.

The white stone had been put beside the path as a marker,

or so it seemed to me; the wide valley of the Eurotas is a place of wheat and barley, and not one of stones and sand. The path born beside this stone climbed the bank at once, crossed fields of stubble far from any house, wound among sheep meadows into the eastern hills, and at last reached a wood of stunted trees—a wood filled with ax-bitten stumps.

It would have been so easy to lose the path in the dim moonlight that I wonder now how I did not; yet it had been trodden by many feet not so long ago. In the meadows, sheep must have crossed and recrossed it, but the marks of their sharp hooves had been blotted everywhere by softer walkers; in the woods my fingers told me of herbs crushed at its edges still damp with their own juices.

Two hills it climbed; the third it seemed rather to split as a man splits firewood with a wedge. When I had passed between those walls of stone, I walked as though in a hall colonnaded with mossy trunks, trees so softly furred that to brush against one was like caressing some vast beast, oaks as broad as boulders and as tall as masts.

A lion stepped from the darkness beneath the trees into a glade filled with moonlight, not half a stade away, and turned its black-maned head to stare at me. An instant later it had vanished in the shadows once more. I waited, fearing I would meet it should I go forward; and as I stood there, straining my ears to catch the least sound, I heard the singing of children.

Something in their song promised I need not fear even a lion in that enchanted place. I did not trust it and waited still; but after a time I went forward again, and soon I saw the red flicker of firelight through the leaves. I had walked quietly before; I sought to walk even more quietly now, so that I could assess the ceremony to which I had come before the other worshipers saw me.

The altar was a flat stone set upon two standing stones, its top only a trifle higher than my waist. The children I had heard were dancing in the space between two fires, stepping slowly and solemnly in the moonlight to the tapping of a pair of stone-headed hammers and the lilting of their own high, clear voices. Behind them, in the shadows of the trees, men and women murmured like willows stirred by the wind. Cerdon had called this a shrine of the Great Mother and indicated I must touch her, but I saw no goddess.

The clicking of the hammers was like the beating of my heart. For a long while I listened to it and to the children's song, and watched their dance; the girls wore garlands of flowers, the boys garlands of straw.

The clicking stopped.

The little dancers froze in their circle. The woman who held the hammers rose, and another led her forward. The child nearest the altar—a girl—went with them.

When they reached the altar, the woman and the girl held the woman with the hammers back; she was blind. She touched the altar with her hammers and laid them upon it. With the help of the other woman, she lifted the girl onto the altar. Slowly she chose a hammer and edged around the altar top until she stood at one end, nearest the girl's head.

As she walked, so I walked too—much more swiftly than she, but I had more ground to cover. I circled the clearing until the altar was between me and those who watched, and as she lifted her hammer I shouted a name and dashed forward.

A sighted woman might have stopped to look; then I would have succeeded. The blind priestess did not. The stone hammer fell, splashing the girl's brains upon the stone.

That was when I saw the Great Mother, an old woman half again as tall as I, leaning over her priestess and dabbling her fingers in the blood. A goddess indeed, but aged and crazed, her gown torn and gray with dirt. For all I owed Cerdon, I would not have touched her if I could. I turned to flee instead; something struck my head, and I lay stretched upon the ground.

Before I could rise, a hundred slaves were upon me. Some had such sticks as could be picked up in the wood; some only their fists and feet. One shouted to the rest to stand aside and raised a billhook. They released me, then turned and fled as though it were they who were to die. I caught the ankle of the slave with the billhook with one foot and kicked his knee with the other, and he fell.

As I scrambled up, Rope Makers were emerging from the trees, their line as straight as on the drill field, their long spears leveled. I snatched up the billhook and killed the slave who would have killed me, finding it a better weapon than I would have supposed.

It was then I understood that the others did not see the goddess: a man took the priestess by the arm and led her away, assisted by the sighted woman; and for a moment he stood within the Great Mother, as a fire within its own smoke. "I drink no blood that has wet iron," she said.

I tried to explain that I had not killed the man with the billhook for her, then Drakaina embraced me. "Thank Auge! I thought they'd killed you."

"How did you get here?" I asked. "Were you watching before?"

She shook her lovely head, making the gems in her ears glitter in the moonlight. "I came with the Rope Makers. Or rather, I brought them. I could find this place—and you, Latro—though they could not."

The Rope Makers reached us as she spoke. Save for the dead man and the dead girl on the altar, the worshipers were gone. So was their terrible goddess, though I could hear her old, cracked voice calling to her people among the oaks.

# CHAPTER XXXI

## Mother Ge's Words

THE prophecy of the goddess still echoes in my ears. I must write it here, though if it is read by the Silent One, by Pasicrates, he will surely try to kill me.

He was not at the shrine of the Great Mother, but because I thought the leader of the Rope Makers (who had gathered to stare at the altar and the dead girl) might be Pasicrates, I asked his name. "Eutaktos," he told me. "Have you forgotten our march from Thought?"

Drakaina said, "Of course he's forgotten, noble Eutaktos— you know how he is. But what about you? Don't you remember me?"

Eutaktos said politely, "I know who you are, my lady, and I see what a service you have done for Rope tonight."

"What of Eurykles of Miletos, who marched with you? Where is he now?"

"Wherever the regent has sent him," Eutaktos said. "Do you think I meddle in such things?" He turned to his men. "Why're you standing there, you clods? Pull her off and tear down that altar."

I asked whether he would bury the child.

He shook his head. "Let the gods bury their own dead— they make us take care of ours. But Latro"—his harsh voice softened a trifle—"don't try to handle something like this by yourself again. Get help." As he spoke, eight shieldmen lifted one side of the altar, and it fell with a crash. There

231

were about thirty shieldmen altogether, one enomotia, I
suppose.

As we stepped beneath the trees, someone threw a stone.
That was how it began. Stones and heavy sticks flew all the
way to the split hill. A shieldman was struck on the foot,
though he could still limp along; soon another's leg was
broken. Two shieldmen tied their red cloaks to the shafts of
their spears and carried him.

In the split the stones were much larger, and they struck
much harder because they were thrown by men on the hilltops. Those who had thrown from behind the trees were
mostly women and boys, I think. Without armor Drakaina and
I hung back, but the shieldmen held their big hoplons over
their heads and advanced. The cries from the hilltops and the
clang of the stones on the bronze hoplons were like the din of
a hundred smiths, all shouting as they hammered a hundred
anvils; they deafened and bewildered us all, or at least all of
us save Drakaina.

She took my arm and drew me away to the thick shadows
we had just left. I said, "They'll kill us here."

"They'll certainly kill us *there*. Don't you see the Rope
Makers aren't getting through?"

Nor were they. The rearmost shieldmen had stopped and
were backing away from the stones.

"They've probably blocked the path in some way. Or if
four or five slaves with weapons were stationed where it
widens out, one or two Rope Makers would have to fight
them all. In their phalanx they may be the best soldiers in the
world, but I doubt they're much better than other men alone."

The rest soon followed those we had seen retreating. Nearly
every man was helping a wounded comrade with his spear
arm while he tried to fend off the stones with his shield.
Eutaktos bellowed, "Back to the fires! It won't be long till
daylight."

Drakaina screamed. I turned in time to see the flash of the
knife. Then she was gone. The woman who had attacked her
shrieked and fell.

Another woman and a boy rushed at me in the darkness,

and I cut them down with the billhook, though I am not proud of it. When they were dead, I examined them; that was when I saw I had killed someone's wife and a boy of twelve or so, she armed with a kitchen knife, he with a sickle.* Seeing the sickle, I wished for my sword, though the billhook was no mean weapon. The woman who had attacked Drakaina was writhing in agony, but of Drakaina herself there was no sign.

I rejoined the Rope Makers, helping carry a wounded man. There were more stones as we fought our way to the clearing. I was struck twice, but I did not fall, nor were any of my bones broken. When we had marched to the split in the hill, the Rope Makers had stayed in file, and often they had seemed not to notice the missiles hurled at us. Now several rushed into the trees again and again. Twice they killed slaves, but one of the Rope Makers did not return.

The fires had burned low, so while some of us treated our wounded, the rest (of whom I was one) gathered such wood as we could find and piled it on the flames. When I heard the voice of the goddess in the oak wood again, I told Eutaktos the slaves would attack us soon.

He looked up from the dying Rope Maker he had been attending to ask what made me think so. Before I could reply, a lion roared from the trees, and a wolf howled. As though they too were lions and wolves, a hundred answered them. Every man had a stone, and each ran close before he threw, then dashed back into the shadows. We picked up such stones as we could find and flung them back, but most were lost in the dark.

They charged our circle at last. I fought with my back to one of the supports that had held the altar, though it was not high enough to give much protection. A Rope Maker fell beside me, then another, and after that I no longer heard Eutaktos shouting encouragement. I fought on alone, ringed by slaves with clubs and hachets. All this took less time than it has taken to write of it.

---

*Latin *falx*. —G. W.

The cracked voice of the old goddess called, *"Wait!"* and though I do not think the slaves knew they heard it, they obeyed it nonetheless.

Long strides carried her to the fires; the spilling of so much blood must have restored her vigor, if not her youth. The lion and the wolf frisked around her like dogs, and though the slaves of the Rope Makers could not see her, they saw them and drew away in terror. When she stood before me I was a child once more, confronted by the crone from the cave on the hill.

"It is you," she said, "come again to visit Mother Ge. Europa carried your message, and my daughter has told me what she promised you. Do you recall Europa? Or my daughter Kore?"

If I had ever known them, they were lost in the mist, lost forever as though they had never been.

"No. No, you do not." Huge though she was, her voice seemed faint when she spoke to me; I could scarcely hear her above the snarling of the beasts and the cries of the slaves. "Why don't you threaten me with that hedge bill?" she asked. "You threatened Kore. Do you still fear my lion?"

I shook my head as she spoke, for as she spoke, what I had known of Kore and Europa came flooding back to me. "If I were to kill you, Mother, who would heal me?"

"By the wolf that gave your fathers suck, you are learning wisdom."

The slaves were staring at me as though I were mad. They had lowered their weapons, and as Mother Ge spoke I dropped mine, went to her, and touched her arm.

The slaves shouted aloud when I laid my hand on her, but quickly they fell silent again. When they came forward, many eyes streamed with tears—the eyes of men as well as those of women and of children. They would have touched her too, I think, if they could; but the lion and the wolf rushed at them, menacing them as the shepherd's dogs menace the sheep.

"Goddess!" one of the slaves shouted. "Hear our plea!"

"I have heard your plea many times," Mother Ge told

him, and now her voice was like the singing of a bird in the sun, in lands that are drowned forever.

"Five hundred years the men of Rope have enslaved us."

"And five hundred more. Yet you are seven when they are one. Why should I aid you?"

At that, they led the blind priestess forward. She cried, "We are your worshipers! Who will feed your altars if we lose our faith?"

"I have millions more in other lands," Mother Ge told her. "And some for whom I am not yet bent and old." She paused, sucking her gums. "But I would have another sacrifice tonight. Give it to me willingly, and I will do all I can to free you. The victim need not die. Will you give it?"

"Yes," shouted the priestess and the man who had spoken before; and after them, all the people shouted, *"Yes!"* Then Mother Ge told them what she required of him, and the blind priestess found a sharp flint for it, searching the ground on all fours like a beast.

Twice he tried to strike but drew back his hand at the first blood. Though Mother Ge had said he need not die, his progeny died that night to ten thousand generations, and he knew it as well as I. He stood well back from Mother Ge and from me; the other slaves crowded around him, cheering him and pledging tawdry rewards—a new roof or a milch goat. I knew then that I might slip away in the dark if I chose, but I waited as fascinated as the rest.

Then there was a stroke in which there was no hesitation. His manhood came away in his hand, looking like the offal from a butcher's shop when he held it up. Someone took it from him and laid it upon the fallen altar, and he stood with legs wide apart, bleeding like a woman—or, rather, like a bull when it is made an ox. The others made him lie on the ground and stanched his flow with cobwebs and moss.

"Now hear me," Mother Ge said. She straightened her back, and it seemed that a great light shone there, a light from which her body shielded us. "This man is sacred to me as long as he lives. In payment, I will fight for you, striving to make his master, Prince Pausanias, king of this land."

The slaves muttered against these words, and a few shouted protests.

"You think him your greatest foe, but I tell you he will be your greatest friend and perhaps your king, turning his back upon his own kindred. Still he, and I, may fail. If so, I shall destroy Rope—"

Here the slaves roared so loudly I could not hear.

"—then you must rise against the Rope Makers, your scythes to cut their spears, your sickles to beat down their swords. But first, your stones against their helmets. So you defeated them on this night. Remember it."

Then she was gone, and the clearing seemed dark and far from the lands of men. One fire was dying, the other already no more than embers. In a litter they wove of vines, half a dozen men carried away the man who had unmanned himself. Others trailed behind them, bearing the bodies of relatives killed in the fighting. Some women asked me to come with them and offered to treat my bruises, but I feared them still because of the woman I had killed, and I told them to follow their husbands. They did as I ordered, leaving me alone with the dead.

Though the billhook was not intended for digging, I was able to scratch out a small and shallow grave in the soft earth of the clearing. I buried the girl I had not saved and heaped her grave with the stones that had been flung at us. I believe one of the dead Rope Makers was Eutaktos, whom I had known in some time I have forgotten. Though I robbed several of their helmets to study their faces, I could not be sure; I had seen Eutaktos only briefly and by firelight.

Nor did I any longer know who Kore and Europa were, nor what they had once meant to me, though I could recall a time not long ago when I had known. Their names and that memory troubled me at least as much as the thought that the lion and the wolf might still be near. I muttered "Kore" and "Europa" over and over as I built up the dying fire and carried blazing sticks to reestablish the other, until at last *Kore* and *Europa* ceased to have any meaning at all for me, ceased even to be names.

Walking up and down between the fires, I waited for dawn before I made my way through the split hill. The bodies of many Rope Makers had laid on that narrow path, and there were still many bloodstains; but the slaves had dragged the bodies away, so that they lay in the shadows beneath the trees, wrapped in the green life of the oaks. I do not think the other Rope Makers will find them there.

From the place where Drakaina had taken my arm, I could see the old goddess walking the valley, a woman taller than women, at once darker and brighter than the treetops touched by dawn. She stopped at the grave, I think, for after a time she vanished from sight and I heard her weeping.

When I had passed the split hill, I cast aside my weapon and hurried through the dew-decked fields to this camp on the bank of the Eurotas, where now I write these words in the morning sunlight. Io met me. After I had told her something of what had happened that night and she had salved my bruises and mourned with many head shakings the blow that had struck me down, she took me proudly to see Cerdon, whom she had hidden among the hay that fed our pack mules; but Cerdon had died while she slept, and already his limbs were cold and stiff.

# — CHAPTER XXXII —

## Here in Rope

STRANGERS are viewed with the greatest suspicion. This morning Drakaina, Io, and I went to see the famous temple of Orthia. Its enclosure on the riverbank must once have been separated from the city, but now the Rope Makers have built their houses right up to the boundaries of the sacred ground. Drakaina said, "In the Empire, we wall our cities properly. When you're on one side of the wall, you're in the city; on the other, you're in the country. With all these straggling hamlets, who knows? Thought was almost as bad, but at least they had guard posts on the roads."

"The Great King tore down your walls," Io reminded her. "That's what the regent said."

Drakaina nodded. "The People from Parsa have a sense of fitness. Its walls symbolize a city, and pulling them down is the destruction of the city. Rope's been destroyed already—or let's say that it's never existed. This is just four villages; no wonder they call it scattered."

Slaves turned their faces to one side when we passed, and even the Neighbors we saw did not wish to speak with us. Rope Makers stopped us and questioned us, women as well as men, and many told us we were unwelcome. We soon learned to reply that we would gladly go elsewhere if only their regent would permit it, which silenced them quite effectively.

Drakaina shook her lovely head after one such encounter. "There's no place in the world where men are less free than they are here, and none where women are freer—save perhaps in the country of the Amazons, the women who live without men.''

"Are they real?'' Io asked. "Once Basias said I'd be a strategist among them.''

"Of course they are.'' Drakaina slipped her arm through mine. "But you'll have to go far to the north and east—much farther east than my own city. And you'll have to leave Latro here with me. The Amazons don't care for foreigners any more than these Rope Makers, and they consider all men spies.''

I said, "There can be no such race; they'd die out in a generation.''

"They lie with the young men of the Sons of Scoloti. If they bear a girl afterward, they sear her left breast so she can use the bow. Boys buy them the favor of their goddess, or so I've heard. I admit I've never seen one of these women warriors myself.''

I thought of the dream I had last night when she said that; perhaps later I will write of it here.

"There it is!'' Io exclaimed, and pointed.

"About what I expected. They don't know what a real temple looks like here. Nobody could who hasn't traveled in the east, though some of these are at least beautiful. This isn't even that. In fact, if this whole city were destroyed, no one would ever guess from looking at the ruins that half the world had trembled at its name.''

The temple was indeed small and very simple, its pillars mere wooden posts painted white. I took off my sword and fastened the belt around one.

Io said, "We're supposed to make an offering. See the bowl? Master, do you have any money?''

Drakaina told her, "I'll take care of it,'' and tossed one of the iron coins of the Rope Makers so that it rang against the bronze rim.

As we went from the brilliant sunlight of the portico into the shadowy interior, Io asked, "Where did you get that?''

"Hush!''

It was the age of the temple that impressed me most, I think, and perhaps it would be just to say that its age was the only impressive thing about it; but that made it truly a sacred place, the home built for a god when the world was young and men had not yet forgotten that when the gods are mocked they punish us by leaving us.

A priestess, white-haired but as tall as I and as straight as any spear, glided from some recess. "Welcome," she said, "to this house in the name of the Huntress, and to this land in the name of the House of Heracles."

"It's true," I admitted, "that we're all foreigners here, madame. But we've come to Rope at the order of your regent, the great Prince Pausanias, who does not permit us to leave."

Drakaina quickly added, "We have the freedom of the city, however, and I am a priestess of your goddess."

The white-haired woman made the slightest of bows. "As such, you may sacrifice here whenever you wish. No one will prevent you. Should anyone question you, tell them you have my permission. I am Gorgo, daughter of Cleomenes, mother of Pleistarchos, and widow of Leonidas."

Drakaina began, "Then the regent is—"

"My cousin and my nephew. Would you care to see the image of the goddess?" She led us to a wooden figure, cracked and blackened by time. "She is called Orthia because she was found standing upright, just where you see her now, in the days when our forefathers conquered this land."

The bulging eyes of the statue gave it the look of a madwoman. In either hand it grasped a snake.

"The wood is cypress, which is sacred to her. The snake in her right hand is the empyreal serpent, the one in her left the chthonic serpent. She holds both and stands between them, the only god who unites heaven to earth and the lower world. When she appears here, it is most often as a snake."

Io asked, "Could she help my master? He's been cursed by the Grain Goddess."

Drakaina added, "I've already offered sacrifices to our threefold goddess on his behalf. Do you remember Basias,

Io? He promised to carry a message to her.'' She turned back to the priestess. "And Latro is much better. His memory was taken from him, and he still can't remember; but now he acts almost as though he could.''

I said, "The goddess is angry.''

"Why?'' Gorgo's eyes were large and cool, the rare blue eyes that shine like ice.

"I don't know. But can't you see the way she looks at Drakaina?''

Io's hand flew to her mouth to stifle a shout of nervous laughter.

"No,'' the priestess told me softly. "I cannot see that. But you do. What has this woman done?''

"I don't know.''

Even in the dimness of the temple, I could see how white Drakaina's face was. She said, "He is mad, most reverend Queen. Pasicrates and I, and the little girl, care for him.''

"Pasicrates is a fine young man, and a faithful servant of the goddess.''

"As I am. If I have displeased her—''

"You will be punished.''

When Gorgo said that, there was a silence that stretched so long that it became unbearable. At last Io asked, "Is this where the boys get whipped?''

"Yes, child.'' One corner of the priestess's mouth lifted by the width of a grain of wheat. "In this city, we girls receive much the same education as the boys, but we are spared that. Here food is placed upon the altar, and the older men stand where you are standing, and on the portico outside, and as far as the sacred precinct of the temple reaches. The boys must dash past them and take the food, then dash past again; they are beaten as they run. See the stains their blood has left on our floor? Thus they learn what women already know: that without women there is no food for men. Because they are beaten that day, they can never forget. There is a statue of the goddess at Ephesos with a hundred breasts. The lesson is the same.''

Pasicrates was waiting for us when we left the temple.

"My slave said you had gone out to see the sights," he told us. "This is the first most visitors want to see."

Drakaina asked, "And are there others?"

"We do not have the wealth of Tower Hill," Pasicrates conceded as he led us away, "and yet our city is not without interest. The well I am about to show you is known these days in every civilized land."

"Really?" She smiled at him; her sharply angled face gave her smiles a disturbing quality. "Is it like the one at Hysiai, that inspires all who drink to prophesy?"

"No," Pasicrates replied. He hesitated. "I was on the point of saying it isn't a magic well at all. Except that now that I think on it, it does have power, and power of a sort you might find particularly interesting. It changes men to women."

Io said, "It seems like everybody's turning against you, even the Huntress."

Drakaina looked so angry that I feared for Io, though she faced up to it as bravely as any child could.

Pasicrates said, "What's this? Tell me, little girl."

"Latro says the goddess is mad at her. Sometimes Latro sees things other people don't. Sometimes he sees the gods; and talks to them, too."

"How interesting. I should have asked you more about him when we met. Foolishly, I wasted my time with one Eurykles. Latro, what did you see?"

"Only that she gave Drakaina a look of fury, just as Drakaina looked at Io a moment ago."

"And it's Orthia who sends sudden death to women. What a pity you're not a man, Drakaina. Is that your true name, by the way?"

She feigned not to hear him.

"She is also the protector of young beasts and of children," Pasicrates told Io. "Did you know that? Our boys pray to her before they are beaten, and dedicate the end of their childhood to her. Yet she favors girls more. It goes ill with anyone who harms a girl here, unless he is high in her favor."

I said, "It will go ill with anyone who hurts Io, while I live."

Pasicrates nodded. "You might well be the instrument of her justice. So might I."

We had been strolling through the city as we talked; when nothing more was said for a time, I ventured to ask about the houses, saying it seemed strange to me to see so many windows in a city of his people.

"Ah, but you've been in Thought, even if you don't remember it. There they think about being robbed. We don't. We're too poor, and there's little here to buy." He smiled. "But here's the well. Look down. You'll find it worth seeing."

Io dashed ahead and pulled herself up by the coping to peer into the depths. *"Skeletons!"* she called.

When Pasicrates arrived he seated himself on it beside her. "Are bones all you see, little Io? Surely there is something more."

"Just mud and water."

"Yes, earth and water. You see, I am a knowledgeable guide. I brought you here at noon, when the sun shines far enough down for you to see the bottom. It's not a very deep well. Perhaps that's why it went dry, or nearly dry. Drakaina, don't you want to look?"

I peered inside. As Pasicrates had indicated, the sun reached more than halfway to the bottom and lent light enough to show the rest. Three black-bearded men were penned there. They had heavy gold bracelets on their arms, and their golden sword hilts were set with many gems. One gripped his wrist, his face twisted in agony; one covered his face with his hands; one wept, face upturned, and extended his hands to me.

Pasicrates said, "The Great King sent his ambassadors here, demanding earth and water in token of our submission. They were bold men when they came, but frightened women when we threw them in to get them for themselves. You should have heard them scream. Drakaina, I think you'd better look. I won't push you." He slid from the coping and strode away.

Io said softly, "I thought he liked the Great King."

"He's jealous," Drakaina snapped. "The regent prefers me. Latro will find that understandable, though perhaps you won't. When we went into the temple, you asked where I got the coin I offered. Prince Pausanias gave it to me, as he's given me other things. Do you like this gown?" Her hand caressed the crimson fabric. "It's moth's spinning, brought from the end of the earth; once it belonged to a noble lady of Susa."

"It's beautiful," Io said with honest admiration. "But now that you're speaking to me again, will you tell me how you explained to the regent? You were a man the first time he saw you, and you're a woman now, and he's not like Latro."

"I told him the truth—that the goddess had given me my desire. It hasn't reduced his esteem for me, believe me."

"Watch out," Io said. "She's liable to take it back."

Drakaina shook her head, and it seemed to me that she was hearing someone other than Io. "I feel I've lived a long, long time," she said. "And that I've been what I am since the first stars took shape."

Afterward we idled about the city; but nothing more was said that I think worth recounting, save that Drakaina remarked that I had given her a slave some time ago. When I asked what had become of him, she said he was dead.

We watched naked women run and throw the discus, which Io thought disgusting, and saw the barracks where the Rope Makers sleep. After that we returned to this hill fortress in the center of the city, stopping for a time to watch slaves at work upon the tomb of Leonidas. This was in the village called Pitana, which stands close beside the hill. I do not know what the name may mean. Perhaps "legion." A least Io says there is a mora of that name in the regent's army.

Here in the fortress I write as I do, catching the fading light of the sun as it shines through the embrasure. Drakaina has just come to say this day will be our last in Rope.

# PART IV

# — CHAPTER XXXIII —

## Through This Shadowed Gorge

DARK Acheron cuts the rocks like a knife, at last plunging into the earth on its way to the Lands of the Dead. Nowhere else are they so near the living; nowhere else are they so readily summoned—so says Drakaina, who is even now preparing for the ceremony. As I watch, Prince Pausanias himself digs the votive pit, while Io feeds ferns to the black lamb and black ewe lamb he will sacrifice. Pasicrates and I have dipped jars of water from Acheron and unloaded the mule, which carried honey, milk, wine, and the other needful things. I am writing this because Io says I have neglected to write for too long; and indeed when I read what I had written last, I saw that we had been in Rope, which the young men of the prince's bodyguard speak of as a place very far away.

But also because I do not wish to lose all recollection of the dream I had last night. It was of a ship, a round-bellied trader with a white swan at its stern, a broad, striped mainsail, and an angled foremast. I opened a hatch on deck and went below to a cavern, where a lovely queen and a grim king sat thrones of black stone amid the smell of death. Three dogs barked, and the queen said, "He passes. His message fulfills . . ."

There was more that I have forgotten. When I told Io of the ship, she said it was the one in which we came here. If that is so, some part of me retains the memory, though I

cannot recall it. Surely that is a good sign. It may be I will
find my past soon, perhaps even here among these damp and
frowning rocks. Pausanias has completed his pit, and Pasicrates
winds dark garlands of hemlock and rue about the lambs.
There are chaplets of herbs for us.

 

It came, and I saw it! Drakaina poured libations of milk,
honey, sweet wine, and water, and strewed the ground with
barley meal. She held the lambs while Prince Pausanias
pronounced the invocation: "Royal Agids come! Advise me,
and I will make your tombs places of pilgrimage and sacrifice
for the entire world. Should I seek peace or war? Was my dream
true, that said this slave would bring me victory? How shall I
know it? Come! Speak! You I love in death as in life."
Though his hand shook, he took up his sword and struck off
the heads of the black lamb and the black ewe lamb so that
their blood streamed into the pit; releasing their flaccid bodies,
Drakaina began a chant in a tongue unknown to me.
  At once the rock behind her split, and there came forth a
king in armor, with a bloodstained knife in his hand, bleeding limbs, and a lolling head. He was terrible to behold, but
he knelt and drank the vapors from the pit as a shepherd
drinks from a spring; as he drank, his wounds ceased to bleed
and he appeared almost a living man—not handsome, for his
face had been scarred by wine as well as the knife, yet
having such an air of command as few possess. Drakaina fell
in a fit, her mouth gaping and rimmed with foam. From it
there issued a man's voice, as swift and hard as the crack of a
lash.

 

"Nephew, seek peace and not death.
Nor drink from the blue cup of Lethe.
Ask who will make the fortress yield,
To those that fought at Fennel Field."

 

At the final word Drakaina gave a great cry; and the stone,
which had closed, opened again to receive the dead king. In
his train now walked an attendant, a lean, fantastically dressed

man with disordered hair. Drakaina was weak and sick when
they were gone. She crawled to drink the milk left from the
libations.

The prince drew a deep breath; his forehead was beaded
with sweat. "Was it good? Who'll provide the exegesis?"
He wiped his hands on his chiton. "Pasicrates, who spoke to
me?"

Pasicrates looked to Drakaina. Receiving no help from her,
he ventured, "Your royal uncle, perhaps, King Cleomenes.
Only he perished—" Pasicrates hesitated, then finished weakly,
"By seeking death."

"By his own hand, you mean. You may say so. He
desecrated the sacred lands of the Great Goddess and her
daughter when he marched to Advent. The nature of his
punishment is common knowledge. What of the second line?"

"He warns you against the wine that drove him mad, and
so by implication against offending the gods as he did. You
asked three questions, Highness. It seems to me the first two
lines of your royal uncle's verse answer your first two questions. You are to seek peace, and you are to trust your
dream, because to distrust it would be an offense to the
gods."

"Very good." Pausanias nodded. "And those who fought
at Fennel Field are the shieldmen of Thought, who are now
besieging the fortified city of Sestos. Cleomenes fought them,
twice invading the Long Coast. I should aid them instead—
seeking peace with Thought now, that I may better seek
peace with Persepolis later. So Cleomenes seems to be
saying."

"Highness, you asked how you might know whether your
dream was truly from the gods. King Cleomenes urges you to
ask who will make a fortress yield to the men of Thought.
Why not send a token force from your retinue to Sestos?
They say it's the strongest place in the world; if it falls,
you'll know your dream was the true speech of the Maiden.
If it doesn't, it will be a failure for Thought and not for us.
That seems to me to be your royal uncle's advice, sir, and I
see no flaw in it."

Pausanias's face twisted in its scarred smile. "Yes, the
risks will be small, and the People of Thought will take it as
a friendly gesture, a personal gesture on my part, since
Leotychides has withdrawn. The aristocratic party there, particularly, will take it so. Xanthippos commands." He chuckled. "And you wouldn't exactly object to leading a hundred
of my heroes on a new Trojan War, would you, Pasicrates?
Or should I say, swift-footed Achilles? It will be a glorious
adventure, one in which a man might win considerable
reputation."

Pasicrates looked at his feet. "I will stay or go, as my
strategist commands."

"You'll go, then, and keep your eyes open." The prince
wiped his sword on his cloak.

I said, "And I, Highness. I must go with him."

Io protested, "Master, we might get killed!"

"You don't have to," I told her. "But I do. If the gods
say I bring the regent victory, I must be with his standard."

"Here's your first volunteer, Pasicrates. Will you take
him?"

Pasicrates nodded. "Highness, I'd like to take all three.
Latro for the reason he just gave: the test won't be valid
without him. The child to care for him, and the sorceress
because it may be desirable to . . . ah . . ."

"Arrange terms of surrender." The prince rose.

"Exactly, Highness."

"All right, then. It will make things easier for me at home
anyway—Gorgo doesn't like her."

When the winding mountain paths had brought us here
again, the regent ordered his bodyguard to form the phalanx;
this bodyguard consists of three hundred unmarried men
chosen by himself. "Shieldmen of Rope," he began. "Rope
Makers! Hear me! You know of the glorious victory of
Mycale. There's not a man among us who doesn't wish he
had been there. Now word has reached me that our allies,
jealous of our glory, were not content with that victory.
When our ships set out for home, they remained across the
Water, and they have laid siege to the Great King's city of
Sestos!"

Though the young soldiers stood rigidly at attention, there was a stir among them, like the stirring of a wood that hears far off the thunder of the storm.

"When we return, I intend to tell the judges we should send an army to aid them—but what if Sestos falls before it arrives? You know how we were late to Fennel Field. You have heard, I imagine, that the men of Thought are claiming credit for the victory at Peace. I ask you, shall we let them say they took Sestos alone?"

Three hundred voices roared, *"No!"*

"And I too say *no!*" The regent paused; the young men waited, tense and expectant. "All of you know Pasicrates, and you know he has my entire confidence. Pasicrates, step out here!"

Pasicrates left the first line of the phalanx to stand beside the regent, and even to me he looked a young hero in his bright armor.

"Pasicrates will lead a hundred volunteers to Sestos. Those who do *not* wish to volunteer, remain in ranks. Volunteers! Step forward and join Pasicrates!"

The formation surged forward as one man. "He'll choose," the regent shouted. "Pasicrates, choose your hundred!"

A moment ago, Io asked what I was writing about. "About the choosing of the hundred volunteers," I told her.

"What about what we did in the gorge, killing the black lambs?"

I told her I had already written about that.

"Do you think it was really real? That King Cleomenes talked through Drakaina?"

"I know it was," I said. "I saw him."

"I wish you'd touched him. Then I could have seen him too."

I shook my head. "He would have frightened you." I described him to her, dwelling on the horror of his wounds.

"I've seen a lot. You don't remember all I've seen. I saw you kill the Rope Makers' slaves, and I saw Kekrops after the sea monster killed him. Do you think Pasicrates understood what Cleomenes said?"

Drakaina sat up at that. "Do you remember? What was it?"

"Don't you know? You said the words."

"No," Drakaina told her. "I was not I who spoke. I remember nothing."

Io recited the four lines as I have given them and added, "I don't think Pasicrates was right. I think Cleomenes wanted a real peace, and not for the regent to send men to Sestos. That was what he meant when he said the regent should ask who took the fortress. If he didn't send men, he wouldn't know."

Drakaina said, "He meant no one would take it. I've seen Sestos, and believe me, what they say is true—it's the strongest place on earth. People talk of the walls of Babylon, but they are gapped to let the river through. That was how the People from Parsa took it the first time. Sestos has no such weakness. As for seeking peace, Cleomenes knows that Demaratus, the true heir to the younger crown of Rope, is one of the Great King's advisers. He naturally hopes for an agreement that will leave the Agids the elder crown and give Demaratus the younger. If such an agreement had been struck two years ago, the whole war might have been prevented."

I asked if she was feeling better.

"Yes, thank you. Weak, but as though I'll be stronger than ever when I'm no longer weak. Do you know what I mean?" She cupped her full breasts and caressed them, savoring delights to come. "Something in me knows the best part of this life still lies ahead."

Io asked, "Just how many lives do you have? And is there a spring where you take a bath to get back your virginity?"

Drakaina smiled at her. Her lovely face looks hungry when she smiles. "Don't flutter too close, little bird of joy, or you'll sing a different song."

Io seated herself at my feet. "You may be the bird who has to learn a new tune, Drakaina. Prince Pausanias likes you, but we're going with Pasicrates, and he hates you."

"Because I came between him and the regent—quite literally, as it happens. When the regent's a hundred leagues away, things will be different; you'll see." With such fluid grace as few women possess, Drakaina rose. "In fact, I think I'll have my first chat with the noble Pasicrates now. He'll be the one who assigns us space on the ship, I suppose. I want the captain's cabin. Would you care to bet I don't get it?" From the sheen of her dark hair and the grace of her swaying figure, it seemed likely enough she would.

When she was out of sight, Io made a face. "I think if somebody sliced her up the way you said Cleomenes was, she'd wiggle till sunset."

I did not want to punish Io, but I told her I thought that an ugly thing for a child to say, even though Drakaina's name was "she-dragon."

"It used to be Eurykles of Miletos," Io told me. "I know you don't remember, Latro, but it was. Eurykles was a man, and when we lived with Kalleos, sometimes he spent the whole night in her room. Drakaina says he changed himself into her by magic. I didn't like Eurykles much, but I liked him a whole lot better than Drakaina. And if you ask me *she* changed him into her, somehow."

I asked her how this Eurykles had looked. Now that she has described him for me, I know he was the man I saw follow King Cleomenes.

A short time ago, the prince regent's runner came to tell me that he will send for me soon. He said I was to wash and put on my best clothes, which I have done. I asked if he would be present, but he said he would be in the town getting supplies for our expedition to Sestos. A shieldman of the bodyguard—one of those who will not be coming to Sestos with us—will probably be sent for me, he said.

Io reports that according to the gossip of the camp, a ship has brought the regent's sorcerer.

# — CHAPTER XXXIV —

## In the Regent's Tent

THERE was no one to meet me. "Wait here," said the young shieldman who had brought me. As he turned to leave he added, "Don't touch anything."

I do not believe I have ever been a thief; but for a thief it would have been tempting indeed. There were lamps of silver, gold, and crystal, and many soft carpets and cushions. A long knife in a green sheath with gold mountings hung from one of the tent poles, and an ivory griffin spread its wings upon a peak of ebony.

I was admiring this last when the regent entered, bringing with him a sly little Hellene with a beard. "This is the slave," the regent said, dropping to a cushion. "Latro—Tisamenus, my mantis."

I did not know the word, and my ignorance must have appeared on my face. Tisamenus murmured, "A mere consulter of the gods, sir, a humble reader of the omens of sacifice."

"Tisamenus advised me at Clay. Those who know the result know why I think highly of him."

"His Highness has told me of his dream. I wished to see the man. It sometimes amuses His Highness to accede to my little requests. Sir, Latro, I noticed you were admiring that statuette when we entered. Do you know of those monsters?"

"Do they actually exist? No, nothing."

The regent said, "I'm told they live in the country of

those Sons of Scoloti who revolted against the royal branch of their people, and that they hoard gold."

I said, "Which can't be as precious as this carving, Highness."

Tisamenus murmured, "I'd understood they're found north and west of the Issedonians. It's said they put out one eye of any man they find trying to make off with their treasure; but if he's already one-eyed, they kill him. However, I think it likely my information is mistaken, Highness, and yours correct."

The regent laughed. "No, you've the right of it, I feel sure. The best intelligence of such things is always that which puts them farthest from us."

Tisamenus nodded and smiled. "I don't suppose you've seen the creatures, sir?"

I shrugged. "I've no way of knowing. From what I read in my book today, I was already with the regent when we were in Rope. If he's told you about me, he must have told you I don't remember."

"Yet you remembered the monster, sir. I saw that memory in your eyes."

I shook my head. "I don't recall what I learned of them, if I did. Or how I learned it, or where."

The regent chuckled. "Sit down, you two. I'm remiss in my duties as your host. Latro, Tisamenus—" He turned to the mantis. "Which do you prefer, Tisamenus of Elis, or Tisamenus of Rope?"

"As Your Highness chooses to honor his servant."

"Tisamenus of Elis, then. Latro, Tisamenus got my permission to visit his family after the battle. That was unfortunate, because he wasn't present to interpret my dream when I dreamed about you; but I've told him that dream now, and in general he seems to feel I've caught the meaning without him."

"To visit my sisters and their husbands, sir. I have not been favored in the matter of sons and daughters." The mantis sighed. "And the Inescapable One deprived me of my poor wife at the time of the last Games."

I cleared my throat. I did not think what I was about to say would lose me my head, but the possibility, however slight, lent a chill to my words. "With your leave, mantis. Why is it you call me 'sir' when the regent has called me a slave?"

The regent said brusquely, "That's just his way."

Almost too softly to be heard, Tisamenus murmured, "Courtesy is never wasted, sir. Particularly courtesy toward a slave. We slaves appreciate it." To me he added, "You will not be able to answer our questions, then. That's a terrible pity, but perhaps you won't object if we beg you to try."

"Fetch some wine," the regent told Tisamenus. "Want a cup, Latro?"

"I can answer that one," I said. "Yes. But Io can tell you more about me than I can tell you about myself."

"I questioned her some time ago," the regent said. "And I was able to pass to Tisamenus all I learned in a few words. She met you in Hill. You were badly wounded. You'd tried to embrace a statue of the River God, and they brought you to the oracle there. It gave her to you and assigned a citizen to guide you to Advent. All three of you were imprisoned in Tower Hill until you were freed by a captain from Thought. In Advent, the goddess came to you in a dream and promised to restore you to your friends. Then the lochagos I'd sent looking for you found you and brought you to me."

Tisamenus poured the wine, so old and good it perfumed even that perfumed air. "Thank you," I said, accepting the cup.

"You don't look pleased. What's the matter?"

"You told me a lot, Highness, but none of it was what I wanted to hear."

"Which is?"

"Who my friends are, where my home is, what happened to me, and how I can be cured."

"Your friends are here—two of them, at least. I'm your greatest friend, and anyone who stands with me will be your friend as well. Do you know of the promise made me in my dream?"

"Yes. We talked of it this afternoon in the gorge."

Tisamenus murmured, "Then perhaps you also know why it should be so. What makes you a talisman of victory?"

"I have no idea."

The regent said, "My first notion was that we'd been born at the same instant—it's well known such children are linked. Tisamenus?"

The mantis looked doubtful. "I'd guess he's the younger." To me he said, "I don't suppose, sir, that you know the day of your birth?"

I shook my head, and the regent shrugged. "So it might be true. I'm in my twenty-eighth year. Think that might be your age, Latro? Speak up. You won't be beaten."

"Twenty-eight sounds old to me, Highness. So I think I must be less."

Tisamenus had risen. "Shrewdly spoken, sir, and I agree. May I call your attention once more to this admirable carving? Can you perhaps inform me as to the name borne by these monsters?"

"They're the Clawed Ones," I said.

"So," Tisamenus whispered. "The god who took away your memory left you that. What man comprehends their ways?"

The regent drank. "A thousand times I've heard somebody say that: Who understands the ways of the gods? Everybody asks the question, nobody answers it. Now I'm a man and nearly a king—do you know many of our Rope Makers already call me King Pausanias, Tisamenus? So I'll try, Latro. You do."

As cautiously as I could, I said, "I'm not sure I follow you, Highness."

"I called you an idiot once. Since then, I've seen enough of you to know you're anything but."

"Yet there's an idiot here, Highness, if you believe I'm in the councils of the gods."

Tisamenus said, "You're treading on dangerous ground, sir."

"Because if you believe it, Highness, it must be true; and I would be an idiot not to tell you."

The regent gave Tisamenus his twisted smile. "You see what I mean? If this were the pentathlon, he'd win every event."

"Good," I said. "Because if we're linked, Highness, it might be that if I were beaten you'd be beaten too."

"And the chariot race. But Latro, my friend—and I'll call you my friend and not my slave—you know things you don't know you know. You didn't remember the name of the winged monsters until you were asked, did you?"

I shook my head.

Tisamenus murmured, "So it is, perhaps, with the councils of the gods. If we recall them to you, will you tell His Highness?"

I said, "If he wishes it, certainly. But though Io says I once swept floors for a woman in Thought, I don't believe I ever swept the hall of Olympus."

"Then we'll begin with speculations humbler still. You acknowledge that there are many gods?"

I sipped my wine. "All men do, I suppose."

"You once told His Highness, no doubt truly, that you were a soldier of the Great King."

"I feel I am."

"Then you must know something of the barbarians, sir. Indeed, you must have marched through Parsa, for the Great King's army did so on its way here. Are you aware that they hold there's only a single god, whom they call Ahuramazda?"

"I know nothing of them," I said. "At least, nothing I can remember."

"And yet they sacrifice to the sun, the moon, and the earth, and to fire and water. It is possible—I speak now as a sophist, sir—that there is but one god. It is possible also that there are many. But it is not possible that there are one *and* many. You disagree?"

I shrugged. "Sometimes a word is used for two things. When I loaded the regent's mule, I tied the load with rope."

Prince Pausanias chuckled. "Excellent! But now that you've bested poor Tisamenus, let me play Ahuramazda's advocate. I say that just as there's only one king at Persepolis, there can be only one god. Why should he tolerate more? He'll destroy them, then there'll be only one. Show me my error, Latro, if you can."

"Highness, if you were truly a magus—I mean a priest of this Ahuramazda—I don't think you'd speak like that. You'd say there can't be a single god, but that just as there are two kings in Rope, there must be two gods also."

The regent held out his cup, and Tisamenus poured him more wine. "Why do you say that, sir?"

"I don't say it, but I think the magi would. They would reason thus: There's good in the world, so there's a good god, a wise lord. But there's evil too, so there must be an evil lord as well. In fact, one posits the other. There can be no good without evil, no evil without good."

The regent remarked, "Here we know that good and evil come from the same gods, having observed that the same man is good one time and evil another."

"Highness, a magus would say, Then I will call the good Ahuramazda and the bad Angra Manyu, evil mind. And if the good is truly good, won't it put the lie from it?"

The regent nodded. "Yet what you say doesn't explain Orith—the other gods. What of earth, fire, wind, and so forth?"

Tisamenus nodded, leaning toward me to listen.

I said, "Now I can speak for myself as well as for the magi. It doesn't seem to me that there can't be good without evil or evil without good. For a blind man, isn't it always night? With no day? It seemed to me that if Ahuramazda—"

A shieldman of the bodyguard entered as I spoke; when I fell silent, he addressed the regent. "The captain has arrived, Highness."

"Then he must wait. Go on, Latro."

"If Ahuramazda exists, Highness, all things serve him. The oak is his; so is the mouse that gnaws its root. Without oaks there could be no mice, without mice no cats, and without cats no oaks. But shouldn't he have servants greater than oaks and men? Surely he must, because the gap between Ahuramazda and men and oaks is very wide, and we see that every king has some minister whose authority's only slightly less than his own, and that such men have ministers of their own, similarly empowered. Besides, the existence of the sun, the moon, the earth, and of fire and water are indisputable facts.''

"But the existence of Ahuramazda is not an indisputable fact. Finish your wine.''

I did so. "Highness, let us think of a great city like Susa. Within the city stands a palace as great again. A beggar boy squats outside the palace wall, and I'm that poor boy.''

"Is Ahuramazda the king in that palace?''

I shook my head. "No, Highness. Not so far as I, Latro the beggar boy, have seen. The servants are the lords of the palace. Once a cook gave me meat, and a scullion, bread. I've even seen the steward, Highness, with my own eyes. The steward's a very great lord indeed, Highness.''

The regent rose. Tisamenus stood at once, and so did I.

"So he is, to a beggar boy,'' the regent said, "though not to himself, perhaps. We'll speak of this again when you've returned from Sestos. Do you want to see your ship?''

I nodded. "Even if it's the one we came in, I'd like to see it, Highness. I've forgotten it, but Io says we came by ship.''

"It's one of those that brought us here,'' he told me as we stepped from the scented air of the tent into night air that was sweeter still. "But not the one in which you and Io sailed with me. I'm taking that back to Olympia. One of the others is going to carry you and Pasicrates to Sestos.''

The shieldman and another man were waiting outside. The regent said, "You're Captain Nepos?''

The captain stepped foward, bowing low. "The same.'' His hair gleamed like foam in the moonlight.

"You understand your commission and accept it?''

"I'm to carry a hundred Rope Makers and two hundred and seventy slaves to Sestos. And a woman, who must have a cabin to herself.''

"And a slave girl,'' the regent told him. "With the slave you see before you.''

"We can occupy the same cabin," I said. "Or we can sleep on deck, if there's no cabin for us."

The captain shook his head. "Just about everybody will have to sleep on deck, and it'll be crowded at that."

The regent asked, "But your ship will hold them all, with their rations?"

"Yes, Highness, only not in much comfort."

"They don't require comfort. You know you won't be able to make port at Sestos? It's under siege, and the other ports of the Chersonese are still the Great King's."

The captain nodded. "I'll land them on this side, from boats. That'll be the safest way."

"Good. Come with us, then. I've promised Latro the sight of your ship, and you'll have to point it out to him." The regent looked about for Tisamenus, but he was gone. The shieldman offered to search for him, but the regent shook his head. "You've got to allow these fellows some freedom, if you want to hang on to them." As we began our walk, he added to me, "He wanted to spare his legs, I suppose. We had to make him a citizen to get his help at Clay, but he's no Rope Maker, just the same."

Though the moon was low and as crooked as my sword, it was a clear night with many stars. We climbed a cliff above the town that gave us a fine view of the little harbor. "There's *Nausicaa*," her captain said proudly. "Nearest the mouth of the bay." His ship was only a darker shape upon the dark water; yet I wished I were on board already, for I feel there is nothing for me here.

The regent said, "You'll be anxious to get back, I imagine, Captain."

"Anxious to serve you, Highness, but—"

"Go." The regent waved a hand.

I thought we would return to the camp, but the regent remained where he was, and after a time I realized he was not looking at the ship, but at the sea, and at Sestos and the world beyond.

When he turned away at last, he said softly, "What if the beggar boy— Let's not call him Latro; his name is Pausanias.

What if Pausanias the beggar boy could become known to the king? You must help me, and I'll help you. I'll give you your freedom and much more.''

I said I did not think I could do anything, but I would be happy to do all I could.

"You can do a great deal, I think. You know the servants, Latro. Perhaps you can persuade them to allow me to enter the palace.''

He turned to go. The shieldman, who had followed us when we climbed the steep path up the cliff, came after us as silently as ever.

While we returned to the camp, I thought about what the regent had said and all the things I have written here. And I despaired of promoting so great and terrible an enterprise, though I could not say so when I parted from the regent. How is a man, even a prince and a regent, to enter a palace no man has seen? To befriend a monarch whose ministers are gods?

There is one more thing to tell, though I hesitate to write of it. A moment ago, as I was about to enter this tent Io and I share with Drakaina and Pasicrates, I heard the strange, sly voice of Tisamenus at my ear: *"Kill the man with the wooden foot!"* When I looked around for him, there was no one in sight.

I have no notion what this may mean, or who the man with the wooden foot may be. Perhaps it was some trick of the wind. Perhaps I am to be mad as well as clouded of memory, and this voice was a phantom of that all-obscuring mist.

# — CHAPTER XXXV —
## Ships Can Sail Dry Land

OUR ship is crossing the isthmus today. I have already read much in this scroll and found in it many things that puzzle me; perhaps I should write of our crossing before it becomes one puzzle more.

I woke with Io asleep beneath my arm and Drakaina awake on the other side. She says we coupled in the night, but I do not believe her. Though she is so lovely, her eyes are as hard as stones, and I would never have intercourse with a woman while a child slept with us. Nor do I believe a man could, without waking the child. Besides, though I cannot now recall the night before, I believe I could remember it when she first spoke, and that I did not credit what she said, though she said also that I had drunk too much wine.

True or not, I rose and dressed; so did she. Io woke too, grumbling because she had no chance to wash her little peplos while we were at sea and had none now, though we rode at anchor.

Our ship is larger than most of the others I saw in the harbor this morning. Io says we waited all yesterday for our turn at the slipway, but it is hard without a bribe for the slipmaster. This morning the young man who sleeps in our cabin roused his hundred (they sleep on the deck with their slaves and the sailors, and it was their feet that woke me) and had them rowed to the city. Io said we watched the ships yesterday, and the oxen draw them along the slip much more slowly than a man walks—that is true, as I see now—and

263

thus we could go into the city, too. If *Nausicaa* were taken on the slip, we could soon catch up to her.

"We've been here before, Latro," she told me. "This is the place where the soldiers came from who took us away from the Rope Makers' slaves. You won't find that in your book, because I had it then. See that hill? Up there's where they kept us till Hypereides came and they gave us to him. Pindaros and Hilaeira and the black man were with us, and I'll never forget how it was when they struck off our fetters— Hypereides told them to, after he'd talked to us—and they led us out into the sunshine. You can see the whole city from up there, and it's really beautiful. Do you want to see it? I'd like to look at the place where they kept us."

Drakaina said, "Yes, let's go. Perhaps they'll keep you again. But will the guards let us go up?"

Io nodded. "They let anybody go. There's a temple at the top to Kalleos's goddess, and some other temples and things."

The city is full of people, all hurrying to someplace else. Many are slaves and workmen with no clothes but their caps; but many are wealthy too, with gold rings and jeweled chains and perfumed hair. Men are carried about the city in litters. Drakaina says that in Thought only women and sick men use them, and this place is much more like the east, where she comes from. The truly rich have their own litters and dress four or six slaves alike to carry them. Those who merely wish to be thought rich hire litters, with two bearers or four.

"If we had the money," Drakaina said, "we could hire two litters ourselves, so we wouldn't have to climb all those steps. You and Io in one and I in the other." (I believe she had at first planned to suggest that Io ride with her but seeing the expression on the child's face knew it to be useless.)

"You've got money," Io told her. "The regent gave it to you, that's what you said, and you paid the boatman. So go ahead and hire yourself a litter, and Latro and I will walk."

I nodded, and in truth I wanted to stretch my legs, which feel as though they have not had much exercise lately.

Drakaina said, "Not enough. But we could sell something."

Io looked at her askance. "What? Sell one of those rings? I never thought they were real gold."

"Not my rings. But we've other commodities, if only we can find the right buyer."

A soldier tried to shoulder past us, and she caught him by the arm.

"Not now," he said, and then when he had seen how lovely she is, "Call on me tonight. You'll find me generous. I'm Hippagretas, Lochagos of the City Guard. Across from the Market Temple of the Stone God, and two doors north."

"I'm not from Tower Hill," Drakaina told him. "Not that I'd mind having a lover so distinguished and handsome. I only wished to ask you who commands the army of this city."

"Corustas is our strategist."

"And where can we find him? Will you guide us?"

"In the citadel, of course. But no." He shook his head, tossing the purple plumes of his helmet. "Much as I'd like to, I have important affairs."

I smiled to hear that even the soldiers of this town hurried about like merchants.

Drakaina smiled too. "Might Corustas not reward an officer who brought him people with information?"

The lochagos stared at her for a moment. "You have a message for the strategist?"

"I have information, which I will give him only in person. But I suppose I may tell you that we have just disembarked from the ship carrying the aide to the regent of Rope."

Soon Drakaina and Hippagretas were in one big litter and Io and I in another, each litter carried on the shoulders of four bearers. "You and the black man had to carry Kalleos like this," Io told me. "But there were only the two of you, and I bet Kalleos is as heavy as you and me together."

I asked whether we had to climb so steep a slope, and she shook her head. "It was uphill, but not nearly as bad as this. I was following you, and you didn't know it." She giggled. "I'd watch the litter and wonder which of you would give up first, but neither of you did."

I told her no man likes to admit he's weaker than another.

"A lot of women do—that's one reason why so many of

us like men better, besides their being easier to fool. Look there, you can see the water already. And there's the slipway. Thirty-six stades from the gulf to the Sea of Saros. That's what the man we talked to yesterday said.''

I asked her whether Drakaina had been with us.

She shook her head. "She stayed on board, because Pasicrates was there, if you ask me. We went with the captain, and they seemed happy enough to see us go.''

I scarcely heard her. With the few steps since she had mentioned the water, the bearers had turned a corner and ascended a bit more; and the bright patch of water Io had pointed out had grown to an azure sea, as a child grows who is a woman as soon as your attention is distracted for a moment, at once restless and restful, alluring and dangerous. And it struck me then that the sea was the world, and everything else—the city, the towering crag of limestone, the very ships that floated upon it and the fish that swam in it—was only exceptional, only oddities like the bits of leaf or straw one sees in a globe of amber.

I was myself a mariner on that sea, a sailor at the mercy of wind and wave, lost in the mists and hearing breakers on the reefs of a rocky coast.

"This is it,'' Io said as the bearers lowered our litter before a frowning building. "This is where they kept us, Latro, in a cellar down a lot of steps.'' Drakaina and the lochagos were out of their litter already.

The interior seemed a cavern after the heat and brilliant sun outside. I understood then why so many gods and goddesses are said to live under the earth or among the everlasting snows of the mountaintops; no doubt we would do the same if only we were not bound to our fields for sustenance.

Corustas proved to be a beefy man in a cuirass of boiled leather molded with lions' heads. The snarling faces woke some faint fear in me, and I seemed for an instant to see a lion rear and threaten a mob in rags with its claws and fangs.

"You were on the ship with the young Rope Makers?'' Corustas said. "I take it you are not Rope Makers yourselves.''

Drakaina shook her head. "I am from the east. The man—who will be able to tell you little or nothing, by the way—is a barbarian, and neither he nor I can tell you his tribe. The child is from Hill."

"And your information?"

"And your price?"

"That must be determined when I have heard you. If it will save our city"—he smiled—"ten talents, perhaps. Otherwise much less."

Drakaina said, "Your city's in no immediate danger, as far as I know."

"Fine. You'd be surprised how often people come here to warn me of oracles and the like." He took out a silver owl and held it in his palm. "Now tell me what you've come to say, and we'll see if it's worth this. My time's not unlimited."

"It concerns an oracle," Drakaina said. "A dream in which the regent places complete trust." She extended her own hand.

"And it concerns my city?"

"Not directly. It may eventually."

Corustas leaned back. His chair was of ivory, inset with garnets and topazes. "Your ship is the *Nausicaa*, out of Aegae, bound for Hundred-Eyed. A hundred young Rope Makers are aboard, sent by the regent to offer praise at the temple of the Heavenly Queen in fulfillment of some vow."

Io smiled behind her hand, and Drakaina said, "You've been questioning the sailors. That was what they were told."

"And the young Rope Makers," Corustas added. When Drakaina said nothing, he muttered, "When we could," and dropped the owl into her hand.

"The hundred men are not bound for Hundred-Eyed, nor for any other place on Redface Island. Nor are they being sent in fulfillment of a vow, nor for any other sacred purpose."

"I know that, naturally," Corustas said, gauging Drakaina with his eyes. "They wore full armor when they went to threaten our slipmaster today. The Argives aren't fools enough to let a hundred armed Rope Makers through their gates." He took out another owl.

Drakaina shook her head. "Ten."

"Absurd!"

"But for nothing I will tell you they are picked men, taking their instructions directly from the regent."

"I knew that as soon as young Hippagretas told me you had said the regent's aide was aboard."

I asked whether *Nausicaa* would be taken on the slip today. "Ah!" Corustas winked. "You can talk after all. But you know nothing about all this."

"No," I said. "Nothing."

"You think a woman can get more and is less likely to be tortured. You're wrong on both counts. To answer your question, whether the ship crosses the isthmus today or never depends on the message I send our slipmaster. That in turn depends on what we say here." He looked back to Drakaina. "Five owls for the true destination."

"One word only."

"Agreed, but no tricks."

"Sestos."

For a moment I thought the strategist had fallen asleep. His eyes closed and his chin dropped to his chest. Then he opened his eyes again and straightened up.

"Yes, isn't it?" Drakaina said.

"And a dream told him to do it?"

Drakaina rose, knotting the six silver owls into her robe. "We really should go. The child wants to see your city from the summit."

"One more for the dream."

"Come, Io. Latro."

"Three."

Drakaina did not sit down again. "The dream—"

"Who was it? The Huntress?"

"The Queen Below. Had it been the Huntress, I wouldn't be telling you these things. She promised him that the fortress would fall soon after the young men arrived, and the regent believes her implicitly. Now you know all I do."

As Corustas counted out three more owls, he asked, "Why the Queen Below? It should have been the Warrior, or perhaps even the Sun."

Drakaina smiled. "A strategist, and you've never seen the fall of a city? Believe me, there's little enough drill or light then, but a great deal of death."

Outside, she asked the bearers whether the lochagos had paid them, and when they said he had, ordered them to carry us to the temple at the summit. They protested that they had been paid only to bring us up from the city and return us to the place where they had found us. Drakaina said, "Don't trouble me with your impudence. We've been conferring with Strategist Corustas, and if you won't earn your money like honest men, he'll have you whipped in the market-place." After that they did as she told them.

The temple was small but every bit as lovely as it had looked from below, with slender marble pillars and elaborate capitals; its pediment showed a youth offering an apple to three maids.

When the bearers were out of earshot, Io whispered, "You didn't tell him about Latro. I thought you were going to."

"Certainly not. Suppose Corustas had decided to keep him here? Do you think the regent wouldn't have guessed someone talked? And that it was you or me? Now have a look at the view; I told Corustas you were going to."

Io did and so did I, feeling the sea breeze would never be so pure again as it was today, nor the sun so bright. The white city of Tower Hill spread in two terraces below us. Its gulf, stretching away to the west like a great blue road, promised all the untouched riches of the thinly peopled western lands, and I felt a sudden longing to go there.

"By all the Twelve, that's *Nausicaa!*" Io exclaimed. "See, Latro? Not on the skid, but waiting to get on. Notice her cutter bow?"

Drakaina smiled. "Quite the little sailor."

"The kybernetes taught me when we sailed with Hypereides. And I talk to our sailors too, instead of holding my nose in the air."

A jeweled and scented woman with golden bells in her hair passed us, jingling as she turned her head to smile at Drakaina; she carried two live hares by the ears.

# — CHAPTER XXXVI —

## To Reach the Hot Gates

A ship can follow either of two courses, as our captain explained. He is a white-haired old man, fat, and stiff in all his joints, but very knowing of the sea. When he saw I did not understand, he sat on a coil of rope and drew the coast on the deck for me with a bit of chalk.

"Here's the skid where we went across." He drew as he spoke. "And here's Water and Peace."

Io asked, "Does that name* really mean 'peace'? That's what Latro says. It seems like there's been so much fighting there."

The captain looked far away, out over the dancing waves. "Because in the old times it was agreed with the Crimson Men there'd be no raiding on the island. In the old times—my grandfather's times—everybody took what he could, and there was no shame to it. A ship came to a city, and if her skipper thought his crew could take it, he tried. If you met a ship that could beat yours, you ran, and if you didn't run fast enough, you lost it. A man knew where he stood. Now maybe it's peace, and maybe it's war, and you don't know and neither does he. Last year the Crimson Men were the best in the Great King's navy. I mean the best sailors—the Riverlanders were the best sea fighters. And the Crimson Men would have fought on Peace if they could have landed. The old promises don't count, and the new aren't lived up to.

---

*Salamis* (Gk. Σαλαμίς). Latro translates the Phoenician root. —G. W.

"Kings used to look for places where both wanted the same. Then they'd make an honest bargain and keep it, and if they didn't, they'd be disgraced, and punished by the gods, and their people too. Now it's all trying to get the advantage by tricks. What's the use of a bargain, when the other man's not going to keep it as soon as he sees it's a trick?"

Io pointed. "Thought must be right about here."

"That's Tieup. Thought's up here on the hill. I don't go there much any more. We're way past all that anyhow. Here's where we are." He continued the coast to the north, then made a long mark beside it. "That's Goodcattle Island, a great place for sheep. With a regular crew, we'd be going wide of it; there's a narrow channel, and the wind's from the north, mostly. But with all these stout lads to pull the sweeps, there's no reason to, as the noble Pasicrates says. We'll spend the night at the Hot Gates, and he can make his sacrifice. There's nothing like a fair wind, but the ash wind blows whichever way you want."

By "the ash wind" he meant the sweeps, long oars that one or two pull standing up. There are twenty on each side, and I took my turn at one with the men of Rope. It is hard work, and it blisters the hands; but it is made easier by singing, and it strengthens the whole body. My head cannot remember for long, but my arms, back, and legs do not forget. They told me they had been wasting in idleness and desired to strive with the blue giant; so I did, and laughed to see men (who so often make poor beasts serve their will) rowing the bawling bullock tied to our mainmast across the sea.

None of these things are of much importance, perhaps, but they are the first I remember; thus I write them, having waked from my dream.

Only eighty could be used at the sweeps, and we have more than four hundred, with Pasicrates and myself and the crew, a number that let all of us rest far longer than we rowed. When the sun was halfway to the hills on our left, a wind rose behind us. The crew hoisted both sails, and we ported our sweeps.

Pasicrates proposed wrestling matches, there not being room enough on the deck for any sport but wrestling or boxing. A lovely woman called Drakaina came to watch, taking a place close beside me. She has a purple gown and many jewels, and the Rope Makers moved aside for her very readily; she must be a person of importance.

Sniffing the wind, she said, "I smell the river—that air has crocodiles in it. Do you know what they are, Latro?"

I told her I did and described them.

"But you do not remember where you saw them?"

I shook my head.

"Are you going to wrestle, when your turn comes? Throw the other man over the railing for me."

It was something the victors often did to show their strength. Our ship trailed a rope, and the loser swam to it and climbed back on board, many saying the cool plunge was so pleasant after the heat of the deck that it was better to lose than to win. I promised Drakaina I would if I could.

"You're a good wrestler—I've seen you. You nearly defeated Basias, and I think you could have if you had wished."

I asked, "Is Basias here?" because I did not know the names of most of the men from Rope and thought I might wrestle him again.

She shook her lovely head. "He has gone to the Receiver of Many."

Hearing that, I feared I was defiled by his blood, for I know something is not well with me. "Was it I who killed him?"

"No," she told me. "I did."

Then it was my turn to wrestle.

Pasicrates had matched me against himself. He is very quick; but I am a little stronger, I think, and I felt I was going to win the first fall; but just as I was about to throw him to the deck, he slipped from under my arm so that I was left like a man who tries to break an unbarred door.

The railing caught me at the hip, and Pasicrates got my right leg behind the knee and tossed me over.

How cold the water was, and how good it smelled! It

seemed to me that I should not be able to breathe it as I did; but though it was much colder than air, it was richer too and strengthened me as wine does.

When I opened my eyes, it was as though I were suspended in the sky like the sun; the blue water was all about me, a darker blue above, a paler, brighter blue below, where a great brown snail with a mossy shell crawled and trailed a thread of slime.

"Welcome," said a voice above me, and I looked up to see a girl not much older than Io. Her hair was darker than Drakaina's gown—so dark it was nearly black. Almost it seemed a cloud or aureole, and not such hair as men and women have.

I tried to speak, but water filled my mouth and no sound came, only bubbles that fell to the pale ground and vanished.

"I am Thoe, daughter of Nereus," the girl told me. "I have forty-nine sisters, all older than myself. We are permitted to show ourselves to those who are soon to die."

She must have seen the fear in my eyes, because she laughed; I knew then that she had said what she had for the pleasure of frightening me. Her teeth were small and very sharp. "No, you are not really going to drown." She took my hand. "Do you feel you are suffocating?"

I shook my head.

"You see, you cannot, as long as you are with me. But when I leave, you'll have to go down there again, unless you want to die. It's just that mortal men aren't supposed to see us too often, because they might guess at things they're not to know; mortal women hardly ever see us, because they know when they do. We can show ourselves to children as often as we like, though, because they forget the way you do."

She wriggled off through the water like a serpent, waving for me to follow. I shouted but produced only a rush of water from my mouth.

"Europa told me about you. She's rather a friend of mine, except that she's too fond of herself because she used to lie with the Descender. Sometimes Father shows himself to sailors before storms, if he thinks the storm will kill them all. Do you know about that?''

Thoe glanced over her shoulder to observe my answer, and I shook my head.

''Then the sailors say, 'Look! It's the old sea man!' and they take in their sail and put out a sea anchor, and sometimes they live. It's good of him to warn them like that, don't you think?''

I nodded. We were swimming up and up, circling as a hawk soars on a rising wind. The brown slug looked very small now, but I saw men's legs kicking all around it.

''And sometimes my sisters and I show ourselves to ships about to strike a reef. We call warnings, but our voices are high when we're out of water, and the sailors tell each other we're singing to lure them to their deaths.''

From what she had said, I guessed why I had been unable to speak. Pitching my voice high as I could, I said that was unjust of them.

She laughed at my croaking. ''But sometimes we *do*. You see, sometimes the ships aren't wrecked, and so we try to call them back so we won't get in trouble. We comb each other's hair then and admire our beauty like mortal women. It usually brings them. We aren't cheating, because we lie, sometimes, with them, if any live through the wreck. We do it before they get too weak and thirsty. Except for me, because I'm the youngest. This will be my first time.''

Until she said that, it had seemed to me I had been flung into another world from which I might never return; and I had been too dazed by the beauty and strangeness of it to try. Now I understood that if only I could reach the air below, I would again be with Drakaina and the men wrestling on the deck. I gestured to show what I meant to do, and Thoe caught me by the hair.

''You need not fear,'' she said. ''We bear your children beneath the sea, so they drown.'' When she saw my horror she said, ''Kiss me at least before you go, so that I will not be shamed before my sisters.''

Slender and cold, her arms wrapped my neck. When her

lips brushed mine, it seemed to me that I had been fevered all my life, and that I wanted nothing more than to cool myself forever in the icy billows of northern seas, where snow drifts from the sky to the waves like the feathers of white geese.

My head broke the surface. I shook sea water from my hair, and when I opened my mouth to gasp for breath, more water vomited from it, as water is spewed from a face of stone in a fountain. This water was bitter with salt; it ran from my nostrils too and stung them.

A wave broke over my head as I spluttered and gasped for air. I could not remember whether I could swim well or not—surely I could not swim as Thoe had—but I felt Pasicrates would not have thrown me over the railing unless he had known I could; and before I had finished those thoughts I was swimming, though I could not have said where.

It was nearly dark, and as I swam, lifted by the waves and cast down again, the stars came out one by one, shaping gods and beasts. I found the Great Bear, and from it, Polaris. The captain had said a north wind would be foul for us; thus we had been sailing north, with the mainland to the west and Goodcattle Island to the east. I kept Polaris at my right shoulder, hoping to find land or the ship.

Thoe leaped across the waves as though springing from rock to rock and stopped to stand upon a beach and laugh at me. When my foot touched the sand she vanished, and her laughter was only the lapping of the waves. For a long while I was too exhausted to do anything but lie sprawled like a corpse driven to shore.

It was thirst that made me rise. Mingled with the soft laughter of the waves, I heard the chuckle of a brook glad to have come at last to the sea and rest. I searched and found it, and drank deeply; and though I saw the red gleam of a fire far away and heard men's voices, I did not walk toward it until I had filled my stomach with water. (Not long ago I asked Drakaina what god it was who shaped the world. She said it had been made by Phanes, the four-winged and four-headed, who is male and female together. How cruel it was of Phanes to make the seas salt, and how many must have died because of it!)

The voices were those of the men from Rope. When I saw them, I could not help wondering whether Thoe had guided me to them, and I recalled our captain's saying Pasicrates meant to sacrifice at the Hot Gates. Stone columns stood there. Before them was an altar, with a driftwood fire on it. Pasicrates held the halter of the bullock; a rude garland circled its neck.

". . . and intercede for us, great Leonidas, intercede for us, all you heroes, when we must recount what befell the slave, Latro. For you know there was no true victory upon him, nor did he carry the favor of any god." This he spoke, and as he said "god," the sacred knife entered the bullock's neck to speed it to Leonidas.

Surely no one could have resisted such a moment. As I stepped into the firelight, I announced, "The gods say otherwise, Pasicrates."

Unable to recall my past, I cannot say whether it has held many such culminations, but I doubt it. To see these men, so hard, so strong, so prideful in their hardness and their strength, with their mouths gasping like children washed the last fatigue from me.

I said, "You were permitted to throw me so that I might speak with a certain Nereid. Thoe is her name. Now I have returned, ready to resume our match. When the others wrestled, it was for three falls—not one."

For an instant there was a hush so complete the crackling of the fire on the altar seemed the burning of a city. Far up the mountain they call Kallidromos, a lion roared. At the sound the men of Rope roared too, so many and so loud as to silence the waves and the grieving wind.

Before their shout died, Pasicrates and I were locked more tightly than any lovers. I knew his strength then, and he knew mine. He sought to lift me, but I held him too tightly, and slowly, slowly, I bent him back. I could have broken him then if I had wished, snapping his spine as a soldier mad for blood seizes his enemy's spear and breaks it; but I was not mad for blood, only for victory. I threw him to the ground instead.

Io rushed forward, laughing like a lark, with a jar of wine and a rag for my face. A Rope Maker did the same for Pasicrates. Another, perhaps a year or two older, asked, "What of the sacrifice? Surely this is sacrilege."

Pasicrates answered, "We give our might to Leonidas, just as might was offered to Patroklos. The winner will complete the sacrifice."

When we closed again, his strength was twice what it had been. For what seemed a whole night we strove together, but I could not throw him, nor could he throw me.

There came a moment when my face was to the fire, and he met my gaze. The lion roared again, nearer now, and loud as a war horn over the shouting of the men from Rope. Pasicrates stiffened. "There's a lion in your eyes," he gasped.

"And a boy in yours," I told him; and lifting him over my head, I carried him away from the altar until the waves licked at my ankles, and I cast him into the sea. The lion roared a third time. I have not heard it since.

# — CHAPTER XXXVII —

## Leonidas, Lion of Rope

"HEAR our prayer," I intoned, dressed again in the chiton Io had kept for me, crowned with a few wildflowers and girded with my belt of manhood. "Accept our homage!" Moved by I cannot say what spirit, I added, "We do not ask for victory, but for courage." With that I cast the bullock's fat and heart into the fire, and the men from Rope sang a marching song.

The sacrifice was complete. Half a dozen slaves fell upon the bullock and hewed it to bits with knives and hatchets. Soon everyone had a stick with a gobbet of meat at the end of it. There was wine too, barley bread, hard cheese, salt olives, raisins, and dried figs.

Io said, "This is the best meal we've had since we've been with these awful people, Latro. You're lucky you don't remember what we've been eating."

"This is good enough for me," I told her. I was so hungry I had to force myself to chew, so as not to choke on the meat.

"For me too. But don't ever, ever try their soup. We have, and if somebody was going to pour that soup down my throat I'd cut it first." She went to the carcass and got another bit of flesh to put on her stick. "This is as good as dining with Kalleos, and I don't know anything nicer you can say about a meal than that. If you want some more meat, though, you'd better get it. There isn't much left."

I shook my head. "I'll have something else. Meat alone upsets the digestion."

Io giggled. "And to think Drakaina's missing it."

"She is? Where is she?"

"Still on the ship." Io pointed toward the bay, where our ship rode at anchor in the moonlight. "Pasicrates thought the reason you never came up was that she'd put a spell on you. Or anyway, that's what he *said* he thought. If you ask me he was looking for somebody to blame, and he picked the right party. So she's back there with her hands tied behind her and a clout over her mouth so she can't work any more magic."

"I must speak to him about that," I told her.

With what remained of my loaf in my hand, I went to the fire at which he sat and seated myself beside him, saying, "Greetings, most noble Pasicrates."

"Ah," he said. "The victor. Yet a slave. Still a slave. I should not have demeaned myself, and the gods have punished me for it."

"As you say. You are our commander, the master of our ship and all on board. But if I'm a slave, I no longer recall whose. Your servant—I will not say your slave—has come to beg you to release the woman called Drakaina. She's done me no harm today. Has she harmed you?"

"No," he said. "We'll free her in the morning."

"Then let me swim to the ship, and I'll tell the watch you've ordered her freed."

He looked at me quizzically. "You'd swim there yourself, if I permitted it?"

"Certainly."

"Then you won't have to." He turned to one of his companions. "Take the boat and a couple of seamen, and tell them to free the woman. Bring her back with you."

The man nodded, rose, and vanished into the night.

"As for you, Latro, I want you to come with me. Do you know what this place is?"

I said, "They call it the Hot Gates, but I don't know why. Since we sacrificed to Leonidas, I suppose he's a hero and that he's buried here."

"He was," Pasicrates told me. "Our people dug up his body—what they could find of it—and sent it back to Rope.

It had been hacked to bits." He spat. "The Great King paraded Leonidas's head on a spear."

As we walked on, I asked him what it was I smelled. It was like the stench of a bad egg, but so strong it overpowered even the tang of the sea.

"The springs. They boil out of the ground, not pure and cold like other springs, but steaming and reeking, sickening to drink and yet a cure for many ills. Or so I've been told. This is my first visit to this place, but they say in Rope that's why it's called the Hot Gates—it's the way to those boiling springs."

"Is that where we're going?" I asked him.

"No, only to the ruined wall. My men and I went to look at it by daylight, before you came out of the sea. Now I want to show it to you, and tell you what happened here. You'll forget, but I've begun to think that's because you're the ear of the gods; they hear, instead of you, or they take the memory of what you've heard from you. This is something the gods should know."

"There it is." I pointed. "Where that man sits combing his hair." I could see him plainly in the moonlight, naked and muscular, plowing his long dark locks with a comb of pale shell.

"You see a man dressing his hair?"

"Yes," I said. "And another—now he throws a discus. But this can't be the wall you're looking for. It isn't ruined."

Pasicrates told me, "Those must be ghosts you see. Here Leonidas and his Rope Makers exercised their bodies before the battle and readied them for burial. You and I are alone, and the wall lies in ruins before us. The Great King destroyed it so his host could pass."

I said, "Then Leonidas was killed, and the army of your city destroyed."

"He had no army, only three hundred Rope Makers, a few thousand slaves—he was the first to arm them—and a thousand or so unreliable allies. But the judges had instructed him to hold this road around Kallidromos, and he held it for three days against the Great King's host, until he and every man who'd stayed with him were dead. The Great King counted three millions all told, about half of them real fighting men and the rest mule drivers and the like.''

"Surely that's impossible," I said. "Such a small force could never defend this place against so many."

"So the Great King thought." Pasicrates turned suddenly to face me. "That was a tear, I think, that struck my hand. You're no Rope Maker, Latro. Why do you weep?"

"Because I must have seen this battle," I said. "I must have taken part in it. And I have forgotten it."

There was a narrow gate in the wall, and as I spoke it opened and a gray-bearded man in armor came out. As he drew nearer, I saw he had only one eye. I described him to Pasicrates and asked whether it was Leonidas.

"No. It must be Leonidas's mantis, Megistias, who spoke the tongues of all the beasts." Pasicrates's voice was calm, but it was the calm of one who uses all his will to hold his fear in check.

In a moment Megistias stood before us. His face was pale and set, his single eye fierce in the moonlight, the eye of an old falcon half-blind. He muttered something I did not understand and passed his hand before my face.

Then he was gone. I stood in the front rank with other men, men armed as I was with two javelins, a helmet, back and breast plates, and a rectangular shield.

Turning to face the hundred, I shouted, "While the Immortals are gone, we could have no higher honor than to be the protectors of the Universal King, the King of the World's Four Quarters, the King of the Lands, the King of Parsa, the King of Media, the King of Sumer, the King of Akkad, the King of Babylon, and the King of Riverland. Let us treasure that honor and be worthy of it.'' Yet I paid little heed to the sense of what I myself had said; it had been in my own tongue, and knowing that my comrades understood it made its cadences more lovely to me than any music.

When I turned again, I saw why I had spoken. A knot of men was breaking from the melee, cleaving a path through the levies driven forward by their officers' whips; but there was small cause for fear: they were no more than thirty at most.

At my command, we cast the first javelin together, then the second. Our javelins were not like the light arrows of the archers; they had weight as well as speed, and they transfixed the hoplons of our enemies and pierced their corselets. Half a dozen fell at the first cast, more at the second, when every man drew his sword.

Another command; we locked shields and charged, the slope of the ground being with us. *"Cassius!"*

The man who opposed me was taller than I, his helmet high-crested and his battered armor traced with gold. He thrust for my eyes; but his own blazed not at me but at the Great King, who sat his throne on the hill behind us. I was only an obstacle that barred his way for a moment, then would bar it no more. I wanted to shout that I was no less a man than himself, my honor and my life as precious to me as his to him. But neither of us had time or breath for shouting.

I swung my falcata with all my strength, and the downward cut bit deep in the rim of his hoplon. Its bronze gripped the blade and held it, conquered in its conquest; a twist of his arm wrenched the falcata from my hand.

Disarmed, I barred his way still, blocking each thrust with my shield, giving way one bitter step at a time. The man on his right died, and the man on his left. I fell, tripped by what I cannot say. He rushed by me, but I slipped my shield arm from the leather loop and still half-recumbent hurled my shield at his back.

Except that it was not my shield, only the cloak in which I slept. I sat up and rubbed my eyes, my ears still ringing with the din of battle. The bodies of the slain drank their own blood, becoming only sleepers, living men who breathed and sometimes stirred. Leonidas was but the dying fire. I rose and saw the army of the Great King, proud horseman and cringing conscript, melt into the slopes of Kallidromos.

I could not sleep again, nor did I wish to. I built up the fire and spoke for a while with Drakaina, who was also awake. She says Falcata is the name I give my sword and not its kind, and that it is a kopis.

Then, recalling the map drawn by the captain of our ship and the way I had wrestled on the deck with Pasicrates, I wrote of those things here, and of Thoe the Nereid, my dream, and all the rest. Now Io has risen too, and she has read the writing on the columns to me. There are three. The first:

> "Redface Isle, four thousand bred;
> Three million scorned, till all were dead."

The second:

> "The wizard Megistias's tomb you view,
> Who slew the foe from Spercheius's ford.
> This greatest seer his death foreknew,
> Yet sooner died than leave his lord."

The third:

> "Speak to the Silent City,
> Saying that in her cause,
> We begged no tyrant's pity,
> And fell obedient to her laws."

A sailor who heard Io read said these verses, which Io and I agreed in thinking very fine, were put here by an old man called Simonides; but he does not know him personally.

# — CHAPTER XXXVIII —
## Wet Weather to Sestos

W<small>AVES</small> broke over the bow all day, while the wild wind the sailors call the Hellesponter laid the ship on her beam ends. If it truly blew from that part of the world, we could have done nothing, as the captain told me, for it would have come across our bow with the waves. It did not, but in fact blew out of those northern lands that are said to be rendered uninhabitable by bees. Thus, by pulling the sail to starboard as far as we could, we plunged across the pounding sea as if our fat, rolling *Nausicaa* were a racing chariot, passing the island the sailors call Boat a little after dawn.

If it is a boat, it is a burning boat; for it is here, they say, that the Smith God has his workshop, and the sail of Boat is in fact the smoke that rises from his forge. They say too that this god once built a metal man to guard the Island of Liars, but his wonderful creation was destroyed by the crew of a ship from Hundred-Eyed.

Save for the captain, a few sailors, and myself, everyone fell prey to the sea disease. The captain assured me it was not serious and would cure itself as soon as the sea was calmer, it being no more than a sleight of the Sea God's to preserve the rations of good ships by ensuring that their greedy passengers eat no more and offer all they have already consumed to him.

Whether that is true or otherwise, this sea disease affected all the Rope Makers, as well as Io, the Lady Drakaina, and many of the crew. With so few able to work, everyone was needed. I joined the sailors who could still keep the ship, sometimes helping with a steering oar, sometimes heaving at a line to trim a sail, sometimes climbing the mainmast (this was difficult because it was so wet) to take in sail or let it out. All this while *Nausicaa* bucked like Pegasus or wallowed like a boar, making what would otherwise have been mere drudgery into a great contention with the sea. I thought then how happy a sailor's life must be and wished I might join the crew and live as they did; but I said nothing to the captain.

Once indeed it seemed the sea played too roughly with me. I was standing on the rail trying to clear the foreyard arm, which had fouled one of its halyards, when I felt the ship drop from under me and I was cast into the water; but a wave lifted me at once and tossed me onto the deck a little aft of the mainmast. By good luck I landed on my feet, and the crew has treated me with considerable respect ever since. However, I feared the same thing might happen again, and that the sea, seeing me grown proud, would drop me on my head or my buttocks; thus I took care to be as humble toward everyone as I could, to praise the wild majesty of the sea whenever we had time to talk, and to offer a coin I found tied into a corner of this chiton—it is my oldest, which Io suggested I wear because of the bad weather—to the Sea God.

Just after the sun had reached its zenith, the waning wind brought rain. The captain came to talk with me, and I happened to mention the coin, saying that though it had been but copper and small, the Sea God must have accepted it.

He agreed and told me the story (which I set down here as a caution for myself in future days) of King Polycrates, who was so lucky he conquered any place he wished and defeated every army sent against him. Besides all this, he was an ally of the King of Riverland, who was in those times the most powerful monarch in the world, and a great friend of his as well; and at last the King of Riverland grew concerned, saying, "Polycrates, my friend, the gods never raise a man high but to cast him down, as boys carry jars up a tower so they can throw them from the top. Some bad luck is bound to befall you. Of all your possessions, which is most precious to you?"

"This emerald ring," answered Polycrates. "It came to me from my father, and because it looks so fine, all the people of my island counted me as a great man from the moment I put it on. At their request I took charge of their affairs, and I have ruled ever since with the success and good fortune you know."

"Then throw it into the sea to appease the gods," the King of Riverland counseled him. "Perhaps if you do, they will permit you a serene old age."

Polycrates thought about this advice as he was returning from Riverland, slipped off his ring, and hurled it into the waves with a prayer. When he reached home, his people held a great celebration in his honor and brought him many gifts, the loot of the cities he had burned and the ships he had captured, one bringing a rich armor, another a necklace of gold and hyacinth, a third a cloak of byssus, and so on. Last of all came a poor fisherman. "Majesty," he said, "I have nothing to offer you but this fish, the finest I caught today; but I beg you to accept it in the spirit in which it comes to you."

"I will," Polycrates said graciously. "Tonight you and I shall dine together in my royal hall, old man, and you shall see your fish upon my table."

At this the old fisherman was overjoyed. He stepped to one side, took out his knife, and opened the fish to clean it for the king's cooks. But no sooner had he slit its belly than a beautiful emerald ring dropped from it and rolled to lie at Polycrates's feet.

At this all the people cheered, thinking it showed what a favorite of the gods their king was. But Polycrates wept, knowing his sacrifice had been rejected. He was soon proved right, for he was lured to his death by one of the satraps of the Great King, who at that time had not yet conquered Riverland and considered every friend of its king his enemy.

Though the wind grew less it did not die, and before night came we saw the dark loom of the land through the falling rain. All the men from Rope whooped for joy and insisted on landing at once. The captain was very willing we should, for there is no port on this side of the land, and thus it is a hazardous spot for ships. But while the boat was being made ready, he tried to buy me from Pasicrates, offering four minas, then five, and at last six, though he said he would have to have a year in which to pay the final two. "You'll waste him ashore," he said. "He's the best sailor I've ever seen and a favorite of the gods to boot."

"I can't sell him for any price," Pasicrates answered. "He's the regent's, not mine. Perhaps you're fortunate at that—a favorite of the gods is a dangerous man."

Thus we landed in the rain, with all the men from Rope rejoicing at one moment to be off the ship and swearing at the next while they tried to keep their armor and their rations dry. I had expected to see a city, but there was only a camp of tents and huts, with ships drawn up on the beach. Io knew nothing of Sestos; so I asked Drakaina, who told me the city was a hundred stades inland. She liked the rain no better than the Rope Makers did, but she looked so lovely with her wet gown clinging and her eyes ringed with starry drops that the men from Rope ceased to complain whenever she was in their sight, throwing out their chests instead and pretending no weather could ever trouble them.

Pasicrates, however, stood upon a great rock and studied the sea. I saw the worry in his face and asked him what the matter was when he came down. "This rain signals the end of the sailing season," he said. "Soon the leaves will turn, and there will be storms worse than the one this morning. It will be hard to get supplies, and to return home when the city falls." He gave me a crooked smile and added, "You must hurry." I was not sure what he meant, but Io says I am to take the city for the regent of Rope, though no one knows how.

Our march to Sestos was long and cold. The Rope Makers wrapped themselves in their scarlet cloaks, and Drakaina hired two sailors to make a litter covered with sailcloth for her. I sheltered Io and myself under my cloak as well as I could, and I think that because there were two of us, we were warmer than all the rest.

"How big you're getting," I told her. "When I think of you it's always as someone much smaller, but your head comes to my ribs."

"Children my age grow fast," she told me. "Then too, traveling with you I've had sunshine and plenty of exercise, which most girls don't get. Good food too, while we were with Hypereides and Kalleos. Kalleos gave you this cloak, master, so you could wear your sword on the streets at night and not be stopped by the archers. I know you don't remember, but it was the night Eurykles bet he could raise a ghost."

"Who's Eurykles?" I asked her.

"A man we used to know. A magician. He's gone now, and I don't think he'll ever come back. Kalleos will miss him, I suppose. Do you still have your book?"

"Yes, I put it in my pack. I've got your clothes and your doll too."

"My doll's broken." She shrugged. "I like keeping it, though. Are you sure all that isn't too heavy for you? I could carry my own things. I'm your slave, after all."

"No. I could carry this pack a long way, and I suppose I'll have to. I doubt that it's any heavier than the loads the Rope Makers are carrying, with their helmets and spears, their armor and their big hoplons."

"But they have their own slaves to carry their tents and rations and the other things," Io pointed out. "When we were on Redface Island, they made their slaves carry everything except their swords. I don't understand why they don't do that here. Do you think they're afraid the slaves would slip in the mud if they had to carry so much?"

"They would only beat them," I told her. "This is the Empire, and they know we might be charged by the Great King's cavalry."

Io turned her dripping face to stare at mine. "How do you know that, master? Are you starting to remember?"

"No. I know those things, but I don't know how I learned them."

"Then you have to write all this down when we get to Sestos. Everything you remember from today, because I may not always be with you. And master, I heard the captain trying to buy you. Write that you're not a slave, even if—''

"I know," I told her. "But I wanted us to stay on the ship, if we could. A merchant ship visits many ports, and there are men in them from many others."

"So maybe you could find your home. I understand."

"Besides, I like the work, though not the idea of deserting my patron."

Io lifted a finger to her lips.

We still have not seen the walls. Darkness came long before we reached this place and pitched our tents. Pasicrates, Io, and I will sleep in this one, with Pasicrates's slaves. Drakaina shares a tent with two Rope Makers, I think so that neither can molest her.

We had beans, onions, and twice-baked bread tonight, and it seemed very little after so long a march through the rain, though there is still some wine. The Rope Makers joked about going to Sestos for more food, and some of them, I think, stole food from the soldiers of Thought. I find it easy to see why there is so much ill feeling between these two cities, even though they are allies—*friends,* as it is said in their tongue. Allies must be friends in deed and not only in word, if they are to have more than a sham alliance.

No moon and no stars tonight, only a thin drizzle that is almost a mist. I sit in the doorway of our tent, where the smoking fire gives just enough light for me to write. They say firewood is scarce already, but with a hundred Rope Makers and more than two hundred armed slaves at his command, Pasicrates will have all he needs, so I throw on more whenever the flames sink too low.

When I was a child, we saved the prunings from our vines to burn—I remember that. I remember my mother's singing as she crouched by the fire to stir a little black pot, and how she watched me as she sang to see whether I enjoyed her song. When my father was there, he would cut a pipe from reeds, and then the reeds sang her song with her. Our god—I have just remembered this—was Lar. My father said Mother's song made Lar happy. I remember thinking I understood more than he, and being proud and secretive (as little boys are) because I knew Lar was the song, and not something apart from it. I remember lying under the wolfskin and seeing Lar flash from wall to wall, singing and teasing me. I tried to catch him and woke rubbing my eyes, with Mother singing beside the fire.

# — CHAPTER XXXIX —
## Engines of War

SIEGE towers and battering rams are everywhere on the landward side of the city, each with a few hundreds to protect it from a sally. That is so the barbarians will not know whence the attack will come, as Xanthippos, the strategist from Thought, explained. Pasicrates of course asked where it *would* come, but Xanthippos only shook his head and looked wise, saying he had several sites under consideration. It seemed to me he had not decided because no place is yet weak enough to permit an assault.

But perhaps I am driving my dog before the cattle. I should say first that Pasicrates, Drakaina, and I went to Xanthippos this morning; and that he is a man of about my own height, gray at the temples, with an affable yet reserved air Drakaina said is characteristic of the old aristocracy of Thought.

He welcomed us cordially to a tent bare of any sign of wealth or luxury, with a worn-out sail for a ground cloth and simple stools that appeared to have been made on the spot. "We are delighted," he said, "that the Rope Makers have chosen to join us. How encouraging to see our ancient friendship renewed in the face of our common enemy. Am I to take it that the other ships were blown from their course by yesterday's storm? Let us hope they arrive safely today."

"Why?" Pasicrates asked bluntly. "Are you in need of troops?"

"No, not at all. What I have real need of is a hole through

those walls." Xanthippos chuckled, his keen gray eyes including all of us in his merriment. "There are only about five hundred barbarians inside, all told. Some thousand Hellenes, but I expect them to change their allegiance once the assault begins."

Pasicrates nodded. "We Hellenes are notorious for it—save for the men of my own city. And our assault will be . . . ?"

"As soon as the walls are breached. That will be in another month, I should say. May I ask whether it is King Leotychides or Prince Pausanias who commands?"

"Neither," Pasicrates told him. "Nor will there be more ships. There was only one, and we have come."

It was not possible to tell whether Xanthippos was really surprised or merely feigning to be. He seemed to me the sort of man who has mastered his feelings for so long that he no longer knows them, and may be furious or overcome by love without being conscious of either.

"I am the regent's man." Pasicrates took an iron signet from his finger and gave it to Xanthippos. "I come for him."

"Then allow me to congratulate him, through you, on his great victory. It will give me the deepest pleasure to do so in person upon some future day. No doubt you yourself took a leading part in that glorious battle. Alas that I was with the fleet! Would you care to cast aside, if only momentarily, that sometimes awkward briefness in speech for which your fellow citizens are so well known and describe for me—for my enlightenment as a strategist, I may say, as well as my delight—just what it was you did?"

"My duty," Pasicrates told him. He then questioned him about the progress of the siege but learned very little.

"So you see"—Xanthippos spread his hands—"the great thing is to retain the flexibility that enables one to seize, and indeed to recognize, opportunity."

"But you expect Sestos to fall in a month."

"Or a trifle longer, perhaps. Certainly before the onset of winter, though we may see some of its earlier stages. There is very little food in the city, I'm told, and they are not Rope

Makers there, accustomed to living on a bite of bread and a handful of olives.''

"Your own men should be planting next year's crop already.''

"They're mostly city men.'' Xanthippos smiled. "You Rope Makers are fond of saying we have no soldiers—only cobblers, masons, blacksmiths, and the like. It sometimes has its advantages.''

"And you,'' Pasicrates told him, "are found of saying we Rope Makers know nothing of sieges.'' He checked himself. "I came to convey the regent's respects to you—''

"Consider it done.''

"I do. And to tell you we will have to draw rations with your own men. We brought only a few days' supplies. You would not want to strain our ancient friendship, I think. For a bite of bread and a handful of olives we will lead your assault. You need only follow us.''

Xanthippos was still smiling. "Your heroic offer is duly noted.''

"You'll find your men inspirited by the knowledge that they are led by the shieldmen of Rope.'' Pasicrates stood, and Drakaina and I rose with him. "As for sieges, we know more than you suppose.'' He held out one hand, its fingers outspread. "Count them, Xanthippos. I say Sestos will fall before you're finished.''

Xanthippos remained unruffled. "Then the news you bring is doubly good. Not only have we received reinforcements from Rope, but the city is to fall within five days. You didn't mean five months, I hope? Before you go, may I ask why you brought this man and this woman when you came to confer with me?''

Without waiting for Pasicrates's answer, he turned to Drakaina. "Are you a Babylonian, my dear? A marvelous city, and one justly noted for the beauty of its women. Prior to this unhappy war I had the pleasure of visiting it. I hope to return, should my fellow citizens ostracize me again, which I fear is more than likely.''

"You may ask," Pasicrates told him. "But you will not be answered."

Outside, Drakaina said, "We should not have come with you. We'll be watched after this."

Pasicrates snorted. "Magical arts, and you can't evade a few of these shopkeepers? How are you going to get into the city?"

"Not by transforming myself into a bat, if that's what you're thinking. Not unless I must, and I haven't had a chance to gauge the problem yet."

"Nor I," Pasicrates admitted. "You're right; let's make a circuit of the walls."

The rain had stopped, but clouds hung gray and heavy over Sestos, and we had to pick our way through mud. I noticed some of the soldiers from Thought had winter boots, but all of us were still in sandals. From the walls to the distant hills spread the melancholy ruins of the houses that had once stood outside the city proper. The holes that had been their cellars were full of black water, and broken bricks and charred timbers protruded even where the men from Thought had made crude paths and roads.

We had gone no more than a couple of stades when Io came running up to join us, splashing through the mud in bare feet. "How was Xanthippos?" she asked.

I told her that if he was half as clever with the barbarians as he had been with us, the city would fall within five days, as Pasicrates had promised him it would.

"That was because you're here. Wasn't it, Pasicrates?"

The Roper Maker pretended not to hear her. He was already some way ahead of us.

"We must get inside," Drakaina told her. "You're a clever child, so keep your eyes open."

Io whispered, "I have already. I can get you inside any time you want, if nobody's watching."

Drakaina stared. "How— No, never mind. When we're alone. But have you ever seen such walls, either of you? The Great King has made this the lock with which he chains the whole coast."

Io said, "Then we've brought the key, if the regent's dream is true. Pasicrates is going to storm the city in a day or two, that's what the Rope Makers were telling each other while you were gone."

I said, "But if the key is in the chest, who can unlock it? I'm going into the city with Drakaina."

"Master, the Maiden sent you here. You don't remember, but I do. She said you'd find your friends here. If you go inside, it might not work. Besides, I'll have to come with you. I belong to you, and I have to remember things for you."

Drakaina hissed, "Certainly not!"

"I agree. I won't risk her life like that. Io, I'll bring you to me later if I can."

Io pointed, no doubt to distract me. "There's a lake!"

"No," Drakaina told her. "That's the strait."

In a few moments we were there. As Io had indicated, the strait was no wider than a small lake—we could watch men working on the wharves of the city on the opposite shore—and though it joined the horizon to the northeast, to the southwest we saw what appeared to be its termination. As we looked over the water, a trireme appeared there as if born of the rocky coast and, beating six white wings, seemed to fly along the waves as it came to join the others blockading Sestos.

Io said, "If this goes to the sea, I'm surprised they don't land the supplies here. It would be a lot safer."

I said, "It would be a great deal more dangerous, if that coast to the east still acknowledges the rule of the Great King."

Pasicrates had been studying the scene in silence. Now he said, "It was here, little Io, that the brave Leander swam from shore to shore to visit his beloved. I see you know the story."

Io nodded. "But he drowned one night, and she threw herself from the top of the tower. Only I didn't know this was the place."

Pasicrates favored her with his bitter smile. "I'm sure that if you were to go into the city, they'd point out the precise tower—her bloodstains in the street too, very likely.''

"It doesn't look so far. I bet I could swim it.''

I cautioned her, "Don't try. Haven't you noticed how fast that ship's coming? There must be a strong current.''

Drakaina added, "You may try for all I care, Io; but your master's correct, and there are frequent storms as well. Pasicrates, you too were thinking that where one swam, another may swim, weren't you?''

The Rope Maker nodded slowly.

"But swimmers could carry only daggers. A dozen shieldmen would be more than a match for a hundred of them.''

"I wasn't thinking of storming the city with swimmers,'' Pasicrates told her. "I was wondering how Xanthippos gets his information.'' He turned on his heel and started back the way we had come.

Drakaina said, "The lovely Helle drowned here too, giving her name to the place, when she fell from the back of the Golden Ram. These are dangerous waters, you see.'' She smiled at Io as a stoat might smile at a starling, though I sensed she was trying to seem kind.

"I *don't* know that story,'' Io said. "Would you tell me about the Golden Ram, please?''

"With pleasure. It belongs to the Warrior, and it lives in the sky between the Bull and the Fish. Remind me on some clear night, and I'll point it out to you. Once, long ago, it came to earth to interfere in the matter of two children, Phrixos and Helle, who had become a burden to their stepmother, Ino. No doubt the Warrior had planned to make Phrixos a hero, or something of that kind. Ino's called the White Goddess now, by the way, and she's an aspect of the Triple Goddess. Anyway, the Ram was determined to frustrate her, so it got itself a golden coat and joined the children as they were playing in a meadow, promising them a ride on its back. As soon as they were on, it sprang into the air, and at the highest point of its leap, right here, Helle fell off and drowned as I told you.''

Io asked, "What happened to her brother?"

"The Ram carried him to Aea, at the east end of the Euxine, thinking he'd be safe there. After putting in a good word for him with the king, it hung its golden coat in a tree and returned to the sky. I was a princess in Aea—"

"Wait a minute! I thought this was hundreds and hundreds of years ago."

"We live many different lives," Drakaina told Io, "in many different bodies. Or at least some of us do. I was a princess in Aea, and a priestess of Enodia just as I am now. I told my father quite truthfully that the goddess said he would be killed by a stranger. Since Phrixos was the only stranger around, that did for *him*. And I set my pet python to guard the golden fleece. Then—"

We had caught up with Pasicrates, who had stopped to examine one of the ramps the men from Thought were building. It was of earth, with logs laid in crisscross layers to reinforce it. "Childish," he said.

I ventured that it looked well constructed to me.

"Yes? How would you continue it when it nears the wall? It must be highest of all there, and the defenders will rain down stones and spears upon your head. Burning pitch too, perhaps."

"I'd assign a shield bearer to each workman," I told him. "A hoplon's big enough to protect two men from stones and spears from above. For that matter a strongly roofed wagon could be used to move the logs, and much of the work could be done from inside it with the floorboards taken out. And I'd station every archer and slinger I had about halfway from here to the wall to make my enemies think twice about showing themselves to throw stones and spears. They could only form a single line along the parapet there, but my archers and slingers would be able to form four or five lines, so that for every missile of theirs we'd return four or five."

Pasicrates stroked his chin and did not answer.

We soon came to just such a roofed wagon as I had spoken of, with a splintered battering ram slung in it; no doubt I had seen it on our way to the strait, and it was the unconscious recollection of it that had made me speak as I did. I stopped and asked the men repairing the battering ram how it had been broken, and one pointed to one of the narrow doors in the base of the wall. "We tried to knock on that, but they've got a log three times as big as this up there. It's hooked to a chain so they can swing it down and pull it back up. When the old ram came out of the barn here, down she swung and snapped it right off in back of the bronze, like you see."

Young though Pasicrates is, he had not seemed boyish to me until then. "Tell them what to do, Latro. I'm sure you know."

I said, "Fundamentally, they have to catch either the log or its chain, holding it with something too heavy for the men on the wall to draw up. This wagon they call the barn seems heavy enough to me; there's a lot of thick wood in the roof, and those wheels are solid oak and as wide as both my legs. The men are putting a stouter timber in the ram already. If I were in command, I'd put spikes on its sides, and on the sides of the wagon too. Then the log would nail itself to one or the other as soon as it struck."

One of the men who had been fitting the new beam into its slings stopped work and stepped over to us. "I'm Ialtos. I'm in charge here, and I thank you for the advice; we'll make use of it. Did I hear the Rope Maker call you Latro?"

I nodded. "That's my name. Or at least, that's what I'm called among your people."

"We've got a captain here—" He pointed. "See that tower on wheels? They're putting leather on the front and sides so it can't be set on fire, and he's superintending the job. He'll talk you deaf, do you know what I mean? But he knows leather and how to get it."

Io shouted, "Hypereides!"

"That's the man—I see you've met him. He goes on sometimes about a slave he used to have called Latro. Sort of a simple-minded fellow according to Hypereides, but you could tell he liked him. He traded him to a hetaera for a series of dinners—mostly, I think, to keep him away from the fighting."

Drakaina said, "I wouldn't call Latro simple-minded, but he forgets from one day to the next." She shot a mocking glance at the Rope Maker. "He's unusual in some other respects too, wouldn't you say, Pasicrates?"

"Even women who speak little talk too much." He took her arm to draw her away from Ialtos.

Io had been studying the tower on wheels. Now she tugged at my cloak. "Look, master! Up on that ladder. It's the black man!"

# ——— CHAPTER XL ———
## *Among Forgotten Friends*

THE heart remembers, even when no trace of face or voice remains. The black man came running to us, shouting, his arms in the air; and though I do not know where we met or why I love him (though no doubt those things are written somewhere on this scroll), I could not stop smiling. Without thinking at all about what I should do, I embraced him as a brother.

When we had shouted together and pounded each other on the back and hugged with all our strength like two wrestlers, Pasicrates tried to question him; but he only smiled and shook his head.

Io explained, "He understands—most of it, anyway. But he can't talk, or he won't."

Drakaina said something then in a harsh and rapid way that seemed to me no better than the creaking and grinding of mill stones; and to Io's amazement and my own, the black man answered her at once in the same language. "Your friend speaks the tongue of Aram," Drakaina told Io. "Not as well as the People from Parsa, but nearly as well as I do myself."

Pasicrates said, "Then ask him how he came to learn it."

She spoke to him again, and when he had replied she said, "He says, 'For three years I was with the army. We marched from Nysa to Riverland, from Riverland over the desert to the Crimson Country, then through many other countries.' He also says, 'My king is not subject to the Great King; but the Great King gave him gold and many fine things, and

swore there would be peace between our lands forever if he
would send a thousand men. I walked before a hundred and
twenty, all young men from my own district, and I learned to
talk in this way that I might know the wishes of the Lords of
Parsa.' " Drakaina added, "I'm shortening this a little."

Io demanded, "Ask how he met Latro."

" 'I saw a god had touched him. Such people are holy;
someone must care for them.' "

Io started to ask where Hypereides was, but Pasicrates
silenced her. "Does he want to go back to his own country?"

Before Drakaina spoke, the black man nodded and began
to speak. She said, "Yes, very much. He says, 'My father
and mother are there, both my wives, and my son, who is
very small.' "

Pasicrates nodded. "Are there any of the other men from
his country in the city?"

"He says he doesn't know, but he doesn't think so. He
thinks they may have gone south with the army. He says, 'If
they were here, they would show themselves to me on the
walls.' And I suppose he's right—he was in plain view
working on that tower; hundreds of people in the city must
have seen him."

"Tell him I require him to carry a message into the city for
me."

Io protested. "He belongs to Hypereides!" I think she did
not want to lose sight of the black man again so soon after we
had found him.

"Who will surely consent for the good of our cause. No
doubt he will be compensated by his city."

"He says Latro and this child must come with him."

I smiled and Io giggled, darting a glance at Pasicrates.

He ignored her. "And why is that?"

Now the black man spoke at length, touching his chest and
pointing with his chin to Io and me, and toward Sestos, and
once pretending to draw a bow.

Drakaina told Pasicrates, "He says he won't do what you
ask as a slave, that a slave remains a slave only as long as
he's watched. If he goes back to the People from Parsa, he
will be a soldier again, and as a soldier he won't do what you

ask unless you free Latro, and Io too. He says you can force
him to go to the city, but that once there he won't deliver
your message—only tell lies.''

Even Pasicrates smiled at that.

"For myself," Drakaina added, "I remind you that I am
the person sent by your regent to the barbarians—not this
black man. Not even you.''

"Yet another messenger may be useful, particularly one
who speaks their tongue. His price is too high, but I imagine
it can be lowered.''

I said I was willing to go into Sestos if he wished me to.

Pasicrates shook his head. "If you were lost permanently,
how could I explain to the regent? No, you must stay with
me until the city capitulates and we return home.''

Catching my eye, the black man motioned toward the
tower, then spoke to Drakaina.

She said, "He desires to show you what he has been
building.''

I said, "And I want to see it. Come along, Io.'' Though I
did not say so, I suspected the black man wished to put
himself under the protection of the man called Hypereides. I
do not remember him, but Io seemed to like him, and it
appeared likely the black man was right in thinking he would
fare better with him than with the Rope Maker.

"You know everything about siegecraft," Pasicrates said
as we came near the tower. "Explain this to me.''

I told him that since he could see it himself, there was very
little to explain. It was a tower on wheels, built of wood. The
back was left open to reduce its weight, but the front and
sides were covered with planks to keep out arrows, and with
leather to prevent the planks from being set ablaze. Before
the tower was pushed against the wall, the leather would be
soaked with water by men using rag swabs on long poles. In
addition, leather buckets of water would be hung in the
tower, to be used by the men inside.

He said, "Our enemies will put their finest troops opposite
this tower.''

I answered, "Yes, but good fighters will be put in the
tower too.''

The black man had gone around it as we spoke. Now he reappeared, bringing with him a bald man in a leather cuirass. The bald man seemed astonished to see us, then smiled broadly. "Latro and little Io, by the Standing Stone! I didn't think I'd be setting eyes on you again till we got back to Thought. How did you get here? Is that fellow Pindaros with you?"

He patted Io's head, and she embraced him and seemed for a moment too moved to speak.

"I don't suppose you remember Pindaros the poet, do you, Latro? Or his wench Hilaeira either."

The Rope Maker stepped forward. "I am Pasicrates, son of Polydectes. I am here as the representative of Prince Pausanias, son of Cleombrotus, Victor of Clay and Regent of Rope."

"Hypereides," Hypereides said. "Son of Ion—" Io whispered afterward that he meant he was of the Ionian people and proud of it, and that Pasicrates is a Dorian. "—commander of the *Europa,* the *Eidyia,* and the *Clytia.* Only my ships aren't in the water right now." He jerked his head toward the west. "They're beached, and most of my men are here working on these things."

Pasicrates said, "I'm told you sold this slave to a hetaera in your city."

"That's right, to Kalleos." Hypereides paused, looking from Pasicrates to Drakaina, as though wondering whether either were out to make trouble for him. "Not legally, of course, because women in my city can't hold property. Everything's in the name of a man she calls her nephew. She pays him so much a year for that."

"We are more reasonable in Rope—we don't love lies. Latro and the child are our regent's now, given him by your hetaera."

Io yelped, "He was supposed to pay!"

"Then he will, you may be sure. But in Rope, children who speak out of turn are whipped for it. Remember that." Pasicrates had never taken his eyes from Hypereides. "As the strategist of the Rope Makers here, I'm interested in your tower, Commander. How could you make it so the top was level with the top of the wall, when you couldn't measure the wall?''

Hypereides cleared his throat. "With all due respect, Strategist, neither one of those is exactly true. We want the top higher than the wall, so we can put bowmen there to shoot down on the enemy. And we could measure the wall. We did. Come around to the front here." He led the way and pointed upward. "See that door? It swings down, and it'll be level with the merlons. There's a stair in the back, as you probably saw, so all our men will have to do is run up the steps and step off onto the wall.''

"It must have taken a brave man to carry a measuring pole to the base," Pasicrates said, "even late at night."

"Oh, no." Hypereides's mouth twitched with amusement. "I measured it myself, and in broad daylight too. First I had a bowman—there he is. Come here, Oior."

A big, bearded man in loose trousers shambled over. He had a hammer in his hand and there was no bowcase at his back and no quiver at his waist; yet I knew the bald man was correct, for the bearded man had the look of a bowman.

"We tied a thread to an arrow," Hypereides continued. "Oior shot the arrow so it stuck in the ground at the foot of the wall. Then we cut the thread and pulled the arrow in so we could measure the thread. That gave us the distance from the place where Oior stood to the base of the wall."

Pasicrates said, "Which is *not* the height of the wall, unless you were very lucky."

"No, certainly not. Then we stuck a sword in the ground so it was exactly a cubit high. When the shadow of the wall touched the place where Oior had stood, we measured the shadow of the sword and divided the length of the thread by the length of the shadow. The answer was the height of the wall: forty-seven cubits."

Oior the bowman smiled at me and touched his forehead in greeting.

When we returned to Pasicrates's tent, he sent Drakaina and Io away, then held out his hand. "I see you're wearing your sword, Latro," he said. "Give it to me."

I unfastened the catch of my belt. "You're welcome to look at it," I said, "as long as you mean me no harm."

"Give it to me," he said again.

The very flatness of his voice told me what he meant to do. "No," I said. I refastened the catch.

He whistled. I suppose he must have decided I required correction before we left to make our circuit of the walls and perhaps even before we called upon Xanthippos, because his slaves appeared at once, one carrying two javelins and the other a whip, a scorpion of three tails. They entered through the back of the tent, and Pasicrates moved to block the front, his hand upon his sword hilt.

"These men may kill me," I told him, "but they will not beat me." I recalled that he had said a woman sold me to the regent. "And if they kill me, what will you tell your master?"

"The truth," Pasicrates murmured. "Sestos did not fall, you were lazy and insolent, I tried to discipline you, and you resisted."

His hoplon leaned against the tent wall near the entrance. With a practiced motion, he slipped his arm through its leather loop and grasped the handle. "Now take off that sword, and your cloak and chiton, like a sensible man."

I said, "No one thinks you Rope Makers sensible men."

"And so they are our slaves, or they soon will be." He glanced at the slaves that were truly his. "Keiros, Tekmaros, don't kill him."

Neither was well equipped to capture an armed man alive, and what happened next would have been ludicrous, had it not been terrible. The slave with the scorpion advanced first, lashing the air to make a savage sound he must have hoped would frighten me. I stepped forward and slashed at the rawhide lashes. He jumped back and in so doing impaled himself on one of the javelins held by the man behind him.

The terrible thing was not that it killed him, but that it did not. With the head of the javelin in his back, he remained alive, bleeding and gasping like a fish on a gig as he dropped the scorpion and flailed about with his arms.

I caught it up—and as I did so, saw that Pasicrates was

almost upon me. Its stock was of some heavy wood, and the lead-tipped lashes looked as though they might easily entangle a man; I threw it at his legs.

He was too quick for me. The stock rang against the bronze facing of his hoplon. I swung Falcata in the downward stroke that is most powerful of all. Again he was too quick, raising his hoplon to block her blade; but it bit the bronze like cheese, cut the hoplon to its center, and leaped free as a lynx springs from a rock.

Pasicrates screamed. It was a high, shrill cry like a woman's, though he thrust at me like a man even as he screamed, and made me skip aside.

The wall of the tent was at my elbow then; this scroll lay on my pallet not far from my left hand. I stooped to pick it up. That saved me, I think. A javelin passed so near my head that the sound was like a blow. Blood streamed from my ear.

The javelin had pierced the side of the tent. A slash laid it wide. I stumbled out and ran east, past the tents and through the little fields toward Parsa and Persepolis—toward the heart of the Empire, though I cannot say how it is I know the names of those places.

When I had reached the hills and could run no more, I found this hollow in the rocks and stopped to rest, the pulse pounding in my head like the laughter of some great river in flood. Soon the gray clouds hanging over the land parted. The sun appeared, a crimson coin set on the horizon behind me. I staunched the blood from my ear with moss, wiped Falcata's smeared blade on fallen leaves, and unrolling this scroll read enough to learn that I must write.

Writing has given me time to catch my breath and listen for pursuit. There has been none. When the moon rises, I will run again. It is important, so very important, that I do not forget I am fleeing, and what it is I fly from. "I have to remember things for you," the child, Io, told me as we wandered among the soldiers and siege engines of Thought. I wish she were with me now.

# —— CHAPTER XLI ——
## We Are in Sestos

THE goddess sent me here, and it was no dream. How easy it would be to write that I dreamed, as so many have written in so many other places. Yet I know I did not, for I dreamed before the goddess came.

It was a dream of love. The woman was raven-haired, or so it seemed in the moonlight, with eyes that flashed with desire. How she clutched me and drove my loins into her own! A lake, dark and still, mirrored silver stars; all along the shore men in horned and leering masks capered with women crowned with the vine, to the thudding of timbrels and the rattle of crotali.

Then I woke.

The woman had vanished, the instruments fallen silent. My torn ear burned and throbbed. The stones stood about me, hard and dark. The air was cold, heavy with snow. I heard the wind muttering among the oaks, and I knew it—though I do not know how—for the thought of Jove, the god who rules the gods and cares little for men. It seemed to me that he was mad, black thoughts repeating one or two words again and again as they brooded upon revenge.

I sat up, and the night was like any other. A wind walked among the trees, and an increscent moon hung low in the west. Far off a wolf howled. My limbs were stiff with cold, but I felt no desire to roll myself in my cloak again; I felt instead that I should rise and fly from some danger, and though I no longer recalled what it was from which I had fled

307

earlier, I sensed a menace that was no less now. Stretching, I looked down to find this scroll, which I recalled having pushed into a hiding place among the rocks.

At once I gasped and nearly cried out, staggering backward from the lip of an abyss beside which I had slept only a few moments before. It seemed a pit without a bottom, or at least without any bottom the silver radiance of moon or stars could ever reach. Trembling, I cast a stone into it and listened. I heard nothing, though I strained to hear for many thuddings of my fearful heart.

Though perhaps my stone is still falling, falling always and without end, something moved in the abyss. If it lacked any termination, still it had sides; and blurs of white and palest green, tiny and remote, swarmed over them as ants may creep across the walls in a sealed tomb. Sometimes it appeared that they flew from one side to another, flitting like bats and flickering like rushlights.

"You would find me," someone behind me said. "I have come already."

I turned and saw a girl of perhaps fifteen sitting on a stone behind me. Her gown was woven of somber autumn foliage, yellow, gridelin, and russet, and a stephane with an ebon gem was on her brow. Though she sat with her back to the moon, I could see her face clearly; it seemed hungry and ill, like the faces of the children who sell their bodies in the poor quarters of cities.

"Soon you will wonder what became of your book," she said. "I will keep it for you; now take it, and leave my door."

When she spoke, I was more afraid of her than of the abyss; perhaps if I had not feared her so, I could not have done as she instructed me.

"I have rolled it tightly for you, tied it, and pushed your stylus through the cords. Put it through your belt. You have much to do before you write again."

I asked, "Who are you?"

"Call me Maiden, as you did when we first met."

"And you're a goddess? I didn't think—"

She smiled sourly. "We still meddled in the wars of Men? Not often now; but the Unseen God wanes, and we are no longer lost in his light. We will never be wholly gone."

I bowed my head. "How may I serve you, Maiden?"

"First by taking your hand from your sword hilt, to which it has strayed. Believe me, your blade is powerless against me."

I dropped my hands to my sides.

"Second, by doing as I instruct you, and so relieving me of the necessity I laid upon myself for Mother's sake. You recall nothing of this, but I have promised to reunite you with your comrades."

"Then you've been kinder than I deserve," I said, and nearly stammered from the joy that flamed in my heart.

"I act for my mother, and not for you. You owe me no thanks. Nor do I owe you any. If you had accepted your beating like any other slave, my task would have been easy."

"I am not a slave," I said.

She smiled again. "What, Latro? Not even mine?"

"Your worshiper, Maiden."

"Smooth-tongued as ever. No man outreaches his gods, Latro, not even in falsehood."

"You said that you've promised to bring me to my own people, Maiden. If that was a falsehood, slay me now."

"I will keep my promise," she said. She licked her lips. "But I hunger. What payment will you give me, Latro, when I do as you wish? A hundred bulls to smoke upon my altars?"

I shook my head. "I'd slaughter every one, and singing, if I had them. I have nothing beyond what you see."

"Your book, your sword, your belt, your sandals, and those ragged clothes. And your body, but I will not ask you for that; it will be mine soon enough, no matter what. Would you heap my altar with the rest?"

"With everything, Maiden."

"And Io?"

I asked, "Who is Io?"

"A slave. She says yours. Will you give her to me freely?"

I nodded, though I sickened to nod. "You have only to show her to me, Maiden."

"Then I will not ask you for her. Nor for your book and sword and the other things. I ask an easier sacrifice instead: a wolf."

"Only a wolf, Maiden?" Now my spirit leaped for gladness. "You are too generous, too merciful!"

"So many have said. Yes, a wolf. The wolf is sacred to my mother, as you would know had you not forgotten it. Furthermore, I will see that this wolf comes to you, and I will place my sigil on it so that you will know it."

"And I won't forget?"

She pointed, and though the hill stood between us and the rising sun, when she pointed I knew that it was there. "In summer, when the days were long, you lost the dawn before evening. Days are shortened now; when the wolves howl again, you will yet remember me and this: The wolf will attack you, yet you will not fear it. He is the one."

"As you command, Maiden, and gladly."

"Not so gladly when the time comes, perhaps. But first you must return to the walls you fled, return with the dawn. Will you do that?"

"It's dawn now," I told her. "Can I run so fast? I will if I can."

"Your foes seek your life. Be wary. As the sun rises, you will see a woman and a child walking hand in hand. Draw your sword and give it to the child. Do you understand?"

I nodded. "I will do just as you've said, Maiden."

"Then when you find the wolf, grasp its ear, cut its throat, and speak my name. Go now, do that, and my promise will be fulfilled."

The city was far out of sight to the west; yet I saw it, its gray walls, grim with a hundred towers, rising high above the tents of the besiegers. I sprinted toward it, and it vanished; but I continued to run, leaping stones and loping across fields of stubble until I reached in truth the tents I had seen falsely through the eyes of the goddess.

Here soldiers woke and spat like other men, goaded by the

braying of the trumpets—buckled on their armor, took up spears and hoplons marked with the inverted ox of Thought, and formed ragged files that were soon straightened by the curses of their enomotarches. Some looked at me curiously, and I waved this scroll above my head so they would think me a messenger; no one stopped me.

The tents ended. I reached a place where houses and shops had stood outside the walls. They had been burned, though whether by the besiegers or the besieged I cannot say. There were towers and sheds on wheels, and ramps of clay and wood. Worse, the tumbled stones and tiles of the ruined houses threatened to trip me with every stride. Once I noted a dented pan among the ruins, and once a scattered string of coral beads. I thought then of the misery of poor women I would perhaps never see.

Soon I was within bowshot of the walls. An archer there kindly told me so, sending his shaft whizzing past my eyes to bury itself in the blackened ground to my right, so that I returned this scroll to my belt and ran wider.

Already the sun was well above the horizon behind me. The Maiden had said I was to give my sword to the child "as the sun rises," but it seemed to me it was impossible that day. Yet I continued to run, or rather to trot, circling the walls in search of the woman and the child.

The temptation always was to go too near, for by curving my path more sharply I could have decreased its length. Twice more archers loosed at me, their long-flying arrows falling at last almost at my feet.

I had made a half circle when I saw them—a woman in a purple gown and a child in a torn gray peplos, hand in hand, so deep in the shadow of the wall that the soldiers on it might have slain them with stones had they wished.

At the same instant a wounded man shouted, drew his sword, and dashed toward me. I marveled at his courage, for he had lost his left forearm not long before; the stump was still bandaged below the elbow, and the bandage was still gay with his blood. I had drawn my own sword before I remembered the words of the Maiden, who had perhaps desired that

I fight this one-armed man without it. That seemed no more than just, for surely he was still weak from his wound. I ran to the woman and the child then with all the speed I could command, extending my sword to the child hilt foremost.

She accepted it readily; but when I turned, others were sprinting after the one-armed man. One fell with an arrow through his throat, but two more caught the one-armed man, wrestling his sword from his hand and pulling him to safety. As I watched them, I was bathed in gold. The sun had risen above the city wall, bringing a second dawn.

Still other men, shieldmen in armor, dashed from the wall to take us. They dragged me, with the woman and the child, into a doorway so deeply set that it was like a tunnel ending in a narrow door. When this door swung back, we were in the besieged city. Houses of two and even three stories were set thickly along the narrow street, many with their backs formed by the wall. The men who held us seemed not otherwise than the men outside who warred on them; but with them were soldiers not like them at all, soldiers whose curling beards were black instead of brown, and who wore loose trousers of yellow, blue, and green.

They bore us to the citadel and took the woman from us, and with her my sword as well. Now we are shut up in this guard room, where at Io's urging (for this child is the slave girl I told the Maiden I would sacrifice if she wished it) I write my account.

# —— CHAPTER XLII ——

## *Though Not Without Aid*

I have defeated three men, guards of the satrap from Susa. They were Hellenes, though in Sestos the Hellenes do not govern themselves, as Io explained when I had finished writing of our capture. So it is, she says, wherever the Hellenes live on this side of the Water.

"All the better for them," I said, "assuming that the men of Parsa are wise and just. These Hellenes are proud, grasping, and turbulent; brilliant, perhaps, but without any real feeling for the duties of the citizen and the majesty of the state."

She agreed, then asked in a whisper whether I thought someone was listening.

"No," I said. "I speak my mind—the simple truth."

"But I'm a Hellene myself, master."

"I was considering the men. The woman are better, perhaps, yet wanton."

"You only say that because you saw them in Kalleos's house, mostly. Do you remember her? Or Phye? Or Zoe, or any of the others?"

I shook my head. "I only know how these Hellenes have seemed to me." I sought to take the sting from my words. "Their children are beautiful and very kind."

She smiled. "I'm the only one you've had much to do with. But maybe you're right anyway about the men and women. What do you know about the People from Parsa?"

"It was they who commanded the soldiers who brought us

313

into this city; but though I feel sure I've seen them before, I
can't remember where."

"I saw them back in Hill. They don't talk like we do, and
they keep their women out of sight even more than the people
do in Thought. And I saw one on the wall yesterday. That
was how I knew how to get Drakaina into Sestos."

I asked whether Drakaina was the woman in the purple
gown, and Io nodded.

"She wanted to get inside so she could talk to the People
from Parsa for the regent, but she didn't know how. Only
yesterday, you and she and Pasicrates walked around looking
at the towers on wheels, and I saw a man from Parsa on the
wall watching her. The jewels on his cap and in his rings
caught the light, so I knew he must be an important man, and
from the way he looked at Drakaina I knew that if she ever
came near the wall he'd have soldiers come out and get her.
Then you fought with Pasicrates and ran away, and I thought
I ought to go in with her, so that maybe I could get him to
help you. The Rope Makers will probably kill you if they
ever catch us again."

"Who's Pasicrates?" I asked, not liking to hear that I had
run from him.

"He's the head Rope Maker out there," Io told me. "Or he
was. I'll tell you about him if you want, then you can read
about him in your book. We're going to have plenty of time,
I suppose."

Io had no sooner spoken than the door swung wide. I
expected to see soldiers like those who had brought us here,
perhaps with an officer from Parsa; but these were all barbarians with long trousers and cloth-draped heads. I found I
knew already what sorts of faces they would have and how
they would be armed. Yet because I did not know I would
recall those things until I saw them, I will write something of
them here.

Their hands and faces are the only parts of their bodies
they do not cover; and sometimes they cover even their faces,
pulling up the cloth that conceals the neck to keep dust from
the nose and mouth. Instead of sandals they wear shoes

(which I think must be very uncomfortable) so that no part of the foot can be seen. Among the Hellenes bright colors are worn often, but garments are all of one hue save perhaps for a band at the edge. The People from Parsa have half a dozen different colors in the same cloth. Even soldiers like those who came for us do not wear much armor.

Their spears are no taller than the men who bear them. Instead of a pointed grounding iron that can serve as a second spear head if the shaft breaks, they have a round weight at the butt. It is wise of them to make them that way, I think, because so short a spear would be useless after the shaft had broken; but the weight should permit the soldier to reverse his broken spear and use it as a mace. This weight shifts the point of balance to the rear, just as the grounding iron does.

The men of Parsa always have their bows and bowcases. I think they must be fonder of the bow than any other race; surely no race could be fonder than they. Their bows are of wood and horn bound with sinew, and they bend backward when unstrung. Their arrows are hardly longer than a man's forearm and have iron points. Some have blue feathers, some gray. They are carried in the bowcase with the bow.

Their swords are short and straight, with tapering blades sharpened on both sides. Those of the soldiers who came for us have bronze lions' heads on their pommels, and that of Artaÿctes, to whom they brought us, has a golden lion's head. It is very beautiful, but the truth is that all these swords are hardly more than long daggers—good for thrusting but for nothing else. Some of the men from Parsa do not even carry swords. They have long-hafted axes instead, and that is what I would choose myself in preference to such a sword. The men who bear these axes wear a knife at the belt.

Artaÿctes is of graying beard, with eyes even harder and darker than is common among his countrymen. Because he wears a jeweled cap and many rings, I decided it was he whom Io saw upon the wall. The woman Io had called Drakaina sat at his right hand, not cross-legged as he himself sat, but with her fine legs to one side and bent at the knee to show their grace. When we came, she drew the end of a many-colored scarf across her nose and mouth.

He addressed her in a language I did not know, and she bowed her head. "Once my lord has spoken, the thing is done."

As the Hellenes speak, he said, "Your tongue is more supple than mine, in this speech particularly. They do not comprehend ours?"

"No, my lord."

"Then explain to them why they have been brought into my presence."

Drakaina turned so it appeared that she looked from the window of Artaÿctes's audience chamber, yet I saw her eyes were on me. "I told my lord what you did to Pasicrates and said you could no doubt kill three ordinary men. He has a guard of Sestians beside his own soldiers, and three have volunteered to fight you. Not with spears, but with hands bare, as contestants fight in the pancratium. Do you know that event? Only weapons are barred."

I was about to ask what I had done to Pasicrates (whom Io had told me I had fled) when Artaÿctes clapped his hands and a sentry ushered in the three. All were as tall as I am, well-muscled men at the height of their strength.

Io protested, "This isn't fair!"

Drakaina nodded agreement. "You're right, but the men of Parsa don't like boasting. I'd forgotten that. When they hear a boast, it's a point of honor with them to make the man perform accordingly, even when it was spoken by another. I believe my lord thinks too that Latro has been my lover, though we both know it is not so."

Io said bitterly, "By no fault of yours."

I was watching the three. If the leader could be killed, it would take the heart from the others. Often a leader stands between his followers, but in battle the place of honor is the right flank. As I took off my sword belt I muttered, "Maiden, aid me now."

At once the door of Artaÿctes's audience chamber opened again, and two more men entered, both as naked as the first three. Neither was large, but the first was so handsome and well shaped in every limb that every other man must have seemed deformed in his presence. The other was older, yet strong still, sun-browned and grizzled, with cunning eyes. Neither made any move to help me, each standing motionless beside the door, his arms at his sides. The three who faced me did not so much as look at them.

Artaÿctes said, "You are three set at one. Kill him and return to your duties."

The Sestians to my right and left stepped forward so that with the third they might enclose me. I knew that was death and edged to the left, so that the man there would have to fight me alone, if only for a moment.

He grappled, and I struck him with my fist below the navel and in the face with the crown of my head. He reeled and fell backward, his nose gushing blood.

At once the older man flung himself upon him, face to face as lover kisses lover. Until then I had not been certain the rest could not see the two who had come last, but when I saw them I knew. I circled and feinted, sure delay would favor me.

Nor was I wrong. The grizzled man rose, his mouth crimson with blood, and seized one of my opponents from behind. Still the man did not see him, yet his movements were slower.

"I am Odysseus, son of Laertes and King of Ithaka," the grizzled man whispered. "We need more blood, for Peleus's son."

"I doubt it," I told him, for I had seen that the remaining Sestian watched my eyes and not my hands.

When the fight was over, Drakaina smiled—I could see her lips through the thin stuff of the scarf. "My lord Artaÿctes feels the news I've brought is too important to remain caged here. Furthermore, there isn't food enough in the city for it to resist much longer—the people are boiling the straps from their beds."

Artaÿctes spoke some angry word, but Drakaina did not look chastened.

"He hoped for relief before this. It hasn't come; so he will go, taking his own people and those from the far lands. He plans to leave the Hellenes here, knowing they'll negotiate a surrender that will spare their houses and their walls. When he's conveyed my news, he'll get an army from the Great King and return to crush the barbarians, if they're bold enough to remain. I've told him you've sold your sword to the Great King, and he's just seen you're a fighter to be reckoned with. He asks if you'll go with him to Susa, where he expects to find the Great King."

I nodded, adding, "Yes, certainly."

Speaking for himself in his harsh accent, Artaÿctes asked, "Are you not of the Hellenes? You look as they."

"No, my lord."

"Then prove it. Let me hear your native tongue. The Hellenes will learn none but their own."

I did as he said, swearing in the tongue in which I write these words that I owed no allegiance to Thought or any such city. I do not think Artaÿctes understood me, but he seemed convinced. He took my sword from behind the scarlet cushions on which we sat and handed it to me.

"We will go by night," he said. "The barbarians will be asleep, save for a few sentries. No one must know. The people of this city tell all they learn to Yellow Horse, no matter how often they swear their loyalty. You are to ride beside me and carry this woman with you. See that she is not harmed." By "Yellow Horse" he meant Xanthippos, but he broke his name as I have broken it here.

When we had left the brightly hung audience chamber, Drakaina said, "Before we go, you must be armed. Wouldn't you like a shield and spear besides your sword? What of a helmet?"

Io told me, "You had round things for your chest and back when I met you, master."

I nodded. "A shield and a helmet, certainly, if there's going to be real fighting. No spear. I'll take a couple of javelins instead."

The armory was in the lowest part of the citadel. I asked

for an oblong shield of medium weight, but those they had were hoplons, round and very heavy, or peltas shaped like the moon and very light.

"These honor my goddess," Drakaina said, holding up one of the latter. "It's the kind the javelin men in Thessaly use."

I told her that leather over wicker would stop only arrows and slingstones.

"That's because that's all they have to worry about," she said. "They stay well away from the spears."

I shook my head, knowing that if there is any fighting at all tonight, it will be hot work. I will not be able to run from the spears.

"Here, sir," the armorer said. "Try this. It's the smallest hoplon in the whole place."

It is a cubit and a hand across (I have just measured it), and faced with bronze, as I believe they all are; but there is wood and a leather lining behind it; and as he said, it was the lightest.

Io called, "Here's a nice helmet."

"Nice for a Hellene, perhaps," I told her. "But I don't want the men from Parsa to think I'm a Hellene in the dark."

The armorer snapped his fingers. "Wait a moment, sir. I believe I've got just what you need." He returned carrying a helmet shaped like a tall cap. As soon as I tried it on, I knew it might have been made for me.

Io said, "I've heard people talk about the Tall Cap Country, where they wear caps like that. And the bowmen on Hypereides's ships had them, but theirs were foxskin. I didn't know they made helmets the same way. Is it far from here?"

"Across Helle's Sea," the armorer told her, "and a good way by land after that; it would probably take you three or four days. Do you have a boat?"

Io laughed and said, "I'm not going," which I thought singularly ill omened.

I got a cuirass as well—not one of the heavy bronze corselets the shieldmen wear, but one of many layers of linen stitched together. It should give a good deal of protection while weighing not much more than a warm cloak. The javelins were easiest of all, for the armory had any number of good ones.

"The satrap has assigned me a house," Drakaina said when I had collected all the equipment I needed. "I'm going there now to get some sleep before tonight. It wouldn't do for him to see me with circles beneath my eyes." She hesitated. "You would be welcome, but I don't know that it would be wise."

I told her I wanted to go up on the wall and have a look at the country.

"As you wish, then."

The armorer said, "I could show you around, sir. Oschos's my name."

Io told him, "My master has no money."

"But he's been talking with the satrap," Oschos answered, smiling. "So perhaps he will have." To me he said, "Our citadel's built right into the wall, sir, on the east side, so you can start from here and go right around, passing through the guard towers."

I studied the plain and the hills beyond as we walked along the wall. The Hellenes will expect any escape to be made to the south and west, so Artaÿctes says. A short march that way would bring us to a place from which we might easily cross the strait by boat, evading the blockading ships. He means to try the northeast instead, making overland for the port cities of a sea called the Propontis. Because Oschos was with us, however, I could not give more attention to that direction than to any other; and so I studied them all, and even the harbor, where the ships of Sestos cant their scorched masts through the soiled water.

When we left the wall we passed a marble building guarded by eunuchs, out of which some slaves were carrying chests and baskets. "What's that?" Io asked.

Oschos looked respectful. "The house of our satrap's women."

Io remarked that it looked more like a tomb.

"It was one," Oschos told her. "I hear that he uses them whenever he can. He feels a gynaeceum without windows is more secure, and who can doubt it?"

When we were alone here Io commented, "I wouldn't like to be Artaÿctes when he dies. The gods below aren't going to like his putting his concubines in a tomb."

"Who are the gods below?" I asked her as I hung up my new shield. The truth was that I felt I already knew one at least.

"The gods of the dead," she told me. "There's quite a lot, really. Their king is the Receiver of Many, and their queen is Kore, the Maiden. They have a whole country of their own under the ground, Chthonios, the world of ghosts."

Now I write and Io sleeps. When night comes I will ride with Artaÿctes and the People from Parsa, perhaps to the world of ghosts, because I have pledged my honor. But I will leave Io here, as she herself prophesied. Perhaps I shall never see her again. A moment ago I brushed her hair from her brown cheek, wondering whether there was ever a face dearer to me than hers; and though I cannot be sure, it seems impossible. How she would laugh at me, if she were to wake and find me weeping for her!

# ─── CHAPTER XLIII ───

## A Soldier of the Mist

Lost in the night and its shifting vapors am I. Already I have nearly forgotten how this night began.

I lay on a pallet in a cold, dark room with a single high window, a window having narrow steps and a vantage for an archer beneath it. I think I had been asleep; a child, a girl, slept beside me.

A lovely woman came for me, and with her a hard-faced spearman. I must have known that they would come, for I rose at once and put on my cuirass and helmet by the light of the spearman's lamp, thrust this scroll through my belt, and took up my hoplon and javelins. I think I knew where we went and why, but that too is lost in the mist. "We will let Io sleep," I said to the woman. "She'll be safe here."

The woman nodded and smiled, her finger to her lips. Before she died, she said her name was Eurykles.

We hurried down dark and narrow streets reeking of ordure and joined a throng of silent people before the gate. The woman led me to the front, saying, "Artaÿctes and his guards will be here at any moment. Then we'll go."

I asked her who the rest were, but men on horseback pushed their mounts through the crowd before she could answer. The chief among them, a bearded man on a white horse, spoke in a language I could not understand; and to my amazement another man, who grasped his saddle cloth, spoke after him just as I write these words. This is what they said:

"In the most holy, most sacred name of the Sun! My

people, does our situation seem desperate to you? Reflect! Here we have been penned like coneys, with scarcely enough to eat and without even clean water to drink. When next the Sun, the divine promise of Ahura Mazda, mounts his throne, we shall be free, every one of us, and once more in the Empire.

"So it shall be if we act like men. Those who fight must press ever forward as they fight. Those who need not fight must turn back and fight to aid their brothers. Horsemen, do not ride off, leaving your brothers on foot to fight alone. Surely Ash will know of it! And I will know of it too, and what I know I will soon tell the Great King. Rather, ride at the flanks of those who press your brothers on foot, and protect my household."

More was said, but the spearman tapped me on the shoulder and I listened no more. He led two horses, and he handed the reins of a champing gray stallion to me. The woman said, "Can you ride?"

I was not sure. I answered, "When I must."

"You must tonight. Mount, and this man will help me up."

I leaped onto the gray's back and discovered that my knees knew something of horses, whether my mind retained it or not.

Grinning, the spearman clasped the woman about the waist and lifted her until she sat behind me. Though I have forgotten so much, I still recall the flash of his teeth in the dark and her arm about my waist, and the musky, flowery smell of her that was like a summer meadow, with a serpent among the blossoms.

"At last I know why the People from Parsa put their women in these trousers." Her voice was at my ear, ecstatic with excitement. "For a thousand years they have not known but that they might have to gallop off with them next day." Someone shouted an order, and the gates swung toward us. "Stay with Artaÿctes," she said. "The best troops will be with him."

As we rode out, the mist from the harbor crept in, meeting

us half a stade from the gate. Covered carts rumbled behind our horses. The woman said, "Now the enemy knows. If the wheels weren't making so much noise, you could hear their sentries shouting already."

Indicating the carts, I asked why they were here.

"For Artaÿctes's women. His wife and her maids will be in the first, his concubines in the others." She hesitated, and I heard how sharply she drew breath. "But where is he? Where are his guards?"

A few dozen foot soldiers with oblong shields followed the carts, and before them marched one who bore an eagle on a staff. My heart nearly burst at the sight of it (as it does now at the thought), though I could not have said why.

There was a shout from a thousand mouths. I swung about in the saddle to see the wide hoplons and long spears of the enemy break through the mist, and above them a black cloud of slingstones, javelins, and arrows. They had waited only until the last foot soldiers were clear of the gate, knowing perhaps that the Hellenes inside would close them against our retreat. Their phalanx was a hedge of spears.

"Go!" the woman cried. "He's tricked us! He must think I'm a spy—he's leaving the city some other way."

Before she had finished, I had loosed the reins and dug my heels into the gray's ribs. It sprang forward like a stag. In an instant, we had passed between the last cart and the soldiers who followed the eagle; but the mist held another phalanx as terrible as the first. I turned the gray aside and lashed it with the reins as I saw a third phalanx wheel to block the road; for there was a narrowing space between it and the second, and in that space only a scattering of archers and slingers.

Fearsome as the close-drawn shieldmen were when they fronted us, they could do nothing as we thundered past their flanks. One of my javelins I cast left, the second right, and though I did not see my foes die, each must have taken its toll. A bearded archer nocked an arrow meant for me, but we were too swift; I felt his bones break beneath the gray's hooves.

Horsemen followed me, iron-faced riders from Parsa with

singing bows. We turned as one and caught the phalanx from behind, scourging the soft back of that monster of bronze and iron, felling its shieldmen like wheat before the reapers. Falcata scythed their spears and split their helmets, and they died, falling onto the dry yellow grass under a sky suddenly blue.

That is all I can recall of that time. When I lifted my head, a rolling mist had covered the lake. Somewhere the woman I had lain with screamed. As I struggled to rise, my hand touched a crooked sword half-buried in the mud. Not certain even that it was mine, I stumbled to my feet and limped among the dying and the dead in search of her.

I found her where the bodies lay thickest. Her feet had scattered gems that twinkled in the starlight, and a black wolf tore her throat. Its forepaws pinned her to the ground, but its hind legs stretched useless behind it, and I knew its back had been broken.

I knew too that it was a man. Beneath the wolf's snarling mask was the face of a bowman; the paws that held the woman were hands even while they were paws. Ravening, the wolf dragged itself toward me. Yet I did not fear it, and only fended it from me with the point of my sword.

"More than a brother," it said. "The woman would have robbed me." It did not speak through its great jaws, but I heard it.

I nodded.

"She had a dagger for the dead. I hoped she would kill me. Now you must. Remember, Latro? 'More than brothers, though I die.' "

Beyond the wolf and the woman, a girl watched me—a girl robed with flowers and crowned. Her shining face was impassive, yet I sensed her quiet pleasure. I said, "I remember your sacrifice, Maiden, and I see your sigil upon it." I took the wolf by the ear and slit its throat, speaking her name.

I had come too late. The woman writhed like a worm cut by the plow, her mouth agape and her tongue protruding far past her lips.

The Maiden vanished. Behind me someone called, *"Lucius
. . . Lucius . . ."*

I did not turn at once. What I had thought the woman's
tongue was a snake with gleaming scales. Half-free of her
mouth, it was thicker than my wrist. My blade bit at its back,
but it seemed harder than brass. Frantically it writhed away,
vanishing into the night and the mist.

The woman lifted her head. "Eurykles," I heard her whisper. "Mother, it's Eurykles!" With the last word she fell
backward and was gone, leaving only a corpse that already
stank of death.

The man-wolf was gone as well. The man lay in his place.
When I touched him, his beard was stiff with blood, his back
bent like trampled grass. His hands thanked me as he died.

*"Lucius . . ."* The call came again. It was only then, too
late, that I sought for him.

I found him beside the broken eagle. He wore a lion's
skin, but a spear had divided his thigh and a dagger had
pierced his corselet of bronze scales. The lion was dying.
"Lucius . . ." He used my own speech. "Lucius, is it
really you?"

I could only nod, not knowing what to say; as gently as I
could, I took his hand.

"How strange are the ways of the gods!" he gasped.
"How cruel."

*(These are the last words of the first scroll.)*

# GLOSSARY

The principal proper names in Latro's account are identified here.
A few (such as "Lands of the Living" and "Shining God") have
been omitted when their meaning seems obvious. Certain other
terms that could pose difficulties for his readers are defined as well.

*Acetes*—The commander of the armored soldiers (hoplites) on
Hypereides's trireme.

*Acharnae*—A village roughly midway between Thought and Advent, but farther inland than either.

*Acheron*—A river flowing through both the Lands of the Living and
the Lands of the Dead.

*Advent*—A small city near Thought, allied with it. The most famous temple of the Grain Goddess, the Royal House, is there.

*Aea*—The capital of Colchis, an ancient barbarian kingdom far
north and east of Thought.

*Aegae*—A small city on the northern coast of Redface Island, the
home port of the *Nausicaa*.

*Aesculapius*—The god of healing, an ancient physician deified.

*Agamemnon*—An ancient king and hero.

*Agathocles*—A famous musician of Thought.

*Agids*—The older royal family of Rope.

*Ahuramazda*—Ahura Mazda. Literally, Wise God or Wise Lord;
the chief force for good in a mythology in which evil occupies an
equal place.

*Alcmene*—The mother of Heracles.

*Amompharetos*—An officer (roughly a colonel) in the army of
Rope.

*Anadyomene*—One of the names of Kalleos's goddess; it means
"Sea-Born."

*Angra Manyu*—The evil god who opposes Ahura Mazda.

*Antaeus*—A Libyan giant, a son of Gaea.

*Apia*—The name given Gaea by the Sons of Scoloti.

*Apollodoros*—A famous choirmaster.

*Aram*—A country lying between the Cities of the Crimson Men and Babylon. Its language is understood in most parts of the Empire.

*Archilichos*—A poet and freebooter.

*archimage*—Great magician.

*Areopagus*—A hill in Thought, the site of murder trials.

*Argiopium*—A village near Clay.

*Argives*—The people of Hundred-Eyed.

*Argolis*—A peninsula southwest of Thought, to which wealthy families fled when it became apparent the Great King's army would capture their city.

*Artabazus*—The wily general who took command of the Great King's army following the death of Mardonius.

*Artaÿctes*—The governor of Sestos, appointed by the Great King.

*Artemisium*—The northernmost point of Goodcattle Island.

*Artimpasa*—The name given the Triple Goddess by the Sons of Scoloti.

*Asopus*—A god of rivers, the father of numerous nymphs. Live coals are discovered in the beds of his streams, which are also called Asopus.

*Auge*—The Huntress. This is the name by which she is known in Bearland; it means "bright light."

*Basias*—An ouragos in Eutaktos's lochos.

*Bearland*—A primitive mountainous area in the middle of Redface Island. It is technically independent of Rope.

*Boat*—A volcanic island in the Water. The metal-workers' god maintains a forge there.

*Boreas*—The god of the north wind.

*Budini*—Fair-haired barbarians inhabiting a densely forested tract northeast of the plains now held by the Sons of Scoloti.

*Celeos*—An ancient king of Advent. The present Royal House is built upon the ruin of his palace and takes its name from it.

*Cerdon*—One of the many slaves who work Pausanias's estate. Cerdon talks with Latro beside the fire on the evening of his capture.

*chalcis*—A bird that never wakes, but flies in its sleep. Its proximity induces sleep in others.

*Chersonese*—The peninsula separating Helle's Sea from the Water.

*Chios*—An isle of the Empire, peopled by Hellenes.

*Chthonios*—The underground Land of the Dead.

*Cimmer*—The eponymous founder of the barbarian tribe displaced by the Sons of Scoloti.

*Circling Isles*—A group due east of Redface Island; they form a rough oval.

*Clay*—A small city near Hill, allied with Thought. It gives its name to the battle in which Latro was wounded.

*Copais*—A large lake northwest of Hill; its waters enter the Lands of the Dead.

*Coronis*—A princess of Horseland, the mother of Aesculapius. The literal meaning of her name is "crooked horned." A more plausible meaning is "of the broken tower."

*Corustas*—A strategist of Tower Hill.

*Cowland*—The area northwest of the Long Coast. It is dominated by Hill.

*Crimson Country*—A coastal strip to the northeast of Riverland, dominated by the cities of the Crimson Men.

*crotali*—Musical rattles normally consisting of tuned lengths of bone or hardwood suspended at one end from a hand-held frame.

*Delian*—Usually the Shining God, but also his twin the Huntress; from their place of birth.

*Demaratus*—The rightful claimant to the younger (Eurypontid) crown of Rope, now in exile at the court of the Great King.

*Demophon*—An infant prince whom the Grain Goddess wished to render immortal by bathing in fire. Her good intentions were frustrated by the arrival of his mother. Priests of the Grain Goddess at Advent must be of his family.

*Dog's Tail*—A sand spit extending from the island of Peace.

*Dolphins*—A mountain town on the mainland west of Tower Hill. Its oracle is the most famous in the world.

*Drakaina*—A lamia. Her name means "she-serpent."

*Eleonore*—One of the courtesans employed by Kalleos. Her name means "merciful."

*Eleusis*—Advent.

*Enodia*—A name of the Dark Mother; it means "of the roads."

*enomotia*—A military unit of 24 men and an officer. Roughly, a platoon.

*Ephesos*—A coastal town of the Empire, inhabited by Hellenes; it is a short distance north of Miletos.

*Euboea*—Goodcattle Island.

*Eumolpides*—The leading family of Advent—once its royal family.

*Eurotas*—A river on Redface Island. It flows almost due south and empties into the sea. Rope is on this river.

*Eurybiades*—A strategist of Rope.

*Eurykles*—A sorcerer and self-appointed priest of the Dark Mother. Kalleos's lover.

*Eutaktos*—A lochagos (roughly a captain) in the army of Rope.

*Euxine*—An extensive inland sea northeast of Helle's Sea. It is linked with Helle's Sea by the First Sea, and is far larger than both.

*Falcata*—Latro's sword.

*Fennel Field*—A battle in which Men of Thought repelled a sea-borne invasion by the Empire.

*Fingers*—Dectuplets borne by Gaea, five boys and five girls. They are friendly to metal-workers and magic-workers.

*Gaea*—The eldest of all goddesses, worshiped by the aboriginal inhabitants of Redface Island and in many other places. The lion is her cat, the wolf her dog; she is also associated with pigs, cats, snakes, and bulls. She once spoke at Dolphins, but has been driven out by the Shining God. Her name means "earth."

*Gates to the Hot Springs*—A point in the northeastern coast of Cowland where cliffs wall the beach. A traveler walking north reaches thermal springs soon after passing them.

*Gello*—A freedman formerly employed by Kalleos to keep order.

*Goodcattle Island*—A long, narrow, rocky island northeast of the Long Coast.

*Gorgo*—The most distinguished woman in Rope, a princess, the widow of its heroic King Leonidas, the mother of its boy-king Pleistarchos, and the chief priestess of Orthia.

*gridelin*—The color of dried flax, a light gray-violet.

*Gulf*—A body of water west of Tower Hill, open to the sea only at its western end.

*hebetic*—Suggesting Hebe, the goddess of youth. Suggestive of a youthful cupbearer at a banquet. (Hebe is a cupbearer to the elder gods.)

*Helle*—The long-ago princess who gave her name to Helle's Sea by drowning in it. Her name presumably means "daughter of Hellen."

*Hellen*—The eponymous ancestor of the Hellenes.

*Helle's Sea*—A narrow strait between the Water and the First Sea. Sestos is on Helle's Sea.

*Heracles*—An ancient hero possessing great strength, who purged Hellas of monsters and was made immortal after his death.

*Heraclids*—Royal or aristocratic persons descended from Heracles.

*Herodotos of Halicarnassos*—Called "the father of history." He titled his book *Historia,* which means "inquiry."

*Hilaeira*—The young woman who joins Latro, Pindaros, and Io at Lake Copais. Her name means "brightness."

*Hill*—The dominant city of Cowland. It is walled, and has seven gates.

*Hippocleides*—The epitome of insouciant indifference. One of the eighteen suitors of an heiress, he performed a comic dance at their betrothal party. On being told by her father that his absurd capering had cost him his marriage, Hippocleides replied that it made no difference to him and continued to dance.

*Hippagretas*—Lochagos of the City Guard of Tower Hill.

*hoplon*—A circular shield of wood lined with leather and faced with bull's hide or bronze. A letter or symbol identifying the soldier's city is usually painted on the face—a club for Hill, for example.

*Horseland*—Thessaly, the country north of the Gates to the Hot Springs, famous for its cavalry.

*Hot Gates*—The Gates to the Hot Springs.

*Hundred-Eyed*—A major city on the east coast of Redface Island.

*Hypereides*—A leather merchant from Thought, and the captain of the *Europa*.

*Hysiae*—A village on the road from Thought to Hill.

*Hysiai*—A town on the road from Rope to Hundred-Eyed.

*Ialtos*—An officer in the army of Thought.

*Iamus*—The founder of a family of prophets.

*Ilissus*—A stream of the Long Coast; it empties into the Strait of Peace near Tieup.

*Ino*—An ancient princess of Hill, the stepmother of Helle and Phrixos. She is worshiped in many places on Redface Island. Her name probably means "my daughter."

*Io*—The child slave who attaches herself to Latro at Hill. As she tells Latro, her name means "joy."

*Island Sea*—A landlocked sea east of the Euxine.

*Issedonians*—A barbarian tribe of the remote northeast.

*Ister*—A great river emptying into the Euxine.

*Kalleos*—A hetaera of Thought. Her name means "my beauty."

*Kallidromos*—The mountain whose cliffs form the Gates to the Hot Springs.

*Keiros*—A slave belonging to Pasicrates.

*Kekrops*—The sailor killed by the Neurian.

*Khshayarsha*—The Great King.

*Kichesippos*—Pausanias's slave physician.

*kopis*—A heavy, curved, single-edged sword having its edge on the inside of the curve. Latro's sword appears to be a kopis. A large knife of similar pattern, used by hunters to skin and cut up game.

*Kore*—The Queen of the Lands of the Dead, Gaea's daughter. Her name means "maiden."

*Lalos*—One of Kalleos's cooks.

*Lar*—A household spirit.

*Latro*—A wounded mercenary.

*Lebadeia*—A small city west of Lake Copais, the site of the oracle of Trophonius.

*Leon*—Kalleos's other cook.

*Leonidas*—A heroic Agid king. A small force under his command fought to the last man at the Gates to the Hot Springs. Gorgo is his widow.

*Leotychides*—The King of Rope who commanded the combined fleets at Mycale. He is from the younger (Eurypontid) royal family.

*lochagos*—The officer commanding a lochos. Roughly, a captain.

*lochos*—A military unit of one hundred men.

*Long Coast*—A more or less triangular peninsula extending from the mainland between Peace and Goodcattle Island; Advent, Tieup, and Thought are on this peninsula. Its name is probably derived from the long and relatively straight coastlines of its eastern and southwestern sides.

*Lycurgus*—The chief author of the legal code of Rope. He was a prince of the younger (Eurypontid) royal family.

*Lyson*—A sailor assigned to guard Latro and the black man.

*Malea*—A rocky cape, the southernmost point of Redface Island, famous for storms.

*Mardonius*—The commander of the Great King's army killed at the battle of Clay. A man of great strength and courage, he led the Great King's bodyguard in person.

*Medes*—A nation closely related to the People from Parsa but subject to them. Because the Medes are more numerous, they are often confused with the People from Parsa.

*Megara*—A small city on the eastern side of the isthmus linking Redface Island with the mainland.

*Megareos*—Captain of the *Eidyia*.

*megaron*—The public room of a type of ancient palace. (The word is sometimes used for the palace itself as well.)

*Megistias*—King Leonidas's seer and sorcerer.

*Miletos*—A coastal city of the Empire, inhabited by Hellenes.

*Molois*—A stream in Cowland.

*Mormo*—A servant of the Dark Mother.

*Mycale*—The battle in which that fraction of the Great King's navy which had survived the battle of Peace was burned.

*Myrrha*—A Cypriot princess, mother of the most handsome of men.

*Naxos*—An island in the Water, belonging to the Empire.

*Nepos*—Captain of the *Nausicaa*.

*Neuri*—A tribe of barbarian sorcerers and werewolves.

*Nike*—The goddess of victory.

*Nysa*—The black man's country, south of Riverland.

*Oior*—A bowman aboard *Europa*.

*Orthia*—The Huntress, called so in the Silent Country. The famous wooden figure from which this name is derived originally represented Gaea. It means "upright."

*Oschos*—An armorer of Sestos.

*ouragos*—The second in command of an enomotia. Roughly, a platoon sergeant.

*Parsa*—The country of the Great King, the location of Persepolis and Susa.

*Pasicrates*—Pausanias's runner.

*Patroklos*—An ancient hero, slain at the siege of Ilion.

*Pausanias*—The Agid regent of Rope.

*Peace*—An island south of the Long Coast. Also the largest town on the island, the narrow channel separating the island from the mainland, etc.

*pelta*—A light shield in the form of a thick crescent, of wicker covered with leather.

*Persepolis*—The capital of the Empire, largely a governmental and religious center.

*Phanes*—An eastern god, said to be the creator of the universe. This name means "revealer."

*Phrixos*—Helle's brother.

*Phye*—The most important courtesan employed by Kalleos. Her name means "tall."

*Pindaros*—The poet chosen by the citizens of Hill to guide Latro.

*Pitana*—One of the villages making up Rope.

*Pleistarchos*—The Agid boy-king of Rope.

*Pleistoanax*—Pausanias's son.

*Polycrates*—An ancient king, long famous for good fortune.

*Polyhommes*—A priest of the Grain Goddess at Advent.

*Propontis*—The First Sea. It links Helle's Sea with the Euxine.

*Redface Island*—A large island south of the mainland, linked with it by an isthmus. The Silent Country and Bearland are regions of Redface Island. Tower Hill is on the western side of the isthmus.

*Rhoda*—One of the courtesans employed by Kalleos. Her name means "rose."

*Riverland*—Kemet, the most ancient of all nations.

*Rope*—The dominant city of the Silent Country. Its soldiers are said to be invincible.

*Sabaktes*—A servant of the Dark Mother.

*Sacred Way*—The road from Thought to Advent.

*Samos*—An island of the Empire, inhabited by Hellenes.

*Saros*—The gulf or sea separating Argolis from Peace. (Also a ruined city on the coast of Redface Island that once controlled this sea.)

*Scoloti*—An ancient barbarian king.

*Selene*—The bright aspect of the Triple Goddess. The others are the Huntress and the Dark Mother.

*Semele*—A princess of Hill, mother of the Kid.

*Sestos*—A walled city on Helle's Sea.

*Silent Country*—The fertile portion of the Eurotas valley. It is guarded by mountains to north, east, and west; its southern side is protected by a swamp. The Silent Country is dominated by Rope.

*Simonides*—An elderly poet and sophist. He wrote the verses inscribed at the Hot Gates.

*Solon*—The chief author of the legal code of Thought.

*Spercheius*—The river separating Cowland from Horseland. It was forded by the Great King's Army on its way to the Hot Gates.

*Spu*—The bowman killed by the Neurian.

*stephane*—A gold or silver headband, widest across the forehead.

*Susa*—The largest city in Parsa.

*taksis*—A large infantry unit of variable size. Roughly, a division. Its commander is one grade below a strategist.

*Tekmaros*—A slave belonging to Pasicrates.

*Teleia*—The queen of the gods.

*Teuthrone*—A fishing village on the coast of Redface Island.

*Themistocles*—Thought's most famous and influential politician and strategist.

*Thoe*—The youngest of the Nereids. Her name means "swift."

*Thought*—The chief city of the Long Coast and the intellectual capital of Hellas.

*Thygater*—The woman reanimated by Latro and Eurykles. Her name means "daughter."

*Tieup*—The chief port of Thought.

*Tisamenus*—Pausanias's seer and sorcerer.

*Tower Hill*—The richest city in Hellas. It is on the gulf, on the west side of the isthmus. Tower Hill built and controls the skid used to take ships across the isthmus.

*triacontor*—A small warship, rowed with 30 oars.

*Trioditis*—The Triple Goddess: Selene, the Huntress, and the Dark Mother.

*Triple Goddess*—Trioditis, the twin sister of the Shining God. Fundamentally a deity of night, she is particularly associated with dogs, which bay at the full moon, course game under the crescent moon, and rush unseen at benighted travelers on the dark roads of Hellas.

*trireme*—A large warship, rowed by 170 oars.

*Trophonius's Cave*—One of the many entrances to the Land of the Dead.

*Umeri*—One of Latro's comrades.

*Water*—The sea east of Hellas. It contains the Circling Isles and many other islands.

*Xanthippos*—The strategist in charge of the siege of Sestos, an aristocratic soldier-politician from Thought.

*Zoe*—One of the courtesans employed by Kalleos. Her name means "life."